Retribution

*Before you embark on a journey of revenge,
dig two graves.*

~Confucius

Also by Marina Cox

Stranded Series;

Stranded: Book One

Vendetta: Book Two

Stranded Series: Retribution is a work of fiction. Names,

characters, places, and incidents either are the product of

the author's imagination or are used fictitiously.

Any resemblance to actual persons, living or dead,

events, or locales is entirely coincidental.

First Printing: 2018

ISBN: 9781732809413

eBook ISBN: 9781732809406

Printed by Lulu Press, Inc.

Published by: Marina Cox

Cover Design: Marina Cox

Illustration: Marina Cox

Design & Layout: Marina Cox

Website: www.Marina-Cox.com

This book is dedicated to Dave Warde,

my brother from another mother.

You left us way too soon, *dude*!

Cast of Characters

Andy Parrish *– married to Jackie Parrish, son of Everett Calhoun, half-brother to Courtney Curwin, father to Brandon Parrish.*

Ava Kincaid *– Casting agent in Hollywood.*

Brandon Parrish *–Legendary Hollywood actor, married to Sage Cassava, son of Andy and Jackie Parrish, grandson of Everett Calhoun, father to baby Tristan.*

Charlie Vega *– Top Talent agent to the stars—manages Brandon Parrish, Sage Cassava and Lola Watters, originally born in Italy as Rodolfo Benenati, first child of Gustavo and Adelina Benenati, twin brother to Roberto (Jack Cassava), brother to Laviana (Meg Jackson), and uncle to Sage Cassava-Parrish.*

Courtney Curwin *–Top News Anchor/Lawyer, biological daughter of Everett Calhoun and Catalina Rocha, half-sister to Andy Parrish, aunt to Brandon Parrish.*

Everett Calhoun *– (Deceased)-Ex-Hollywood Actor/Gangster, father of Andy Parrish and Courtney Curwin, grandfather to Brandon Parrish.*

Frank Hartford *– (Deceased)-Business Tycoon/Founder and former President of Hartford Enterprises, first husband of Margot Hartford, father of Kelley Hartford-Cassava, grandfather to Sage Cassava-Parrish.*

Frederick *–Judge of the Circuit Court, personal friend of Frank Hartford.*

George Paul *– Margot Hartford's Personal Assistant, head of the entire household staff at Providence Estates.*

Hans Mobley *– Chauffeur/Head of the Parrish household cabin in Montana, married to Lydia Johnson-Mobley.*

Jack Cassava – *(Deceased)-Attorney/Business Entrepreneur, married to Kelley Hartford-Cassava, originally born in Italy as Roberto Benenati, second child of Gustavo and Adelina Benenati, twin brother to Rodolfo (Charlie Vega), brother to Laviana (Meg Jackson), father to Sage Cassava-Parrish.*

Jackie Parrish – *married to Andy Parrish, mother to Brandon Parrish.*

Karly Driggers-Rocha *–Daughter of notorious mob boss, Victor Rocha.*

Kelley Hartford-Cassava – *(Deceased)-Junior VP of Hartford Enterprises, married to Jack Cassava, daughter of Frank and Margot Hartford, mother to Sage Cassava-Hartford.*

Ken Barker - *Law Enforcement/Semi-Retired Sheriff, married to Margot Hartford.*

Lola Watters – *Hollywood actress/Sex symbol.*

Lydia Johnson-Mobley – *Runs the Parrish household cabin in Montana, married to Hans Mobley.*

Margot Hartford-Barker *–President of Hartford Enterprises, married to Ken Barker, mother to Kelley Hartford-Cassava, grandmother to Sage Cassava-Parrish, great-grandmother to baby Tristan.*

Meg Jackson – *Owner/Editor of WE Magazine, married to Peter Jackson, originally born in Italy as Laviana Benenati, third child of Gustavo and Adelina Benenati, sister to brothers, Rodolfo (Charlie Vega) and Roberto (Jack Cassava, aunt to Sage Cassava-Parrish.*

Michael Buchanan – *TV News Director.*

Peter Jackson – *CEO/Owner of Jackson's Publishing Company, married to Meg Jackson.*

Sage Cassava-Parrish – *Writer/Author, married to Legendary actor Brandon Parrish, daughter of Jack and Kelley Cassava, granddaughter of Frank and Margot Hartford, mother to baby Tristan.*

Victor Rocha *– (Deceased)-Notorious mob boss/Gangster in Italy, late husband to Catalina Rocha, father to Karly Driggers-Rocha.*

ret·ri·bu·tion

retrə'byo͞oSH(ə)n

noun
1. punishment inflicted on someone as vengeance for a
   wrong or criminal act.
   synonyms: punishment, penalty, one's just deserts;

…He will come with a vengeance;

with divine retribution he will

come to save you.

Isaiah 35:4

PROLOGUE

Late one night, she'd been playing with her beloved tea set, when a knock had sounded at the front door. From there, she honestly doesn't remember leaving the parlor *or* who let the strange men in the house, but in the next memory, they were standing just inside the foyer, having a serious discussion with her mother. She remembered being both scared and mesmerized by their accents, even though they talked in her native tongue. And she recalled only a few sentences from their entire conversation.

"How do I know you're not here to kill us?" Her mama had questioned in a very quiet voice.

"If we were here to kill you, we wouldn't have knocked," came the response.

From there, the memory ends.

She guessed that she couldn't have been more than three or four years old at the time, maybe even younger. Or at least that's what her child-like voice had said on the recording. The one her therapist had documented, *after* her first session as an adult, *under* hypnosis.

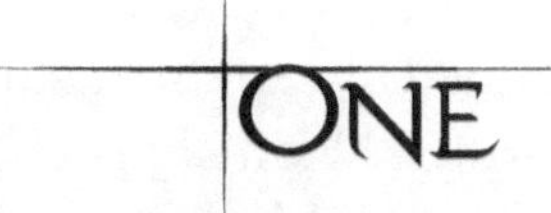ONE

Charlie Vega stared out onto the bustling city of LA, from the rooftop of his office building. He puffed steadily on a cigar as he leaned on the ledge and studied the early evening traffic on the streets, three stories below. For some, the work day was over. But for an elite few, it was just beginning.

The six-lane street that ran north and south in front of his agency, were already congested and almost at a standstill. Somewhere in the distance, the shrill sound of brakes rose above the racket and car horns blared. Loud radio music reached his ears and the smell of exhaust fumes invaded his space, even this far up.

The jam-packed sidewalks were equally full of people, weaving in and out of each other, like an orgy of ants. Most of them either had cell phones glued to their ears, gabbing a mile a minute or they were pecking and swiping on the screen, without even looking up.

Charlie sighed and puffed again on his cigar. A lot had changed from when he'd first purchased this building, over thirty years ago. The storefronts facing him below, used to house mom-and-pop businesses, up and down the strip. The boulevard was always clean and safe— day or night—with the typical California palm trees spread out along the medians, their tops gently blowing in the breeze.

Streetlights had been diligently maintained and lit up just about every inch of the sidewalks. It was an invite for couples to stroll to and from the diners, shops or the movie theatre on the corner. Hell, life in LA was so different then, he and Jack had kept a spare key hidden in the fountain outside the back door, without so much as a second thought.

Now the buildings contained cheap thrift stores, pawn shops and greasy food joints. Neon signs cheapened the windows of every storefront by blinking and advertising their specialties, instead of creatively displaying their goods. The city's talented graffiti artists had long ago covered their ground-level walls, with a mesh-mash of drawings, in an intense rainbow of expression. And the billboard signs above them, obscured the skyline, advertising boldly of ambulance-chasing lawyers and eager plastic surgeons. The once-thriving theater on the corner, now had its windows boarded up, with a badly deteriorating marquee sign that hung lopsided above its door. At the moment two thugs stood under the shadows of its eaves, hands in pockets, looking around at the activity in the streets.

The smog that LA was famous for, had begun to settle heavy in the air. It made the concrete below look dark and dirty and the cracks on the sidewalks appeared deeper and wider.

Due to the spike of crime in the area, Charlie had been forced to upgrade the security on his building a long time ago. The agency was now lit up like Fort Knox, with motion and sensor detectors *completely* surrounding the entire structure. Sure he had thought about moving his business to a better part of town, the more this one seemed to decline. But for now, Charlie did not feel threatened enough to rush that into the present. Sometimes he wondered why his gut had him procrastinating. Other times he figured it was because he wasn't that far away from *real* retirement and found it ridiculous to uproot this close to the end.

Someone yelled below and Charlie glanced toward the street, just in time to see a beefy fist swinging in the air, from an open car window. A bicycle messenger darting in and out of the traffic jam, was his obvious intended target. He glanced further to the right and noticed a homeless man sitting against the wall of the pawn shop across the street. He was begging for some spare change from a woman, dressed all in white, who was walking quickly by. She blatantly ignored him as she jumped into the back of a taxi, waiting at the curb.

Two teenaged-boys on skateboards, sporting backpacks, began plowing through the crowds on the sidewalk, going in the opposite direction. In the process, they were pissing a trail of people off. The two youths' response was to flip them all the middle finger! *Typical!* Kids today were totally out of control and had no respect, not for anyone— including themselves. Charlie shook his head in disgust.

L.A. was very *well-known* for having its fair share of people with overblown egos. The eclectic mixes he mostly dealt with, were famous celebrities, musicians, head studio execs and the millionaires and billionaires who invested in them. Most everyone thought they were someone which caused all those ego-fueled personalities in one place, to either mesh or clash. Unless of course, you *were* Brad Pitt *or* Brandon Parrish! The two of them had blazed such a deep trail through the dense forest of Hollywood, that even their peers were as star-struck as the fans, when they were present at an event. Which was the reason why agents like Charlie *never* booked the two of them at the *same* time. There wasn't enough security *available* to handle it! Charlie chuckled to himself out loud.

If any of those thugs down on the street had a clue that famous icons visited *his* building on a regular basis, he would have to immediately relocate. But he'd already thought about that a long time ago, when he began to collect an elite slew of famous clientele.

Any idiot knew that a parade of limos pulling up in front of a business was something that attracted a lot of unwanted attention. So Charlie had added a three-car garage on the back of the building, so his clients could depart from their limos, without being exposed. Once they were both safely inside the building, there was also a private elevator provided for them, that led up to the rear of his third-floor office. That way, any caliber of celebrity could come and go without being bothered by visitors or staff. It made his clients feel special and it kept the drama to a minimum, which was all Charlie cared about.

He took another strong draw off the cigar and began to lose interest in the comings and goings below, as he now settled his sight again, on the skyline. The sun was already halfway below the horizon and casting shadows on the adjoining buildings. His thoughts began to backtrack through his day. Thank God no serious contracts or meetings had been scheduled because it would have been an epic fail on Charlie's part. His mind was too consumed with the fallout that transpired after they had left Margot's. Once he had unloaded the story on them all that night, Brandon's attitude towards him, seemed to abruptly change. The lighthearted, humorous and playful side he often exhibited, seemed to vanish the next morning after Karly Driggers was arrested. Many times Charlie had wanted to tell Brandon *everything* so he would be prepared just in case a threat like *her* were to come along. But it was one of those situations where your dammed if you do and dammed if you don't. In this case, he was currently just dammed no matter which way he looked at it. Charlie tried to tell himself not to take it personally. Brandon had been through a hell of lot in a very short time and he hoped eventually, the shock of it all would wear down and he would look at him the way he used to.

As for Sage, unlike her famous husband, she was smart enough to understand that all the fault did not lie at Charlie's feet. Margot was flying almost solo on this one. She had forbidden Charlie or Meg to have any contact with Sage after Frank died. Her leverage was the excuse that to do so, might put her life in danger. Charlie had believed it for a little while. Until the danger, in the form of Karly, had solely been brought on, by none other than Margot herself. He scrubbed his face with his hand and then shifted his weight on the brick ledge. An image of Courtney's face briefly flashed across his mind. In Charlie's opinion, she was the one who got the worse end of the deal. At least Sage knew *who* her father was, even though he had lived under an assumed identity, whereas Courtney would never know Everett personally, only the legendary stories he'd left in his wake. Charlie was sure, that learning she had been the *love* child of a secret affair, was going to take some time for her to adjust to, on her part. As one last effort of respect towards the man who'd saved his life, he would do whatever he could, to keep his only daughter safe. And no matter how many strings he had tried to pull on her behalf, the story of Courtney shooting Karly Driggers had been too big, to keep a lid on. He hoped in the long run, her innocent efforts to save them all, would not lead to exposing their true identities and connections to the notorious Victor Rocha.

A subtle noise from behind, interrupted Charlie's thoughts. In a knee-jerk reaction, he spun around in defensive mode, his eyes darting to the lone access to the rooftop. Because he didn't trust the automatic lock on the heavy door, Charlie had a habit of propping a brick in-between the threshold and the frame, to keep it ajar. It was the perfect way to ensure that he never got trapped on the rooftop. Getting locked out was a stupid phobia of his but a phobia nonetheless and obviously the source of the noise. As if right on cue, the door opened towards him slightly, catching in the draft and then it rested against the brick again, becoming still. He walked over to the front of the structure and looked down to the sidewalk below. Just like clockwork, he saw the top of a grey head as it disappeared inside the back seat of a bird-yellow taxi. The door closed and the car entered into the traffic from hell.

It was Peggy, his personal secretary. She was always the last one to leave. In the process she'd caused a draft to make the rooftop door move. It always did that whenever other doors in the structure below, were opened and closed. It was all that scientific bullshit that fell under *action* and *reaction* he'd learn years ago in school.

Charlie relaxed his shoulders and tried to settle his gut but that creepy feeling he had been experiencing all day, came over him again. He took another draw off the cigar and exhaled. The smoke bled out into the sky and dissipated. It was getting darker, the traffic below had started moving at a faster rate and the sidewalks were finally thinning.

Charlie scanned the streets below and saw nothing that stood out. Once again, he had to remind himself that Victor's lunatic daughter was locked up somewhere tighter than a drum and her father long ago shanked to death in a federal prison. The days of looking over his shoulder had finally come to an end. Or so his mind hoped because his gut kept telling him otherwise.

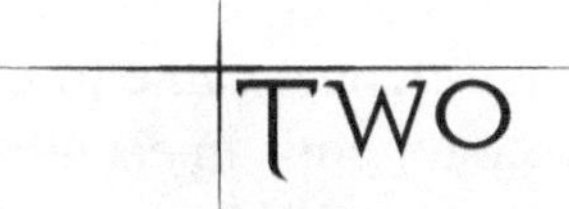

TWO

News of the infiltration and seizure of the famous Somalia Pirates hideout, began to spread *fast* among the locals of Africa. Thanks to Courtney Curwin and her crew, the U.S. would soon be informed as well. Just an hour ago she'd uploaded the last of the script she'd written in her words, to the main news department in New York. An email confirmed it had arrived at the other end and had already been forwarded to the guys in editing.

Now came the boring part—to sit and wait!

The most populated town nearest the pirate's site had been Kenya. Since the news had already broken there the day before about the seizure, media crews and the curiosity seekers from neighboring towns began to fill up the local hotels. That left few options for Courtney and her crew of six when they'd returned to town. Because of limited space, she had no choice but to share a room with her boss, Michael Buchanan. Not exactly the arrangements she would have preferred but at least the two bedrooms that were offered with the suite, were separate with doors that closed, which afforded her some sort of privacy. The secret mad crush she'd had on Michael for eons didn't help make their temporary situation on her any easier. Being confined to a room all morning just added to her current *sour* mood of already feeling closterphobic and restless. At least the unit came equipped with a tiny kitchenette and dining room space that gave her a place to work while they played this waiting game with the Feds. Until they were allowed back at the site to continue coverage, there was nothing else for them to do and it was too hot to be prowling the streets.

Not long after she'd emailed the script, she heard the click of the lock behind her, indicating that her boss had returned. Within seconds Michael came through the main door, juggling two styrofoam cups in each hand.

"Don't shoot, I come bearing gifts!"

He kicked the door shut behind him with his foot as the smell of fresh coffee filled the small space. As much as she wanted to ignore his presence and his ridiculous comment, the desperate need for caffeine won over. She didn't verbally reply, just grabbed the cup he offered, giving him a look that needed no words.

"Your quite welcome, *Princess*." Michael said sarcastically, amusement written all over his face.

"Don't *call* me that!" she spat, not in the mood to be playful. "And *thanks*!" she added, referring to the coffee.

He stopped in front of the table she was sitting at and studied her for a second.

"Courtney, you know there is *nothing* I can do about what happened back at the site. We're only the *press*! We're not the *government*, or the *local* police or in the *states* anymore! We can't just go around making *demands* in a *foreign* country where we have no jurisdiction. We are nothing more than *guests* here and we have to tread lightly if we want to continue to have access!" He stressed. "I thought you said we *already* had *exclusive* access Michael!" Courtney stated.

"We did!" Michael confirmed.

"Exclusive does *not* mean sitting in a hotel room doing nothing." She debated.

"You didn't see any other news crews there, *did* you Princess?" He asked. "That's the part that was *exclusive*. Everything changed when you brought everyone's attention to that piece of tin on the wall!" He added.

"That *piece* of tin belonged to a plane that crashed over two decades ago, Michael! Anyone who knows that would question *how* the serial number—*in* flawless shape—got from the *belly* of that plane to *hanging* on a wall in a hut that belongs to a bunch of pirates!" She threw a twist of sarcasm in that last sentence.

"Those pirates have covered hundreds of miles by boat and by land during those few decades and stole a lot of shit in the process, Courtney. They could have stumbled upon the wreckage clear up near the Indian ocean, where it went down." he said, just as calm as ever.

"Who says?" Courtney asked him. "The government?" When he didn't immediately respond, she added.

"Hmmm…. wouldn't be the *first* time they swayed a little from the truth."

"Ok." he said. "So let's just say they lied about the location of the crash? What would be their gain?"

"Who knows?" Courtney offered, shrugging her shoulders. "But it's got some kind of value on it, otherwise we would still be out there, covering the story like we're supposed to be doing, instead of wasting time in a hotel, sipping on mediocre coffee."

He took the chair next to hers. His knee touched hers under the table and she quickly moved her leg. Then the wickedly delicious smelling cologne he wore, saturated her senses.

"Want to know what the buzz is around town about it all?" he asked, leaning in, making it worse. "The leaders of Kenya are thinking about making the seizure a *local* holiday. Word is that the natives up and down the waters for hundreds of miles each way, are celebrating."

"The natives are partying prematurely, if you ask me." Courtney said, returning her eyes back on the screen, trying her best to keep a straight face while her insides were mushing with him so close.

Michael's brows drew slightly together. "You still strongly believe the leader was not among them?" He said, more as a statement.

"Absolutely." She confirmed, without a hitch. Michael sighed and leaned back in the chair. "Let's hope your wrong." He said. "It's highly possible that a few of those bastards could have been somewhere else when that raid took place, but if the leader happened to be one of them, well that would make the seizure almost pointless."

"Which is *my* point." Courtney said. "Without a confirmed identity, no one knows who the leader is or what he looks like. So how can the Feds strut to the world like peacocks, that they've captured this ring, until they're sure they have the head guy? Because they don't and that's why I believe it was one of the reasons why we were abruptly told to leave."

"Well *hell* Princess, keeping something that *big* out of the hands of the media is a no-brainer! The last thing our government wants is for us to let the cat out of the bag that they captured everyone *but* the most dangerous guy in the bunch!" He shook his head. "And you can bet, if this so-called leader wasn't already captured when our boys hit that camp, he's well aware now that it's been compromised and he'll be long gone before anyone figures it out. He might never be caught."

"I'm sure he has plenty of resources in this country that would be more than willing to smuggle him out." She said. Michael's brows drew slightly together. "You think he's got *that* many friends?" She nodded. "Even with the United States Military on the ground everywhere, armed to the max, as well as highly trained FBI agents? Who would be that stupid?"

"Locals!" she simply stated, looking over at him. "People who he's already manipulated and brainwashed to protect him, should a time like this arise! They're loyalty is *not* going to lie in us foreigners, Michael. Even though he's a bad seed, he's symbolic here, kind of like royalty in a bad way, but respected all the same. I definitely believe that *someone* would be stupid enough to get him out, right under all their guarded noses."

Michael's face formed in a smirk. "They'd turn on their own people?"

"Someone in the bunch is *always* willing to, if the price is right." She said.

"That's the sad part about the human race." Michael said. "Everything has its price."

"And those pirates they captured are not going to give up their boss." Courtney said. "It's back to that loyalty thing again. They'd die before they'd point him out."

"They can always do a line-up and let the *victims* point him out." Michael suggested. "It would probably be a whole lot quicker."

"Those poor people have a long road ahead of them. Once the families are reunited there will be tons of therapists and lawyers coming out of the woodwork offering their services. It will turn out to be a fiasco and could take months before any of them are willing to cooperate. This guy could be anywhere in the world by then."

"Your absolutely right about that, Princess."

"Did you find out anything else out about that hut we were in?"

"A lot of things." He began.

"Such as?" she urged.

"They found records."

"*Records*? What *kind* of records?"

"The kind you'd find in a business office for inventory. The house boy, Bram, told me that this country is very poor in education. He said most of the natives don't know how to read or write. So I'm gathering this is why it had everyone's undivided attention at the site." Michael said. "Because whoever kept those records had *exceptional* skills above and beyond a common river thief. And they went so far as to bury them in a steel footlocker under the dirt floor."

"Pirates are known for burying their treasure. That's nothing new." She said. "So what were they inventorying?"

"Just about every movement *made* in that camp."

"Like logs?"

"Yes, filled with details of their attacks, lists of all the loot that was taken on each one, the dates it happened and the names of the dead that piled up through the years who were involved."

"They let you see them?" She questioned.

"Hell no! They won't let someone like me near that."

"Then how do you know this?"

Michael broke into a grin and winked at her. "I don't give up my sources, Princess, you *know* that."

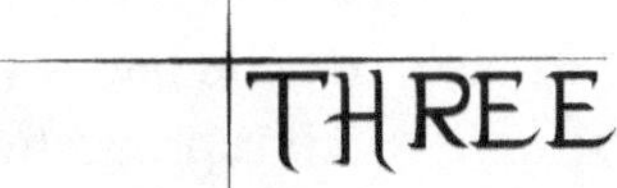

THREE

Meg was humming softly to herself while she arranged an assortment of snacks on a tray, that consisted of two kinds of cheese, chunks of turkey, wheat crackers, some luscious grapes, apple slices, roasted almonds and a bowl of garlic hummus in the center. Now all she needed was the pita chips and some good wine and they were all set. She was looking forward to spending some quality alone time with her husband Peter. Since it was late in the evening, he had suggested some healthy snacking instead of a full-on meal. Then he threw in the idea of bringing it into the bedroom and catching a movie while they ate. He didn't need to ask her twice. It was a perfect way to round off the intense, emotion-filled event, that they both had just experienced. Meg had lied earlier to Peter when she'd told him she was fine. She was far from fine but it was easier to lie than to go through any more drama. There was a time when you just had to shut down and let the dust settle. But the unsettled feeling she'd been experiencing after the events that took place at Margot's, had her more rattled now, then before. Standing in the security of her kitchen, she'd tried to reassure herself that it was just leftover tremors from the 'earthquake of a story' that Charlie had unloaded on them. After all, there were several parts of her brother's tale that she was hearing for the *first* time that night, as well. And it was very upsetting to realize just how much she really didn't know about the details surrounding their parent's death or the death of her mother's friend, Catalina. Also learning that Courtney was Isabella—well she was having a more difficult time wrapping her head around that one. It wasn't that Meg doubted her birthright. It was just too surreal for her to digest right now. Courtney had not only been a college friend of Peter's but she had also, over time, become a close friend of Meg's. To reprogram her brain cells from just being their *friend* for years to actually being Everett Calhoun's *daughter*—it was just going to take some getting used to.

Wow—just wow! Meg thought.

At least there was a silver lining in all this mess. Not only did Peter now know her secret, but Sage *finally* knew *who* she and Charlie really were. For Meg it meant that she might have a chance at a *real* relationship with her *only* niece without Margot further interfering. Of course the bonus there was that Sage *just* happened to be married to one of the biggest legends in Hollywood. A legend that Meg was obsessed with, when it came to having him on the front cover of her magazine.

She knew Sage was going to become a very important part of her life in the near future which meant there were some sacrifices that she was going to have to make on her part, pertaining to her famous husband. Learning to become *un*-obsessed with a hot idol like Brandon Parrish, was going to be a struggle on the professional end of things. She'd been chasing him for years, using any little tidbit that was thrown her way and now, here he was, a part of the *damn* family—totally accessible—only to become '*off limits*' to her, *virtually* overnight.

Strange how life works, she mused.

And it didn't stop there. She was going to have to walk on eggshells, at least until they all became more comfortable around each other. Brandon would require more time to warm up to her than his wife, since he detested what Meg did for a living. There would be some very awkward family get-togethers until everyone got used to the new dynamics. She just hoped Brandon would not pick up where Margot left off and shield Sage so she wouldn't be allowed to spend time with her. Somehow she was going to have to gain his trust in believing that Sage's welfare would always come before her position as editor of a magazine. Her brand might suffer because of it. But from this point on she couldn't cover anything about them randomly or without their permission. It was the respect thing. Hopefully Sage and Brandon would continue to give her the exclusive, like they did when she covered their wedding. That would be the best compromise ever! Meg hummed some more as she began visualizing *We* magazines' future covers featuring Sage's Stranded movie in production, starring Brandon Parrish. She smiled to herself as she grabbed the pita chips from the pantry shelf and added them to the plate. Yes, there were several silver linings that came from Charlie finally spilling the beans. And the best of all was no more worries about the Rocha family getting in the way.

She was at a place in life that the past wasn't going to be her crutch anymore. Just like Peter had said to her on the flight home, it was all over for them now that Karly had been arrested. And maybe, just maybe once this all died down, her and Peter could finally start working on a family of their own. She always wanted to have a baby but would never dare bring one into *her* world where there was danger always lurking. Now that the threat was over, it was suddenly a big possibility.

On that note, she grabbed the platter and entered the hallway that led to their bedroom. She sat the platter down on his nightstand, along with two plates and a small stack of napkins.

"*Peter*?" she called out. "It's *ready*!"

When he didn't respond right away she figured he must be in the bathroom. She walked back to the kitchen and grabbed the chilled bottle of red from the wine fridge, removed the cork and topped off her glass. She then poured one for Peter. She returned it to its place on the rack and grabbed both the glasses and headed back towards the bedroom. She sat one on his nightstand and walked around the bed and sat the other on hers.

"*Peter*?" She called again.

No answer.

She left the bedroom and headed back down the hallway, entered the living room and found it empty. Then her eyes caught sight of the sliding glass door that was slightly ajar. She walked over, and that's when she saw him and realized why he was not responding.

He was outside, on the far end of the terrace, with his back to her. When she walked closer to the opening, she could hear him talking and realized he had his cell phone up to his ear. She did not hear the entire conversation—only the end.

He had ended it with the words "*Miss you*!" He had said it with emotion.

She wanted to believe for not *one* second, that her sweet, *devoted* husband Peter would *ever* cheat on her. *Never*! But *who* in the hell would he be saying that to, with *endearment* in his voice, on the phone? Maybe his father?

He pulled the cell away from his ear, stuck it in his pocket, turned and began walking towards her, just as she opened the door wider.

"Hey babe! Everything good?" he asked, when he looked up and saw her. A smile replaced the deep frown that had been there seconds before.

She hesitated for a moment, then returned his smile and said, "Yes, everything is just fine." This was the *second* time tonight she'd lied to him because right now she just didn't want to deal with any more drama. "Everything good with you?" she asked, in return.

"Everything is always wonderful when I'm with you!"
Peter said, flashing her a handsome smile as he wrapped an
arm around her shoulders.
The gesture had been effective.
Any previous doubts she'd had before, had quickly been
diminished.

FOUR

Lola Watters sat in an overstuffed chair, facing a huge pane of glass. Relaxed after a very hot shower, she was wrapped in an ankle-length, white thick robe and nothing else. Her bare feet were tucked up underneath her hem for warmth. Her dark hair—still damp—was piled high on top of her head and in her hand, a very tall glass of red Italian wine. Inside the hotel room, the precious silence surrounding her was both welcoming and appreciated. So was the view beyond the glass doors that led to the balcony. She could see a full view of the sun that was setting in the far distance. Pooling around it in all hues of orange and yellow, were what looked like streaks of fire, in an otherwise waning blue sky. Its descent seemed like it was creating a vacuum effect, almost as if the colors were being pulled down with the weight of the sun.

It was synonymous with the way she'd lived for *most* of her life—with the feeling that some *unforeseen* gravity was always there, pulling *her* down, trying to stop her from accomplishing her goals.

She'd always *thought* her issues now, had something to do with the significant losses she'd experienced along the way. And now she thought she *finally* knew what it was. This was one of those times when she wished *so* bad, that her mother was here so they could talk.

But that would never again be.

Ever…

A lone tear slid down Lola's cheek, as she watched the last of the hues in the sky, dip below the horizon.

I hope your resting in *peace*, momma!

FIVE

"Are you *ready* for your surprise?" Brandon asked, beaming a smile at her that was infectious.
"Your scaring me." Sage simply said, resisting slightly, not sure what he was up to. At the moment he was walking backwards through the doorway of their bedroom, hands entwined in hers, pulling her with him, his beautiful blue eyes pinned on her with excitement dancing in their depths. "There is nothing scary about *this* surprise." He reassured her, as they passed the fireplace and stopped in front of the French doors. At the moment they were closed.
"Awesome!" Sage said with feigned excitement. "French doors! Your right! What a *surprise*! This isn't scary at all!" Brandon let go of her hands and put his finger gently to her lips. The warmth of his touch, just that small bit of contact, warmed her entire body. The whiff of his sexy musky scent, the long strands of hair he'd carelessly tucked behind his left ear, the way his mouth moved when he spoke, never ceased to make her weak in the knees. "My surprise is *not* the French doors *my* love, but what's on the *other* side of them!"
His voice had turned husky and seductive. Before she could react or speak he swiftly walked away from her, grabbed both knobs and pulled them open wide in a dramatic fashion. Sage giggled because she always loved it when he went into acting mode but this time she stopped short, when the sight past his shoulder, caught her eye. The view beyond the railing took her breath away and would never get old. The enormous mountains in the distance, with deep valleys full of lush green vegetation,

seemed to go on forever. And the brilliant hue of blue in the late afternoon sky, offset them both so perfectly, that it looked like a painted masterpiece, that belonged in a museum. But this time, it was upstaged by something else. A few months back, before Tristan was born, Sage had come across an image on Pinterest that made her pause. It was the scene of a cozy little seating area for one, on a balcony almost *identical* to theirs, that led off from the master bedroom. The focal point of the photo, was a wellworn leather chair, complete with an Aztec-upholstered ottoman. In the picture, a book was open and lying on the foot stool with a pair of reading glasses resting on its pages. It had been positioned at an angle, about a foot from the railing, on top of a small, solid red rug. On the floor beside the chair, was an old pottery mug and next to it were a pair of well-worn fuzzy slippers. A moonlit view of a dark blue sky outlined the massive mountains in the distance beyond. The picture had spoken a thousand words to her all at once, so she saved it. Later, she had shown it to Brandon and asked his opinion. They hadn't even talked about it long. Soon after, he'd hopped on a plane to London and she had discovered her grandfather's journals in the barn. Then Tristan had been born and the hope of creating such a space, had quickly been put on the back burner, in her mind.

But *obviously* Brandon hadn't forgotten her desire to recreate that sanctuary on their balcony. The scene in front of her, looked as if the photo had come to life. A soft leather chair and ottoman, close to the size of the one in the image, rested generously, on a charcoal-gray area rug. A pewter-finished floor lamp, towered over the back of the chair, its neck made of a flexible material that bent in any direction the user chose. A sturdy looking side table held a copy of her novel, *Stranded* and beside it, her piecedtogether *Wicked* cup that she had a hard time letting go of. He had even laid a thick lap blanket across the foot of the ottoman in her favorite shade of violet. It was a perfect addition for those chillier nights, paired with an electric, outdoor fire pit, that sat a few feet away.

Omg! Could she love this man *any more* than she already did?

She tore her eyes away from the inviting space, long enough to direct her gaze at Brandon, who was standing just over the threshold of the balcony. His smile was still intact and his eyes searched hers for a reaction.

"You *did* this for me?" She asked, still in disbelief.

He was nodding. "You bet your *perfect,* sweet ass I did!" His grin grew bigger. The dimple on one side slightly appeared.

"But *how*…?" She was at a loss for words. "*When* did…?"

"Doesn't matter!" he said, walking over and taking her hands in his. "It's done! *And* it's *your* own *personal* space." He guided her over to the leather chair and made her sit. "You can read or work on your laptop while it's nice out." He said. "You see this table?" He pulled the side table over to her with ease. "It has wheels on it so you can move it around. It can be used as a temporary desk. The lamp behind your chair is adjustable in height and it has three settings, from low light to really bright light and it comes with a remote," he said, pausing to point at one on the table. "so you don't have to get up when your seriously buried in a chapter!" He tapped one of the buttons and the light got brighter. "And the rug is a little thicker and twice the size as the one in the picture but I thought it would be warm on your feet on those extra chilly nights. And because it reaches the threshold of the French doors, *physically* your feet will never touch the cold flooring underneath, to and from our room. And with the nights being a little on the cool side right now, I couldn't pass up this nifty little device." He picked up another remote on the side table and aimed it at the fire pit that was only a few inches away. Instantly a flame shot up out of the gravel base and she began to feel the heat emitting from it. "I know there wasn't one in the photo you showed me but I figured we'd cheat just a little." He winked at her, laid the remote on the table and sat down across from her on the ottoman. He scooted it closer, intertwining his legs with hers.

"You just thought of *everything*, didn't you?" she asked, amazed that he would do something like this for her, making sure to add in all the comforts she would need while immersed into a late night writing session.

"I had to tweak it just a little from the original idea so it fit *you* and our environment we live in but yeah, I think I nailed it!"

"You nailed it alright! I absolutely *love* it! It's so charming, so comfy, so…*inviting*! It's a brilliant and inspirational work space to write in, yet also the perfect place to read a good book! I can't believe you even paid attention to the picture I showed you that day and yet," she glanced around at the space. "You captured the ambiance that drew me in. It's just like the photo, only better! Oh I *love* you so much for doing this!"

"And I love you more!" he said. "And I'm glad you approve."

He was proud of himself. There was a slight curve to his beautiful mouth, a relaxed set to his jaw and his piercing blue eyes went right through her. His blond, shoulder length hair, had grown since the premiere and had natural strands of gold running through it that shimmered in the lamplight.

He was so damn perfect in a rugged sort of way, Sage thought and still found it hard to believe he was hers. This was one of those times when she felt like pinching herself just to make sure she wasn't dreaming. Instead, she kissed him full on the lips and wrapped her arms around his waist, resting her chin on his shoulder. She briefly closed her eyes and inhaled the scent of his hair, snuggled into the warmth of his neck. No one had to tell her to savor every moment or to appreciate every milestone, not when she had something as special as he was within her grasp every day. She held onto him for a moment, the embrace lasting a few seconds. She was content to stay just like this all evening if she could get away with it and they didn't freeze to death. Fall was knocking at their door and the evenings were getting quite nippy. If it wasn't for the fire pit putting out such great heat, they'd already had to go in. She reopened her eyes and looked out over the railing and into the horizon, appreciating the moment and that's when she noticed that the view beyond that side of the cabin was different.

She pulled slowly away from him, her eyebrows drawn in confusion.

"What's the matter?" he asked, slightly alarmed as he turned to see what had her frowning.

"The tree…" she began, when it finally dawned on her.

"Oh yeah…about *that*…" he said hesitating and turning back to face her, a sheepish grin on his handsome face. "I've been meaning to tell you that I reworked the landscape a little." He said, "I remember while I was stranded here, you told me that this was one of your *favorite* spaces in the cabin. Well, I couldn't help but notice lately, that you hardly come out here anymore. I figured redoing this space like that photo would change the *energy* and make it *inviting* to you again. I didn't want you to be reminded of Jeb every time you saw that tree," he nodded towards the space where it used to be. "so I decided to have it taken down. As the saying goes, 'out of sight, out of mind'. Well, you now have an *unobstructed* view of the mountains because of it and it made a *hell* of a side table!"

He winked at her again, then ran his hand over its smooth wooden surface.

Sage gazed down at the exquisite piece next to her leg that used to be covered in bark and then looked back up at her husband. "*That* is part of the *tree* that Jeb was *in* that night?" She asked, pointing at it.

He nodded. Then made a grimace. "*Yes!*" He was hesitant. "Is that going to *bother* you?" He asked quickly. "The tree itself was pretty fat around so I didn't want to let it go to waste or burn it all up in a fireplace. I mean it wasn't the trees fault and it's really not a good idea to burn pine in the fireplaces anyway."

She leaned forward and put her hand over his mouth to silence him, her face inches from his. He had no choice but to stop speaking.

"I *think* that is the most *beautiful* side table I've ever *seen* in my life! There is not a *another,* for *any* price, that could compare to *its* value! To *know* that *you* made this for *me* with *your* hands and *your* heart, so that I could sit out here with a surface to write on, means the *world* to *me* and so do *you*, so *damn* much it's scary!" She hesitated but only for a second. "Brandon, when I use this table, I won't be *thinking* about Jeb Perkins. I will be *thinking* about how *lucky* I am to have *you* love me *enough* that you turned a *negative* in my life into a *positive* and that *surpasses* everything!"

Brandon studied her while he gently removed her hand that was over his mouth. He bent slightly forward and kissed her, *long* and *hard* and then brought both of her hands to his lips. The warmth and softness of his mouth, *even* on her fingertips, sent tingling sensations racing throughout her body.

Brandon pulled her hands away from his lips and laid them with his own, in his lap. "I *wanted* a life like this." He said, his tone serious. "I *dreamed* about having a life like this!

When I thought *everything* in my life was *perfect* as it was, *everything* went *terribly* wrong. But it wasn't until it went terribly wrong, that I found out it was *far* from perfect. *You* changed my life Sage! I was in that bed across the hall, nearly *half* dead, an absolute *stranger* to you! You nursed me back to life—*literally*—in more ways than you can imagine and *you* think *you're* the only one who's *lucky*?" One of his hands left his lap and gently grazed the side of her cheek. "I can *never* repay you for that Sage, nor do I ever want to. I *want* to be indebted to you forever, if this is what *forever* feels like!"

Sage thought about how they had been thrown together as strangers by fate, only to quickly become enemies, which slowly and miraculously turned into a friendship, that led to a passionate love affair, and then eventually into marriage and now they were parents. It was amazing how life works sometimes.

"Our fairytale family." She said, summoning their story up in a nutshell.

"Our fairytale family who got their *happily ever after*!" he said, referring to the little inside joke they had acquired between them. He kissed her again, lightly.

"If you don't stop doing that, we'll soon be buck-naked and charged with child neglect."

"Hans and Lydia are pulling baby duty right now so the neglect charge is out the window." He began a trail of kisses down the side of her neck. "I'll settle for the buck-naked part. It'll give us a chance to break in your new chair."

"Dammit Brandon, let me at *least* spill coffee on it first." She protested.

He laughed and abandoned her neck long enough to kiss her again on the lips. "I'm glad you like your little Zen space." He said with sincerity.

"I *love* my new Zen space. It's going to be perfect for all kinds of things." She kissed him back.

"On HGTV they would refer to your Zen space as very *functional*." He said, smirking, the corner of his mouth slightly curving.

"You've been *binge* watching again, haven't you?" she questioned, teasing him.

"It's possible!" he admitted. "Is there any other way?" He wrapped his arms around her then, nice and snug. She melted into him as he kissed her brow. They stayed like that as the world around them progressed. The crickets played their music down below as an owl hooted in the distance. Sage loved the sound of the wind, as it picked up and caused the branches from nearby trees to sway in its breeze, signaling that fall was near.

"This is the first time we've had a moment to be alone since we came back from your grandmothers." Brandon said softly in her ear, breaking the brief silence between them.

"I know." Sage sighed into his warm neck. "This past week has nearly sucked the life out of me. I'll be really happy when everything gets back to normal."

Brandon paused for a second and then said, "At the rate this family's going, *normal* might not be an option for us."

"It's got to be. I don't know how much more I can take." She said, snuggling closer. While her last comment hung thick in the air, he tightened his embrace, bringing her closer.

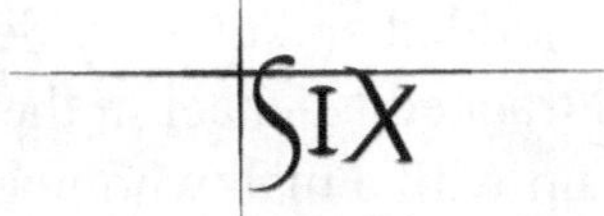 SIX

It had been raining for well over an hour in Kenya. Fat drops of water continuously slammed against the panes of the windows in the hotel dining room. The tin roof magnified the patter to sound more like hard-hitting hail, than simple raindrops. The lights inside flickered almost in perfect beat with the thunder, threatening to put them all in a blackout. Lightning that followed the rumble, streaked across the skies as the rain continued to drop, flooding everything in its wake.

The hotel had become quickly packed, in both the lobby and restaurant area—if you could call it that. On the far left side stood a bar, complete with stools. On the far right were a set of well-worn sofas and two armchairs grouped together near the front windows of the building. Wedged in-between were a cluster of tables and chairs that served as the restaurant part for the guests that wanted to dine. At the moment, Courtney, her boss and her cameraman, Tony, were occupying one of those tables, wrapping up a late lunch.

Michael had finished first and was now surveying the crowd in the room. Courtney noticed that he seemed to be very interested in the vicinity of the main doors. Then, without warning, he quickly stood up, murmured something to them both and abruptly left. Courtney didn't hear what he said because the waitress approached the table and spoke to them at the same time. "Can I get you anything else?"

"I'm good!" Tony said, flashing a smile her way.

"Courtney?" He nodded towards her.

"Can I get a large coffee to go please! Just cream!" she said this to the waitress.

"Sure!" The woman nodded and quickly departed.
Courtney found and tracked Michael in the crowd with her eyes, just as he met up with a man who was dressed in army fatigues over by the bar. He and Michael shook hands in a business-like manner and the two began to converse. She turned her attention back to Tony.
"Did you get a chance to copy that footage for me?"
"Yes *love*!" He turned slightly from the table and pulled on the strap of his backpack, that was hung on the back of his chair. He unzipped a side pocket and pulled out what looked like a red-colored thumb drive. "Here you go!"
"Thanks!" He leaned over and dropped it in her outstretched palm. She slid the small device deep in the pocket of her jeans.
"Anytime!" Tony said, replacing the bag on the back of his chair.
Courtney glanced over her shoulder again in Michael's direction. He was still deep in conversation with the man at the bar and both of them were sipping on a bottle of beer.
"Any idea who the guy is that Michael's talking to?" she asked Tony.
The cameraman's eyes searched the room, then landed on the target. "I have no idea what his name is but I've seen him around!" Tony said.
"Well, we know one thing, he's military!" Courtney said, stating the obvious.
"Yep! No doubt!" Tony agreed, as he glanced over at the two men again. "And judging by all the metals hanging off his chest, he has to be pretty high up in rank."
Courtney glanced at the two men again, briefly before turning back to Tony.
"He has a silver insignia on his collar and on his garrison cap. That makes him a *five*-star general." She said.
"Oh dude," Tony gave a low whistle. "That must be *the* General Bradley!"

"*Who*?" she asked.

"General Bradley! He's the *head* dude that's over the *military* dealings with the pirate's lair. That's how we got first priority on this gig above the other networks. Guess the gossip is, he and Buchanan go way back to elementary school days or something."

"*Really*?" Courtney said, cocking her head and taking a second look. Both of the men did look quite comfortable with one another. She could believe that.

"Maybe he's working his magic right now to get us back onsite!" Tony suggested, referring to the ban in place at the moment against all media.

"Have you heard anything about *why* it's restricted access all of the sudden?" Courtney was just fishing, simply because he moved in circles that she straight up didn't. He always knew the latest gossip among the locals of any town, city or country that they visited.

Tony began to nod his head slowly. "Bram, the house boy, has a cousin on the police force that patrols the water. Says he's had plenty of dealings in the past with the pirates. Because of it, the military and the Feds sought him out to help untangle the mess out there. He told Bram that they found a *dead* body of a woman in one of the huts. He said that they called in *more* sky police to handle the problem."

"*Sky police*?" Courtney questioned.

"It's what the natives refer to as the FBI because they all flew in by helicopters."

"Oh!" She paused. "So they said *more* came?" Courtney asked.

Tony nodded. "Bram said that his cousin told him a *second* team arrived yesterday, *exclusively* to handle the body."

Courtney studied Tony for a second, as the realization took hold.

"If that's true, then it can only mean one thing," Courtney began. "The deceased was *American*." Tony nodded. "Does

Michael know about this?"

"No, you're the first one I've told." He said.

"And you *believe* this house boy?" she asked.

Tony nodded. "Like I said, he's got a cousin…" he began.

"I got that part!" She said. "I'm just curious on how you got this house boy to speak so freely, when all the other locals won't talk to us."

Tony grinned. "Bram is a cool little dude. He just happened to take a smoke break at the same time that I did last night. We hung out for a bit and bumped gums. If you can get him going, he likes to talk."

The waitress suddenly reappeared with Courtney's coffee. She thanked Tony for the info and the thumb drive and headed to her room. Once inside, she made a straight shot to the room she was staying in. Leaving the door ajar, she headed to the desk, where her laptop was waiting. She sat the container of coffee down beside it, took a seat in the chair, opened the device and began tapping on some keys to wake it up. She sipped as she waited for the screen to load and stared out the window for several seconds, watching the rain. She began thinking over the conversation she'd just had with Tony, concerning the *second* FBI team that had been dispatched and the tortured victims, that she had witnessed, boarding the buses.

Michael had told her later that they had taken them to a government hospital to 'sort it all out'—which meant they needed to identify them, provide any medical attention and hopefully obtain statements of how they got there and when they were taken.

The beep on the laptop brought her attention back to the screen. A search box appeared with a cursor prompting her to type something in the blank field. She typed—*Kelley and Jack Cassava—Images.*

It seemed like it took forever to assimilate a list to work through but eventually some articles began to load in the window, of possible matches. The first one—of course—was about the plane crash itself involving the couple, that took place in 1987. The facts were vague and hinted that a plane headed to the United States with American passengers on board, had been lost on radar somewhere over the Indian ocean. But there wasn't an update, not one that she could find online anyway, to confirm the crash site had been located. Of course they *eventually* found it because the government had sent the remains back to the states so the Hartford's could give their daughter and her husband a proper burial. Sage and Brandon had found the document in Frank's safe in the library that said so.

 She backed out of that page and went on to the next listing. It opened to the familiar picture of Frank and Margot Hartford's cabin in the newspaper. She'd found this once before when digging for the goods on the famous icon and his new wife. The article was highlighting the fact that most residents from up north have a home they flock to in the south, to avoid the tough winters. But the couple from Florida, had done totally the opposite, by building a winter retreat in the '*Great State of Montana*'. She guessed that made news in some sort of *odd* way, enough to put it on the front page of the Leisure section.

Judging by the style of their clothing and hair, the shot had to have been taken some 15 years ago. Mrs. Hartford hadn't seemed to age a bit between then and now. In the pic, the smile on her face was genuine and it reached her eyes. The shoulders were completely relaxed and the arm around her husband's waist was confident. They both looked *very* happy.

She backed out of that article and clicked the next listing below it. This one was highlighting Kelley and Jack's genealogy, which really wasn't theirs. It was more of a marketing ploy, to get the user to pay a fee to find the ancestry of deceased loved ones. She backed out of that and kept going down the listings, through article after article, trying to find a pic of either Kelley Hartford-Cassava or her husband Jack Cassava but found nothing.

Then she tried to find out if they were ever issued a death certificate since their remains had been acknowledged by the government and buried in the ground on U.S soil. After almost thirty minutes of not finding that either, she gave up. Of course, she had to rationalize with herself that this happened over two decades ago. Unless someone dumped that info into the internet from their archives, it wouldn't come up in any database in the cyber world. Nor would a pic of them unless it was from a yearbook, again dumped into the archives by a real person. After another fifteen minutes, she gave up.

Remembering the thumb drive that Tony had given her she fished it out of her pocket, took the protective cap off and stuck it in the USB port side of her laptop. She opened the files and began watching the coverage that Tony and his crew had filmed at the pirate's hideout. There were several, but none captivated her like the *last* one.

The bus that took the captives to safety, was dead center of the lens when the camera began to roll. Tony had zoomed in on the hostages faces, that were freed from the pits, as they were boarding, secretly on the other side through a protection of trees. The soldiers were guiding some of them to the open door of the bus. Most of the victims were covered in mud. It made it hard for her to tell which of them were male and which were female.

They continued throughout the video to come in groups, in pairs—some with children. The soldiers had to help a few of them walk onto the bus, they were so weak. Courtney focused on their features. The video played itself out as she reached over and grabbed her coffee. She sipped, keeping her eyes on the screen and silently prayed that the victims would eventually find peace once they were reunited with their loved ones. It was a miracle that any of them were still alive because of the deplorable conditions they'd been living under.

Towards the end, two soldiers carrying a gurney between them, came into view. On it was a body covered with a sheet. The soldiers abruptly stopped at the front bumper of the first bus. A third soldier stepped down from the side door and walked around to meet them. They talked for a moment but Courtney couldn't make out what they were saying. The men weren't facing the camera so she couldn't read their lips.

The soldier that had stepped off the bus, pulled his radio and talked into it. Within a few seconds, a military van pulled up alongside the first bus. A fourth soldier jumped out of the driver's seat and opened the double doors on the passenger side. The two soldiers that were carrying the gurney, walked over to the open doors of the van and tried to make it fit. The jarring of the movement unsettled the covered body. A lone foot fell from the confines of the sheet. It slid out as far as the ankle. One of the soldiers casually shoved it back under. In the process, something shiny caught the right light and flashed for a second at the camera.

What the hell was that?

Courtney paused the video, moved the timeline back a few frames and then hit play. At the precise time the foot slid out again, the sharp flash repeated itself. She paused it and zoomed closer.

It almost looked like a *gold* ankle bracelet which would make sense why it caught the light in the lens. It was not uncommon for women in Africa to wear trinkets around their ankles and arms. In fact, she'd seen most of the locals decorated in that fashion and they sold them by the dozen for dirt cheap, in the markets. But what was *not* common, was one who sported gold, out in the middle of a jungle.

But then again, it was a camp full of looting pirates. They could have taken that from *anybody* they robbed. Courtney paused the video again and stared hard for a moment at the screen. This *had* to be the dead body from the hut that Bram had told Tony about. Because a gut feeling told her to do so, she captured that part of the video and attached it to an email of a graphic designer she'd worked with in the past, requesting her to enhance it. She had no sooner clicked on the *send* button, when the power in the suite went out and she was plunged into complete darkness.

SEVEN

Sage stared out with appreciation, at the second-story view beyond the railing of the place she now called *home*. The night sky had taken over, the stars were present and the degrees in temperature had dropped. The electric fire pit that Brandon had added to the mix, was doing an excellent job of keeping her pretty warm and toasty. The leather chair he had chosen for the space, was incredibly comfortable. It gave her a bird's-eye-view of their property below, as well as a clear view of the mountains in the distance. She glided her hand over the smooth surface of the side table, that he had custom-made from the tree, then gently pushed the edge with her finger and was surprised at how easy it moved.

She glanced down at the floor, admiring the plush grey rug, when she noticed the tote bag leaned against the base of the chair. With growing curiosity, she bent forward and slid her hand inside and pulled out one of the journals they'd found in her grandfather's safe. It was the same type of notebook as the ones she'd found in the box out in the barn. Except this one was in better shape than the others.

Opening the cover, she noticed right away that the ink on the pages weren't as faded either and they separated easily. She thumbed through, all the way to the back. This particular one seemed to have more entries in it, than any of the others did. She flipped back to the front again and also noticed that the very first entry was the month and year that her parents had died in a plane crash.

She quickly closed the cover upon seeing *that* and took a moment to collect herself. A wave of nausea rattled her gut. Her heartbeat quickened. She felt sort of jittery inside all of the sudden so she glanced out at the view beyond the railing, hoping it would quiet the rush of fear and help her concentrate on something more pleasant until she settled down. Taking a few deep breaths, she then exhaled slowly, closed her eyes and tuned in to the music of the night. In the distance the two owls still called to one another. The crickets sang in unison and the breeze picked up. She could hear the rustle of the leaves as they danced in the wind, branches swaying, then falling silent again.

This was going to be hard, she tried to rationalize with herself. Reading the entry about her parent's crash from her grandfather's point of view, was going to stir up a lot of painful, buried feelings. It was bad enough to have experienced it as an eight-year-old when it happened. Now she was going to know what it was like, to deal with it as an adult.

Was she really ready for the pain to come crashing back into her life, right when she had just learned it was okay to be happy again?

She let out an unsteady sigh and at the same time opened her eyes and looked down again at the journal she held in her hands. Aside from the harsh truths it may contain, it was something that had to be done for her, as well as everyone else's peace of mind. And possibly shed some light as to why her grandfather had thought it necessary to later exhume the graves of her parents. Her need for those answers at the moment, overwhelmed the need to protect her delicate side.

Taking a deep breath, she opened the cover again. The top of the first page had the same style as the others, the date written and underlined in black ink, headlining the entry.

June 1987

I am a completely broken man.
As I write this I am trying my best to hold it together but my heart is literally ripping apart.

I am numb and I don't know how I am going to go on—

Sage paused. The lump that was trying to form in her throat was already doing a terrific job. The pressure on her chest began. She was already feeling a magnificent amount of sorrow just from those first three lines.

Oh God, could she really do this?

Could she withstand the intense pain that was jumping off the page?

She took another deep breath and forced her eyes to devour the next sentence.

A few weeks ago, we received the horrible news that the plane my precious daughter Kelley and Jack were on, is missing and presumed to have went off the radar somewhere near the Indian ocean.

Oh God!

Sage quickly glanced up at the view beyond. She subconsciously bit her lip and fought back tears that threatened to escape. Keeping her emotions in check was the key, she kept telling herself in her head.

An old memory of her parent's smiling down at her, as she last remembered them, flashed in her mind, almost as a form of encouragement.

You can do this! It seemed to say.

She looked back down at the entry.

I am frantic and not sure what to do while I wait for more news concerning the search efforts that are underway to locate it.

There is a sick feeling in my gut that tells me the end result is not going to be in our favor. Never in the history of missing planes has one later been found intact and everyone on board found alive.

Sage could hear the echoes, in the deep recesses of her mind, calling out for her parents at their funeral. She had been young then, confused and in agony all at the same time…
Mommy!
Daddy!
Another flashback of the caskets being lowered into the ground soon followed. So had the expressions on her grandparents' faces when it was happening. To an eightyear-old child, they had looked dazed and shocked. Now, as an adult reading this entry, she realized the incredible grief that they were suffering from.

It's so hard to stay optimistic for Margot—that they might still be found alive.
Especially now that this package arrived confirming what I was already afraid of.
I swear, if I find out he had anything to do with this, I'll call in my own markers!!
I won't rest until he's dead!

Who was *he*?
Sage felt the knot in her gut tighten. Was her grandfather insinuating that *someone* might have had something to do with the plane going down?

Oh, my sweet baby girl Kelley.
What have we done?
It hurts so bad to think that I will never see you again. Or to convince myself that I will never hear your voice or be able to talk to you or wrap my arms around you in a loving hug. The precious memories of you as a little girl have become my nightmares. Last night I thought I heard you running the hall, calling out for me and you sounded so scared! And Jack, my precious son, whom I loved as if you were my own flesh and blood. So young and full of unbridled promise. I

can't even begin to understand why God would allow this to happen after everything Everett and I did to save you. It's just not fair!
Why couldn't it have been me?
Why?
And what will I tell our darling, sweet baby Sage? Now she will have to grow up without either of you and this could all be my fault. How did it all come to this?
God please let this be a terrible mistake.
Please let them find that plane!
Oh Lord, I beg of you, let them find my kids alive.
What have I done to us Sage?
What have I done?

Sage quickly closed the cover and lifted her head, her eyes searching the dark shadows of the land in the distance. Even though the fire pit was still emitting a good amount of heat, she suddenly felt very cold *inside*. A lump began forming at the back of her throat and she tried to swallow it down. An odd sort of pressure began to build in her chest. A soft whimper escaped from deep within. It was followed by a floodgate of tears. She quickly pushed the journal off her lap, jumped up, leaned over the railing and heaved violently.

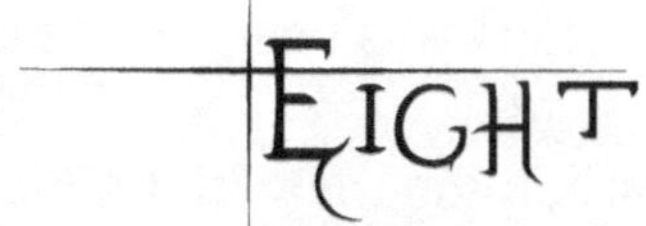

EIGHT

"Would you like me to do that for you sir?"

Brandon jumped at the sound of Hans' voice. It pierced the silence of the dimly lit kitchen. He turned to see he was halfway across the room before he was even aware. "*Shit!*" he responded. "Where in the hell did you come from?"

"Sorry, sir." Hans neared the island where Brandon was standing, a look of concern on his face. "I didn't mean to startle you. Is everything alright?"

"Everything is fine, Hans. You must have super *bionic* hearing. I have been the quietest ever, I swear." Brandon said, earnestly. "I should be the one apologizing if I disturbed *you* guys."

"No need for apologies sir. Lydia and I were in the lounge watching the telly." He said.

"I shouldn't be much longer Hans. I'm just making some late night coffee for Sage." He explained.

Hans looked down. "There are *two* cups sir. Is Miss Sage on a writing frenzy this evening?"

"No, I'm making one of those for me." Brandon said, flashing him a smile when he glanced up.

"Ahhh." Hans said, smiling back and winking. "Planning on a *late* night sir?"

"It's always *possible* Hans, when you're the *father* of a newborn." Brandon said.

Hans chuckled. "And *how* did the unveiling go of the new space out on the balcony?"

Brandon grabbed for Sage's favorite hazelnut creamer from the fridge. "She *flipped,* just like I knew she would." He said, as he walked over to the cup and added some to her coffee. Hans automatically picked up the spoon and began to stir.

"That's just *lovely* sir!" Hans was beaming. "I knew it would please her!"

"By the way, thanks for helping me with hiding that chair and ottoman." Brandon said, reaching up and playfully tapping his shoulder. "If I would have hidden it anywhere else other than your room, she would have sniffed it out before it was put in place."

"Your welcome sir. It was my pleasure. Lydia and I are always glad to be of help."

"She's sitting out there right now." Brandon found it hard to contain himself. "She wants to test it out for a little bit, so I offered to pull daddy duty inside. I think she's wanting to go through the journals and paperwork we found in Frank's safe for a little bit. I opted to go the extra mile and fetch the coffee."

"She will spend hours out there, sir. It's just marvelous what you've done. That's going to be a nice work space for her, until a few months from now when she'll have to start writing inside." Hans said.

"*Dammit*, that reminds me!" Brandon said. "I need to get online right away and order the wood." He removed the second cup and sat it on the counter. "She asked about the desk again tonight, the one she wants for our room. I have her believing that it's going to be *custom* made in a factory. I need to get moving on it."

"Did you tell her the story behind the side table?" Hans asked.

"*Yes*! She noticed the tree missing not *ten* minutes in the chair. She's so damn *observant*! But she was cool about it, just like she's cool with everything." He stirred the creamer in his cup, then threw the spoon in the sink. "That's one of the things I love *most* about her."

"I know sir!" Hans said, smiling himself. "Will you be needing anything else in here tonight?"

Brandon reached for both handles on the cups.

"No, I'm good!" He lifted them off the counter, simultaneously. "Sleep tight old man. See you in the morning."

Doing a pretty good balancing act, he headed towards the main hallway.

"Would you like for me to help you with that, sir?" Hans offered, trailing slowly behind him with the dish towel.

"No, I got it." He managed to leave the kitchen without spilling a drop and entered the hallway that led to the stairs.

"Make sure you turn off the baby monitor Hans. He's mine for the next couple of hours." He added, almost to the first step.

"Lydia and I fed and changed master Tristan not more than a half hour ago sir. He should be out for a while." Hans said behind him.

"Thanks Hans! You guys are awesome! I don't know how Sage and I would manage without you both." He took the first step, then the next and was on the third when behind him he heard Hans say, "*Sir*?"

Brandon, still balancing the cups and a step at a time, said over his shoulder. "What is it Hans?"

"I almost *forgot* to tell you." He said, reaching the bottom of the stairs. "Lydia went out to the barn today to dust and straighten up the office. She said when she walked in, the picture of Charlie, Mr. Hartford, Mr. Cassava and your grandfather had somehow fallen off the wall and was lying on the floor."

"Ok, *well*, did she put it back up?" he asked, thinking; simple problem, simple fix.

"Not *exactly* sir. She said the frame was broken on one side and that the glass was still intact but shattered. She put it on the desk exactly as she found it, for you and Miss Sage to have a look at."

Hans sounded distressed having to tell him this last bit of news. Brandon hated to hear it as well. The frame was just as old and priceless as the picture. And it was happening at the *wrong* time. Especially after the story Charlie had just laid out to them. Sage was not going to be happy.

"Did she mention *what* she thought made it fall?" Brandon asked, almost to the top. "I hung that picture myself and made double sure it was secure."

"Lydia said the hanger was still anchored in the wall and almost looked like someone had walked up to it and knocked it off on purpose."

"That's strange." Brandon stopped and looked down at Hans over the railing. "And nobody's been out there?"

"Nobody since we all left to go to Mrs. Hartford's. This was the first time the office has been unlocked since we got back."

"Hmmm." He said, thinking to himself. "Well, there's nothing I can do about it now."

"I know sir. We just wanted you to be aware." Hans said.

"I appreciate that. We'll deal with it in the morning. Goodnight!"

Brandon resumed climbing the stairs when Hans spoke again.

"Sir, I wouldn't want her to go out there and find it on the desk like that before you told her in the morning." he said from below. "After what has happened."

Brandon cleared the last step, stopped at the beginning of the landing and looked again down at Hans.

"I will *tell* her now, *ok* Hans?" Brandon did not wait for an answer as he turned and began walking past Tristan's door and on to theirs.

Faintly, from below, he could hear Hans muttering. "That would be *splendid*, sir!"

As Brandon neared the doorway to their bedroom, he thought about Hans comment and immediately decided he could not agree. Right now, *splendid* was the last word he would use to describe the *eerie* shit that had been going on long before he and Sage had met. And hearing that the pic of the four men—who helped *mold* their present chaos—just happened to fall off the wall for *no* apparent reason, just added to the ever-growing list of *unexplained* phenomenon.

 NINE

The small living area of Courtney's suite was sparsely illuminated by only two hurricane lamps. Michael had warned her it was all the hotel could spare and the oil had already burned a quarter down in the chambers. Which meant they had about three hours left until their artificial light ran out and they would be plunged into even *more* darkness.

There were three emergency candles lying on the table. She was saving them for later in case it got late and still no power. She would keep one in the bathroom, give one to Michael for his room and the other would be for her room. But she hoped it wouldn't go that far. She absolutely *hated* being in a power outage during the nighttime. A lot of bad things occurred in the dark when people were helpless without electricity. It was giving her anxiety just thinking about it. She started to pace hoping it would release some of her pent-up tension.

Where was Michael?

He had been gone for well over an hour now and she was starving. Not to mention the room had become stuffy without circulation from the overhead fans.

As rain continued to pound the roof, lightening periodically lit up the sky outside the window. She walked over to the nearest one by the dining table, parted the drapes and flipped the latch. The window was old but with some guided force, it lifted up about six inches from the sill before stopping. The cool night air rushed in, along with the strong smell of rain. The window was void of a screen, so the casing quickly began to collect heavy rainwater. She grabbed a hand towel from the bathroom and doubled it up on the sill.

That's when she noticed movement to the right out of the corner of her eye. She hesitated, then leaned closer to the glass, her nose almost touching the pane. She swore she'd seen a flicker of light. Who would be crazy enough to be outside in a storm like this? As if on cue, lightening at that moment, lit up the sky and everything below it, for all of ten seconds. It was then that Courtney saw three figures wearing black rain ponchos. They were walking rapidly towards her, down a narrow alley that ran a story below her window, alongside the hotel. One had a flashlight in his hand which was probably what the flicker of light was that had caught her eye.

As they neared her window, one of the dark figures seemed to slow down. As if he *knew* she was watching, he tilted his head up and looked right at her. Lightening marked a jagged pattern across the sky turning everything bright at the same time. A loud crack of thunder followed directly after and shook the pane she was standing next to. It illuminated the man down below in the alley. There was something about his eyes that sent chills immediately throughout her body. It only magnified the moment. She took a step back and then another until he was out of her sight. The heavy rain was beating down on the pane, soaking the towel on the ledge to the point, that it was starting to drip pools of water on the floor. Her heart raced a little in her chest. Why was this person being so aggressive to someone who was innocently peering out into the night from a hotel room? Maybe it wasn't such a good idea to open the window while she was alone, after all. If this man were athletic enough, he could scale the wall in no time and come right through the opening. The thought gave her chills.

Now all she thought about doing was quickly closing it before he did.

She sprang into action, moving two steps to the right, staying parallel with the curtain, keeping out of his line of vision, in

case he was still right below. From there, she could see the view of the alley to the far left. Another bout of thunder boomed overhead, lightening followed and lit the area.
A sigh of relief flooded her. The man had moved on and was making strides to catch up with the other two. Apparently stepping away from the window had caused him to lose interest. She watched as he began moving at a brisker pace and then they all three disappeared in the dark. Didn't they know the alley was a dead end?
Abruptly, a dull thud from behind made her jump. She turned quickly and her eyes landed on the main door to the suite.
The lock was still engaged and the chain was still on.
What the hell was that?
The sound came again. Another loud thud, almost as if someone were kicking the door from the other side. Then the knob started rattling. Someone was out there…
"*Courtney*!"
She barely could make out the voice but she certainly heard her name.
"Who is it?" she asked, moving closer, her heart thudding.
"It's me! Open up! Hurry!"
"*Michael*!" She said, as she turned the bolt lock, slid the chain off and opened the door wide to indeed find him standing there. In both of his hands he was carrying bags that looked pretty heavy. She bent to grab one as he was passing through the doorway.
"I got this, just shut and lock the door!" he said and headed straight to the dining table.
Once the chain was back in place she met up with him just as he was unloading the first bag. The delicious aroma hit her in the face. He had an assortment of styrofoam containers he'd arranged on the table. He was pulling off the lids, one-by-one to reveal mounds of fluffy rice, steamed mixture of veggies with grilled sausage and potatoes.

"Where did you get all this food?" Courtney asked, her mouth instantly began to water.

"Mambo is out back under a covered porch, whipping up food for the guests on a big square grill-looking thing. They also have an enormous fire pit, a *real* one, not anything you could buy in Walmart." He joked. "There's a ton of people gathered around it, drinking, eating and hanging out. I had to wait for my place in line, for the food that is. I wasn't sure what you would or wouldn't eat, so I just grabbed a variety of what he had to offer. Looks like the people who run this place are prepared for outages like this. And the way they were set up down there, gave me the impression that this black-out situation is a regular occurrence."

The other bag he unloaded held the paper plates, plastic silverware, napkins, packets of salt and pepper, ketchup, mayo, two throwaway cups and two very cold bottles of wine. Courtney raised an eyebrow when he sat them on the table along with a bottle opener.

"Are we celebrating something?" she asked.

"Yeah." He said off-handedly. "We're celebrating the fact that we have a roof over our heads and food in our belly and a dry, warm place to sleep." She grabbed the neck on one of the bottles and tilted it enough in the dim light to read the label. It was a good one and *white—points* for Michael! He tossed the empty bag in the trash can and grabbed the opener and the bottle that Courtney wasn't currently holding. "It's a big no-no in some areas of Kenya, to drink the tap water and they were out of *bottled* water, *Princess*. The only soda in the house is the carbonated Coke from the bar and as you guessed it, the tap doesn't work when the power is out. The only choice left for us was wine or cheap ass beer and you nor I need to wake up in the morning with a shitty headache. So this is the reason for the wine. We need something tasty to wash down all this heavy, greasy food we are about to indulge in." He removed the foil, worked on the cork as he looked back up at her. "*Sit*. Eat!" He instructed. She did as she was told and began helping herself to a little bit of everything. Michael eventually worked the cork out and began filling one of the Dixie cups. He then passed it over to her. He poured another for himself and took a seat next to hers.

As he heaped food onto his plate, Courtney took a sip of the wine and to her surprise she found it to be delicious and refreshing. The food was just as tasty and she dug in not realizing until now, just how famished she had been.

"So does anyone think that the lights will be restored soon?" Courtney asked in between bites.

"Not a chance." Michael said, tearing into his own plate with gusto.

"Do they even know what happened?"

Michael paused from shoving food in his mouth and chewed as he eyed her.

"This *isn't* New York, Courtney." He said, once he swallowed. "They don't have electrical trucks with high-tech lifts to come out at this time of night and restore electric. They will have to wait until the rain stops tomorrow and then figure out where along the lines, the problem is. I think Mambo said there were a total of seven guys—local—who even *know* what the hell they're doing. Three of them are extras out at the pirates site, putting out *other* fires which leaves four here."

He grabbed his wine and took a healthy gulp. He sat his cup back down, uncorked the bottle and topped his and hers off. Courtney wondered if the three people she'd seen below in the alley earlier, were the three guys Michael had just mentioned. It made more sense now to her on why they would be out in weather like this. They had journeyed back from the hideout to help in the morning with the restoration.

"How's the crew doing?" Courtney asked.

"Tony was the only one I ran into downstairs. He was the designated one sent to pick up food for all of them. He's going to stay put once he gets back up to the room. I guess there's a curfew in effect during power failures. The staff is letting everyone know that the hotel will be put on lockdown by midnight. I guess when there's a black-out they don't want to take any chances. When I asked Mambo about it he said it can get pretty rough out on the streets, especially if the rain stops before the sun comes up. Locking down the hotel until then is just an extra precaution. Since that was the case, I took the bottles of wine and Tony took a case of beer up for him and the guys."

"Did you and Tony have a chance to talk?" Courtney asked, finishing up and tossing her plate in the trash.

Michael glanced her way as he took the last bite of food off his plate. "Tony told me about Bram, the house boy. He knows what he's talking about because I checked." He chucked the utensils and the paper plate in the trash, wiped his mouth and hands on a napkin and then threw it in there too.

"So the second team of feds are here because of the deceased in the hut." She confirmed. "Did your source tell you a name perhaps?" she asked.

"No, they weren't at liberty to discuss that with me, Princess."

"Would that source your referring to be the general I seen you talking to in the bar downstairs?" she asked.

He studied her for a moment before answering. "No, I got this straight from one of the feds."

"Where and when did you have the opportunity to talk with one of them?" she asked skeptically.

"Downstairs." Michael said. "He was hanging out next to the fire pit. I noticed him when I was putting our food order in. Coincidently, he was an old buddy I knew back in the college days. While I waited for Mambo to cook our meal, we caught

up. Conversation steered around to the lair. That's how I got confirmation that the person was American. And then, he told me something else that I found quite interesting." "What else did he tell you?" Courtney asked, on the edge of her seat. "He mentioned an incident, back in the states, he thought I should know about." he said, with a touch of gravity to his tone.
"An incident? *What*?" she was perplexed.
"So quick of you to forget, Princess. I hear you had *front* row seats to a shooting!"

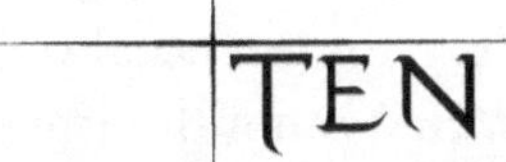

TEN

When Brandon entered the master bedroom, the drop in temperature was immediately evident. The reason why—the French doors were still open to the balcony and the fireplace was void of a fire. He'd been so wrapped up in surprising Sage with her new space, that he hadn't even thought about starting one yet, for the evening. That would be the next thing on his list as soon as he delivered her coffee.

Brandon effectively navigated his way through their master, both cups still balancing in his hands. He stepped out onto the balcony and to his surprise, found it empty. On the ottoman lie what looked like one of Frank's journals but Sage was nowhere in sight. He sat both cups down on the side table and softly called out her name, thinking maybe she might have wondered off to another part of the upper tier. But a quick scan in both directions of the porch, also appeared to be empty. With very few options left, he walked back inside the bedroom and headed towards their bathroom. He found her when he rounded the corner. She was standing at the sink with a towel in her hands and she was pressing it to her face. The fringes of her hairline were wet. It appeared that she had just washed or splashed her face with water. There could be only a few reasons why she would do that.

"You okay?" he asked gently.

She locked eyes with him for a second in the reflection of the mirror and briefly nodded before she resumed drying her face with the towel. The nod did not reassure him and her eyes seemed red and irritated. He immediately figured it had something to do with the notebook that he'd seen lying on the ottoman. She hung the towel back on the bar and turned to him. Now, face to face, he could see that he'd been right and she *had* been crying. He reached out his hand and offered it to her without saying a word. She took it without hesitation and he swiftly guided her back to the balcony. Once he got her settled in the chair, he handed her the fresh cup of coffee. She accepted it with both hands and managed to flash him a half-smile. Brandon glanced at the monitor where his precious son could clearly be seen, sleeping soundly. He gave her a moment to collect herself while he picked up the journal and pulled the ottoman closer, then took a seat. He laid the book in his lap and grabbed his cup. He was quite comfy between the warmth of the liquid and the heat from the fire pit on his back. It not only heated the area thoroughly but the visual of the flames lent an ambiance in the space, that was desperately needed right now. He finally cut the silence and gave his full attention to her.

"Baby, *what* happened?"

She closed her eyes for a second as if to block out a terrible vision and then reopened them and shook her head. "I opened *that*," she said referring to the journal on his lap. "And stepped into a childhood *nightmare* right out of the gate!" Fresh tears shimmered in her eyes. "I didn't make it past the *first* page."

Brandon sat his cup down and opened the cover. He began to read the entry. Right away he could see why she had become so upset. The contents were of Frank Hartford just learning her parents plane was missing. Of course what made matters worse, was that his emotions were raw and bleeding all over the page. Further down, Frank was declaring that he wouldn't rest until the person responsible, was dead. Brandon stopped and looked up at Sage. "I assumed the plane went down because of system or pilot failure?" he asked her.

"That's what I thought too." She said, throwing one hand up in the air.

"Frank sounds as if he's convinced otherwise."

"Exactly!" Sage said, dotting the corner of her eyes with a Kleenex. More fresh tears gathered and escaped from her eyes. He reached over with one hand and lovingly squeezed her leg for comfort. Then he returned his attention to the journal. But the rest of Frank Hartford's rantings, just confused him that much more. He literally seemed to be blaming himself for something he'd had no control over. Brandon closed the book and looked up at his distraught wife. He sighed and scratched his head.

"You think maybe *reading* this right now is such a *good* idea, Sage?" He asked, tapping his finger on the cover of the book. "I mean; we just went through some pretty *heavy* family drama that we haven't even processed yet. Maybe we should try to sort that out *first* before we take on any more?"

"I'm afraid there isn't *any* part of this drama that's going to be *easy* to sort out, Brandon. My grandfather's entry and Charlie's story are just pieces to a *bigger* puzzle, than I think any of us realize." She said.

The picture that Hans had told him fell off the wall in the office earlier, entered his mind. He pushed it aside for the moment.

"I'm sorry this is all happening." He said soothingly. "It's as much out of *your* control, as it is *mine*. This ship sat sail long before we were born." She said, staring off into space.

"This is true." Brandon agreed. "And there's only two people left that I think know more than they're telling about the events that went down *after* the crash."

"We were in a room full of strangers." Sage said. She turned from staring out into the night and looked at him.

"Maybe they didn't want to blindside me too bad that night in front of everyone. Maybe one-on-one, both Charlie and my grandmother would level with me about the details, in a more intimate setting. Or maybe my grandmother doesn't even *know* the truth behind the crash, if indeed it was a result of Victor's plot to seek revenge. My grandfather could have spared her the pain and kept it to himself."

"For all we know Frank could have *told* Charlie to spare you *and* Margot the details." Brandon offered. "Maybe he never intended for these journals to be found either. It's possible that leaving them behind in the safe, was not in his original plan."

She tossed the used tissues on the edge of the table and picked up her cup. "He took those two specifically from the cabin, back to Florida with him and hid them in the safe for a reason. Otherwise, if he didn't want them found, he would have thrown them in the fireplace right below it. That much I know about him."

"Unfortunately, as much as I want Charlie's story and Karly getting arrested to be the end of it," Brandon said, "I have to agree with you. There's too many holes. I tend to believe he was holding onto them for a reason."

"Unfinished business." Sage suggested, deep in thought.

"And you and I have no doubts that the '*he*' my grandfather was referring to in that entry, *was* none other than Victor Rocha."

Brandon thought about this for a minute.

"Yeah but why would he personally go after Frank? Victor could have put a hit out on me or my dad if he wanted to continue to get at my grandfather. Charlie gave me the impression that Rocha had a bigger hard-on for him because of his affair with Catalina."

"And I'm sure he did but put yourself in Rocha's evil mind for a second. My grandfather and yours were partners with him in the furniture trade. He got butt-hurt when he was cut off doing business with them. He probably lost a lot of money and was made to look like an ass to his peers. It wasn't enough that he got his revenge on Everett when Catalina drown. He went further by shooting my grandparents down in cold blood and would have done the same to their children and Everett, if they'd hadn't got out that night. But he didn't stop there. He teamed up with his brother and came all the way to California with intent to kill Everett that night they broke into the furniture store. Who knows what would have happened if he'd been successful. Would he have shown up at *our* house next? And then *yours* to complete the Vendetta? Doing so would have wiped both of our bloodlines off the map."

"When you deal in massive quantities of drugs Sage, there's always several hands in the pot. It's impossible for it to function effectively under a one-man operation. When our grandfathers cut Rocha's trade off, it put a major kink in his plan and humiliated him in front of his business partners which I have no doubt he had. In order to gain some of that respect back, he had no choice but to retaliate. Taking out the men who caused it and their families in Victor's eyes, was the golden ticket for revenge."

"Victor Rocha *murdered* my grandparents, and now possibly had something to do with murdering my mother and father. And all for *what*?" she asked, new tears forming in her eyes.

Brandon reached over and gently squeezed her hand in comfort. "Bastards like Victor Rocha don't have compassion for human lives, Sage. Sometimes there is no reason."

"But I need one." She said. "I need answers in order to find closure."

Brandon sighed. "For you, I'm willing to put my feelings aside and arrange a time we can go see Charlie, if it's the only way we are going to get to the bottom of this and find the closure we *both* need."

"And what if Charlie or anyone else involved doesn't have the answers? Then what?"

Brandon could see and clearly hear the worry in her words. "The answers are out there somewhere and we have many resources to go to *if* we need to dig deeper. Don't forget my love, that our newly *acquired* females of the family make a living out of digging up dirt," Brandon said, rolling his eyes. "And since they *enjoy* it so much, I'm sure they would love to help us out, if needed. Then there's always Madison, the private detective. He seems to be able to dig in places that no one else can. Don't worry. We'll figure this all out."

Sage nodded, looking a little more relieved. He squeezed her hand gently again.

"Don't keep *anything* from me." She said, her eyes pleading. "No matter how much you think it's going to hurt Brandon, *please* don't do it. Don't try to protect me or my feelings from the truth. I know going in, that the closure for this is not going to be pain-free."

"I won't." he said.

"Promise?" she asked.

"I promise." He agreed. Again the picture of the four men flashed in his mind and what Hans had told him, right when he was coming up the stairs.

"On that note, I do have something to tell you." He began, slowly. "It doesn't have anything to do with what we were just talking about. It's about the picture of our famous foursome that we have hanging out in the barn."

"What about it?" Alarm immediately showed on her face. He knew how much she loved that picture now that she knew its significance.

"Nothing has happened to the picture itself, but Hans said Lydia found it on the floor in the office. The way he tells it, sounds like it just didn't want to hang there anymore. Apparently it broke the frame and the glass." She sighed.

"As long as there's nothing wrong with the picture, the rest can be replaced." Her shoulders relaxed slightly, which made him glad he had decided to tell her now.

The baby began moving around in the monitor, causing both of them to turn their attention to the screen. Tristan made little grunting noises, blew some bubbles from his tiny lips and then tooted some air. Both of them laughed and it broke some of the tension. Then the baby grew still and his soft snores began to take up rhythm again. Brandon felt the cool air push at his back. He glanced at his watch. It was getting late. "I need to start a fire in our room. It's pretty chilly in there."

"Go ahead." She said. "I'll be right behind you."

He stood up and smiled at her. "Of course." He leaned over and kissed her.

"I love you." She said.

"I love you *more*!" He lingered close for a moment, to search her eyes. "Are you sure you want to be alone?"

She nodded. "I need a moment."

"Ok, take your time. I've got a few things that I need to wrap up online before bed." He collected his cup and the baby monitor. "I'll take this with me and keep an eye on our little man. I can take this in too." He offered, referring to the journal.

Sage glanced over at the black book still resting on the side table and slowly began to shake her head no.

"Don't worry about it." She said casually. "I'll bring it in with me when I come."

"Ok." He nodded and moved towards the French doors. "You know where to find me." He winked at her, blew her a kiss and headed inside, hoping for her sake, she would leave that *damn* journal closed, for the rest of the night.

ELEVEN

The man was alone in the *'time out'* room when they'd first brought the aggressive female patient in. He'd been sitting quietly in the corner, his eyes glazed over from being heavily medicated. His lips were clamped together tight and his big hands were clasped and resting on his chest. His breathing was shallow. Before she'd entered the room he had been staring intently at the television mounted high up on the wall. Now, he glanced away from it for all of two minutes, blood shot eyes following their movements. The woman was wrestling with the two men who had an iron grip on both of her upper arms, on either side of her. Halfway towards what was referred to as the *glass room*, the woman went limp, refusing to take another step on her own. So they hauled her up by her armpits and dragged her the rest of the way.

The bad-tempered nurse—who always *stayed* inside the room—had been anticipating their arrival. She already had a pair of gloves on and was preparing a needle. Once the patient caught sight of the syringe, she began shouting obscenities. Most had this reaction when they knew they were about to be sedated against their will.

He turned his head slowly back to the room before him. He was still the sole occupant. The chairs around him were empty but before long, the woman would join him. She would sit in this room for thirty minutes, in front of the TV, while being observed by the scowling nurse. They would wait for the drugs to neutralize her system and calm her down before the orderlies would come and escort her back to her room.

His attention turned back to the images that filled the TV screen. They were flashing so fast; his drug-laden mind couldn't keep up. It began to mesmerize him until the orderlies blocked his view. They were back with the female, who they deposited in the chair about three down from his. When they left the room he dared to turn and look at her. She was already swimming in the drugs, mouth agape, eyes transfixed on nothing in particular, the fight in her completely gone, for now. She was probably not even aware he was in the room, much less within her reach. Soon losing interest, he stared at the television. Before long, the orderlies appeared again and escorted him back to his room.

TWELVE

This was going to be one long night, Courtney thought. The pissed-off look Michael had on his face right now, told her it was going to be as turbulent as the storm outside. He was angry with her and he had every right to be. Second hand stories from somewhere else tend to muck up trust in any relationship. Hadn't he preached that to her during the entire time they'd known each other? But he hadn't been totally honest with her either, so didn't that make them even?

"I was going to tell you—."

"But you didn't!" He cut her off again.

"I know I didn't. We've been caught up in this mess—."

"We've been idle *all* day, Courtney, don't give me that excuse!"

"This is the first time, other than lunch, that we've had time to sit down together. I couldn't talk to you in the middle of that chaos in the dining room, in front of Tony—."

"He *knows*!" Michael cut her off again. "Everybody at the station *knows*! It's quite the story back home. As a matter of fact, it will be *breaking* news tomorrow on the evening edition, right about the time we should be *landing* in New York."

Courtney just stared at him. It hit her a little hard what he'd just said. She hadn't put much thought into the press side of the nightmare she'd experienced at Margot Hartford's home. Sure they had skated right by the cops with Karly's delusional story, claiming they were the missing Rocha and Benenati kids. If the cops hadn't been long-time fans of hers and Brandon's and the chief of police a major fan of Sage's book, it could have gone in a totally *different* direction.

But luck might not be on their side when it came to the media storm that would follow, once the story aired. Journalists would be coming at them from every angle possible and who knows what they might dig up or who's interest they would attract, dragging it out all over *national* television. There could be more of their enemies out there that would want them dead. Giving credit to any of Karly's story could leave them like sitting ducks. They would *all* be exposed. The whole idea of it was making her ill. She was beginning to understand now why Brandon loathed her *kind* so much.

"Is *our* station breaking the story?" She dared to ask.

"*Of course!*" he said in a tone that made her feel like it was the stupidest question on the planet. Which it was because she already *did* know the answer. News was news, no matter who you were. A notorious, dead criminal's daughter, trying to murder a house full of prominent, well-known celebrities, was *definitely* a headliner. Especially when one of their own major network journalists, were among the ones targeted. She sighed out loud, swallowed what wine was left in her glass and poured more. She emptied the bottle.

"Now you see why I brought *two* bottles of wine instead of one?" he asked, as he reached over and began working the cork off the second.

She sat the empty bottle down and sighed again. "So what exactly is the story?" she asked, having a hard time keeping the dread out of her voice.

"I don't know. I was hoping *you'd* tell me." He replied curtly, twisting the corkscrew deeper inside the top of the bottle with a little more force than necessary.

"There's nothing to tell." She began, her tone sounded a little too defensive. "I went to the Hartford house to—."

"Don't *patronize* me Courtney." He said, interrupting her.

The cork popped and he tossed it and the opener on the table. He sat the bottle down between them and his eyes were piercing at her.

"I'm not patronizing you Michael, *honestly*, with everything going on here, it just slipped my mind."

"Don't give me that *bullshit*, Princess." He said "Putting a bullet in a mobster's daughter isn't something that just *slips* your mind! Furthermore, what *really* pisses me off, is that *you* weren't the *first* one I heard it from."

In her defense, she wasn't keeping it from him on purpose, nor had she anticipated dealing with this so soon. My God, she hadn't even had time to process it herself yet. This time it didn't count.

"Who are *you* to talk?" Courtney asked, feeling the anger and defensiveness in her rise. "Why was I the *last* one to learn about your *personal* connection to the general who's running this show?"

"It's been *common* knowledge since we got here. How in the hell did you think I got us an *exclusive* on that site and myself, *inside* that hut? You've just been too preoccupied to pay attention. Now I *know* why!"

"I've been preoccupied with the story we're working on!" she protested.

"Well, you *best* start worrying about your *own* story right now, since our current segment is on hold. It's a no-brainer that the station is going to want a statement from you about what happened. I'd like one *now*!" He demanded.

"There's no story to work on." She simply said. "I was at the Hartford home when they figured out they had a rogue maid on their hands. The authorities stepped in and arrested her and we all went our separate ways, *after* we gave our statements."

Michael just stared at her for a few seconds before he spoke. "You must take me for a *fool*, Princess. Your audience might buy *that* story, but I don't. And once your competition figures out that the perpetrator is Victor Rocha's daughter, they're not going to buy it either. All the people you pissed off in this business along the way to the top, will start digging for any dirt they can find to *bury* you with. You're the *queen* of your game Courtney and your sitting in the *hot* seat. Those reporters that you *think* are your friends, will turn on you at the drop of a hat and throw your ass off that throne *without* thinking twice."

"Gee! Thanks for the lecture, *dad*!" She replied, sarcastically.

"Your welcome!" He responded with equal passion in his tone. "It's called the *'prelude-to-a-kiss'* version. You think I'm kidding, your delusional as well. I'm not being hard, I'm being *real*. You know how this works, Courtney. One silly mistake or scandal, can change your *whole* life. So you better work long and hard on your statement while you have time on your hands. Because everything you say is going to be critiqued to the last detail. One wrong choice of words can cause an avalanche to come down on your head and you can lose everything you've worked for, overnight!"

"What would *you* have done any different?" she asked, growing more agitated.

"This is *your* circus and *your* monkeys!" he said, throwing out the old adage she often used, when referring to drama.

"You *left* me out of the loop! Your seriously not going to start *asking* for my advice now?" He threw his hands up.

"I wasn't planning on leaving you out of the loop! Regardless of whether you *believe* me or not, I had *intended* on telling you. I just hadn't found the time—."

"Again I ask, what's wrong with *now*?" He stared at her. She stared back.

The rain seemed to slow in its pace and become a steady hum.

"I went to the Hartford mansion—."

"The truth *this* time." He said, interrupting again. "*Because* if your trying to make me believe that it was *only* to advise Charlie Vega on a *legal* aspect, then we're done!"

He meant every word, Courtney knew it. The tone of his voice said he had been pushed too far.

"It was *my* initial motive." she said, point blank.

"I doubt that." he said, not being catty but truthful. "It was your way *in* to a bigger prize. There was a five-million-dollar *bonus* up for grabs if you could snag an interview with his *star* clients!"

"*You* dangled that five-mil like a *carrot* in front of my face!" She reminded him.

"I didn't *dangle* a carrot—as you put it—to *cushion* your bank account, Courtney. I presented the idea to you because I know how *hard* you've worked and how much you wanted your *own* show."

"The big guys set me up to watch me fall. Giving me an assignment to nail down one of the most hard-to-get-at celebrities in the business, was the first sign."

"Which you managed to *pull* off anyway." he said, matter-of-factly. "*regardless* of the odds in the beginning. Hopefully if you get that interview done quick enough, it might air in time to cast a shadow on the news that you *shot* somebody!"

Courtney tensed up. "The cops determined it *was* self-defense." She said. "There are no *legal* ramifications."

"There are *always* legal ramifications when someone gets shot by a *famous*, public figure, Courtney!"

"I didn't do *anything* wrong. The two people present when I shot her *will* testify to that, if it were to get serious."

"It's *already* serious! The FBI told me about it!" He sighed heavily. "Where did you get the *gun* that you shot her with, Courtney?"

"It was Brandon's," she said.

"Brandon Parrish's?" he questioned. She nodded. Michael scrubbed his face with his free hand and then sipped heartily from his glass. She waited. "*How* did you get your hands on Brandon Parrish's gun?"

"I *took* it from him." she said.

"*Great*!" Michael said, exasperated.

"Brandon froze up and someone had to *shoot* that crazy bitch!" she said, in self-defense.

Michael closed his eyes all of two seconds. When he opened them again, he pinned them on her directly. "Please tell me that you *didn't* give that *exact* statement to the *cops*?"

She let out a snarky laugh. "How *stupid* do you think we are?" she asked.

 Michael just shook his head and rubbed his brow in bewilderment. "Who is *we*, Courtney?"

"Me, Brandon and Peter."

"So you were in a room with Brandon Parrish and Peter Jackson?"

She nodded. "And that lunatic!"

"Why were you the one that ended up shooting her?"

"Because Peter was no match for her, he only had the poker from the fireplace and I had nothing but my shoes. Brandon was the only one who had something that would knock her on her ass, guaranteed. But he froze when he thought she was going to stab his newborn. So I took it out of his hands and shot her myself. She had a *butcher* knife and I wasn't going to be stupid enough to try and take it from her emptyhanded, Michael. Neither was anyone else. She had to be stopped."

"Why did she want to *stab* Brandon's newborn, Courtney?"

"She's a psycho Michael! She wanted to stab all of us!"

"Why? *Why* does Victor Rocha's daughter, the *same* Victor Rocha *you* interviewed on death row, want to stab *all* of you for? What's her motive?"

"The cops said she had an obsession with Brandon. She's went after him before. She's just crazy Michael and crazy people don't necessarily need a reason."
"But according to my fed friend, she has some wild story to tell."
"I don't think anyone's going to believe her. She's the one behind bars, not us!"
"A good defense attorney could change that."
"I have *no* ties to Victor Rocha other than that *one* interview." Courtney had not validated anything yet, concerning *her* part in Charlie's story, so she could still safely say that, without the guilt of lying. But Michael, the way he was staring so hard at her, made her rethink her comment. This man was smart and unfortunately there were a thousand others like him in the field, that weren't necessarily on her side. She would definitely need him to get through this. And with the way he was coming at her, it was like he already knew Karly's story she'd told to the cops and he was waiting to see if Courtney would fess up on her own.
"Why were Meg and Peter Jackson there?" he asked.
"Peter is Sage Cassava's publisher." She simply answered.
"And his wife is one of the *biggest* platforms of tabloid trash on the celebrity circuit." Michael said. "If there's one thing I do know about the *famous* Brandon Parrish, it's that he *hates* the tabloids and doesn't mingle with anyone in that category on a *private* level, *especially* Meg Jackson from *We* Magazine."
"Wasn't my party." Courtney said. "I was just a guest."
"*Guest*?" Michael repeated. "And Charlie Vega was the host?" She nodded. "And the theme of the party was legal advice?" Michael stared her down, just waiting for her to falter. "Charlie Vega has a *slew* of lawyers on hand but yet, he steps *out* of the safety of his inner circle and calls *you*?" He cocked a brow. "But yet, you two have never met!"

God, he was so good at finding all the holes in the white lies.

"Unfortunately, I am bound under a client/attorney confidentiality agreement—" She said.

"*Ok!*" He sighed out loud and pushed his chair back. "I'm not going to play this game with you anymore." He said, looking her directly in the eye. "You want to keep dancing around the truth, you can do so *alone!*" He stood up from his chair. "I'll leave the rest of the wine for you. You're going to *need* it, Princess, while you *fabricate* a good story for your audience!"

He bent over and pulled something out of the bag he'd brought their dinner in, earlier. The light from the lamps reflected long enough on the object for her to make out a fifth of Grey Goose.

"I could definitely use a shot of that." She said, trying to instill some dry humor.

With bottle in hand he gave her an apathetic face. "*Nah*! I only share *my* vodka with *my* friends."

His words were meant to cut her and they did a good job. She couldn't respond, could only watch as he turned around and began the short trek to his room.

Yeah, he was royally pissed, Courtney thought and she had to make a quick decision. She hadn't uttered a word to anyone about the outrageous story that Charlie Vega had conveniently dropped in her lap before leaving for Kenya. The pirate's logs that were discovered and the dead American in the hut, had become priority while her personal issues had been put on the back burner. She seriously had not even given it much thought since, about how she was going to proceed in the matter. Nor had she had any time to do her own research to validate Charlie's story. Sharing it with anyone before her DNA could be tested, was like pulling the cart before the horse. But Michael wasn't just *anyone*, she kept reminding herself, as she stared at his retreating back. He was one of the few people that she could trust and who actually gave a damn about her. Was keeping the secret worth the twenty years of solid friendship and support she'd received from this man? After all, the Benenati case had been *his* story in the beginning. Didn't he have a right to know the truth after all these years, of what really happened to those kids? Did she even have the right to tell their story to someone outside their tight circle without the rest giving her permission?

"*Wait*!" Courtney said, halting Michael in his tracks. He was only a few steps away from his bedroom door. The sound of the rain outside, had slowed down its rhythm to a low, consistent vibration, enough, so she didn't have to yell.

"Charlie Vega *did* call me, that much is true and I have the phone records to prove it." She hesitated but he still did not turn around. "And he did ask for me to come to the Hartford's for *legal* advice. Or at least that's what I was under the impression that I was going there for. I had no idea that Brandon Parrish, or his wife Sage, or Meg and Peter were going to be there and they had no idea in return that I was coming. I guess that was Charlie's way of being clever, by getting us all there, in one place."

Michael turned and made eye contact with her. "And *why* Courtney, would Charlie Vega want *all* of you in one place?"

Courtney took a deep breath and while she slowly exhaled, she came to a decision.

"Because…he wanted to *share* something with us, something that we weren't aware we all had in common." The rain filled the pause between them as he stared hard at her.

"And just *what* was it that he wanted to *share* with all of you, Courtney?"

She thought about the words that had haunted her all the way to the other side of the world. The ones that had spooked her to the core from the beginning.

"For starters, Charlie Vega *told* me, that in reality, I was *a* famous, *missing* baby. You know, the *one* from the story in Milan, Italy that *you* covered years ago? The *baby* that belonged to Catalina and Victor Rocha?"

She let that sink in a minute. Her eyes began to water and her emotions began to waver just thinking that it *might* be true. But then again, it *was* true…and she had just made it *real* by speaking for the first time about it to another, out loud, from her own mouth.

Michael just stared at her from across the room. Disbelief and shock were evident in his eyes. She had to say something. She couldn't stand the way he was looking at her.

"Charlie also told us that he *and* Meg Jackson were *two* of the *three* missing *Benenati* children—Sage Cassava's father, Jack, who died in the plane crash—was the *third!*" She added, heaping it all on him at once. And now for the finale… "And Brandon Parrish, the legendary Hollywood actor I'm supposed to conduct an *unbiased* interview with? His grandfather is *Everett Calhoun*—who Charlie said was really my *biological* father, not Victor Rocha, thank God! Apparently Everett had an affair with my mother, Catalina—the one who drowned in the family pool? Well that was a lie. She didn't drown, she was murdered because she fell in love with my…*Everett!*" She couldn't bring herself to say the *other* word. "And it started a war between the families for decades because Everett found out Victor was trying to smuggle *drugs* into the states through his furniture business and he cut him off."

Michael didn't respond, he just walked silently across the room and dropped heavily in the chair he'd just vacated in a huff. The look of uncertainty was very pronounced in his expression.

"*Holy shit*!" he said, as if the story had worn him out. He unscrewed the cap of the vodka and poured both of them shots in the Dixie cups on the table. He pushed one over to her, took his down in one swig and then refilled it. His eyes locked with hers. "*Holy shit*." He repeated, staring at her still in disbelief.

"Now you got an idea of where I'm coming from."

"Your dead serious?" He wanted confirmation.

"I wish I wasn't." she said.

He poured another shot for them both.

"Ok! I *need* you to run this by me one more time. Start from the beginning, Princess. From the time you first got the call from *Vega*."

She reached for the shot he gave her, took it down and winced at the bite it had.

Yep, Courtney thought, this was definitely going to be one *long* night.

THIRTEEN

The key people who were going to be in charge of bringing Stranded to the big screen, met with Charlie the next morning in his conference room at the agency. Surrounded by the producer, director and his assistant, the scriptwriter and three members of the casting company, they had together compiled a *wish list* of actors they thought suitable for the characters in the book. It had only taken them two hours to cast twenty-nine hopefuls for ten spots. And that was supposed to have been the easy part, Charlie thought. Now he was curious how long it would take them to conquer the hardest part which was finding the lead female role to cast opposite of Hollywood's *sexy* bad boy, Brandon Parrish. They'd already spent a half hour throwing out names of popular actresses and every one had ended up on the chopping block because they were either already under contract on other projects or caught up in a series that could last for several more seasons.

Feeling like they were getting absolutely nowhere, Charlie was quickly running out of patience. Sometimes, on days like this where the brainstorming started to tire, it was best to end the torture and reconvene another day, when everyone had time to sleep on it and refresh their minds. Losing interest with the topic at hand, he glanced up at the clock on the wall and saw that it was close to noon. He could often get grouchy if meetings ran over into his lunch hour. This one had all the makings. But before Charlie could stick his two cents in, the head joker spoke. "Read the personality and physical traits again please?" The producer asked one of the casting crew members seated next to him.

"The character is a plain jane. She's pretty, but naturally pretty. There's nothing described as flashy in her appearance when it comes to makeup, clothes or accessories.”

“Diamond in the ruff.” Another added. “Remember, Brandon’s character stumbles upon her in a remote cabin. It’s not until he almost loses his life that he wakes up and sees that real beauty comes from a selfless heart.”

“Yes!” the scriptwriter said. “This story projects a lot about feelings, emotions, strong connections and passion in every aspect. We must convey that at all times when it comes to the two main characters. The actress we end up choosing must possess strong charisma skills, in general, in order to connect with Brandon’s equally strong screen presence that he’s known for.”

“And don’t forget the character is curvy.” The casting director said. “She’s not a size zero and take it from me, makeup has tried it before on past projects. It’s almost impossible to pad up some of these anorexic actresses and make the adjusted weight appear real, even getting the graphic guys involved which can blow the budget. It would be a big advantage to *all* of us if the one we cast has her own curves in real life.”

“She’s right.” The Scriptwriter said. “Mr. Parrish’s character does make it a point more than once in the book about his rescuer having a body shape *nothing* like the Hollywood starlets he’s used to mingling with.”

“So, what Hollywood starlet doesn’t *look* like a Hollywood starlet?” The producer asked with a grin. “Who first comes to mind that is a natural beauty in the land of plastic surgeons and Botox? Who has tons of charisma, curves and sex appeal and could easily *seduce* the viewers and Brandon Parrish’s character, right in front of God and everybody on the screen by literally just standing there?” The assistant director gave a short laugh. All eyes turned to him as he opened his mouth to speak. “That would be an easy answer if Marilyn Monroe were still alive. You just described her perfectly.”

A few more laughs followed all around. Charlie remained stone-faced. Marilyn Monroe was dead and *ten* more minutes had gone by unproductive.

"She was too sexy to play a plain jane part like this." One of the men from the casting crew said as he tried to contain a grin.

"That's not true." The woman on the end said. "Marilyn Monroe didn't always play the sex symbol in her movies. Her more serious roles highlighted her beauty without having all her assets on display."

"I agree." The director said. "If the actress is good enough, she can play any part thrown at her and be convincing no matter how gorgeous she is."

Charlie thought about this for a second.

"The author did not intend for the audience to view the star of her story reminiscent to *Beauty and the Beast*." He said, looking around the table. "She's a beautiful girl, inside and out and Brandon's character is just lucky enough to find her because of a twist of fate and a snowstorm. The girl had locked herself away from the world because of all the bad she has suffered in real life, not because she was *hideous*!" Charlie barked the last word.

Yep, he was getting grouchy and everyone at the table knew it. A moment of silence took over the room. Then the woman on the end dared to speak.

"There's only one person who *fits* the description of a modern day Marilyn, in the present." She said, quite serious now. "Only difference is, where Miss Monroe was pale and platinum, this beauty I'm thinking of is exotic *and* dark. But makeup could lighten the skin and the hair and adding extensions for length would have to be adjusted…*but* the curves would definitely *be* real. And the charisma—well anyone here would agree, she's *dripping* with it!"

"*Who* do you have in mind?" The producer asked.

"Lola Watters." The woman said.

The room was silent for a few seconds. Charlie was the first to speak.

"Lola Watters is the total *opposite* of the character we are searching for. *Absolutely not!*"

"That's why it works!" The woman continued, not taking Charlie's comment as a final vote. "Think about it. She's sexy, naturally beautiful and legitimately curvy with tons of charisma bursting at the seams!"

"The only thing *bursting* at the seams when it comes to Lola Watters, is her clothes!" Charlie said. "And that's what roles she's known for. Not for playing a *passive* woman out in the middle of nowhere in Montana during a snowstorm."

"She's an actress!" The woman on the end spoke up in her defense. "She might be wild in real life but she knows how to take on a part and make it hers. I've worked with her before and I've witnessed it myself. And she *does* fit the body shape criteria, in fact, she's *perfect* if you think about it."

"I have *thought* about it and I don't agree." Charlie said. "She's too high-strung for this character and her look is theatrical while this role is humble as hell."

"Our makeup people are some of the *best* in the business." The woman on the end professed. "They can tame her look down and lighten her up in no time into a believable character."

"It wouldn't hurt to run a test." The assistant director said. Charlie sighed in response. His belly growled loud enough for only him to hear.

"I can see it." The director said.

"I *don't!*" Charlie simply said.

"It might work now that I'm really visualizing it." The casting director said. "She definitely has the curves and the sex appeal on-screen."

"That's the problem." Charlie said. "Our character is sweet, innocent and totally the *opposite* of a diva. I've never seen Lola play a character like that. I'm not so sure she could pull it off."

"That's the whole point." The assistant director said. "She's never played in a role like this so people will be curious. We will attract the male side of the audience because it's a love story starring the notorious sex symbol, so they will be hoping for a boob shot or something."

"This is not a soft *porn* film!" Charlie said rather curtly.

"But the male population doesn't know that." The kid laughed. "We can get the censorship to give it at least a '*sexual* situations' rating which to men *means* sex. And because another famous sex symbol is playing the male part, the wives will be coming right along with them, their *drool* buckets in tow. It would be an explosive headliner!"

"You got a point there." The producer spoke up, dreaming of the headlines with his name close by. "*Sexiest man of the year Brandon Parrish and luscious sex symbol Lola Watters, heating up the screen!* Tickets would be sold out during the release of its first launch. They both have very strong followings at the box office and it wouldn't be hard since you manage them both, Charlie."

"Not to mention that you manage the *author* as well." The woman on the end said. Charlie eyed her longer than he had intended to. She was a good looking woman, maybe ten years younger than he and she had a set of balls. The look on her face told Charlie she was aware of it and she held his eyes as long as he was giving them to her. "Have they ever played in a movie opposite each other before?" The eager scriptwriter asked, his pen poised in the air waiting to make more notes on the paper before him.

"Yes!" The woman with the balls answered before Charlie could. "And they were sizzling." She added, smiling at him. "In fact they nailed it at the box office where the numbers were concerned, didn't they, Mr. Vega? I clearly remember agreeing with the critics when they reached out to you *personally* in their reviews wondering *why* you had not paired them before since they had such chemistry." She finished, quite smug with herself.

"She was a *stripper* in that particular piece." Charlie persisted, giving her that look that usually scared others away.

"Doesn't matter *what* her role was." The woman said, bolder than ever. "When they were both on the screen, it *sizzled*."

"I agree." The assistant director said.

"Well," Charlie said, feeling suddenly feisty. "Too much of a good thing spoils the pot!" he said, directly at her. "The pot for this pair has grown quite cold, Mr. Vega." The woman dared to retort but totally in a mannerly way.

"How long has it been since they worked together?" The director asked.

"It's been a while." The assistant director said.

"If it's been more than five years, which it has," the woman *with* the balls said. "then the audience would be eager. Especially if Stranded is marketed in the right way with both of their names screaming to the crowds. And it should be announced at least three weeks earlier than the usual run before a premiere. It will get the fans hyped up to where the first opening weekend, will be in a *complete* frenzy!"

Charlie stared at her again longer than he intended to but this time with a more serious interest. She was right, he had to give her that. The magnitude of people Brandon's iconic name had drawn in, from all over the world during his last premiere, had been astounding. Adding another well-known, hot, curvy actress who was literally busting at the seams like Lola Watters, was box office overload. The numbers in the end would be appealing and would set them all up for a hell of a franchise but his job was to stand for the client *first* and in this instance, that was his niece, Sage.

And she had specifically requested that she approve of who was going to play her part, opposite of her real-life husband. One look at Lola in the flesh and Sage would do *him* the favor of sending another actress to the chopping block without him even lifting a finger. He turned his attention back on the ballsy woman.

"What's your position here?" Charlie asked her directly. The table grew very quiet, almost as if they were suddenly the only two people in the room. The woman had obviously done her research opposed to the other five in the group. With casting companies, they had so many titles he was curious which this one held.

"I'm the one in charge of making it happen!" She said, looking directly in his eyes with pride in her voice. "I'm the one who's *responsible* for finding the talent and shaping them into the character."

"She has a gift." The woman sitting next to her said. "She's usually right on the mark."

"In other words," Charlie began, "You're the role and actor matchmaker in the movie industry."

"That's a strange way of putting it, Mr. Vega but you've got the idea." The woman stated, not wavering one bit.

"And how long have you been doing this?" Charlie asked because honestly her face was not ringing a bell and he didn't even know her name.

"Ten years, Mr. Vega." She said, holding her own.

"And you said you hired the best?" He turned then and directed this question to the producer.

"And that she is." The producer said, not missing a beat.

"She hasn't been wrong, not once." He said in her defense, as if the woman were not present.

"And you think that Lola Watters is our damsel in distress?" Charlie asked her rather sarcastically, turning his attention on her again.

"Totally!" she said without delay.

He studied the woman for a moment, wondering why she was pushing so hard to put Lola front and center of this project. Sure the actress was good or else she wouldn't be one of his clients but Lola had no experience carrying a heavy lead in a movie.

"This might be the first time you break record." Charlie warned her lightly.

"Before we get too carried away, does Miss Watters have any projects lined up in the near future that would knock her out of the running?" The producer asked Charlie.

Charlie shook his head, answering honestly. "Nothing too pressing at the moment. She has a trail of endorsements and something pending but that project doesn't even start until the end of next year."

"Is she local?" The director asked.

"She has a home in Beverly Hills and New York but last I was aware, she was on vacation in Costa Rica somewhere." Charlie said, shrugging his shoulders.

"If everyone is in agreement I would be willing to do a screen test." The assistant director offered.

"I'm *not* in agreement." Charlie said.

"It still wouldn't hurt." The woman with the balls spoke up again. "Makeup is on standby *and* idle. We can get her right in, if you and her are willing and start working on the look. I've seen Lola study a script and be ready to test in under an hour."

"She's right Charlie, we have nothing to lose." The producer said. "Lola is a focused actor."

Charlie sighed as he shut the cover on the file he'd been taking notes in. "I know what my client is capable of and I also know her many talents. But personally, I just don't see her as primary on this film. You have one chance to convince me. In the meantime, don't stop thinking about *other* possibilities. Email, text or fax them to me for consideration. If I think they are worthy, I'll share. We'll meet again next week and go over and hopefully *vote* on a possible lead so we can get this show on the road, no pun intended. Very soon I'd like to get a date set on when we can actually start shooting."

"The faster we find our female star and nail down a location, my people are ready to go." The director said. "Of course, once all the supporting actors are in place, we can shoot around the main characters until she's named, if you're in that much of a hurry."

"What's going on with location?" Charlie asked, looking around the table, glad to be changing the subject. "Has the scouts found anything yet?" He directed this at the producer.

"Finding that perfect setup close to the description in the book has been a challenge." The producer said, answering in his place.

"But I happened across *something* this morning." The woman with the balls interceded with confidence. Again Charlie turned his attention on her and felt the stress factor on his meter slide lower just a little bit. He took the piece of paper she held out to him. It looked to be a flyer of a two story cabin, similar to the one in Montana, that Brandon and Sage owned now.

"Not bad." Charlie admitted out loud. "Have you checked this out?" He looked directly at the woman who seemed to be the one on the ball in this group, totally ignoring the producer who wasn't *producing* very much at this meeting, even though the location was *his* job!

"It's up for sale but the owner has not had any hits for over three months." She said. "I contacted him this morning and he is *more* than willing to hand over exclusive rights as a shooting location for the next six months to a year."

"This movie shouldn't take more than eight if everyone is on their toes!" The director said.

"Then *get* on it!" Charlie said. "Line up a team to fly down with the production and prop crew to get the layout on this place inside and see if it will work." He handed the flyer back to the woman on the end. "Make sure my secretary makes a copy of that for me before you leave." He said directly to her and she nodded.

"There's only so many rooms in the cabin that the author emphasizes on in the book. The biggest fabrication might be the inside pool scene." The man from production said.

"We can shoot a pool scene anywhere." Charlie said.

"Hell, there's a million *inside* pools in the mountains right here, we can use in California."

"Not necessary." The woman spoke again. "This location has one, solar panels and all, complete with a barn out back of the property that overlooks the mountains in the distance."

"*Perfect*!" Charlie said and for the first time felt progress was finally happening. He turned to the producer. "You need to get permission for the crew to head out ASAP. If it's a go, then get your financial guys in touch with the owner and negotiate and secure that location."

The producer nodded and began making notes on his tablet in front of him.

"We'll run the screen test on our end and get it back to you within the next twenty-four hours." The woman on the end assured him. "That is *if* Ms. Watters is back from her vacation in Costa Rica."

She must be a fan, Charlie thought. Her admiration for the woman was certainly shining through. As much as he wanted to disagree with choosing Lola, he couldn't deny that the woman obviously had a vision in her head and was anxious to convince him of it on the screen. And he had to admit even to himself, as much as he wanted to dislike her in the beginning, he admired her work ethic towards the end. Besides the assistant director, she had been the most outspoken one of the bunch. Her ideas might not be brilliant to him but nonetheless she never stopped pitching and that's what got you somewhere in this business.

Everyone began packing up files and tablets in briefcases, signaling that the meeting was now coming to an end. It was finally his lunchtime. The part of his day where he got sixty minutes to get away from everyone and just listen to the silence in a place where he was not responsible for anything and anyone but himself.

"It will be good working with you again Charlie." The producer said, once Charlie stood, extending his hand. Charlie shook it and nodded as he did with every one of them in the room except when it came to the woman with balls from the casting group. She was the last one to leave and in fact was still packing her satchel at the conference table when Charlie turned and glanced over his shoulder. He watched her for a moment while she was unaware. Now that she was standing, he saw what had possibly urged her fight in defending Lola's body type. The woman before him was curvy herself and wasn't doing a very good job of hiding it in her business suit. Before, the strong confident personality was what made her stand out from the crowd. But now, seeing the *entire* package, made Charlie realize, there was more to her than meets the eye. He watched as she absently pushed a stray hair back while she worked in her task. Her shoulder-length, wavy, dark hair, was a nice shade and he wondered if she was of Spanish or of a Romanian descent. Either way, she was incredibly easy on the eyes.

Sensing he was watching her, she glanced up at the same time as she rested the satchel strap on her shoulder. She smiled and walked over to him, still direct, still bold and still confident, even in her steps. Charlie's stomach growled loud enough this time in the quiet room, that she probably heard. He mentally told it to shut the hell up just as she stopped a few feet in front of him.

"Sounds like somebody's hungry." She said.

"I eat pretty early in the morning." Charlie said. He glanced at the wall over her head and back into her eyes. "It's *past* lunchtime." He confessed.

"We must be on the same schedule." She replied, not glancing once at her watch. "Is there someplace *you* would suggest?"

"*Absolutely*." Charlie said. "Downtown, where it's *safer*."

"Is that where *you're* going?" she asked.

"No," Charlie said. "I'm ordering and staying in."

As if on cue the intercom buzzed in the middle of the table.

"Mr. Vega, will you be ordering the usual from Dagwood's?" Peggy, his secretary, was confirming his lunch order.

"What's the *usual*?" The woman asked Charlie, still locking eyes with him.

After a brief hesitation, Charlie said. "It's called *The Dagwood*."

"Sounds *exactly* what I had in mind!" The woman said. "And since I have to wait for your secretary to make copies of the possible shooting location, I have time."

The room was suddenly so thick with silence that Charlie could have heard someone's contact lens hit the ground.

"Mr. Vega?" Charlie heard Peggy over his shoulder, calling out from the speaker because he had not answered. She was totally oblivious to the conversation that was going on in the room. He hesitated, weighed his options and it was then that he noticed the woman's color of her eyes. The nostalgia of the moment hit him with force as a memory pushed to the front of his mind. He was barely ten when he'd first noticed his mother's beautiful amber-colored eyes and of course his father gushed about them on several occasions. They'd had these onyx flecks in them that made them unique. He'd never seen another with the same color combination…until now.

"Peggy?" he said out loud.

"Yes sir?" came the crisp reply from the speaker.

"Order the *usual* from Dagwood's *and* make it a *double*!"
The woman with the balls smiled in such a way, that it
made something in Charlie's stomach *almost* flutter.

OURTEEN

The office was small, maybe five-by-seven, with no windows and two doors and was housed on the fifth floor, of the main FBI building in Washington. The only furniture in the room was a desk and two chairs. Margot was currently sitting in one of them on the receiving side. The female agent by the name of Fields, sat in the other one across from her with a thick folder open in her hands. There were no other folders on the desk, no personal photos or the normal clutter one would expect a working surface to look like.

There weren't any achievement or milestone plaques on the wall behind the woman's head either. Or any diploma's or pictures of her shaking hands with important people. She didn't even have a name plate on the door. The space didn't look lived-in much less resemble an FBI office, or at least what she thought one should look like.

 Where was the cork board with Post-it notes stuck everywhere and mugshots of America's Most Wanted, tacked up for quick reference? Or the popular red telephone that had square buttons that start blinking when someone important like the President calls? There wasn't even a simple computer on the desk. In fact, the room was so bland that it almost reminded Margot of an interrogation room. Like the ones on television in the cop shows that Ken watched, where the detectives would question the guy who was under arrest. The ge*nuine* five-by seven, two-way mirror that was behind the woman's head, also was a dead ringer for the ones in the movies. Of course it had all the characteristics of a mirror on *her* side—glass and a frame and a reflection—but anyone with half a brain knew it was like looking through a window on the *other* side. It suddenly made her question why they would put her in a room with a two-way mirror? Was someone standing right now on the other side watching them? And if so, *who* and for *what* purpose?

"Mrs. Hartford, first of all, *thank* you for coming so quickly." Agent Fields said, looking up from the file she held in her hands. "I trust your accommodations on the flight and transportation from the airport has been satisfactory?" she asked.

"I have no major complaints, as of *yet*!" Margot replied, her hands folded smartly on her pocketbook, her gaze direct. "*Unless* I have to sit here *much* longer while you go through that folder again!"

"I do *apologize* for keeping you waiting, Mrs. Hartford but I wanted to make sure everything *was* in order." She explained.

"You *people* have had plenty of time to check if everything was in order, a long time ago!" Margot stressed, looking at her watch. "You've already wasted *thirteen* hours of my life and you're just now *familiarizing* yourself with my file, to waste *more* of my time?" Margot stared the woman straight in the eye. The irritation in her voice was loud and clear.

Agent Fields held her own stare as she forced a smile. "*Mrs*. Hartford, I am already *very* familiar with the *main* facts concerning your daughter's case. It's the *small* details that need *double* checking. After all, it's been a few *decades* since this incident occurred!"

"It's been over *twenty* years Agent Fields, since the *incident*—as you *refer* to it—*occurred*!" she said sternly. Most of the time Margot prided herself on having control of her emotions, but considering what her entire family had just been through, her nerves were not in the *best* condition right now.

"My deepest sympathies to you and your family for your loss." Agent Fields said, the smile disappeared.

"*Great*!" Margot said briskly. "Now that we have the *insincere* condolences out of the way, let's get down to business. Why in the *hell* am I here?" she demanded, her brows furrowed.

Agent Fields cleared her throat and presented her best business face. Her dark, perfectly-straight hair moved like a silk curtain. The slight slant at the corners of her eyes gave Margot the impression that she must be from Asian descent, although she didn't carry an accent. She called herself an FBI agent but she looked awfully young. Margot swore she couldn't have been any older than Sage.

"With all due respect, Mrs. Hartford, this case has been a mystery to the bureau from day one and as much as I hate to admit it, it just got even *more* complicated in the last seventy-two hours."

"Complicated for *who*, Agent Fields?" Margot asked, leaning slightly forward, eyebrows drawn down in a frown.

"Unfortunately Mrs. Hartford, it's become complicated for *all* of us!" Agent Fields said.

"I am beside myself with curiosity as to what the hell you are talking about!" Margot said, her face stoic, one eyebrow cocked.

"It's quite simple really." Agent Fields said with a cool tone of simplicity. "Recent *unexpected* developments have surfaced that might have a tie to the plane your daughter was on."

A nerve began to throb somewhere in the back of Margot's neck. "Let's just *cut* the bullshit, shall we?" She asked candidly. "What kind of *unexpected* developments are you people talking about here that involves *my* family?"

Agent Fields finally broke direct eye contact with Margot, closed the file she still held in her hands and laid it down on the desk.

"Mrs. Hartford, did you happen to *catch* any of our *national* news in the last twenty-four hours?" She asked.

"No!" Margot answered, shaking her head. "I haven't had time."

"Let me catch you up then." Agent Fields said with a twinkle in her eye, as if she were enjoying this little meeting. "Are you aware of the *notorious* Somalia Pirates, Mrs. Hartford?"

"Of *course*!" Margot answered almost immediately followed by, "*Who isn't?*"

"You'd be surprised!" The agent replied, a shrewd smile threatened the corners of her mouth. "There are still *many* citizens living *in* the United States who can't even tell you the *name* of their current vice-president, much less anything about *turf* wars that are taking place in *third-world* countries!"

"Ignorance is in *abundance* right now, Agent Fields, in *all* categories and countries." Margot said, sternly. "but I highly *doubt* you brought me all the way here to discuss *willful* illiteracy in the world!"

"No, Mrs. Hartford, you are right! I did not!" The agent said curtly. "Are you aware that the Somalia Pirates lair has been seized off the coast of Africa by our troops?" she asked, point blank. Margot nodded her head 'yes' without speaking. Agent Fields took that as her cue to continue.

"As you probably already know, the pirates have practically *evaded* prosecution by *any* law enforcement of any rank throughout the country, whether local *or* abroad, for several reasons over a *very* long period of time. They've ruled the canals and waterways for hundreds of miles in *either* direction off the African coast. They have pilfered, looted, murdered, kidnapped and bullied their way through *three* decades of countless victims. They are ruthless and violent pirates that take *whatever* they want, *whenever* they want, *however* they want, leaving destruction, misery and loss in their wake. Rumors began to circulate during the early 80s among the fishermen that somewhere, deep in that dense jungle, just off the African boarders, the Somalia pirates had a *secret* hideout. It was supposedly where they lived, stowed all their confiscated loot and planned out their next moves on unsuspecting targets. When the local officials could not find any credibility behind the rumor that this lair existed, they began to believe it was derived more out of *an* urban myth, than reality. That is, until a few weeks ago."

Margot interrupted, finding this history lesson all unamusing.

"Agent Fields, what does *pirates* looting in *Africa* have to do with my daughter's plane?" Margot asked with an annoyed sigh.

"Back in 1987, do you recall an agent by the name of Phillip Greene, who contacted you or your husband, regarding the remains of your daughter and son-in-law, Jack Cassava?"

"My *late* husband handled *all* correspondence with *your* people and the burial decisions, Agent Fields. I personally *never* spoke to an Agent Greene or *anyone* else with this bureau for that matter, about the crash." Margot said.

"Mr. Hartford ever mention his name at the time?" Agent Fields asked.

"No, I was too distraught to even *digest* what was happening, much less care who the person's name was that he was talking to. Why are you asking me when it should all be right there in that file?" Margot questioned, gesturing at the closed, thick folder that lie between them.

"The original reports concerning the crash that happened *in* 1987 are *in* that file, Mrs. Hartford. But about a week ago, a suspicious envelope arrived here at the bureau that says *otherwise*."

The two women eyed each other in a second of silence.

"Otherwise *how*?" Margot asked, not liking the direction in which this was going.

Fields let out a short sigh. "At the time of the crash, Agent Greene was appointed as lead investigator of the case. According to his reports in *this* folder that I pulled from our archives, the end result was that they never *found* the plane. But yet last week, we received an envelope citing a *different* result—also handwritten by Agent Greene—dated the same day as the original. Only this one states that the plane was *found* and that the remains were returned to the family, at the expense of the government."

Margot took a second to digest what this woman had just said. The ticking of the clock above the door reverberated in the silent room.

"Who *mailed* you the conflicting report?" she finally asked.

"We don't know. It came anonymously. We've tried to track its origins but with no luck."

"Why would there be *two* conflicting reports?"

"That's what we are also trying to figure out. We hoped by talking with you, it would give us some answers."

"The obvious answer I can give you is the *first* report is wrong, *dead* wrong." Margot pointed to the file. "The plane was *found*, that much I know because *your* people told my husband that it was."

"The original report in this file *is* the correct version, Mrs. Hartford. We *never* found the plane in '87 and to this day, the case is still *open*."

"Agent Fields," Margot began, leaning slightly forward for emphasis. "I *stood* at the end of my daughter's gravesite and *watched* her and her beloved husband's coffins being *lowered* into the ground with my *own* two eyes. Her *father* was right there beside me, as well as her *orphaned* child and *all* of the family and friends who *adored* them! The report in your file is *false*! The plane was found and no one has ever contradicted that fact in over twenty years. Who would orchestrate such an elaborate lie? And what would they gain by doing so?" Just as the words left her mouth, the exhumation paper that they'd found in Frank's safe, flashed briefly in her mind. She vaguely remembered Charlie explaining what had prompted her husband to dig them up. Had he somehow learned that there were no remains in the caskets? But how? And by who?

What in the hell was going to surface from the past now?

A sick dread began to form in her gut.

"You can believe we are working diligently to find that out, Mrs. Hartford." Agent Fields said. "All we know at this time, is that someone went to great links to carry out an elaborate *sick* hoax. They either threatened or bribed Agent Greene to write that false report and to go through the motions of making you and your husband believe that the plane had been found and the remains recovered. Whoever did, had a lot of time on their hands, a lot of power play with some pretty prominent people and plenty of money in the bank to finance the entire affair." Agent Fields said. "Does anyone or anything you know of, come to mind back in '87, that fits that criteria?"

"If I didn't know any better, I'd say that the description you just gave, *fits* your operation here, Agent Fields!" Margot said. "You *did* just admit you had a *rogue* agent who you *already* know falsified some records."

"I can guarantee you that we have already checked out all the other agents who were working closely at the time with Agent Greene on your case. All of them are either retired or deceased." Agent Fields said. "We are currently delving into that side of it now but so far, it looks like Agent Greene was acting alone."

"Who paid for the caskets to be delivered to the cemetery? Money *always* leaves a paper trail. Find the records the day they were received and you find your culprit." Margot said, literally fuming under the collar but not daring to let any of it show.

"Our agency contacted the current caretaker at the cemetery and he verified that the graves exist but he couldn't tell us much else. Apparently they lost records in a fire around the same time which seems suspicious all by itself. We also checked with our accounting department and they verified this morning that there was *nothing* in the expense budget in '87 that showed we paid out for any caskets. And the exhumation order that was inside the envelope with the false report, tells us that your husband didn't quite buy the story either, after a while."

There was another pass of short silence. The agent stared straight at Margot as if she had just read her mind.

"Ok, so again let's cut the bullshit here." Margot said. "Why are you *telling* me this, Agent Fields? Why not keep it quiet about this mystery report that was mailed to you? Another *quarter* of a century might pass and none of us *surviving* family members that had loved ones aboard that flight, would be the wiser! So why bring me all the way here to point out to me that your system is flawed? Do you like being sued?"

Margot was on fire! This was the last thing she needed to deal with right now.

"That's where the mystery comes in." Agent Fields responded calmly.

"What *mystery*?" Margot demanded.

"You were the *only* family involved!"

"We were the *only* family involved for what?" Margot repeated.

"Your file was the *only* record that Agent Greene *falsified*. According to this second report, your husband was the only one he actually called and made this false claim to! We already interviewed the surviving families of the crash and not one had ever been contacted by Greene professing to have *found* the plane." Agent Fields said. "Every one of them was told the plane had not been located and might never be."

"And just *what* is the purpose of all this, Agent Fields?" Margot asked, the hairs on the back of her neck beginning to rise. "Why *my* family?"

"We don't *know* why. We were hoping during this interview it would shed some light on the story but it seems you're in the dark just as much as we are." She said.

"*That's it*?" Margot asked incredulously. "You bring me all the way here hoping I can help you clear up a *discrepancy* in your paperwork? Well, I'm not buying it Agent Fields and neither will the ten top attorneys I have on speed dial! Someone *will* answer as to why we were lied to!" The thick silence engulfed the small room as Margot's words now hung in the air.

It was obvious the agent was sizing her up, calculating her next move.

"You are *more* than welcome to *involve* an attorney Mrs. Hartford, but in doing so, you yourself know that it will only *pend* or possibly *halt* this investigation *dead* in its tracks, once the legalities get involved. Being a *savvy* business woman, I don't need to remind you that sometimes litigation on cases as *old* as this, can go on for *years* tied up in courts and it benefits no one. The leads we have in place now, are *fresh* and hold a very *strong* chance of *leading* us directly to the *location* of the crash site, possibly *within* a few days or weeks, putting an end to this nightmare once and for all, for *everyone*."

Margot pondered this over for a minute. As much as she hated to admit it, the agent was right. Bringing the lawyers in would only complicate things and halt progress. It was indeed time to put this nightmare to rest.

"Does this Agent *Greene* still work for the bureau?" Margot asked instead.

"No Mrs. Hartford, he does not." Agent Fields assured her.

"So since finding out he falsified *federal* documents, have you tried to *locate* him so we can all find out why?"

"*Yes*, Mrs. Hartford, we did start the steps in *locating* him with the intent of charging him to the fullest extent of the law." She confirmed.

"*And*?" she demanded. "Have you *arrested* him yet?"

"Unfortunately, Mrs. Hartford, ex-agent Phillip Greene is *deceased*. He died not long after he wrote both of those reports!" she stated.

"Oh how *convenient*!" Margot huffed with sarcasm. "Let me guess, how did he die? Is this where the history lesson comes in? The one you just gave me on the *Somalia* pirates in *Africa*?"

"No," Agent Fields replied, still just as composed as before. "Their reign of terror was just barely off the ground when our agent met his demise in Italy."

"*Italy*?" Margot repeated.

"Yes, *Italy*!" the agent confirmed.

"What happened to him or is that confidential?" Margot asked, trying to keep her emotions in check.

"It's not confidential, Mrs. Hartford. As a matter of fact, it's on *public* record. Agent Greene supposedly drown. Some fishermen from a nearby port found him floating, face down about fifteen miles from shore."

"What *port* was that?" Margot had to know, bracing for the answer.

"*Venice*." The agent replied, studying her a little bit too close for Margot's comfort. "You or your husband ever have any *connections* to Venice, Mrs. Hartford?" This woman was two steps away from making the connection between Victor Rocha and her family, Margot thought. Or she already had because of Karly's arrest and was *toying* with her. Either way, the sick dread in her gut began to grow heavier.

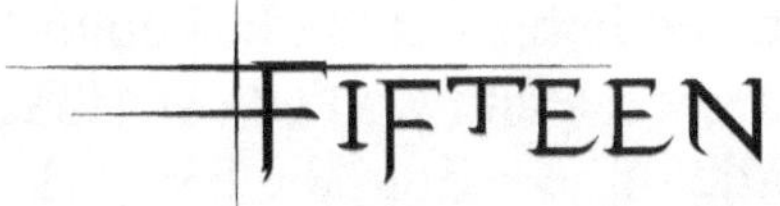FIFTEEN

Brandon unlocked the door to the office with his key. He flipped on the switch just inside and the spacious room was bathed instantly in light. He remained at first in the doorway, just taking in the scene. The room was spotless and there wasn't a thing out of place.

He turned the flashlight on he'd stuffed in his back pocket and shone its strong beam of light on every inch around the lock, on both the inside of the door and the frame it was housed in. He found no scuff or cut marks that might indicate someone had tried or successfully pried their way past a heavy duty deadbolt. The seam where the door met, showed the hinges had not been moved or altered either. Finally, he stepped through the threshold. Because it had been shut up for over a week, the chill in the air was enough to warrant a jacket. Brandon snagged the remote to the fireplace inside the room and turned it on. The flames instantly danced inside the glass panel and he could hear the heat kick on.

He laid the remote back on the desk and saw the broken frame—picture still intact but askew—that Hans had mentioned, laying on the corner. He didn't need to pick it up in order to see the shattered glass or the busted wood that had splintered on impact. There was also no doubt in his mind that it could not be saved and that a new one would have to take its place.

He turned and glanced behind him where it use to hang and where it had approximately landed when it fell on the floor. Lydia had done a fine job of making the evidence disappear on the rug. But it puzzled him as to why it would cause so much damage on impact, when it didn't have far to go and had landed on a padded surface. Just looking at it made one think it was knocked off the wall by force.

He turned back and stared at the four smiling faces in the photo. Something stirred in his gut but he couldn't put his finger on it. He left the desk and walked over to the bar and pulled out a cold bottle of beer from the fridge. He popped the top and flipped the cap into a spin and aimed at the trash like a pro. The rush of the air and chill of the drink omitted some steam at the mouth of the bottle. He took a nice long drink. The bite of the yeast was what he totally needed at the end of a very long-ass week.

He walked over to the wall of windows that faced the south of the property and examined every last one to make sure there was nothing disturbed or odd around the casings. Finding nothing he made a mental note to check the outside as well, on his way back up to the house. After dealing with the likes of Jeb and now Karly, he'd leave no stone unturned. It was obvious his family's life depended on it. Once Brandon walked the rest of the room and found nothing unusual, he settled himself down in the chair, in front of the computer. He powered it up and clicked through a series of security questions before arriving at his private account online, where his security system was monitored. He accessed the cameras that were located outside the barn, mainly around the office and any other door or window that could be breached, or allowed access into the building. Reports of non-stop monitoring, had been added underneath, of security techs signing in and signing off, at different times. Everybody attested in their end notes, that no criminal activity had been reported on their watch. Brandon then accessed the camera inside the office. The personal footage in this section however had an asterisk beside a time in the frame, when something was noted as unusual activity inside.

A chill traveled up his spine.

He clicked on the highlighted note and read the time stamp. He then accessed the footage and time and played the portion back. The camera could be seen in the lens, panning past the desk and the picture was up on the wall. But when the camera panned back the other way in less than thirty seconds, it was no longer on the wall and could be clearly seen on its side, glass broken and resting on the floor. No signs of a person being in the room were reported or seen in the footage. The end result on the notation at the bottom, had the tech chalking it up to '*non-threatening mishaps*" after a close investigation. Since there was no disturbance reported *outside* at the time and there were obviously no motion and sensor detectors going off on the *inside*—in other words, it was safe to blame it on the *ghosts*, if not a faulty nail that just gave way.

Brandon played the short footage a few times again before he finally logged out of his account and off the Internet completely. He powered down the computer and picked up his beer and took another sip. He stared again at the picture of the four men. Then he turned the chair around and stared at the spot where it had previously been hanging. He got up, closed the distance and examined the screw that was still protruding from the wall. He used his free hand to test the movement of the nail. *There wasn't any*. It was as snug in the wood as it had been the day he had put it there. He walked back over and abandoned the beer on the desk. With both hands he carefully picked the damaged frame up and tilted it enough that he could get a clear view of the back. Other than a few tears in the paper backing from the fall, the hanger was intact. It was not loose in the least bit so the theory he'd had of it giving way because the frame was old, was quickly debunked. He returned the frame to rest on its back again and a piece of sharp jagged glass had worked free and fell beside it. Brandon was worried that Sage would cut herself when she changed out the frames, so he began removing the glass himself to save her the trouble. He carefully wiggled only one loose piece from the wooden frame when his cell phone started to vibrate in the front pocket of his jeans. Thinking it might be Sage in the house, he abandoned the photo long enough to pull it out and make sure. It was a text from her informing him that lunch was ready. He texted her back and then laid it down and grabbed for another jagged piece, when it began ringing. This time it was the private investigator's name that appeared on the screen. So much for trying to get something done!

"Great timing." Brandon said, as soon as he put the phone to his ear.

"I hear you have something you would like to discuss with me." Madison's deep, business-like voice responded on the other end, wasting no time by getting right to the point.

"Then you heard right." Brandon said. "I have some work for you, if your available." He added. He shut off the electric fireplace, then grabbed what was left of his beer while he held the phone with the other.

"I'm always available to help you out Mr. Parrish. Would you like to arrange a meeting in person?" he immediately offered.

"No, this won't take long." Brandon took one last look around the room. His eyes came to rest for a few seconds on the photo, still trapped within the damaged frame, lying on the desk. Then he turned from the room and headed to the door.

"What kind of service would you be needing from me?" Madison asked.

"*Research*." Brandon said, as he turned off the light and stepped through to the other side.

Brandon disconnected the call, then made his rounds to the rest of the rooms inside. Satisfied that nothing was disturbed and no one had broken into the structure, he locked the main door and headed back to the cabin.

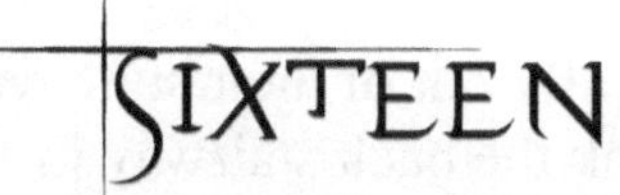

SIXTEEN

Much to everyone's relief, the rain finally stopped the next morning in Kenya. The clouds began breaking apart and exposing glimpses of blue skies above. The sun made an appearance now and then, trying to push through in order to dry the streets below. Puddles were still prominent in dips along the uneven terrain and walkways. The air was thick and muggy and smelled of rotten fish.

But the aftermath of the storm hadn't stopped the people or the town from resuming life where they had left off before the first drop had fallen. Dozens were out and about, especially in the mainstream of the market, just a few streets over from the hotel.

Even though they hadn't found the problem on Courtney's side of town yet, word was out that the electricity *had* been restored on the northwest side, near the market. Which meant her favorite place that sold delicious coffee was open for business and her vodka-soaked brain was in desperate need of a fast wake up call.

She had dressed, covered her stringy hair with a ball cap—emblazoned with the stations' logo on the front—grabbed her hotel key and some cash, and quietly opened her door. Michael's bedroom door was still shut and the suite was incredibly quiet. She imagined he was probably still sleeping off the effects of vodka and the horrors of the elaborate tale she'd told him last night. She decided not to disturb him quite yet, since they still had a few hours to kill before boarding a flight for home.

She wondered if he would be pissed when he did wake up and find her gone. He had done nothing but preach to her, the entire duration of the trip, about the dangers of being unescorted, even in the day time, in a foreign country. But her desperate need for coffee and the freedom to get outside after being cooped up the entire evening before, won over.

She slipped successfully out of their suite without making much noise, then took the back stairway just in case any of the camera crew were up and about. Halfway down the second flight, she ran into the house boy, Bram, carrying a stack of folded towels.

"Miss Courtney, is everything alright?" He stopped on the landing. A look of concern clouded his face.

"Yes Bram, everything's fine." She said, flashing him a smile as she passed.

"Is there something I can get you, Miss Courtney?" he asked, still standing there, looking down at her puzzled.

"No Bram, I'm fine. Thanks!" she waved over her shoulder.

"Mambo has heated water to make coffee down below. We should have power soon." He said.

"Ok, thanks again Bram."

Courtney left him behind and descended the last set of steps. She made her way towards the main doors. For a second her heart raced, thinking that she would find them still locked and curfew still in effect. But the worry was gone the second the door gave way and she stepped outside, into the sunlight.

She navigated down the first block with ease. The flow on the sidewalks were fast-paced and it felt good to stretch her legs. She kept her head slightly down, trying not to attract too much attention. Her hands were shoved into the pockets of her jacket. The fishy-smelling air was causing her stomach to roll and the crowd around her were extremely loud to her delicate ears.

When she approached the second street where she needed to turn left, the pace of the crowd slowed considerably down, almost to a standstill. Up ahead, carts being pulled by donkeys, were neck-to-neck and someone had the nerve to try and mix a small herd of cattle in the bunch. The heavy stench of the farm animals assaulted her nostrils, making her stomach roll again. She pulled her hand out of her pocket and used the cloth of the sleeve to cover her nose. She breathed in through the material and looked around for an alternative route to get to the coffee shop. A very narrow alleyway to the left, looked to be her best bet. She slipped out of the crowd and made her way past the people who were milling about at the entrance. It appeared that she'd have to navigate around a few trash cans but at the other end of the passage, it looked as if it opened up right next to the Kenya bank. The coffee shop she was looking for was on the corner, across from it.

She walked past the break of people and entered the mouth of the alley, making her way gingerly past water-soaked bins and around a few pieces of hanging laundry and *right* into three, heavily-cloaked men, coming from the opposite direction.

They were swathed in black from head to toe, almost resembling the attire of a Ninja's, with face coverings that only revealed their eyes.

"Ahhhh," The one in front with the chocolate eyes spoke first. His accent was thick. "Look what the *Yehova* has sent as a gift this fine day!"

Courtney glanced briefly to the other two behind him. The male in the front who had spoken English and the male on the end, appeared to be very dark-skinned. The man's accent and the fact that he used the word *Yehova* in reference to God in Swahili, confirmed to her that he was of African descent. But the male in the middle, his skin tone was on the lighter side, compared to his comrades and his eyes were a much softer shade of brown, almost like a deep caramel.

"Excuse me!" Courtney said, trying to be pleasant and ignore the first one's rude, flirty remarks. She then made motions to get past but the man in front wasn't finished with her yet. "She has manners too." He said in a rather cocky tone to his cohorts over his shoulder. Courtney glanced at the two behind him to see their reaction. The one in the middle, had his eyes on the one in the front and the look he gave, seemed uneasy. The one behind him, stood ridged with no expression, almost as if he were on guard. He was scanning the alleyway around them continuously. He finally opened his mouth and spoke in Swahili, to the man standing in her way.

He returned the conversation in his native tongue over his shoulder, but not taking his eyes off her. The male in the middle shifted his position somewhat. The look in his eyes told Courtney that he not only understood the language but was obviously not liking what they'd said. And whatever it was, she didn't think she liked it either and her patience with this whole bully mess had come to an end.

"Are you through yet?" she demanded of the man in front, folding her arms to her chest.

He threw his head back and bellowed out a laugh. When his flashing black eyes landed on hers again, the look in them was in no way friendly.

A chill danced down her spine. Her gut, although still uneasy from the Grey Goose the night before, were sending warning signals straight through to her foggy brain. "I will be *done* with *you* when I say so!" The condescending tone was gone and a more serious one took over. The color of his eyes seem to darken, if that were possible, which usually happened when someone was becoming angry. If he or any of his friends thought they were going to toy with her, they had no idea who they were messing with. Courtney was not in the mood for this kind of crap this early in the morning, especially before she'd had her coffee.

She glanced back in the direction from which she had just come, weighing her options of the best way to resolve this dilemma, by removing herself from the equation.

"Don't *think* you can run away from me." the man in front
said, as if he were reading her mind. Before she could react
he reached out and gripped her wrist hard, meaning to
restrain her. Again the man in the middle shifted his weight
and stepped forward, as did the man behind him. Fear
coupled with anger, began to escalate in Courtney, as the
seriousness of the situation seeped deeper into her foggy
brain. It was *one* thing to mouth off to her but it was whole
other ballgame if someone put their *hands* on her!
"Get your hand *off* me!" she again demanded, holding those
black eyes with angry ones of her own.
"Aww, you *are* a wild one." The man said, not even
flinching at her tone or manner as if it meant no threat to
him. He gripped her arm tighter and drew her closer. The
strength in his hand was locked down like a vise on her arm
and the look in his eyes were full of anger. The dark mark
he had tattooed near his eye just made his whole
appearance that much more monster-like. "You will be a
welcoming challenge to tame!" He spat, through gritted
teeth.
He'd made a mistake, Courtney thought in that short
second. He'd gotten right into the perfect position and if
she didn't react now, she might not have another chance.
Without any further delay she lifted her foot and brought it
down *hard* on the side of his knee with all the strength she
could muster. It was an old trick she'd learned years ago
from a defense class she'd taken in college. If the maneuver
was executed properly, it could maim or break the kneecap
which gave the victim time to escape and get help.
Apparently she still had it. Her deed was followed by a
muffled sound of bone splintering and he immediately
released her arm, letting out a yelp of pain. She made eye
contact briefly with the man in the middle. She swore if she
were reading his eyes right, she could have pulled the
fabric from his face and found he was smiling. But the third

man, the one that had spoken in Swahili, wasn't amused at all. He had a look of surprise that registered prominently in his dark eyes. He made a move forward and the guy in the middle reacted. Courtney took a step back just as he raised his arm high and quick and slammed his elbow into his side. The third man lost his balance and teetered backwards and that's when Courtney saw he held a knife in his left hand. It all happened so fast. The guy in the middle was on him, intending to disarm him. The one she'd slammed in the kneecap was trying to stand up and reach her on his bad leg. What part of his face that was visible, was mottled in a mixture of severe pain and rage.

Courtney spared no time in hanging out any longer. She broke into a panic run, heading back to the mouth of the alley where she'd just come. Her heart was rapidly beating in her chest. She wanted to get as far away from them as she could and back towards the throng of people where it would be safe.

A few feet away, Bram, the house boy from the hotel, miraculously stepped into the alleyway from the edge of the crowd. He had a look of concern on his face, his eyes moving between her coming towards him and what was happening behind her. She dared not turn around, not once. "*Miss Courtney*!" he said, sounding relieved. "Thank goodness *we* find you! "He waved his hand in haste. "*Hurry*!"

It didn't take long for her to figure out who the '*we*' was he happened to be referring to. She ran right into the arms of a frantic-looking Michael. Behind him, Tony and the rest of the crew were in tow.

"We've been looking all *over* for you!" he stressed, bringing her to his chest in a protective embrace, his brows creased deeply in a frown. She suddenly felt so guilty for shagging ass and not telling him or anyone else where she was going. The worry in his face were genuine and heavy and his heart was beating rapidly. Courtney normally would have pried out of his arms without a second thought, but after what she had just experienced, she was shaken up more than she realized. She took advantage of his broad chest and leaned into him for a moment instead, trying to slow her breathing and get her bearings.

It wasn't just breaking into a run that had her gasping for breath but the *fear* of the moment that had stolen her stamina. Courtney was an avid runner for years, heading out most mornings before work, running five miles at a time. The short sprint from the alleyway was nothing and Michael would know that. To keep him and the rest of the crew from investigating further, she had to keep her cool. Her loyalty was to protect them first. They were boarding a plane in a few hours and none of this would matter anymore.

"Are you like, *okay*?" Tony asked. He and the rest of the crew gathered around her, all of them stealing glances down the alley to see what had sent her running.

"*Courtney*?" Michael said, still holding her in a strong embrace. It was then that she realized she was trembling pretty bad. The rich scent of him and the security and feel of his arms around her, wasn't helping matters any.

"I'm *fine*." She said, trying to calm herself down inside, for if she didn't, her stomach was threatening to heave.

"What *happened*?" he asked, not letting her out of his grip just yet.

"Nothing I couldn't handle myself." she said, looking over her shoulder again, confirming that the threat had passed. The alleyway still appeared to be empty. "I ran into a dog that wasn't in the mood to play nice." She said, trying to make light of the matter, omitting the fact that the dog might now have a severely injured kneecap.

"Are you hurt?" Michael asked, pulling her away from him long enough to look her up and down.

Courtney shook her head no.

"Bad freaking *Kenya* dog!" Tony said, in a scolding tone, glancing back down the empty alleyway.

"This is *why* I told you not to venture out by yourself!" Michael said, not hesitating to bring out the *I-told-you-so's* mantra he had been preaching to her all along.

"I was just *one* street over from the hotel Michael, trying to get some coffee." She stressed, as if that explained why she had tread lightly over his warnings. "I didn't want to *disturb* you. I thought it would be fine to venture a few blocks away and stretch my legs. I was planning to be back before you woke up." That was the moment she realized he didn't appear to have been aroused from sleep, less than ten minutes ago. On closer inspection she saw that he was freshly shaven and neatly dressed and on top of that, he *smelled* dreamy.

"I've been up for a *few* hours, Courtney." Michael stressed. "I was downstairs getting *you* coffee when Bram came and told me you left."

Courtney turned and looked at the house boy whose brows were still creased.

"I saw you leave the hotel, Miss Courtney." Bram explained. "Mr. Michael said I was to tell him if you did." She couldn't be upset, learning this. Michael hovering over her sometimes too much, had just paid off, in more ways than he would ever know.

"It's okay Bram. You did *nothing* wrong." She said, trying to ease the guilt off the boy's shoulders. "In fact, you did the *right* thing."

She patted his arm and gently forced her way out of Michael's protective embrace. He seemed reluctant and it just made the guilt in her deepen that much more, that she'd made all of them this worried. Obviously he *had* been speaking the truth when he'd warned her of the dangers in this city.

"You did good, little dude!" Tony said, patting Bram encouragingly on his back. The rest of the crew nodded in agreement.

"We need to get you back to the hotel." Michael said, taking charge as always. She felt nauseated as hell and a headache with its own heartbeat, had formed in her temples. All she wanted to do at this point was get some damn coffee.

"I need some pain meds or something." She muttered. "I'm not feeling too well!"

"I have some in the room." Michael offered, his hand still supporting the small of her back as they walked in that direction.

They didn't make it.

One block from the entrance of the hotel, Courtney ducked into a random alley and began vomiting into a trash can.

SEVENTEEN

You or your husband ever have any connection to Venice, Mrs. Hartford?

Margot sat for a few seconds just staring at Agent Fields. It was *too* much of a coincidence, *especially* after the recent events that had just taken place at her house. Victor Rocha—father of Karly Driggers who had just tried to murder her *entire* family—had carried on an affair with a mistress in *Venice*, Italy. The same *Venice* that Agent Greene was vacationing in, when he met his death, who was *also* at the time the *agent* assigned to her daughter's case. *Venice*…the last known place where Victor had lived before he'd been stupid enough to travel all the way to a furniture store in the states to seek revenge, only to end up in jail and then dead! Margot had no doubt the agent was baiting her. She was sure that word had traveled fast about Karly being arrested in her house and they were waiting for her to slip up and confirm it. Even in death the man was still a monkey on her back. Would his vengeance ever end? Margot cleared her throat and decided to try a different approach.

"Why in the last twenty-four hours has my daughter's case become a priority?"

Something had sent up a red flag to the bureau and she was determined to find out what.

"Your daughter's case at the moment is *not* our priority Mrs. Hartford. But more of a *link* to one that currently is."

"And what case is that?" Margot pushed.

"The search *and* seizure of the Somalia *Pirate's* hideaway." Agent Fields said with conviction. "We have recently discovered during our investigation that the pirates were dabbling in more than just monetary value."

Margot narrowed her brow.

"What do you mean by *more* than just monetary value?"
This time it was Agent Fields who paused a few seconds
before responding.
"I have something I need to show you, Mrs. Hartford."
She finally said, sounding a little too serious for it to be
anything good. "And it's not going to be easy." The
agent reached up underneath that dark curtain of hair and
Margot got a glimpse of what looked like a Bluetooth
device, attached to her ear. She pushed an invisible button
on the apparatus and began speaking low to someone.
"You can come in now."
"*Who* can come in now?" Margot asked, her eyes
immediately darted to the fake mirror facing her on the
wall.
Maybe she hadn't been *imagining* it. Maybe her instinct
had been on point, when she'd wondered earlier, if
someone *was* watching her from the other side of the glass.
And if they'd been watching, they'd been listening in to, on
their *entire* conversation as well.
Margot watched as the knob on the door—the one she'd
thought in the beginning *might* be a closet—began to turn
and *open*.

EIGHTEEN

"Talk about *delicious*!" The woman with the balls from the meeting, said. "What's on this again?" She took another healthy bite of the sandwich.

Charlie looked up at her from his own and couldn't help but smile inwardly. Finally, he'd met a woman who ate like a human *instead* of a bird in Tinsel Town and who obviously had great taste when it came to a good, sloppy sandwich.

"It's ham, salami, roast beef, pepperoni, cheddar, lettuce, pickle, tomato, onion, green peppers and banana peppers." Charlie said. "Throw in a little oil and vinegar, some pepper, oregano…and of course they make their own bread the morning of."

"All I have to say is '*yum*'!" She said, wiping the mayo that escaped to the side of her mouth with a napkin. "You sure have *great* taste in sandwiches, Mr. Vega." She added.

Charlie finished chewing and wiped his own mouth.

"Of course I do." He said, smiling at her. "And please, call me *Charlie*." He said, hesitating before taking the next bite. "You know; I'm having a hard time recalling your name."

"It's ok." She said, flashing a quick smile his way. "We were introduced rather quickly. I didn't expect you to remember. It's Ava. Ava Kincaid." She took another bite.

"Nice to meet you, Ava Kincaid." Charlie said.

She nodded and in between chewing she said, "It's nice to meet you too, Charlie."

They ate for a few more minutes in silence.

The weather on the rooftop could not have been better, Charlie thought. There was a slight breeze that kept the heat at bay and the umbrella over their table was wide enough, that it kept the sun from beating down on their backs. Impulsive moments like this, was not something that

Charlie did on a regular basis but then again, Ava was not a *regular* woman. She was a straight shooter, just the kind of female he liked to deal with, especially when it came to business.

"Ya know," Ava said, just as she finished with the last bite of her sandwich. "This movie is going to put Lola in the *hot* seat." She began thoroughly wiping her fingers of oily mayo residue.

Charlie took the last bite, wadded up the sandwich wrapper and threw it in the paper sack they'd been delivered in. Ava did the same with hers, along with the napkins she'd used. Charlie took a drink from his soda cup, swallowed and then stared at his lunch guest for a few seconds. She stared back.

"What *are* you, a fan?" he asked.

 Ava laughed. "I *could* be."

"It's more than obvious that you are in her corner." He said.

"Being a fan doesn't *cloud* my judgement. I'm speaking from a professional point of view when I say I am confident that she *is* the lead and *will* fit this part."

"Why are you so sure?" he asked.

"She's a *strong* female role model for a lot of *insecure* women." She simply said.

"Well that's an interesting take on that assumption because I would never think *insecure* women would gravitate towards someone *like* Lola."

"She catches *our* attention and holds it longer than most because she's more relatable to the viewers. She's a very interesting celebrity because she makes you feel that she's reachable. She's also as real as it gets and unpredictable as hell with just enough hint of a mystery. She doesn't act like the regular Hollywood *polished* and poised star, who is *always* trying to be politically correct. She shows up in public places with no makeup on, hair in a ponytail, in sweats and doesn't give a shit because she's *that* comfortable in her own skin. She's entertaining because you *never* know what's going to come out of *her* mouth and half the time she's speaking what we're already thinking, when it comes to *most* of *her* peers in Hollywood. She's as classy as she is trashy but demands respect just the same. I know several female entertainers in this industry who admire and support her and several who steer clear because they know she won't hesitate to call them out, if they rub her the wrong way. Look what she did to Jenna Adams."

Charlie let out a chuckle. "Jenna Adams did it to herself. Lola just exposed her fake ass!"

"True." She agreed. "But Lola's no angel. She's had *more* than her fair share of scandals but her fan base obviously doesn't care because her numbers are always steady. She has a *large* following Charlie and it grows a few at a time every day. You know those numbers will *triple* if you take her off the back burner and put her *in* the spotlight. You've never done that yet."

"I've tried to a couple of times but she just didn't fit the character that they were looking for. *Casting* always picked someone else." He said, defending his past decision.

"Well, I'm the head of *casting* on this project and I'm determined to prove all of them wrong." She said. "*Including* you!"

Charlie sighed and leaned back in his chair. "Ava, with all due respect, this movie is *not* just any ordinary romance novel. It is a *special* project that I need to make sure is executed to the best that it can possibly be and that includes making sure I appoint the *right* people to play the roles, that will make it come alive on the screen. You may be *lead* in the casting department but Sage has the final say on the *entire* production. I can't and will not play any favorites. Nor will I allow someone to be cast in a role I do not think they can carry. I can say with *confidence* that Brandon Parrish, being the *male* lead, is going to bring to this project *exactly* what it calls for in the story. I cannot say that, with as *much* confidence, when considering Lola for the *female* lead."

"Why?" she asked, her poker face intact.

"Because the lead female role is an innocent, naïve and modest character whose personality and dynamics are the total *opposite* of what Lola extrudes. She's always gravitated towards the eccentric and wild roles. She does them quite well, don't get me wrong but that's the part that worries me. Seeing her name connected to the movie I'm afraid, might send out the wrong—*first*—impression to the public of what Stranded is really about. It could turn off a lot of potential viewers because of her well-established, brash reputation. Think about it—a well-known sex symbol, *alone* in a remote cabin with a movie star for a few weeks. What the hell does everybody *think* is going to happen? *Sex* everywhere is what! They won't take it serious. With Lola Watters name attached to the marquee, add a cheap soundtrack playing in the background and you got all the makings of a *soft* porn. Brandon is *not* going to want to be portrayed like that and the writer damn sure is not going to want her story *portrayed* like that."

"I disagree." Ava said sharply, shaking her head. "Brandon Parrish is the *serious* side of sexy while Lola is obviously more on the *wild* side of sexy—that is very true. But it's also *what* will attract the viewers in hordes. They won't know which one is going to come to the *other* side in this movie and that *part* of the mystery, is what's going to make the viewers curious. His legendary reputation will counterbalance Lola's and the both of them together will bring the house down."

Charlie sighed and leaned back in his chair. "I would have to see Lola test before I could make that decision." He said. "And I'll have one for you as soon as you give me her contact info."

"You have to go through her agent." Charlie said, dryly.

"I thought that's *what* I was already doing." She said, a smile spreading on her face.

"I'll give her a buzz and let *her* contact you." He said, returning the smile. "After all, Lola *might* not be interested in the part. Don't you think we should ask her *first*?"

"Oh, *believe* me when I tell you, Charlie Vega, Lola will definitely be *interested*!" She plucked her phone from the satchel on the floor. "In the meantime, while you *play* the big, *macho* agent," she said, with a teasing smile. "I'll need *your* contact info."

The smile still stayed on Charlie's face as he recited his *personal* cell to her, *instead* of his office number, *on* purpose. He watched as she swiped her fingers on the screen and then tapped on the keys. Within a few seconds his own phone lit up next to him, alerting that he had a *new* text message.

"Now you have *my* info." She said, just as smooth. She slid her phone back inside the bag, glanced at the watch on her arm and stood up. "I *have* to go." She said abruptly. "I have a meeting downtown I have to get to." She then proceeded to dig further in her bag and produced a wallet. Charlie waved her off before she could start dispensing dollar bills. "*Please*. Lunch was *my* treat, Ava." He said and flashed a crooked smile her way. "And I certainly *enjoyed* the company."

Ava studied him for a moment, then flashed a smile of her own, as she shoved the wallet back in her bag. "Then I must say '*thank you*' for your hospitality, Charlie. I enjoyed the company as well *and* that *delicious* sandwich concoction of yours."

"It's called a *Dagwood*." He said, smiling back.

"Yes, the *Dagwood*." She repeated, staring a second too long at him. "You know," she started, then hesitated.

"*Yes*?" Charlie prompted. This woman had not been at a loss for words during the *entire* meeting or during lunch, so he was definitely curious about what had her stumbling now, at this late in the game.

"You said a few minutes ago that you didn't think Lola would *fit* this role because she's the total *opposite* of what is required, *correct*?" Charlie nodded. "You also said that attaching Lola's name to the movie might give off the wrong impression because of an already-established *reputation*." Charlie still nodded. "And that it might throw off some *potential* viewers from the get-go and that you didn't want the movie or Brandon Parrish portrayed like that, *right*?"

Charlie knew she was going somewhere with this, he just didn't know where. If nothing else, he'd learned, in the short time they'd spent together, that she didn't mince words.

"That *is* correct." He said, regardless because he found her interesting.

"Well, you just poked holes through your *own* theory about Lola."

"I'm not following you." he said shrugging his shoulders, being honest.

Ava sighed and yanked the straps of her bag over her right shoulder and then she smiled as her eyes locked with his.

"Before I came to this meeting today, I was *warned* about you, Charlie Vega! I was told you were a *hard* one to get along with. That you *are* rude, mouthy, grouchy and you cuss *worse* than a sailor, whether there are women present or not. I've also heard your notorious for ripping up contracts with millions at stake, over the slightest discrepancy and then leave a room abruptly and loudly, without compromise. In fact, my coworkers were drawing straws yesterday, because *no* one wanted to volunteer to help cast this movie, with your *name* on it. They say it's tough enough to deal with *you* and *one* client involved, much less being the agent of *three,* that is connected to *one* project." She paused briefly and probably because Charlie was making such a stoic face. "My point is," she continued, letting out a short sigh. "I have to agree with *a few* of the things that are being said about *you* and *disagree* about all the rest. You *are* a hard one to negotiate with in this business and you *are* excellent at being an *arrogant* asshole when you're trying to get your point across but it's a role that you play. It's business, I get it. I *saw* the big-shot agent in action downstairs for myself, in that meeting this morning but this afternoon, you've turned out to be quite the *charmer*. If I hadn't of taken out the few minutes that I did, to *see* you in a *different* setting, I would have missed a great opportunity to finally meet the *real* Charlie Vega and everything everyone said about you would have held true. It's no different with Lola. Putting her in a different setting, might make you *see* her for *who* she really is. And I think, *seriously*, you would be *very* surprised." She smiled and it was warm and genuine. Charlie felt the heat of it touch his face, if that were possible.

Damn this lady was smooth in her deliverance. When was the last time anyone associated the word '*charm*' anywhere near Charlie's name? What in the *hell* had the corner deli put in that *Dagwood*?

"*Charmer, eh*?" He repeated one word out of the *entire* paragraph she'd just laid on him. That crooked grin returned but only to one side of his mouth.

She glanced at her watch again, returned the smile, then turned on her heels and headed towards the door. "I'll be sending over the tape in a few days, tops!" she called to him, over her shoulder.

"And *you* will be delivering it in *person*, I assume?" he responded, as he watched the nice view from the back. She reached the door, grabbed for the knob and turned slightly his way. The smile was still in place.

"I'll treat next time by bringing lunch when I do." And then she was gone.

This one, Charlie thought, *doesn't miss a beat. Plus, she had a nice pair of legs...*

NINETEEN

Courtney was still not feeling well a good hour after returning to their suite. She'd abandoned the coffee that Michael had brought to her after the first few sips. She'd fought several urges of nausea while she'd finished packing. She'd splashed her face several times with cold water, hoping it would bring some color to her cheeks. Feeling sorry for her, Michael had somehow miraculously scavenged up a couple of nausea pills from one of the crew and it had eased up somewhat. *Damn* if she was ever going to drink like that again, the night before a flight! Hopefully she would never encounter anything close to what Charlie Vega had dropped on her, right before she'd boarded for this mission, that would make her want to. Talk about right out of the fire and into the frying pan. That cliché fit when it came to describing the last few weeks of her life. First she finds out from this stranger—in a room full of strangers—that she might not be who she *thinks* she's been, all of her forty-something years. Then immediately after, she's flown down to the depths of Kenya, covering one of the most barbaric situations of all time. Seeing first hand, the devastation caused by the Somalia Pirates, had been a lot to handle.

Suddenly all that mattered right now was just getting home to her big king-sized bed. Of all the exquisite pieces she had throughout the rooms of her apartment, that was the one piece of furniture she missed the most. Especially after sleeping on such a firm, hard mattress and living out of such a primitive space. She swore to herself that the moment she stepped over the threshold of her apartment again, she was going to shut the ringer off her phone, close the black-out curtains, take a nice long hot shower and curl up in her bed and sleep for a whole day.

Before another thought could enter her mind, Michael abruptly opened the main door, causing her to jump. Bram walked in behind him.

"Are you alright?" he asked with concern.

She just nodded.

"Sure?" he asked.

She nodded again.

"What happened to your *other* earring?" he asked.

Out of reflex, Courtney reached up to both sides of her ears and felt a pearl stud on the left but nothing on the right.

"Oh, crap!" she said and began looking at the floor around her. Michael and Bram joined in the search but several minutes later, all three turned up nothing.

"We gotta go or we'll *miss* our flight!" Michael warned her. "A new pair is cheaper than to buy another round airline tickets. In fact, I'll buy them myself, when we get back home. *Bram*, you go ahead and take these on down, my friend." Michael directed the boy to where the three cases of luggage were lined up by the door.

Bram nodded in their direction politely, but had a worried frown on his face. He lingered a little too long at Courtney. "I will inform Kioni, who will clean your room after you leave, about the earring, Miss Courtney. No fear, if she finds it, I will get word to you!" he promised.

"Thank you Bram." Courtney dug in her purse and produced her business card, flipped it over to the back and wrote her cell in pen, on the back. She handed it to Bram, who took it and slid it into his pants pocket.

"I have a car waiting downstairs to take us to the airport." Michael said, grabbing a carry-on bag and looping it over his shoulder. "You ready?"

Bram finished loading the luggage on the cart and departed ahead of them.

Courtney nodded. She'd eat something light once they were in the air, to help settle her stomach. Then she'd sleep, probably *most* of the trip home, she told herself. Once they arrived in New York, she'd feel much better because it meant she was that much closer to her bed.

Courtney grabbed her own carry-on bag from the chair next to her and slung it over her shoulder. Michael took one last look around the room and then they both headed out the door, down the hall and began taking the stairs to the bottom floor.

The main doors to the hotel were propped open and Bram was already there with the luggage. Both cabs had their trunks open and were trying to fit all the pieces in like a puzzle. Two of them were scratching their heads. That's when Bram stepped in and took over. Courtney figured it was going to take a few minutes to sort out the mess and thought it'd be a good idea to hit the public restroom before they headed to the airport. She told Michael where she was going and headed back inside.

To make matters worse, the lighting in the restroom was horrible. Courtney's ashen face stared back at her, void of makeup and sporting dark circles under her eyes. *She needed some vitamin D,* her reflection said. She needed a vacation in St. Tropez or St. Bart's for a couple of weeks. Something tropical, with endless beaches, fruity island drinks, her toes in the sand and *hot* cabana boys. Suddenly wanting to escape her reflection, she quickly exited out the door and into the short hallway. Making a quick right, she'd almost cleared the empty bar when she spotted Bram on the other side of the room, talking animatingly in Swahili, to a man dressed in a Kenyan police uniform. He was pointing off in the distance over the man's shoulder and the fact that he was annoyed and revved up at the same time, meant the subject was heated. The officer was engaged in what Bram was saying, taking it very seriously and began speaking into what looked like a short wave radio. They were across the wide expanse of the room away from her and apparently both made no indication that they knew she was there. The officer turned abruptly and left the room. Bram turned as well and headed back towards the main entrance, still *oblivious* to her presence on the other side of the room. Courtney figured the officer must have been his cousin, the one Tony had mentioned that was working the Pirate's site.

She shrugged it off and made her way back towards the front entrance that led outside, where the cars were being loaded. Just as she stepped out into the sunshine, a police car with a loud siren, sped past and headed towards the market area. The shrill piercing that filled the immediate space, caused a sharp pain to stab at her temple. She glanced over at the progress the men had made on the luggage and found to her delight, that the two trolleys were empty and the drivers were just closing the trunks on both cars. With a sigh of relief, she climbed into the back seat of the front car, while the crew filled the second. Michael climbed in beside her, behind the driver.

"Everything okay?" he asked, when they met in the middle, each closing their door at the same time. He sat his carry-on and his laptop bag down on the floor space and began strapping himself in the seat belt.

Courtney nodded.

"Wouldn't fit?" she asked, referring to the extra bag that carried his prized device inside.

He shook his head.

"It's a long flight. I'm going to catch up on some paperwork." He said,

"Not me. I *need* some sleep. In fact, I *need* a vacation." She stressed.

"You might not have a choice, once we return home." He leaned back in the seat as the car pulled away and headed in the direction of the airport. "The station's attorney is advising that once you make a statement, regarding *your* part in the Karly Driggers incident, that you take a break from being on the air for a few weeks. Give everything a chance to die down."

"Well *hell*, that *should* do it." Courtney said, sarcastically. "Admit on air that I shot some *psycho* bitch, disappear for two weeks, then return with a tan *and* whiter teeth, like *nothing* happened? That will keep my reputation *intact* for sure. Why didn't I *think* of that?"

"It's *their* rules Courtney," Michael reminded her, in his own sarcastic, boss-like tone. "We have to play by them, you know that."

"I didn't do anything wrong, Michael." She stressed.

"No one is saying that you did." He replied.

"The incident was investigated and the police came to the conclusion, beyond a doubt, that it was self-defense. That Karly *bitch* is a psycho fan as far as the police report is written up. She went after Brandon before. *I told you that*!"

"That is not *what* worries the big guys and why they called in the top attorneys on this one. It's the small parts of the story that concerns them. The part that none of the other stations know about yet but with some successful digging, could uncover."

"Like what?" Courtney asked, anger evident in her expression and tone.

"Like the fact that you *shot* that psycho bitch *with* Brandon Parrish's gun and how *you* ended up with it in *your* hands, in the *first* place."

"That's easy," Courtney said. "He froze up and she lunged. I had to defend us all."

"She's Victor Rocha's daughter." Michael said, dryly, with a direct stare.

"*So?*" Was her curt reply. "With his legendary *thug* reputation, it only lends more credibility to the fact that she's as psycho as her old man was."

"Once the press makes that connection, they are going to dig relentlessly into her background, Courtney. You know the drill."

"Charlie Vega says that there is nothing of Victor Rocha on record, that would remotely lead back to me, other than the interview, which I did on orders from the station."

"He also told you that there were no paper trails of all four of your original births and *yet* yours is *found* in a safe in Frank Hartford's library, that says otherwise!" he argued.

"I have no proof yet that it's mine…" Courtney began.

"And how will you validate proof of your biological stand on this?" he asked her. "How will you be able to get a DNA test to prove you even *belong* to Everett Calhoun and Catalina Rocha, *without* it raising some kind of suspicion?"

"Andy and I can do it quietly." She stressed.

"If your results become public, Courtney—and that's *always* a possibility when you're a famous figure in the spotlight—if enough money is thrown on the table, the mouths will start wagging."

"Everett was a smooth-talking Casanova. He could have impregnated a number of eligible women in his time that could have been my mother. Besides, no one outside of us, knows he took Catalina as a lover. And although it's more than obvious that I can't do the genetic numbers with my real mother or father, at least thru Andy, I can prove to myself, that I'm Everett's."

"He's the grandfather of one of the most *famous* legends in Hollywood. It won't take somebody long to connect the dots. One thing leads to another and just like I did, an ambitious-driven journalist will make the trek to Italy and find that *one* person, who happen to be around when this was all going down."

"By now, everyone involved is *dead*." She simply said.

"Don't *count* on that, Princess." Michael warned. "Because to do so, would be your first mistake!"

TWENTY

The man sat alone at the table in the big empty room. He kept his head down with his eyes on his tray. He methodically used the fork in his left hand to spear food and shove it into his mouth without missing a beat. He did not look up even once. Not when he paused in chewing to take a drink or when he used the back of his hand to wipe his mouth. He didn't have to look up to know, that all eyes were on his every move. Nor did he have to look up to remember, where all of the six-armed guards stood, strategically placed around him, as he ate his meal. Because every night, it was always the same routine. Nothing about it had changed since they'd brought him to this place. In return, he would continue to act as ignorant and drugged as they thought he was, while he bided his time to escape. Without warning, the silence in the room was suddenly disrupted. The movement came from a side door in the front part of the cafeteria. It opened abruptly and then closed directly to his right. It was followed by the shuffle of feet, maybe three sets. They were accompanied by a rhythmic clinking sound, which meant one of them were bound in shackles.

Still the man dared not to look up. Even though there was activity other than his presence in the room now, all eyes would not be on the new interruption. *Someone* would be watching him and to look up would mean he was *too* aware and being *too* aware, brought on the *wrong* kind of attention and he didn't *need* any more attention on him, than he already had. So he continued to eat, spearing pieces of food on his plate and shoving it in his mouth, until every bit was gone. And only then did he lay his fork down, slowly next to the tray. A hand came into view and snatched it up rather quickly and it was gone, just like that.

"Time's up!"

Hands forced their way under both of his armpits and jerked him to his feet. Both guards began to walk/drag him down the row of empty tables, towards the front of the room. He briefly scanned the space and saw what had caused the intrusion.

Facing them, seated only three tables away, sat another prisoner, dressed in a similar jumpsuit like the one that he wore, only this one was female. Her hands were indeed shackled and lying still in her lap. She was bent so far over, that her greasy hair acted like a curtain and blocked him from seeing the features on her face.

It didn't take a rocket scientist to figure out that she was so heavily sedated, that eating on her own, was *literally* impossible. But no one in this room cared. *No one*. All their prisoners could starve to death as far as the guards here, were concerned.

He neared the table the female was sitting at and her head snapped back at that moment when he dared glanced her way, as if she had no control. All her hair moved with it and exposed the features on her face. For a second her eyes tried to focus on the movement coming at her and then, just as fast, her head snapped forward again, hair falling down, hovering over the untouched tray. He recognized her as the woman who'd been dragged into the glass room. The one they'd sedated when he'd been in there the day before. He dropped his gaze and stared at the passing tiles on the floor. Taking too much interest in his surroundings, would mean he was *more* alert than he should be and that would draw attention…the *wrong* kind. So he continued to play *dumb* and act sedated…as they half-walked, half-dragged him back to his cell.

TWENTY–ONE

Agent Fields glanced over, as a man stepped through the doorway of her office. He wore a very stern expression on his face and he was carrying a small briefcase.
"Mrs. Hartford, this is Agent Metz. He's head of our Forensics department," she explained, as her colleague walked over and rested the case on the corner of her desk. Agent Metz did not speak any pleasantries but nodded in her direction.
"What is this?" Margot Hartford asked, irritation clearly reflected in her voice and in her expression.
"We recovered some items from the Pirates burrow that we suspect were acquired during their pilfering and thievery." Agent Fields said. "We would like to show you some of those items and see if you recognize any of them."
"*Things*?" Margot Hartford repeated, looking from one to the other, as if they had lost their minds. "Why would you two even *think* that I might recognize *anything* that Pirates *stole* from others in a remote country, half-way around the world?"
"We believe it's *possible* that your daughter's plane *might* have gone down within the borders that the pirates often patrolled." Agent Fields explained. "It's even *more* likely that during their travels they could have come upon the wreckage and without a doubt, looted it. There are several items that have been recovered so far, in the seizure, that is extremely foreign to their native culture and availability."
"What do you mean by that?" Margot asked.
"Well for instance, finding a machete in a hut out in the middle of the jungle would not be considered *foreign* or out of place in *that* environment." Fields said. "But a woman's

white ivory *engraved* hair brush from the 1800s would stick out like a sore thumb."

"So your agency thinks that these pirates stumbled upon the wreckage—that *your* bureau can't find—and took items of value that possibly belonged to my dead daughter?" Margot Hartford asked, in that haughty tone she'd presented to her from the get-go.

Agent Fields silently reminded herself to tread carefully with this woman. She was not in the least bit to be taken as someone's little old harmless and naive grandmother. Margot Hartford was a shrewd business woman with an impeccable reputation and rumored to have a set of steel balls between her legs and a razor sharp tongue that can cut down the wittiest opponent. Fields should know, she'd been getting a taste of her own blood almost through the *entire* interview.

"We can't disclose that kind of information right now, Mrs. Hartford. The bureau is in the middle of an ongoing investigation that has been classified as top-secret."

"That's what they *all* say!" Margot Hartford retorted. "Which translated means that—*Yes*, I'm right but you're not going to admit it!"

"*Legally* we can't confirm anything until the investigation is concluded and all the facts have been presented. And in order to further aide *us* in the progress of our investigation, we would greatly appreciate *your* help in *this* part of the process," Fields emphasized but the woman still looked as if she wasn't going to cooperate, so she pressed further. "Mrs. Hartford, we have captured the pirates and right at this moment, they are in military custody. With todays' technology, all we need from just *one* of those prisoners, is the coordinates and we can locate that plane. But we can't do it without some sort of leverage. We need something *tangible* to prove that they were at that site. Going through these items with you might get us the evidence we need to use for leverage, to get some answers. I know it might be *difficult* but if you could just take a look. That's all I'm asking."

Fields held the woman's stern gaze. The silence was thick in the room as they waited each other out. Metz stood like a statue beside Fields not saying a word. He knew his place. She was the lead on this investigation while he ran the labs, simple as that.

"Do you have any children, Agent Fields?" Margot asked, rather sternly.

"Yes, I do." She quickly replied, hoping it would make the woman see her as a compassionate equal. "I have a *daughter*."

"How old?" she asked, her eyes narrowed and brows drawn.

Fields felt this was leading somewhere she might not want to go.

"She's eight."

Margot Hartford smiled but it was not in amusement.

"That's the same age my granddaughter was, when her mother and father were tragically *ripped* out of her young life." She said, in a snarky manner and then she leaned slightly towards her, totally ignoring Agent Metz. "Just *think* for one moment, *Agent* Fields, what it would be *like* for *your* precious daughter, if something ripped *you* away from her, in the *same* fashion!"

"I can't imagine!" Fields said, not missing a beat. "She would be devastated, as I'm sure *your* granddaughter must have been."

Margot studied her for a moment and then spoke. "There is no *word* in the English dictionary to describe *what* that child felt and *is* still feeling as an adult."

Agent Fields did not hesitate. "Which is *exactly* why I thought it best, as one mother to another, to contact *you*, instead of *your* granddaughter. If for one second I could spare my child from dealing with something like this, I would go to any lengths to do it!”

“Are you telling me that if I *refuse* to look at these *items* you have, you would *contact* my granddaughter to do so, in my place?”

“I’m not going to *lie* to you, Mrs. Hartford. That would be our *second* recourse.” Fields confirmed.

The two women eyed each other. The room was deathly silent.

“Oh *hell*!” Margot Hartford finally said, shaking her head in anger. She waved her hand at them and in an irritated tone, said, “Just get *on* with it! I’ve got a *plane* to catch soon.”

Finally, progress, Fields thought.

“Thank you, Mrs. Hartford. We *really* appreciate your cooperation.”

Fields nodded in Agent Metz’s direction, indicating for him to proceed. He opened the lid to the case and produced a large envelope. He stuck his hand inside and extracted a clear plastic bag the size of a sandwich Ziploc. He laid it in front of Margot. “Feel free to pick it up.” Agent Metz said, finally speaking for the first time since he’d entered the office. “Just *don’t* open it.” He warned.

Margot glanced down at the item in front of her and stared at it for a second. She didn’t bother to pick it up and in fact kept her distance, as if it was riddled with disease.

“Do you recognize this?” Agent Fields asked. Immediately Margot shook her head from side to side, indicating no. Metz then retrieved it and laid it aside. He reached into the envelope for another and laid it in front of her as well. Fields watched as again, she stared at the object for a few seconds and then shook her head ‘no’ without even bothering to pick it up.

This went on for several more minutes, item after item. Nothing in the woman’s eyes, mouth set or expression indicated that she was familiar with anything that Metz had to show her. *Until* he laid down the evidence baggie marked number *15*.

Margot Hartford's entire demeanor changed. The careless detached aloofness, did a one-eighty into a more serious interest. The ridged set of her jaw relaxed. The disbelief of what she was seeing began to grow unguarded right in front of their eyes. Margot leaned forward in one swift motion and picked the bagged item up. A breath hitched in her throat and the words *"Dear God"* escaped her lips. They were followed by a shimmer of tears that began to gather in her eyes. As if the woman had been holding her breath in those brief seconds too long, she let out a gasp as she flipped the bag around and looked at the backside. From somewhere in the depths of her purse she produced a fancy pair of glasses and sliding them on her nose, she brought the item closer for inspection.

"Do you *recognize* this piece, Mrs. Hartford?" Agent Fields asked, feeling a twinge of excitement building within herself.

"Oh *dear* God!" the woman repeated, still staring hard at the piece in her hand, obviously in a state of disbelief. *"Kelley*…Oh *dear* God, *Kelley*…"

Tears began to slide down her cheeks.

The possibility that this could be a major breakthrough in both the pirate's lair *and* the decade-old missing airplane, had Fields feeling a surge of excitement, fluttering in her gut. Dozens of agents had worked the plane case for years, baffled and resigned to believe that it had simply *vanished* into thin air. Not a wing, or a piece of luggage, or a body had ever turned up. One second they were on the radar and in the next they were gone. Not a bleep, not an SOS, no alerts, warnings or explanations as to where it went and what had happened. And it had been a thorn in the bureaus side from day one. This woman, if she was truly *recognizing* a piece that they could prove was *on* that plane at the time of its disappearance, it meant there was hope in finally closing this case.

"Mrs. Hartford…," Fields began, but was cut short. The woman raised her hand to her chest and pressed it near her heart. Her face was pale. "Are you *ok*?" Fields quickly stood and came around the side of the desk.

"I'll get some water." Agent Metz said and turned towards the door he'd come from earlier.

"Mrs. Hartford, take some deep breaths." Fields suggested as she placed a gentle hand on the woman's shoulder.

"*Oh dear God…*," Margot Hartford said again, in-between sobs, as she kept staring at the item in the baggie.

"It is *hers*, isn't it?" Fields asked, squeezing her shoulder gently in support.

This time, Margot Hartford frantically nodded her head *yes*, never taking her eyes from the item she was holding. Agent Metz returned to the room with a glass of water and offered it to the distraught woman. She gladly accepted and both agents waited while she took a few sips and tried to regain her composure. Fields slid a Kleenex box in her direction. Margot took a few and patted around her eyes and sniffed. She seemed to be calming down, somewhat, so Fields gently squeezed her shoulder again before leaving her side and returning to her own chair.

"I know this is difficult, Mrs. Hartford and I do apologize for the discomfort this might be causing you." She said, once she was seated. "But you *obviously* recognize this piece?"

Margot Hartford slowly nodded, "That necklace *belonged* to my daughter."

"And just for the record, Mrs. Hartford, the daughter you *are* referring to is *indeed* Kelley Hartford Cassava, one of the *missing* passengers of flight 317537, on June the 8th, 1987, *correct*?" Fields confirmed, for recording purposes.

"*Yes*." Margot Hartford stated, her voice slightly faltering.

"And to the *best* of your knowledge, do you know *if* she had *this* piece, exhibit number *15*, in her *possession* while on that particular flight, Mrs. Hartford?" Agent Fields held her breath, waiting for that answer to confirm what they already knew.

"How else would the *bastards* have acquired it?" Margot Hartford asked, with conviction. Tears filled her eyes again.

"We *know*; we just need to *hear* the words from you to make it a *legal* statement, in order to proceed." Fields explained.

The room grew silent for a few seconds as Margot stared down at the piece in her hand. She closed her eyes for all of two seconds and then released a weary sigh. "She was *wearing* it around her neck the morning she left for the airport." She said. "It was one of her most *prized* possessions. In fact, she hardly *ever* took it off."

Once Fields felt she had gotten all the additional information she was going to get from Margot Hartford, she ordered a car and requested that an agent escort her back to the airport, where she was to catch a flight home. The moment the main office door closed behind them, the other door next to the two-way mirror opened and in walked a tech from Forensics. He was carrying a large, clear baggie and a pair of oversized tongs. He was dressed in a white lab coat and wore gloves. He nodded to both the agents and then stepped around to the side of the desk that Margot Hartford had just vacated. He used the large pinchers to grip the inside base of the glass that the woman had drank the water from. He maneuvered it into the baggie, released the tongs' grip and sealed the top of the bag.

"I want a *rush* on that!" Agent Metz said to the technician. "I'll start testing it myself as soon as I get back to the lab." The tech reassured him, nodding again to both Metz and Fields before leaving the room.

"I want to be notified the minute he *has* the results. I don't care what time of the day *or* night it is." Fields said this to Metz.

The agent nodded. "I've already pulled the DNA samples on the Jane Doe. Once we can make an accurate comparison, I will contact you immediately." He confirmed.

Fields nodded, then sighed and released a stressful breath. Another agent interrupted them when he stuck his head in the door.

"Agent Mullins said you gave the go-ahead to call the general?" he asked, one eyebrow cocked.

Fields nodded. "We got it, on record. Tell him one of the items has been *positively* identified."

"I'll contact him now." He disappeared and shut the door.

"That poor woman." She said to Metz, shaking her head as she picked up the baggie still lying on the desk, that held a gold heart. She studied it for a moment on both front and then back. "I just can't imagine what she's feeling right now, from a mother's perspective." She added.

Metz shook his head, a rather strained look settled on his face as he took the bagged item from Fields and slid it into a new envelope and wrote in black magic marker—*Kelley Cassava necklace*—on the front.

"As a parent myself, I can't imagine either. It's shocking enough to find out a precious family memento, that was last seen on the neck of your missing daughter, *who* has been presumed dead for twenty years, has been miraculously recovered, thanks to a gang of *filthy* pirates." He said.

"However, *if* those DNA comparisons come back *positive* for a match, Margot Hartford is going to be severely devastated, when she finds out that after all this time, her daughter *had* been alive and we managed to miss saving her by a measly *few* hours." He closed the briefcase and made eye contact with Fields. "*If* the woman is still standing *after* you break that to her, she's not only got balls of steel but a *heart* made out of the *same* shit to match it!"

TWENTY–TWO

Halfway into their flight from Kenya to New York, the entire crew had fallen into a deep slumber. Sleep shades had been drawn, seats had been reclined, overhead lights had been dimmed and soft snores could be heard throughout the cabin. Michael Buchanan was the only one awake.

And mainly because he had a *lot* on his mind.

He'd been texting for the last half hour trying to get a jump on the long list of things he had to do. At the top of that list, was to contact his secretary and have her upload some digital files to his laptop that had been archived. He had twenty minutes to kill before they were accessible. He sat the phone in his lap and reached quietly in the seat to his left and unzipped his computer bag. He slid his laptop out, sat it on the fold-out table in front of him and opened it up. The screen came to life. He keyed in the password that connected him to the plane's Wi-Fi, heard the soft ping that confirmed it was successful and immediately muted the volume. He quickly glanced to his right to see if the sound had disturbed a slumbering Courtney, who was in the seat across from his.

But it hadn't.

She was in the *exact* same position as she'd been, the last time he'd looked. Her body was turned slightly towards the wall of the aircraft, away from him. Her breathing was minimal but the features on her face was set in a peaceful tone, one that told Michael she was in a very deep sleep. He had covered her with a blanket a long time ago.

She was still pale from this morning's hangover and a faint shadow had settled around her eyes.

While he patiently waited for the files he needed, his thoughts of course, turned to the staggering revelation that

Courtney had made just last night about being Everett Calhoun's *illegitimate* daughter…the *missing* daughter that was originally peddled to the world as belonging to Victor Rocha and his deceased wife, Catalina.

And yet, he *knew* the minute she'd spoken the words, that Charlie Vega *was* telling the truth, simply because of her *face*.

The similarities in her features compared to Brandon Parrish and his grandfathers' were uncanny, now that he knew the truth…and she'd been right *under* his nose the *entire* time, since the night of her graduation. Everett had *led* Michael to her and practically on a silver platter and he'd had *no* clue. And now here she lies, next to him, unaware that he was staring at her, as she slept. His mind was steady working the pieces of the puzzle into place…*click, click, click.*

Courtney Curwin was one of the most well-known and highest-paid news journalist in the business. If the information she had shared with him last night was to fall into the wrong hands, her life would become a media circus of endless proportions. If Brandon Parrish thought he hated the paparazzi now, just wait until they get wind that he's *secretly* related to the equally famous Courtney Curwin, illegitimate *love* child of *his* grandfather's, who committed adultery with an Italian woman, that later committed suicide by jumping off her balcony into her own pool below. No *wait*! Michael thought. That was the story the world knew! The real one, according to Courtney, is that Victor's daughter, the crazy Karly Driggers, was really the one, as a child, who pushed Victor's wife *over* the balcony out of jealousy.

Oh boy…that was a whole *other* story. And he hadn't even *begun* to digest the fact that Charlie Vega *was* the missing *oldest* child of the Benenati trio. His twin had been Jack Cassava, Sage's *father* and Meg Jackson was the *baby* sister.

Click…click…click.

Isabella Rocha…the *baby*, who everyone speculated had been dead a long time ago.

The Benenati children, who everyone *thought* had been murdered a long time ago.

He stared at Courtney…deep in thought…until he felt a slight vibration on his leg. He looked down and saw he'd received a text message on his cell he'd been waiting for. He read it, replied with a short answer and then deleted the entire thing. He shut the phone down in silent mode and laid it on the empty seat to his left. He turned his attention back to his laptop and tapped the built-in mousepad. The screen lit up. In the right hand corner, a dialog box alerted him that the recent downloads were ready to be assessed. He clicked the first folder and opened it up.

The file was named, '*Benenati Murder Investigation*'. He began to read the old random notes he'd written on the case over twenty years ago, with a totally *new* perspective.

TWENTY-THREE

Margot stared out the small window of the airplane. For the last two and a half hours the view had never changed. Puffs of white clouds floated by within the perimeters of an endless, sky-blue background. The patchwork quilt of land below gave way now and then to cities and bodies of water and then over to more patchwork green. Life in general, all around her, felt like a broken record that just kept repeating itself.

She sighed heavily and took a generous sip of her cocktail. She had been very persuasive when pressing the stewardess into giving her a double. But she'd desperately needed something to slow down the rapid heartbeat in her chest. It seemed to be beating extra hard after the meeting she'd had with the feds. *Especially* after seeing that locket again, the one Kelley had been *wearing* around her neck, the last time she'd seen her alive...

Oh dear God! Margot thought to herself as tears threatened to spill. It had been a really *long* time since she'd allowed herself to walk back *through* the nightmare of that *last* day, that last *moment* before Kelley and Jack had walked out her front door, never to be seen again. It had hurt too much to remember and time had done nothing but enhance it.

Kelley had been the center of Margot's world, from the time she took her *first* breath, until she'd taken her *last* on that fateful day, somewhere over the ocean, a *million* miles from home. Even though they clashed often throughout her short life, it had been strictly out of defiance on Kelley's part and Margot *now* would certainly admit, stubbornness on *her* part. The girl had merely wanted to grow up and find her *own* identity and Margot, the overbearing mother that she was, wasn't ready to let her go, just yet. She'd had a hard time controlling herself from doing the smothering act with her granddaughter. It would get even worse right before Sage was about to board a plane. Just the possibility that something could malfunction while she was in the air, threw Margot into a full-blown panic attack. The fact that time *could* repeat itself, had Margot locked into a nightmare of fear, on a *daily* basis that no one around her, would *ever* comprehend. Now that Sage was married to a wealthy movie-star, who came equipped with his *own* personal plane and flew as much as a person drives a car, well her nerves were just about at the end of their breaking point. The old adage that lightening never struck twice in the same place was an epic lie, as far as Margot was concerned. She'd seen it strike wherever and whenever it *damn*-well pleased!

Now, thanks to Charlie Vega *and* the FBI, everything was going to get worse. It was already *blatantly* obvious that the feds were hot, on some kind of trail that involved *her* family. That much they'd made *very* clear in a round-about way. And the story about the rogue ex-agent who falsified records, then turned up dead in Venice the *same* year the plane went missing, had her baffled as well. And *who* in the hell had sent copies of the documents Greene had falsified, to the bureau? Who had *access* to something like that and *what* was it they were trying to gain, by doing so?   All of it to Margot, felt like a *warning*. A warning that if they wanted to, they could dig some more and start a full-on federal investigation. Margot was afraid that it would lead them to take a *closer* look at Everett and her husband. Before too long, Brandon's famous name would be pulled into this mess and that would automatically *involve* her granddaughter as well. Whom, up until now, she had successfully protected from all of this.

And *damn* Charlie for dragging Courtney Curwin into the mix. He could have told the rest of them without involving her. Margot didn't trust her, after all, she was a news reporter who stuck her nose *gladly* in other people's business for a living. And people who did that, liked to gossip. Who was Courtney going to tell their secret to, that would in turn, blab it to someone else? She had no emotional connection to this family or the Benenati's so what measure was her loyalty to them? What would it matter to her if someone she told, spilled the beans to the world? Courtney was an attention seeker. It would only give her more of what she already craved. There was no loss here for her.

In Margot's opinion, they were all stirring a dangerous pot and she needed to be prepared for the shit storm that would be caused by their recklessness. The first thing on her list to do tomorrow morning, was to contact her legal team and set up a meeting ASAP and figure out a way to keep George from knowing about it.

Just in case…

The sins of the Fathers—echoed the famous Deuteronomy verse in Margot's head. She would *die* before she'd allow *any* of this mess to fall on Sage's head.

She sipped from her cocktail and dared to let her mind wander back to the time when her and Frank's *perfect* marriage had begun to dissolve…

Of course, it had begun when poor Frank started blaming himself for the kids' death in the aftermath. He had stated to her several times out of his own mouth, that *if* it had not been for him falling ill before the scheduled business trip, he would have been the one who had died on that flight, instead of Kelley and Jack. And Margot had not been much help when it came to easing his burdens, simply because she'd been too busy fighting demons of her own at the same time.

For a couple who had always been in each other's constant shadow since day one, the jump in separation was instant after their death, starting with Frank spending long hours, locked up inside his damn library, grieving and doing God knows what. Margot herself had resorted to seeking solitary refuge in her bedroom for a spell to try and pick up the pieces. If it hadn't of been for dear, *sweet* Lydia and her right-hand *man*, George, the House of Hartford would have greatly suffered. It was one of the reasons why she had made sure, long after her death, that *both* would be well taken care of.

Margot paused in her troubled thoughts, took a deep breath, another healthy sip and swallowed, choking back the urge to burst out in tears. The recent incident with Karly Driggers had left her more rattled than she had cared to admit. The nerve-racking interview just now with the FBI, had left behind a *worse* feeling. The whole incident seemed so surreal. Just holding Kelley's precious locket in her hands once again was almost like having a piece of her daughter back, the precious child she'd so adored, the beautiful young woman she had lost. The whole affair had made her quite emotional and she felt as if she were teetering on the edge of mental and physical exhaustion. She was suddenly so…*tired*.

An image of Kelley's necklace flashed across her mind. Agent Fields had confirmed that it'd been found among the pirate's belongings. Apparently the FBI were guessing the thieves had stumbled upon the plane wreck in their many travels up and down the water channel. At the moment, they were interrogating every one of them in hopes to learn of its location. It seemed that Margot might live long enough to learn what *really* happened to her child. Another lone tear escaped and she wiped it systematically away. Margot had wanted to take the necklace with her. She'd wanted to take Kelley's necklace home where it belonged and not leave it behind in some baggie that had to be locked up in a *cold* evidence locker. But Agent Fields explained that they had to keep it a while longer. She promised that one day soon they would release it to her.

And when they did, Margot, of course, would give it to Sage.

Margot's thoughts turned to the graves of Kelley and Jack. What had made her husband suspicious enough to have them dug up? Had someone tipped him off about Agent Greene? And why had he not confided in her if they did? Did he think that she was too fragile at the time, as Charlie had suggested, to handle it? And why hadn't Everett come to her when he'd had a problem with Frank? He'd come to her before, why not when he and Frank had become suspicious about the graves? Maybe Everett never knew that Frank had them exhumed. Maybe her husband had kept it from him too. But yet, he had reached out to their friend, the judge, that something was amiss.

And why had Frederick, who signed the exhumation papers, not ever come forward to tell her about it after Frank died? They had talked many times since, so the man had had ample opportunity. Maybe he assumed that Margot already knew. Or he had been instructed by Frank to keep his mouth shut, even in death!

Eventually, everything comes out in the wash, as her mother always liked to say.

If Margot had ever decided to sell Providence, then sooner or later she or someone on her staff would have discovered the safe. Or if not and she had died without knowing, Sage would have found it. The point being that one of them, eventually, would have learned the truth.

So why not *destroy* the documents? All of them? Why hide certain pieces in a safe and yet leave the journals in a box, in a closet, for anyone to come across at the cabin? The only thing that made sense was that Frank's health had failed him faster than he'd anticipated and there had been no last minute left, to take care of loose ends. He had just simply run out of time. Otherwise, *maybe* he would have burned them out back in a barrel and no one would have been the wiser.

Another tear escaped, this time from both sides. She wiped at her face furiously.

Her gallant, loving, powerhouse husband Frank, the love of her life, her best friend who had been her rock, had been the next who walked out her front door, never to return. He was only supposed to be going to the doctor for a routine check-up. He said he'd been feeling a little under the weather. That afternoon he'd been admitted for tests and…well, he just never came back home.

It almost seemed like the house had a *curse*, taking her loved ones away, one by one and all she had left, was her darling Sage...that is, until the day the famous Brandon Parrish walked into their lives.

If it hadn't of been for the legendary movie star breaking down, not even a mile from the cabin, the current chain of events would not be transpiring. Sage would have come home, possibly still *working* on that bestseller and no one would have yet, found the safe in the library. But then again, if Sage hadn't been at the cabin on that fateful night, the world might have awakened the next morning, to the terrible news that Brandon Parrish and his driver had been found, frozen to death in a limo, on the side of the road in Montana. Where was the lesser evil in all this? The cabin…with its majestic mountains in the distance, where beauty comes hand in hand with danger. That cabin was Frank's favorite sanctuary in the *entire* world. With his *many* millions and social status he'd acquired, the man could have vacationed *anywhere* in the world, yet he was the *happiest* at that God-forsaken, overgrown, tree-fort he'd had built, *squat* in the middle of the mountains in Montana. What he and Sage loved about being in such an isolated and barren place, was beyond her but they fought tooth and nail to do so every chance they could. It was one of the major contributing factors she had considered, when signing the place over to her and Brandon as a wedding present. Frank would have been happy with the decision. Especially since it provided the privacy that a high-profile celebrity like Brandon needed, to hide away from the world. It was now *his* perfect sanctuary.

The captain's voice broke over the speaker above her head. The announcement was to inform the passengers, that they were to return to their seats and prepare for a landing. Relief swept over her.

Within a half hour she would finally be back in her beloved home. Her *safe* haven. A place where she could think. A place that no one had *ever* considered it home but her.

She had been well aware of the fact that between Frank, Kelley and Sage, that the mansion she dearly loved, had not given them the joy of residing there, as it did for her. And it was only in that split second she'd realized, they'd all given up their needs to make her happy and it left a sour taste in her mouth. That's the funny thing about life, Margot thought. It took until you were *old* to figure out just *what* kind of person you had really been, all your life. And in Margot's case, she'd been a pretty selfish woman and in all actuality, she *still* was. Ken was *another* person she loved that *hated* living in her mansion. But yet, she had chosen to ignore it, hoping that over time he would adjust and come to love it as much as she did.

But he hadn't and she knew for a while now that her wonderful husband was suffocating, just like Frank had. In fact, Ken often *indirectly* referred to her home as a *mausoleum*. George had suggested, too many times lately, that Margot needed to consider making a *life* change. His real meaning behind his idea of a *life*-change, was *selling* the mansion and *building* a rustic cabin of their own on a parcel of the hundred-acre-land in Montana, to be closer to Sage. As if to make her feel even more guilty, he reminded her that in order to be a stable presence in baby Tristan's life, it would help if she was a few yards away instead of a few *thousand* miles, *clear* across the state. His suggestions aggravated her because she knew deep down he was right. Everyone would eventually be happy if she'd do just that…everyone *but* her.

Again, every aspect in her life was a broken record.

It was a lot of stress for one person to handle in a lifetime and Margot was no exception. An odd kind of tired began to take over, a mental and physical combination that settled in her core. Under the quiet demeanor, she felt like she was about to erupt. A rumble in her chest, deep in the cavity, quickened her heart rate. For most of the flight she'd felt like she was on a roller coaster, her gut going up and down, her chest tightening and then receding, her mind spinning in all directions. She thought the cocktail would help settle her nerves but instead, it seemed as if it were escalating them. The last thing she needed to do right now was have a panic attack in front of all these people.

To deflect, she tried to slow her breathing. She gave up her glass and buckled in and told herself that once they landed and she was on home ground again, her nerves would subside. Then she would deal with the two men that was awaiting her arrival back home, that she'd lied to, in order to make this trip. As far as Ken and George knew, she had gone to console a friend in Tennessee, who'd recently lost her husband…and she wasn't about to tell a different story for now.

This family had been through enough and she'd be *dammed* if she'd add more drama until the most recent escapades had died down somewhat.

Twenty minutes later, she tried to call Frederick again from the terminal in the airport. After a few short rings, it went straight to his voicemail and she waited for the beep before leaving a message. She didn't specify what she was calling about, just that it was important she speak with him as soon as possible and provided him with a number she was sure, he already had. She disconnected and slid the phone back inside her bag.

She shouldered her carry-on and joined the crowd of people on the escalator. For the first time, Margot felt closterphobic. At the baggage claim off to her right, the crowds of people waiting there, were doubled in size. She had never seen the airport so busy. Thank God she didn't have any baggage to claim because there was no energy left in her, to wait in line.

She felt a film of sweat break out on her forehead as she weaved in and out of bodies, heading for another escalator that would take her to the main floor where her car awaited. She paused long enough to remove her sports jacket and pull the silk shirt away from her damp skin. The roar of the crowd seemed to get louder around her until she felt like it was going to make her ears bleed. A pain shot down the right side of her chest, almost like a stab from heartburn. For a moment she felt like her eyesight had blurred and it had caused her to stumble slightly in her step.

"Ma'am, are you ok?"

Margot glanced towards the voice and saw a pair of airport security cops standing a few inches from her.

"Of course, I'm *fine*!" Margot replied and then everything went black.

 TWENTY-FOUR

Brandon was on the tail end of a phone call with Madison out in the office, when Hans made an appearance. He'd been nursing a cold beer and a Cuban cigar for the last thirty minutes while the PI updated him on the progress. By the time Hans had quietly fixed himself a bourbon and settled down in the wingback chair across from Brandon, he was ending the call.

"Perfect timing!" Brandon said, discarding the cell on the desk. He leaned back in the office chair, sighed heavily and relit the end of an already-blackened cigar. He then slid the Baroque box over to Hans, who helped himself to one. Brandon hit the remote button and the exhaust fan overhead kicked on in a low and soothing hum.

"Mr. Madison was rather chattier than usual tonight, sir?" Hans asked.

"Yes!" Brandon said, still tossing around in his head the conversation he'd just had with the investigator.

"Anything new, sir?"

"Yes and No!" Brandon answered, as he furiously rubbed his brow. "The most important questions I *need* answered are not producing any results just yet but there seems to be a lot of *other* things popping up in their place."

"Like what?" Hans asked, suddenly curious.

"Well, for one, Madison was looking for any Jane Doe deaths that were recorded around the time Victor's mistress disappeared from her home. He didn't find any that matched her description *or* age. Doesn't mean she *isn't* dead, just means that her body hasn't ever turned up to be identified. For all anyone knows, her bones could be somewhere at the bottom of the ocean, off the Venice coast and tied to a concrete block as an anchor."

"Oh *bloody* hell!" Hans said and swallowed a good bit of his bourbon.

"Exactly, but what did stick out to Madison, was that a US Federal Agent was listed among the city of Venice's *deceased*, back in the 80s. The authorities listed his cause of death as an '*accidental drowning*' and documented that he was there on vacation. The reason his death stood out was because Madison noticed that the *same* coroner that signed off on his certificate, was the same one that signed off *on* Victor's wife, Catalina, when she supposedly *drowned* in the pool!"

"Which we know was a lie!" Hans inserted, a stern look crossing his face.

"According to Karly it's a lie, but how do we know *she* was telling the truth? Her mind is so twisted when it comes to reality, for all we know, she could have witnessed her father push Catalina over that railing and then fantasized it had been her instead."

"That's true sir, I never looked at it that way." Hans said, nodding his head in deep thought. "So does Madison think Victor was involved with the Federal Agent's death?"

"Victor was already in prison. Doesn't mean he didn't have anything to do with it, just means he didn't do the deed *personally*. From the way it looks, Victor had the coroner, that worked both cases, in his pocket for some reason. If he signed off on Catalina's death as accidental, then I'm sure he did it for other victims who died at his hand."

"Blackmail, sir?"

"It's possible, since that was Victor's specialty. Madison is going to dig a little further past the paperwork and find out what he can, surrounding this agent's death. He's got a couple of retired feds who are buddies, that worked in the same Washington division where this guy operated out of. He's also put a few of his men on foot in the area, where the mistress lived in Venice."

"What about the mistress' child?" Hans asked. "Isn't that what all this digging is primarily about?"

"Both the mother *and* the child disappeared right after Victor was killed in prison. He wasn't getting out and his old mobster connections knew that. And because Victor had a reputation for running his mouth and boasting to his bed partners, the mistress suddenly became a liability, no different than he was. So in my opinion, it looks like they might have quickly cleaned house, which saved my grandfather and Frank from having to deal with him anymore. Victor is shanked in prison shortly after he's institutionalized and his mistress and child disappear into thin air. It was a quick and guaranteed way of tying up the loose ends back in the day. But why they allowed Karly to live is a mystery to both me and Madison."

Hans shook his head in disgust.

"Even though I'm not a man of violence sir, I have to say, on that last note, I agree. That Karly woman is as *barmy* as her father was."

"Victor was a monster and I'm surprised someone didn't take him out years before he went to prison. Sage read an entry to me this morning from one of Frank's journals that we found in the safe. It paints a clearer picture of how much havoc that man brought upon our two families before, during and long after the Benenati murders. By the time the shoot-out in the furniture store occurred, my grandfather had been pushed to his limits, according to Frank. I think he had every intention of killing them both that night but the cops got there before he could finish Victor off."

"Who could blame them?" Hans asked.

"My grandfather wanted Victor to *suffer* the way he had made Catalina *suffer*. Putting a bullet between the eyes was too *easy* of a death for him. Also according to Frank's notes, Victor Rocha had a catchphrase that he liked to use when threatening his enemies. You know that old biblical saying, an *'Eye for an Eye'*?"

"Ahh, yes." Hans said, eyebrows raised as he gave a curt nod. "*Eye for an Eye*, a *Tooth for Tooth*. The original meaning of that phrase, was *meant* to stand for justice and balance."

"Exactly, but that's not what Victor *intended* for it to mean. The *eye for an eye* scripture was *his* interpretation that God was giving him permission to seek revenge however he saw fit. He said it to my grandfather right before he was hauled away in an ambulance the night he tangled with him for the last time. Madison said it was in the police report. And so the way it's looking so far, the game continued between my grandfather and Victor, even though he was locked up! He still had his connections to pull some strings on the outside and apparently he was working it like a master puppeteer. Frank talks about receiving something anonymous in the mail at Providence Estates. It came in the form of a letter, with no return address. Inside was a single sheet of note paper. Typed in the middle was the name of a popular TV news segment, along with the time and channel it was airing. The program was a special about inmates on death row. Victor Rocha just happened to be one of the inmates that were interviewed. But that wasn't what sent Frank scrambling to call my grandfather immediately. It was when he saw that it was *Courtney* who was the one *conducting* the interview!"

"Oh, *good Lord*!" Hans said, becoming antsy in his chair. "What did Mr. Hartford and your grandfather *do*?"

"Frank said that gramps instantly kicked into action and called his contacts at both the TV station and the prison, intending on telling them to get her the *hell* out of there. But the segment wasn't live at the time it aired. It had been pre-recorded and was shot about two weeks prior."

"Oh, *thank* God! So Miss Courtney wasn't in danger right then?"

"No, Courtney was safe! At the time, she was *at* the station watching it *with* her boss and crew. Evidently it was her first big break in the spotlight. She was quite young and just getting a foothold into the business. She had no idea just how dangerous the man across that table from her could have been, *if* he'd had the *slightest* idea of *who* she really was."

"He would have tried to harm her!" Hans said, worry gathering at his brow. "How ironic!"

"Without a doubt, ironic is an understatement. Remember, Victor was on death row and had nothing to lose. I watched the segment that the note was referring to. It's more than obvious that Victor was seething with rage, on the camera. He was in quite an agitated state and had interrupted the interview towards the end, by abruptly standing up and shouting at the camera his '*Eye for an Eye*' catchphrase, in Italian. Fortunately, the guards surrounding him were on their toes and he was quickly subdued and taken from the room. As a precaution beforehand, they had shackled both his hands and feet. After his outburst everyone was glad that decision had been made. Frank wrote that Courtney appeared to be shaken up but managed to hold it together on air, long enough to conclude the interview as a professional and sign off. But the whole episode did not sit well with my grandfather and Frank. The catchphrase Victor shouted into the camera during that interview, they felt, was a *personal* message intended for them both. They began to worry about *where* he was going to strike next. If he had ways to orchestrate threats from prison, via mail and send evidence that he might be responsible for taking down an *entire* plane, then he could also *hire* a contract killer, to wipe out both of our families. I don't think either Frank or my grandfather took his threat lightly. Because immediately they started covering all their bases. Courtney was the first one. My grandfather thought it was too coincidental that Victor just *happened* to be on that list of interviews she did, so he hired a few goons to watch over her. She had no idea the entire time of course because they were highly trained to stay hidden in the shadows."

"And no harm ever came her way?" Hans asked. Brandon shook his head.

"Not that we know of and she didn't say anything about feeling threatened while she was with us that night at Margot's."

"She was probably still in shock from finding out her true identity, sir." Hans offered.

Brandon nodded in his direction but didn't speak. Both remained quiet for a moment, each deep in thought over what had just been discussed. Hans spoke first.

"It's terrible sir, that one man has destroyed so many lives." he said, shaking his head. Brandon nodded in agreement.

"How is Miss Sage holding up after learning all of this new information?"

Brandon sighed heavily and took a healthy sip of his beer he'd almost forgotten about. He pondered Hans' question for a second and gave himself time to swallow before he spoke.

"Sage truly believes that Victor had something to do with her parent's plane crash."

"Oh no!" Hans said with emotion in his words.

"She thinks somewhere in Frank's journals she's going to find the proof that Victor took their lives in retaliation, as part of the vendetta."

"Even if it's true, I hope for her sanity that she *never* finds it in writing!" Hans said, the strength of his voice was hard when he said it. "She will never get over the idea that her parents were killed because of some *stupid* blood war! That poor girl has been through enough!"

"I know Hans, your preaching to the choir *here*." Brandon said.

"Sorry sir! Just thinking about it gets my blood to boiling."
Hans said, trying to calm himself down a notch.

"I *totally* understand, my man! Believe me, I *know*."
Brandon threw his hands up in surrender. "I mean, *shit*, I
loved my grandfather. I always thought he was a badass but
now I *know* he was truly a *hero* in real life. And I'm glad
he was the one who eventually put that son-of-a-bitch
behind bars where he belonged! Victor took the life from a
woman, that my grandfather *dearly* loved and then laughed
in his face for years after. It was only fitting that he had a
hand in *his* ending."

A light rapping, sounded at the door and both men shot
each other a quick look of puzzlement. Hans responded by
giving a shrug of the shoulders and mouthed his wife's
name. Brandon knew it had to be because Sage *wouldn't*
knock. But just to be on the safe side, he reached inside the
inner wall of the desk, where he had anchored a holster,
that housed a fully loaded nine millimeter. The door
opened and Lydia slid into the room, shutting it behind her.
Brandon, let out a long slow sigh as he retracted his hand
and relaxed his weight against the back of the chair.

"Am I interrupting?" she asked, walking towards them,
flashing a smile.

"Not at all." Brandon said.

"Never." Hans said, patting the seat next to him. Lydia
glided over and sat down. "Would you like some wine, my
dear?"

"No darling. I've got some chilling inside. In fact, I'm
going to also pour a glass for that darling wife of yours."
Lydia said, winking at Brandon. "It's a great aid in relaxing
the mind so she can get some rest."

Brandon tensed up again, an alert expression on his face.

"What's the matter with Sage?" He began stubbing out his
cigar and checking the time on his wristwatch. My God it

was already getting late. He swore he'd been out here no longer than an hour.

"Sage is having nightmares over her parent's crash. She tries to play it off that she's fine but she's not." Lydia said, never beating around the bush. "She's depressed as hell and it's the entire reason why I came out here and interrupted your *man* time!"

Brandon laughed lightly. "By all means Lydia, lay it on me!" he encouraged.

"And that's exactly what I plan to do," she said. "Some of this you probably already know and some of this you might not but I'm going to fill your ears anyway." Brandon nodded, always amused when talking to the woman, he felt, was an *expert* on his wife. "We all know Sage is pretty angry at Margot for not telling her about this whole mess before Mr. Vega did. I can't say I blame her way of thinking." Lydia said. "Not that anyone cares to hear what I think about all this but I'm going to voice my opinion anyways!" She winked again at Brandon.

"I love it when she speaks her mind!" Hans chimed in, smiling with stupid love. He looked like a complete doofus right now and it made Brandon smile because, finally, for once in his life, he knew what that felt like.

"Charlie is as *much* to blame as Margot when it comes to keeping this secret about our families." Brandon said. "If that blizzard had not come at the precise time it did, Sage and I would *still* not have a clue the other existed. *Well*," he recanted, when he realized they were both looking at him funny. "*She* knew about *me* because she was *obsessed*, but that's *beside* the point. What I meant *was*, we'd still be *ignorant* about our past, if the chain of events hadn't occurred the way they did. Thank God for that *strange* hand of fate, that put all of the obstacles in my path that night and stopped me from getting on a plane. Otherwise, if Margot had her way about it, Sage would never have found out about Charlie and Meg!"

"So *your* angry with *both* of them?" Lydia asked.

"*Damn* right I am!" Brandon said. He grabbed his beer and took a quick drink.

"Well, Sage told me earlier that she's planning a sit-down with Margot sometime soon. And pardon me for saying this Brandon but *you* need to do the same with Mr. Vega! In fact, at one point or another, everyone needs to regroup and converse with one another and get your feelings out on the table, so y'all can move *forward* as a family, from here. If this experience taught anyone anything, it should be that this vendetta has been going on long enough and together, you need to put an end to it before it bleeds into baby Tristan's life."

Brandon sighed heavily and nodded in agreement. "Sage and I have already discussed a possible trip in the very near future to see Margot. But she wants to finish reading the last two journals before that happens. We both believe that there's more pieces to this story, then either one are willing to tell."

"That is possible," Lydia began, her demeanor seemed to change somewhat into a more serious tone. "I believe now as I did back then that there were several things amiss in that house," she hesitated. "*Especially* after the plane crash."

"Like what?" Brandon asked. He had been meaning to ask her some questions.

"Both Margot and Mr. Hartford went through separate bouts of grief after their daughter died. For a while there, George and I both thought for sure they were going to divorce."

"*Really*?" Brandon said, more out of reflex than to be sarcastic. "So there was *trouble* in paradise?"

"Of course there was!" Lydia said. "They just lost their only child. The odds were against them."

"So terrible." Hans muttered into his glass of bourbon.

"It *was* terrible!" Lydia reaffirmed, glancing her husband's way briefly before turning her attention back to Brandon. "Margot withdrew to her rooms in the South wing while Mr. Hartford took up temporary quarters in his private office, in the library. For days they didn't speak to each other. George and I took turns tending to Sage just to give them the space to mourn, at least that's what we *thought* we were doing. Your grandfather was there a lot." Lydia said. "He stayed over for a few weeks in the beginning and spent most of his time with Mr. Hartford in the office. Sometimes they'd be in there until way up into the night, drinking and who knows what else, for hours on end. Mr. Hartford had the space soundproofed for privacy some years before. And it worked well when it came to hearing anything on the other side in the hallway. I passed by those doors a million times while they were in there and I never heard a peep! Guess it served its purpose."

"Did you know about all the kids, Lydia? Jack, Charlie, Meg and Courtney?" Brandon asked.

"Absolutely not!" Lydia said, shaking her head vigorously. "I wasn't employed by the Hartford's when that poor couple was killed in Italy. I came into the household *after* those Benenati kids were all young adults and Kelley and Jack were already married. I think Sage was around four then and I fell in love with her immediately. I always wanted babies of my own and since that wasn't going to happen, Sage was the closest thing to a daughter I was going to get. So I loved the *hell* out of her is what I did, *especially* after she lost her momma. And over the years I've learned a lot about her. Sometimes I think I know her better than she knows herself."

"I don't know what to do." Brandon said, being honest. "She's not going to let me take those journals away from her before she's read them cover to cover, so I can't stop her from seeing whatever she finds in them, that could lead to further depression."

"You don't need to take the journals away. It's her *right* to finally know the truth about her past, no matter how hard it's going to be or how much it's gonna hurt." Lydia said. "Her elders have already shoved too much under a rug which has caused all this chaos in the first place. She doesn't *need* shielded from anything else. Learning the truth is what will help her heal."

"I thought about taking her away from here for a few days, just the two of us but she's not going to agree to leaving the baby behind." Brandon said.

"I'm not suggesting that you take her anywhere." Lydia said, shaking her head. "There's no vacation place in the world that can beat the beauty that surrounds her here, every day on this property. Her soul *feeds* off the peace here."

"Are you suggesting I leave, to give her some space?" Brandon asked, cocking his head to the side.

"*Heavens* no!" Lydia laughed. "That would be the *last* thing in her life she could ever want. That and to have you upset with her in *any* way."

The look on her face had Brandon feeling as if there was something underlining in what she'd just said.

"The good Lord above knows that to be true." Hans chimed in, grinning himself, as he stubbed out his cigar in the ashtray. "She *adores* you." He added.

"I *adore* her," Brandon simply said. "I would do *anything* for her and my son."

"*Anything*?" Lydia asked, almost as if she were confirming.

"Of course! She completely changed my life!" Brandon said, looking from one to the other. When neither elaborated and held their tongue, he threw his hands up. "What am I missing here? You have *something* you want to tell me?"

Lydia jumped right in at his prompting.

"Sage *desperately* wants to spend some bonding time with *her* aunt and *yours*."

The silence suddenly hung very thick in the air. So thick that Hans had to clear his throat.

"Why in the *hell* would she want to do something like that?" Brandon asked them both.

"Because Courtney and Meg are part of this great *big* story that just got heaped on her." Lydia said, as if he needed reminding. "Regardless of the fact that you hate what they do for a living, they could help in how she deals with all this right now. Sage is more torn up about what's happened, then she's letting on. And she's very worried about how it's affecting Miss Courtney. She wants to spend some time with her and Meg, to sort some things out but knows in order to do that, she'd have to leave the cabin, baby Tristan and you *because* you wouldn't agree to let them come here. Basically, she's torn between her needs and yours, *simple* as that."

Brandon just sat there for a moment, speechless. He loved a person who was a straight shooter and he definitely got that when he was speaking with Lydia.

"She's not mentioned this to me." He finally said.

"Why would she?" Lydia asked. "She already knows how you *feel* about them and to put her own wants on the back burner is *easier* than to disrespect yours. After all, you and that baby are the *center* of her life. She's very loyal and would never do anything against you, no matter what. And besides, she's use to it, putting someone *else* first before herself. She's had *plenty* of practice with *her* grandmother." Her last sentence was intended to strike a chord in him and it was doing its job. It was well-known now, that after Sage's mother died, she became her grandmother's primary focus. Margot barely let the child out of her sight and when Frank died, the smothering became worse. When he'd first met her in the cabin, she had told him she'd come for the solace and to write a book.

But later, through her own admission, she had confessed that it was mainly to escape her grandmothers constant hovering. It had caused a wedge between her and Margot, something he didn't ever want to happen to them.

"I don't *trust* those two women, Lydia." He simply said.

"It's because you don't *know* them." She retorted. "Your *public* perception of them is what your basing your decision on. But when the ladies come here to be with Sage, Miss Meg is no longer the editor of a magazine you don't like. She's Sage's *blood* aunt, her fathers' sister, who she never knew until now, even *existed*. Can you *imagine* the *precious* stories and *vital* information about her family that Miss Meg can provide for Sage about her father, that no paperwork in any public files, could reveal to your *Investigator*?"

Hans cleared his throat and finally emptied what was left of his bourbon. He quietly swallowed and sat the glass down on the desk. For the next thirty seconds he only made eye contact with the floor.

Brandon didn't speak at first. It was obvious, *once* again, that Hans had told his wife something that was supposed to be *secret* between them. He tore his eyes away from glaring at him, long enough, to settle them back on Lydia, who was probably tapping her foot under the desk, by the look on her face.

Regardless of Hans' blabbermouth, Brandon had to admit that Lydia was right. Madison would never find, written down on paper and stored in archives, the background of her family, that Sage could easily get from Meg Jackson, in one afternoon.

"Ok, I can see Sage wanting to spend a little time with her aunt but *what* does Courtney have to do with this?" he finally spoke. "She can't provide anything from her past that would help my wife. She herself, had no idea who *she* was until Charlie told her."

"Just because Miss Courtney was tossed to another to be raised, doesn't mean she should be treated any different." Lydia said, in the woman's defense. "None of what happened was *her* fault. She may be a well-known news lady to the world but to Sage, she's another helpless victim of this tangled mess. Those three women instantly *bonded* back at Margot's house and every one of us in this room knows it, whether we like it or not." Lydia said. "All I'm asking for is a *few* days that they can be together, in a *safe* environment and away from public scrutiny, so they can talk, relax and lean on each other for a while."

"Your plan sounds great Lydia, except for *one* thing." Brandon said, happy to think he found a loophole in her plan.

"What's that?" She was ready.

"Isn't Courtney on location somewhere?" Brandon said, thinking that ought to buy him some time.

"Miss Courtney *was* on location." Lydia said and then a snarky smile dominated her features. "But right now, she is *actually* on her way home. Her plane should be landing in about an hour."

Brandon couldn't believe his luck. This wasn't going his way at all.

"I suppose you have all the specs on Meg and her availability too?" Brandon asked her, with slight sarcasm and a touch of amusement in his tone. A stealing glimpse at Hans proved he was still staring at the floor.

"Of course I do. Meg is how I learned that Courtney was on her way home. Since she isn't returning to the magazine until *next* week, she's idle as well." Lydia said.

"So what's your plan?" Brandon prompted, wanting to see just how far she had thought this out.

"Hans and I can take over the majority of care for baby Tristan during the day, so Sage gets quality time with them." She plunged right in. "That also means you don't have to be inside and it gives you an excuse to hang out in

the barn during the day, to avoid them. Hans can even bring your meals out here and make excuses on your behalf, that your tied up in business dealings, is why you're not inside."
"You do complain sir, that you don't get to spend enough time out here lately, to work on Sage's desk." Hans said, finally speaking. He had lost interest in the floor and was now looking straight at Brandon. "You said you were way behind schedule yesterday…"
"I know *what* I said Hans!" Brandon blurted out, interrupting him.
"If Miss Sage is busy with the women, she wouldn't be out here underfoot." Hans reminded him. "A couple of eight hour days could get you back on track when it comes to finishing it, within the deadline you set."
Brandon glanced from Hans to Lydia.
"And just *what* are the sleeping arrangements for these two women while they are here, *invading* my house?" he asked.
"The only place empty inside, is the room *next* to yours. And since there's *two* of them, which one are you going to put out here in the barn by herself? The barn that I'm *supposed* to seek solitude in? How does that figure into your plan?"
Lydia smiled a little too confident for his liking. "The king bed in the room *next* to ours can be separated into *two,* full-sized beds to accommodate *two* people.
Neither one of them has *any* reason to come out to the barn." Lydia confirmed.
Brandon just looked at her and slowly began shaking his head. "*Famous* last words."

TWENTY-FIVE

Ken Barker was just about to join George on the back porch for a beer, when his cell phone began ringing in his pocket. He fished it out, glanced at the screen and then abruptly stopped short in the hallway when he saw who it was. He glanced up just as George was passing him.

"I need to take this." Ken said, pointing at his phone. "Give me a minute, will ya?"

"Sure! I'll grab the beers and put them on ice. Take your time!" he said and disappeared around the corner. Ken stepped away from the main area of the foyer and headed across the hall to Franks old haunt. He shut the door behind him and answered the call at the same time.

"Sheriff Clark! How are you this fine evening, sir?" He asked.

"Oh, can't complain Mr. Barker. How 'bout yourself?" Came the southern drawl across the receiver.

"Fair to midland." Ken said.

"Glad to hear it, and the family?"

"All safe and sound, thanks to you and your fine lawmen." Ken said, not mincing any words.

"Well I thank you kindly for the compliment, Mr. Barker. Course we all should thank the gracious Miss Curwin, for making it easy! Putting a bullet in a perp's leg is one way to keep them put until law enforcement arrives."

"Makes our job easier, that's for sure!" Ken said. "You aren't kidding! Anyways, you asked me to keep you updated about Karly Driggers. We've been running the basic background search. Looks like she's been in and out of trouble most of her life which is no surprise here. She's racked up some priors in Italy that were minor but looks like she saved the more serious charges for us to deal with in the states. The second stalking offense on Mr. Parrish's residence, is what will keep her in for a while, that and the fact that her clear intent—*both* times—was to do *bodily* harm with a deadly weapon. Her mental state of mind will determine if she serves her time in a maximum prison or a mental facility. I hope they put her behind bars myself. Deserves her right to be among her own kind. We don't think that Mr. Parrish is the *only* one to fall victim to this perp."

"What makes you say that?" Ken asked.

"When we checked into her background, we found some very disturbing reasons. There's been quite a few accidental deaths involving her family members. Of course, we all know her father was a notorious criminal who got shanked in prison some years back and obviously Karly had nothing to do with that. But the rest of her family is *another* story. Her stepmother *mysteriously* drowned in the family pool, her younger sister fell off a third-story roof, when she was seven and died instantly. Her mother committed suicide in the bathtub right *after* the death of her two-year old baby sister, who *accidently* got run over by a car. Which I *might* add, *Karly* just happened to be the *driver*. But on the flip side of all this, I wanted to prepare you and your family. It's the least I can do…somewhere there was a *leak* and the *press* has got a hold of the story…"

"*Son-of-a-bitch*!" Ken muttered when he ended the call ten minutes later, left the library and made his way to where George was relaxing on the patio. He was already working on his beer and shuffling a deck of cards. A stack of singles rested in a neat pile next to it. Ken pulled one of the ice cold beers out of the bucket he had on the table and popped the top. He settled across from George and fished a cigar out of his pocket. He dropped his phone in its place. He lit the end of the cigar and then pulled a stack of singles out of his pocket and laid it on the table. He began telling George about the nature of Sheriff Clark's call.

"He said legally they can't stop the press from running the story and in fact it will air tonight." Ken said, looking at his watch. "He warned us to be ready for the onslaught."

"That means we are going to have to deal with Margot flipping out for a while." George said with a sigh, not missing a beat as he continued shuffling the cards. He too glanced at his watch. "Speaking of…have you *heard* from her recently?" George's brow creased in sudden concern.

Ken had to think for a moment. "Not since around noon." He said.

"That's odd. I haven't heard from her since then, either." George confessed. "It's going on *seven* o'clock."

"Well, you know how it is when women get together." Ken said. "They yack for hours and never have a clue what time it is."

"That holds true for *most* women, but Margot isn't one of them." George said. He stopped shuffling and rested the cards in a neat stack on the table in the middle. "Her mind is always working and delegating a mental timetable. Idle chitchat with another female does not *ever* trump that." Ken sighed, reached into his pocket and pulled his cell out. "Now you got *me* worried."

Before he could get to the screen where her number was stored, it started ringing. The caller ID displayed Margot as the source. Both Ken and George each had a look of surprise, as they made eye contact.

"She must already know!" George said, when he saw the screen. "Glad I'm not the one answering that!" He laughed and began dealing the cards out, shaking his head.

"Thanks!" Ken said as he pushed the button to answer and held the phone up to his ear. "Your ears must be ringing," he said, speaking into the mouthpiece. "We were just talking about you!" Ken chuckled and then his face lost all amusement. Margot's voice wasn't the one that greeted him on the other end.

"*Mr. Barker*?" the male voice asked.

"Yes, this *is* Ken Barker. Who's *this*?" A mask of concern and confusion came over him all at once. George picked up on the seriousness of his tone and immediately stopped dealing.

"Mr. Barker, I'm calling on behalf of your wife, sir. There's been a *terrible* accident."

 TWENTY-SIX

She's going to be flipping out, Peter thought as he watched the story unfold of Karly Driggers' arrest on the local news. *She's going to see this on television and flip out when she hears my name mentioned.*
He had no clue whether something like this was being televised all over the world but he did know that it was spreading like wildfire here in the states. Especially when the famous names of Brandon Parrish and Courtney Curwin were said in the same sentence as the topic of *'attempted murder'*. Then they'd named him and Meg as part of the victim lineup at Margot's Mansion when the incident occurred. Meg winced and glanced sideways at him.
"Sorry." She muttered.
He reached over and reassuringly squeezed her shoulder. "I don't give a shit about that. I'm just thankful that no one was hurt. We'll get through this. All of this." He was genuinely worried about Meg and everything she had just been through. He was hoping, for her sake, that the interest in Karly's arrest would die down quickly. It wasn't uncommon in the world to hear reports about stalkers when it came to the rich and famous. Usually they ended up running the news circuit for about a week and then were overshadowed by the next headliner. They might recap when Karly is sentenced but that would be about it. The only part that had them all worried was the backstory and the connection to the Hartford's and Karly's father. If that was delved in to, there could be some problems for all involved. Especially if the rantings and ravings of what she'd said in the interview about his wife being one of the

missing Benenati children, were to come to light. That would open a whole *new* can of worms.

Once the story ended and the anchor moved on to the next, Meg checked her phone. After texting a few times, she spoke.

"I *need* to call Charlie."

Peter nodded as she rose and walked off in the direction of the kitchen.

As soon as Meg was out of sight, he pulled out his own phone, hoping *she'd* responded by now. But to his dismay, there was still *nothing*.

Peter sighed and rubbed his brow in frustration, double-checked to make sure the volume was still on mute and stuck it back in his pocket. Eventually *she* would contact him. He just had to be patient and wait.

TWENTY-SEVEN

The churning in Charlie's gut intensified when the video of Karly, shackled and handcuffed, was shown on the local news. Completely surrounded by several law enforcement officers, she was being led down the steps of Margot's mansion. Cop cars and rescue vehicles filled the circular driveway, red and blue lights blazing! Flashbulbs were going off constantly from the crowd of media at the main gate. The anchor, who was narrating the segment, began throwing out the list of famous names that had been in the mansion at the time of the attack. He scowled when he realized how impressive the lineup sounded on TV. That many famous headliners in one show, was going to attract a *lot* of attention, *unwanted* attention and it was making him nervous.

When the segment was over he muted the volume on the TV and stood up. He walked over to the bar that was situated cozily between the kitchen and living room and poured himself a shot of his best vodka. He downed it immediately and then made himself a vodka and soda to take along with him to his home office.

Just as he was sitting down in the chair, his phone lit up in his hand. Earlier, he had put the cell on silent, so he wouldn't be interrupted once the story aired. At a glance he now saw that a flood of calls and texts had come through from business associates and friends. Meg was one of them who had sent a text requesting that they talk. He took a good portion of his drink down and texted her back. Within seconds his cell lit up again. It was her now calling. She was frantic when he first answered but as always, Charlie did what he does best and that was putting *out* the fires. He calmed her down by reassuring her that this would all blow over. And even if they made the connection between Frank and Everett and Victor Rocha, that was as far as it was going to go—that it was just a bad business deal and a coincidence. He advised her to just lay low for now, be aware of paparazzi if she ventured out and NOT, under *any* circumstances was she to give an interview or speak to anyone about the incident. He suggested that maybe it was best if she and Peter got out of town for a week or two until everything died down. And then he hung up.

He was surprised he hadn't heard from Margot yet. But then again, it was her *ass* in a sling this time, for what was happening, so maybe that was why. After all, she'd been the one to hire Karly—*opened* her home right up to her—so he didn't want to hear *any* of her bitching. But on the flip side, there was always a silver lining. This one had forced the door *open* to their past. A door, Charlie felt, should have been opened a *long* time ago.

What was it Jack used to say?

"It's all in the timing, *brother*." He said out loud to the empty room.

He took another generous drink of his cocktail as tears flooded his eyes. He winced at the bite, swallowed hard, then pulled the top drawer of his desk open. He fished out a business card and sat it down in front of him. It was the card his attorney had passed to him, at the beginning of the week with his personal number scribbled on the back. He picked up his cell and dialed it.

After a few rings a male voice picked up on the other end.

"You know those documents we talked about the other day? I'm going to need that to happen much quicker than I anticipated." Charlie said into the receiver.

"I would be more than happy to assist you Mr. Vega." The smooth professional voice responded.

"I need to *amend* my will for both the *business* part, as well as my *personal* assets. When it's time to sign, I need your firm to *witness* my signature on a letter that I'm going to give you, along with my sealed DNA. I'll also need to change the beneficiary I had listed. I need all of this done as *fast* as possible and in *strict* confidence!"

"Not a problem, Mr. Vega. I'll have the papers drawn up as soon as tomorrow." The voice said. "Will that be fast enough?"

"Perfect!" Charlie said, then hung up his cell and laid it face down on the desk. He took down what was left in his glass, swallowing it whole. From this point on, he had no idea what they would be up against next, with that psycho Karly, running her mouth to anyone who would listen. So he was getting his ducks all in a row, just in case he *had* to *sacrifice* himself, to save them all.

TWENTY-EIGHT

"Oh *dear* Lord!" Lydia said in exasperation as she stared at the TV. One hand was resting on her chest, the other on Hans' arm. "Them *damn* vultures!" she hissed. Hans patted her hand with his other one, his eyes not leaving the screen. The story had broken of Karly Driggers arrest at the mansion. The newscaster listed the celebrity figures that had been inside at the time of the attack. He also used the word '*stalker*' several times and relayed to his audience the background information so far, that they'd found on Karly. Victor Rocha and the words '*notorious criminal*' were mentioned, along with other priors that the perp had committed in the past. They had also learned that this was Karly's second offense of breaking and entering into a home where the famous Brandon Parrish was in residence. The anchor finished by saying that charges and sentencing would be determined once Karly Driggers had a full mental health assessment.

"I'll save you time!" Lydia shouted at the screen. "She's a *damn* looney toon and so was *her* father!"

"You can say that again!" Hans chimed in. On second thought he glanced over his shoulder at the closed door that led from their personal family room and out into the hallway of the main cabin. He suddenly was worried about Brandon and Sage and wondered if they had seen it themselves. "Do you think they had the news on?" he asked his wife, looking back at her and nodding in the direction of the upper floor above them.

"You're asking me that like I got x-ray vision or something." Lydia said, grabbing the remote and turning the volume considerably down on the TV to almost a whisper. "How in the *hell* am I supposed to know if they have the TV on, Hans Mobley?" She cocked her head slightly, as if listening for something, and not hearing it, turned to look at her husband. "I *hope* they didn't! Lord knows it's enough to get everyone's tongue wagging!" Lydia picked up her cell and looked at the screen. "I'm surprised Margot hasn't called yet!" She laid it back down on the coffee table. "On *second* thought, I better shut up and not *jinx* myself." She muttered. "*Dammit*!" she added. "My poor Sage just can't catch a break! Right on the *eve* before Meg and Courtney's visit and this happens! They're not going to want to be in a *festive* mood now! Who can *relax* and have girl time with all this crap going on? I'll just cry if they call and cancel."

"Lydia, dear," Hans interjected with a smile, trying to calm his wife down. "Look at the *bright* side of this." He took both of her hands gently in his. "It's the *perfect* time for the women to visit. I'm sure they want to get away from the media coverage that is surely hounding them right now. What better place to hide out then here, for the next few days until *all* of this blows over?"

Lydia stared at him in silence for a few seconds. The distressful look on her face turned from irritation to confusion, then to clarity and a pert smile tugged at the corners of her mouth.

"Hans Mobley, of course your so right!" she said, leaning forward and kissing him full on the lips and then on the top of his bald head. "Why didn't I *think* of that myself?"

TWENTY-NINE

Lola sat in the silence of her hotel room, sipping on a tall glass of her favorite chilled, Barolo red wine. Her mind was working a mile a minute. She was still dressed in the black, ankle-length, form-fitting dress, that she'd worn for her dinner date. The fancy, black-matching, ankle-strap heels she'd worn, were now cast aside on the floor by the foot of her chair. Her curly dark hair hung in a wild assortment of natural curls and perfectly framed her face. She plunged her free hand in it absentmindedly and began to twist a curl out of nervous habit.

She took another sip of wine. Her dark eyes continued to move from one end of the plush suite to the other, while her mind was working overtime, thinking and pondering. A sealed, ten-by-twelve envelope rested on the table in front of her. She would glance down at it every so often and a sigh would escape her lips from anxiety, before she'd turn away again and take another sip. She didn't need to open the envelope to *know* what was *inside*. She just needed to make sure it went straight home to her safe, where it would stay locked up for a while with the *other* one. That is until she decided what she was going to do with it.

Lola begin to feel *more* anxiety building up. The wine wasn't relaxing her at all. If anything, it seemed to be intensifying her mood. Feeling like some fresh air might do the trick, she stood up, reached for a cigarette and a lighter and headed to the terrace. She flung open the glass doors and walked out as the cool night air hit her in the face. She slid the cigarette in her mouth and lit up, exhaling as she wondered over to the railing. She leaned on it and looked three stories down, where the city was alive with lights, the sound of laughter and the rhythm of music.

The sidewalk was pretty busy for this time of night. People were walking in and out of pubs and shops and the smell of something delicious reached her senses. A male bicyclist, with a basket full of two wine bottles and a bouquet of flowers, whizzed by. He was probably on his way to meet his love. *Some girl was going to get lucky tonight*, she thought and wondered when would it *ever* be *her* turn to find the *right* guy.

She watched a few minutes more of the activity down below, long enough to finish her cigarette, then finally left the terrace and stepped back inside the room. She heard her phone vibrating on the table when she entered but there was no one that she wanted to talk with tonight. She walked past it and headed down the hall to the bedroom. The maid had turned the bed down and a complimentary chocolate mint was laying on one of the many pillows that covered a quarter of the king-sized bed. She sat the bottle on the nightstand, along with her glass of wine and practically threw herself across it, face down in the white fluffy mounds of cotton and percale. She stayed like that for all of two minutes, taking deep, extended breaths. At last she rolled over onto her back and stared at the ceiling for a moment, then sat up and looked around the room. Beside her, on the nightstand, was a remote to the flat screen on the wall. How long had it been since she'd just laid in bed and immersed herself into a good movie? She grabbed it, hit the power button and the TV came to life, the sounds of some game show filling the screen. She then fixed all the pillows in one big mound and then rested her weight against them, wiggling around to get comfortable. She picked up the remote again and began flipping through the channels, hoping to find a good movie that would put her to sleep. But what she stopped on instead was what must have been the *local* news. There was a breaking story being broadcast from the states. Any other time, Lola would have surfed right past it but the *huge* image of Courtney Curwin's face, staring back at her, made her pause.

"*What the hell*?" She said out loud, sitting straight up in bed.

The anchor was saying something about *attempted murder*, and the famous face of Brandon Parrish replaced Courtney's on the screen. Then *chills* began to crawl up her spine when Meg and Peter Jackson's names and faces followed.

She quickly threw the remote on the bed, slid off the side and raced from the bedroom to the living room where she had abandoned her phone on the coffee table. She picked it up and tried to call Meg but the signal inside the hotel would not let her connect.

"Oh God, *please* let them all still be *alive*!" she said, through the panic and tears that were filling her eyes. She threw her phone down and grabbed the hotel landline and pushed the button to the front desk. Within seconds someone picked up on the other end.

"I *need* to catch a flight to New York, as soon as *humanly* possible. Can you connect me?" She said to the woman on the other end, her voice shaking. "It's an *emergency*!"

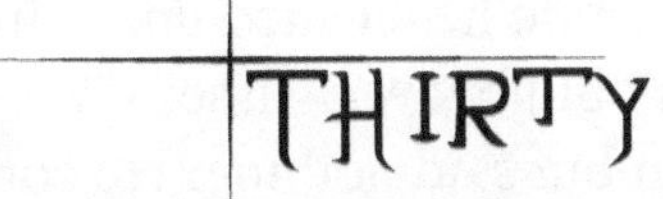

THIRTY

"You just keep on aggravating them on purpose." The doctor said, lecturing, as he cleaned up the man's face, that was smeared with cuts and blood.

The man grunted, knowing it was wiser not to comment. "Looks like this time your nose might be broke." The old man sighed and grabbed more gauze soaked in alcohol. When he pressed it to the cut on his lip, he winced. "You know they are going to write in the report that *you* started it, *again!*" He threw some of the soiled gauze in the pan on the table and grabbed fresh. This time he pressed it to the cut on his cheek. The man flinched. The doctor leaned in for a closer look. His white lab coat smelled like alcohol and cigarettes. "Your eye is going to swell shut if you don't keep the compresses on it I give you." He removed the gauze from the cut, threw it in the pan and put a warm pad in his hand. He directed it up to cover the eye. "Leave it there for the next ten minutes at least." He picked up the pan and began tossing butterfly bandage wrappers and adhesive tabs in with the soiled gauze. "You keep this up and you will never get out of here." He cautioned.

A small flat screen TV was on and playing low in the background. The doctor had been in the middle of his dinner break when the man had been shoved by the orderlies into his care, beaten. He'd got into a tussle with the red-headed fucktard that someone was stupid enough to give a little bit of authority to. The guard enjoyed aggravating him whenever he was on duty. He'd even go as far as to bang on his cell door with his nightstick during all hours of the night, making it impossible for him to sleep. After a while, he just couldn't take it anymore and it was worth the punishment and a trip to the infirmary, just to knock the guy on his ass. "They *enjoy* harassing you." The

doctor still rattled on, while he cleaned up. "They do it to get a reaction and you oblige, *every* time."
The man grunted again but said nothing. He continued to hold the warm compress in place while he watched the doctor move about the room.
"I'm going to get you something for the pain and inflammation. Keep that *on* your eye until I get back." The doctor exited the small office through a side door that led to a locked medicine cabinet, in another room. The only sound now was the hum of the air conditioner overhead and the rattle of his arm shackles every time he moved. The sound of the TV lured his attention and a pretty brunette filled the screen. She seemed pretty excited about something. Soon she was replaced by a video of a female being led away in handcuffs. In the background, a huge white house loomed behind them. The entire driveway was filled with cop cars. Right before the female was put inside one of them, the camera caught a close up of her face. All it took was a *second* for him to *recognize* her.
Growing more curious, he leaned forward, *straining* to hear the details of *why* she was being arrested because the doctor had the volume so low. But images of her victims she had tried to kill, began to flash on the screen, one right after the other. And he didn't need anybody to tell him *who* all of them were. Their *famous* faces were very familiar to him, most of them anyway.
It took a moment for his drug-laden brain to comprehend that he'd just been handed a *gift* and then a slow, *nasty* smile began to spread across his bruised and battered face.

THIRTY-ONE

'One thing about them tables, they can always turn'.
Somewhere along the way, Courtney had either heard
someone speak that slogan or she had read it someplace,
she couldn't remember which. But what she *had*
remembered, was how the idiom had made her feel. It was
a reminder that no one was safe when the *shit* started
flying—*her* included.
The frenzy of reporters that met them at the airport once
they landed, were totally unexpected. The continuous
flashbulbs from the cameras had almost blinded her, when
their small group stepped out into the main terminal. The
shouting voices, all hollering at once, just exacerbated what
was left of the headache she was still nursing from the
Kenya hangover.
When they'd first disembarked from the plane and
Courtney saw the crowd, she had hoped they had
assembled because of the top story they'd just covered, on
the Somalia Pirates seizure. But her hopes were soon short
lived when some of the reporters started shouting out *her*
name, with *Karly's* connected to it. Understanding what
they were really there for, Michael and the guys quickly
formed a protective barrier around her as best they could.
"Keep walking." She heard him say close to her ear. *"Don't*
comment!"
As they pushed their way through the crowd, mics were
being shoved in her face from all sides and a few reporters
were pressing her for a *'statement'* about the incident at
Margot's. Another boldly asked Courtney if she used her
own personal handgun to shoot Karly with. Somewhere
over her left shoulder she heard a woman ask if she were
worried about any charges coming from the State. Yet, still
another wanted to know what her relationship was with

Brandon Parrish and why was *she* in his mother-in-law's house, in the first place. And another asked if she had caught a glimpse of his newborn son and could she *debunk* the theory that the famous couple were keeping him hid because he had been born with *Down Syndrome*?

That last one about the baby struck a nerve in Courtney. She suddenly had this overwhelming feeling of wanting to throat-punch the one who said it. Michael must have caught the look of vengeance on her face. As if reading her mind, he said out loud to the impending crowd, *"No comment!"* as he continued to nudge her quickly forward, towards the elevators.

The rudest reporters in the bunch—to her surprise—were people in the field she knew on a *first*-name basis. She'd had *lunch* with them throughout the span of her career, had bought *gifts* for their children and had even participated *numerous* times in celebrating their individual birthdays, anniversaries or big milestones at work. It was unbelievable how *detached* they seemed towards her, right now. Was this *really* happening?

Cockiness…arrogance and *betrayal* of the worst kind…

"Miss Curwin! Miss Curwin!"

The shouts around her increased in volume. Airport security began showing up in pairs of two. They worked to push the crowd back to make a path and began guiding them out of the stampede and into an empty elevator. *"No comment!"* Michael had shouted again before the doors closed. "Miss Curwin will release a *formal* statement shortly."

On the ground floor, a few more security guards escorted them to the loading pick-up area in front of the airport, where a company car from the station was waiting. Reporters began shouting Courtney's name from somewhere behind her as Michael and her small entourage climbed quickly into the limo. It pulled away at once and drove them straight to their main building in downtown New York. There, she was thrown into an emergency meeting, with not only the *big* guys present, but their committee of *corporate* lawyers as well.

Michael—as tired as he had to be by now—never left her side. He even intervened on her behalf a few times during the heated discussion. He had no qualms about letting the bigwigs know that he was totally on her side. She had no idea what weight he carried in this room but the group almost acted like they took orders from him and not the other way around. A statement had been drawn up for the station to release and Courtney was finally free to go home.

And that was where the *second* nightmare had begun. Gathered in front of her building, were another slew of reporters. Some of them had the audacity to be there after having been previous guests in her home. As much as she wanted to call them every name in the book, she ignored their ridiculous questions and fought her way through to the entrance of her building.

The doorman was waiting for her so she didn't have to waste more time to use her key. He blocked the ones that tried to follow her in, threatening to call the cops on grounds of trespassing. She didn't stop to see if the ploy worked and instead, murmured her thanks and made her way quickly to the elevator.

Once inside her apartment, she disengaged the alarm and locked the door, then re-engaged it. Other than the hum of the refrigerator, her place was deathly silent. She leaned against the door for a moment to catch her breath. Why was all this *happening* to her?

Later, as she unpacked and showered, she couldn't help but worry over her present situation. After all, within a matter of weeks her life, as she always knew it, had been *seriously* turned upside down. Since the night at Margot's, Courtney had been thrown in front of one train wreck after another, with no time in between to process any of it. This was the *first* time she had been alone long enough to focus on herself and even begin to sort out some of the pieces in her head. But now, with the shooting incident involving a notorious mobster's daughter turning into a headliner, well that just changed the *whole* agenda she had previously planned. And if she wanted to keep her career *and* her image intact, she had to do *exactly* what the station's attorneys told her do and that was *lay* low until it all blew over. Being in the spotlight and keeping your name out of the mud, carried a *great* deal of weight and became a balancing act all of its own. Courtney had witnessed numerous times; how one *negative* action could cause irreversible damage to some of the most famous celebrities on the market— *virtually* overnight.

Now that people had easy access to speak their minds on social media, it was apparent how '*black and white*' the world could be when it came to *their* perception of something. They left no room for any 'grey' areas when judging someone from the comfort of their homes. Which left Courtney wondering which direction the public was going to take, now that the word was out, that she'd shot Karly Driggers. Would they support her actions and view it as self-defense or would they turn on her?

In the middle of all the sorting in her head, Brandon Parrish's face flashed across her mind. She thought about how much he *hated* the paparazzi and the press, for meddling in his private life. He'd angrily told her back at Margot's, that she'd *never* know what it *felt* like to be hounded by cameras, until it happened to *her*. Was this *her* karma coming around that he'd warned her about?

One thing about them tables, they can always turn. For the *first* time in her career, Courtney found herself on the *other* side of the story…and she didn't *like* it. *Not one bit*!

THIRTY-TWO

It was two in the morning when George finally left the Florida hospital and headed home. There was nothing more that could be done on his part. Margot was stable but weak once she'd regained consciousness and so her doctor had decided they were going to keep her overnight for observation. Ken had stayed behind because of the fear he swore he saw in her eyes. She'd had a scare—they all had—and George finally admitted to himself, in all the years he'd known Margot, she fully *looked* her age laying in that bed. With the heart and blood pressure monitors keeping time, the IV snaking around her arm and her pale coloring, well it just added to the *theatrics* of the setting. What had landed her a trip to the ER, was that she had basically *passed* out at the airport. The paramedics said when they arrived on scene, she was soaked in sweat and unresponsive. When she arrived at the hospital, the staff had immediately begun to access all her vital organs. But so far they'd found nothing amiss—her lungs were clear, her valves around the heart showed no blockage and her brain scan showed no signs of abnormal activity, that would indicate a possible stroke.

Once they were able to communicate with her, she claimed she was as clueless as they were as to why her collapse happened. She had admitted that her last meal of the day had been breakfast and that she hadn't slept very well the night before.

The doctor overseeing Margot, told them that she had seemed very emotional when she'd first awakened. He said she had immediately burst into an uncontrollable flood of tears and he'd had to prescribe a mild dose of Valium, to calm her down. One of his staff, who recognized Margot's name on her chart, explained to the doctor the loss of her daughter over twenty years ago and more recently, the loss of her husband as well, in this same hospital, about seven years ago.

On that note, he truly believed that Margot was having what most people referred to as a '*mental* breakdown'. He advised Ken, to be on the safe side, he needed to convince her to follow up with therapy, once she was released, to help her work through some of her emotional stress or next time, she might not recover so easily.

Around midnight they finally transferred Margot from the ER to a private room. George inquired as to whether she would like him to contact Sage now that she was settled. She stressed it was too late to make that call tonight and since her health was not in immediate danger, that it could wait until the morning. Neither one felt it was necessary to argue with her, for fear it would spike her blood pressure. When Margot began later to yawn excessively, George used this as his excuse to leave and let her rest. Right before he left the floor, a nurse approached him and had in her possession, Margot's purse and her carry-on bag, she'd had with her on the flight. Instead of running it back into her room, he'd just take it home with him.

She didn't need anything from either one anyway. She wouldn't be driving, so no reason for her to need her license nor would she need any currency while lying flat on her back, with her husband not a few inches away. Twenty minutes later, as he drove into the garage and parked the car, two things from tonight's events stuck out heavily in his mind. The first was when the doctor had said that Margot broke down and *cried* in front of him. Margot was *not* the kind of person, who cried easily in front of anyone, not *even* her family. For her to break down in front of the doctor and nurses in the ER, was very telling about where her mental state was at the moment.

Which brought him to the second thing that was out of the ordinary about tonight. And it was the fact that not *once*, while he was visiting for *two* hours in her room, had she noticed her purse was missing. Which further put an emphasis on just how out-of-it she was. On any other normal day, she would have been asking for her bag the second her eyes opened in that bed.

He put the car in park, shut the engine off and retrieved both the bags from the front seat. As he made his way inside, he glanced at his watch. It was close to three AM and he was feeling the fatigue. He also had an unsettling feeling come over him when he entered the empty mansion. This was the first time in his *entire* career under Margot's employ, that he was going to be in the house the rest of the night, totally *alone*! Because of that realization, it added to the dark and spooky undertones to the vast space. He figured Karly Driggers had something to do with that and he silently thanked her and added a slew of curse words to go with it.

He crossed the marble floor in the foyer and took the main stairs up to the second floor. Some of the running footlights along the hallways were already lit up and cast a creepy glow in dimmer areas of the hallways. Trying to shake that eerie feeling of stepping into a scene from *The Shining*, he stopped in front of a panel on the wall that controlled the South wing and started flipping switches. All the overheads in the hallway began to light up, all the way to the end. George walked to the first door on the left, produced a key, unlocked it and stepped inside.

A soft overhead light spotlighted Margot's desk. He walked over and sat her carry-on in the chair and her purse on it near the computer keyboard. It must have bumped the mouse in the process because the screen lit up and came to life. George glanced absentmindedly at the pop-up dialog box that was displayed in the middle. It read, *"Thank you for flying today with us!"* across the top. It was an airlines follow-up flight itinerary for the trip Margot had just came from. The details in the travel route was just a click away. George touched the screen and the box expanded and the details loaded in a bigger drop-down box. The state it had listed that she'd flown from, was *Washington.* That was odd, George thought.

He pulled his reading glasses from his breast pocket and slid them on to get a better look. He grabbed the purse to move it out of the way so he could have more room to control the mouse, when instead, he lost his grip and it tipped over. The majority of the contents spilled out on the floor in *every* direction. It sounded like an avalanche in the quiet room.

He cursed under his breath, abandoned the computer for now and turned the dimmer switch on the wall to a brighter setting, so he could see. He then knelt down on his knees, next to the leather bag on the floor, turned it right-side up and began putting her things back in it—starting with her wallet, all the way down to her prescription glass case. He hoped he hadn't broken or spilt anything she'd had stuffed in there in the process. Lord knows she was going to have a fit as it was, with everything a mess she'd have to sort out later.

Just when he thought he'd gotten it all, something up underneath the base of her office chair, near one of the legs, caught his attention. He stooped lower, extended his hand and closed it over what felt like a wad of folded up papers and a square of something less flexible, like plastic. When he brought it out into the light, it took him a second to realize what he was holding in his hand.

The bendable plastic piece was a *visitor's* pass. Margot's name, along with yesterday's date were written on the front, along with the words *Federal Bureau of Investigation* and below that, the address to the division in Washington.

It had a clip on the top, one that's used to attach it to some part of clothing. It was currently being used to secure the pieces of paper he had found with it. He removed them from the clip and began unfolding them.

The first page was a copy of the exhumation order on Jack and Kelley, that Frank had secretly orchestrated behind Margot's back. Except this one had the words, *FBI copy,* written in a thin black marker across the top of the page. If it truly belonged to the FBI, then what was Margot doing with it?

He sighed out loud and opened the second folded piece in the bundle. This was the original copies of Margot's airline ticket stub. Just like the message had indicated on the screen, the documentation verified that undeniably yesterday, she had flown to Washington from Florida in the morning and had caught a return flight back that evening. He sat up straight and took another peek at her computer screen. The message was still clearly displayed with her boarding in Washington, *not* Tennessee, as she had claimed she was headed to, when she'd left out yesterday morning. *'Thank you for flying today with us!'* What the *hell* was going on?

And what the *hell* was Margot up to now?

George looked down at the visitors pass again with total bewilderment. Margot was *supposed* to be visiting a friend, at least that is what she had told him and Ken, yet it looked like instead, that she had taken a trip to Washington to meet with the Feds.

But for what?

Was she in trouble?

Little things began to click into place in George's mind, things that had occurred before her trip. For one, she'd made her *own* travel arrangements and two—she packed only a carry-on. That alone should have been a red flag. Another sigh escaped him as he unfolded the third piece of paper. It was a photocopy of a necklace. Written on the side of the picture, in that same thin black marker as the exhumation paper, were the words—*FBI copy—Exhibit 15.* In the photo, the chain appeared broken but the thin gold heart seemed well-worn but intact. It looked like it needed a good cleaning, almost as if it had come from being buried in the dirt. He studied it for a few seconds longer. A familiarity began tugging at his memory and he swore he had seen it somewhere before.

But the exhaustion won over so he gave up trying for now and grabbed the handles of the purse and stood up. He sat it once again on the desk, this time well in the center so it wouldn't do any more dives to the floor but he didn't return the visitor's pass or the paperwork back inside. Instead he slid out his cell and snapped a pic of the computer screen, then returned it back into his pocket, along with the FBI pass and the papers he'd found with it.

He reset the dimmer switch back to a warm glow. His eyes glanced down at the carry-on in the chair and he couldn't help but wonder if she had something hidden in there as well. On second thought, he decided to leave nothing to chance when it came to Margot and took it with him, as he headed for the hall.

He locked her door and began his trek to the West wing to his own quarters. The sound of his footsteps echoed off the walls as if he were walking in an empty concert hall. When he reached his room he entered and shut the door behind him, locking it as well. Only then did he realize how pissed he was at Margot for lying to both him and Ken, about *where* she was going yesterday. And it irritated him to know that he would also lie awake for another hour, trying to figure out *who* he was going to approach first about his little discovery in the morning—*her* or *Ken.*

THIRTY-THREE

Peter had been at work not quite an hour before he received a call from Meg. She sounded excited and for once—to his relief—tragedy was not going to be the subject. She explained she had just gotten off the phone with Sage and Brandon's housekeeper, Lydia. She and Courtney were being invited to the cabin in Montana for the weekend, to spend some quality time with Sage. Lydia made sure to emphasize that the property the cabin was sitting on, was *secluded* and its location was *unknown* to the public or the media. It was also situated directly in the path of a *no-flying* zone, courtesy of the mountains that loomed not far off in the distance. Meg instantly read between the lines. It was a place for her to hide until the reporters grew bored and left their doorsteps and she was seriously considering the offer. Even though it was exactly what she needed right now, she felt *guilty* about leaving her husband behind, in the middle of this media circus surrounding Karly.

Peter thought it was a great idea for her to take some time away and the invite couldn't have come at a better time. He encouraged her to accept and shot down any guilty feelings she had about leaving him behind to 'fend' for himself. He overdramatized when he told her he had tons of work to do at the office and it would give him the time to catch up while she was away. Then he told her how jealous he was that she was going to see this majestic place they had heard so much about, before he did.

Once they'd hung up, Peter immediately called the number he had been trying to reach for days. To his surprise, she picked up on the *second* ring, almost as if she were *waiting* for his call.

"Where in the *hell* have you been and why haven't you returned any of my calls?" he said, somewhat irritated with her.

"I've been busy working." She answered. "I just walked in the door!"

"*I was worried sick*!" Peter hissed into the receiver. "Well then, that makes *two* of us." She said, with heavy sarcasm.

He hesitated for a brief second.

"I take it you've *seen* the news?" he said.

"Yes! I *saw* the news! So that would make it my turn to ask you—what in the *hell* is going on?"

"There's something I need to tell you. That's *why* I've been calling." He stressed.

"I would say so!" She responded, sounding catty. "Meg is going away for the weekend. I'm free once she boards the plane. I can meet up with you tomorrow morning and explain everything."

"Tomorrow *isn't* good; I have to work."

"All day?"

"It's possible. I'll let you know."

"Please do. This is not something that can wait."

"Sounds important." She said.

"It's going to *blow* your mind!" he promised.

"Well then, my darling, I can't wait to *hear* all about it. When I saw the news and they said '*murder*'…,"

"*Attempted*." Peter said. "None of us were hurt—*thanks* to Courtney!"

"So I *heard*! What on *earth* was *she* doing there?"

"That's the *part* I can't *wait* to tell you *all* about!" Peter said.

THIRTY-FOUR

The knock on Courtney's front door was abrupt, which meant she was probably going to get an earful, when Michael Buchanan entered her apartment. He had been detained by the two extra security officers, that were checking ID's at the building entrance, downstairs. They'd called her up to confirm his before he'd been allowed through. She'd heard that he hadn't been too happy about it. But to her surprise, he never mentioned the incident and instead got straight down to business, once he stepped inside.

"Are we alone?" he asked, his eyes scanning the spacious living room, kitchen and dining room that all flowed together as one, around her.

"Of course, who in the *hell* would want to come visit me right now with that mob downstairs?" She asked and shut the door. "Would you like something to drink?"

"Water." he said, following her across the living room and into the kitchen.

She extracted two bottles from the refrigerator, handed him one and kept the other for herself.

"What's up?" she asked, dreading the answer. Had the station sent him to fire her?

"A lot." He answered after taking a drink.

"Is this something I need to sit down for?" she asked.

"I think so." He said and turned from her and headed towards the sofa in the adjoining living room. "Have you had any sleep?" he asked, as he maneuvered himself around the coffee table and sat down.

"Not much." She confessed, following suit and sitting across from him on the matching loveseat. "I was dead to the world on the plane but once I landed in New York, well let's just say it's been a struggle since. What about you?"

His demeanor was morose and he looked either tired around the eyes or something weighed heavily on his mind. "I've slept very little because I have a *lot* on my plate, too." He said.

"If I have something to do with that, then I apologize."

"You have a hell of *lot* to do with it Princess but I'm not looking for an apology. Have you decided if you're going to skip town for a few days?"

"Funny you should ask." She said, flashing a smile his way. "I just got off the phone with Lydia. She said she was calling on behalf of Sage, to invite me down for the weekend. She and Brandon live in some secluded rustic cabin in the wilds of Montana. She made it a point to tell me how *private* it was because it had been built in the middle of a forest."

"You should go." Michael urged. "It sounds like the perfect place to hide for a few days. At least there you can step outside the door without being mobbed by our *own* kind."

"I thought about that," she admitted. "But jumping right back on a plane so quick, is just not what I had in mind or hanging out all weekend with a nephew that literally *hates* my guts."

"Stop making excuses." Michael said. "It's only a four-hour flight if you factor in the time change on different coasts. And besides, you're not *flying* the plane. You can sleep the entire stretch and be well-rested when you land in God's great country."

"It does sound tempting." Courtney said. "Especially in light of what's happening right now. But I know you didn't come by to get updated on my *personal* calendar of events for the weekend."

"Your right Princess, I didn't. But I still agree that you should go."

"What's up then, Michael? Did the station send you?" Courtney asked, steering the conversation back on a business level.

"No, I came here on my own to see you for entirely *different* reasons."

"Such as?" Courtney was curious.

"Such as the part about the FBI and *why* they sent in a special *second* team to investigate the Pirates lair. At the time, I didn't think there was anything to it. The standard protocol for anything as big as this, is to call in the FBI so they can take control and run a detailed investigation. The agents that were originally sent to work this case, are some of the *best* the bureau has to offer. So why they'd send a *second* team out, just didn't make sense to me either, once I thought about it—unless something bigger was at stake. So I made a few phone calls and dug around and I found out that something very serious indeed was discovered during the takeover."

"Like *what*?" Courtney asked. Michael had her undivided attention.

"General Bradley, who is in charge on the military side, is still on the site in Kenya and he won't be *leaving* anytime soon, from what I hear. You were right about his boys looking for *something* in the jungle, I just don't know what. But the talk is that the FBI has suddenly become very interested in the *daily* functions of that camp." Michael continued. "They're trying to pin down *who* it was, that worked out of that hut where the ledgers were found. And apparently there's some sort of a connection to a plane that's still *missing* from *1987*."

"The plane Sage's parents were on was the *only* one reported *missing* that year. I never came across *another* in my research." She said, perplexed.

"Because there wasn't *another*." Michael said. "But you just said they were *looking* for a plane that was *still* missing." She stressed.

Michael changed the subject. "The hut that had the plane's serial number on the wall, held more *secrets* than just that and the buried steel box."

"Like what?" she asked, hanging on the edge of her seat.

"They found a *diary*." Michael simply said.

"A *diary*?" Courtney repeated.

Michael nodded.

"It seems the ledgers weren't the *only* contents of the steel box." He said. "A *personal* diary was found in there as well."

"I guess that solves the mystery of *who* lived in the hut then. Whoever the diary belonged to, would *also* be the owner of the ledgers, wouldn't you think?" Courtney asked.

"No." Michael shook his head slowly from side to side. "The ledgers dates spanned from the beginning of '90 and ended somewhere around *last* month."

"*And*? What's so compelling about that?"

"The diary's last entry was in 1987."

"So what does *that* mean?" Courtney asked, not catching on at first.

"Something inside that diary, indicated that it belonged to a passenger, whose plane is *still* missing. That's why a *second* team got called in. The first one was to handle the pirates lair and the second one came after the *discovery* of the diary and the dead *American* woman in the *same* camp."

Courtney narrowed her eyes, completely puzzled at what he had just said.

"*Wait* a minute! Your saying they found a diary that, *beyond* a doubt, came from a plane, *missing* the same year as Sage's parents did?"

Michael slowly shook his head no. "There's only *one* plane that went missing in '87 Courtney. It was *the* plane that *her* parents were on. It was *never* found. That's why the feds are so *hot* right now in discovering its whereabouts."

"But there's no way," she said, trying to get it straight. "Her parent's plane was *found* years ago by the FBI and they sent the Hartford's their remains. Margot said they were even buried on the state's dime!"

Michael kept shaking his head no. "That's what Charlie Vega told you *because* that's what *they* told the Hartford's at the time. But I have a very *reliable* source that read it straight to me from the *actual* report, archived in the FBI's records. The plane that Sage's parents were on, was never *found,* Courtney! Whoever told that to those people *lied.* Which is the reason *why* the second team was sent in."

There was silence that fell between them while Courtney computed all this in her brain.

"*Oh my God.*" She said at first. "I never did find anything online about the recovery of their plane. I thought it was odd at the time but now…" she trailed off, biting the inside of her lip out of habit.

"Why would someone tell the Hartford's a plane was found when it wasn't?" she directed this to Michael.

"I don't know." He said, shaking his head. "I checked out some things once I got off the phone with the General. I didn't have any luck either and that's why I came over. I knew your version of the story had been different." "You didn't *say* anything to the General about me?" she asked, holding her breath.

"No, *hell* no!" he said. "You know me better than that, Princess. Your secret is safe with me."

"I know, I'm sorry." She said. "I just had to ask. I mean, this is still all new to me *too*! I'm not even sure where to go from here. And now, finding out that these poor people have been lied to about their loved one's death. Why would someone go to such great lengths to make Frank Hartford believe that he was burying the remains of his daughter? Now the Order of Exhumation we found in his safe, is beginning to make a whole lot *more* sense. He must have learned something that made him suspicious enough to request it."

"That's why you need to bite the bullet and take that ride out to Montana." Michael advised. "That's your *family* now Courtney," he stressed. "Regardless of *how* you and Brandon feel about each other; you need to tell him what is going on. Let him prepare his wife for the day the FBI shows up at her door, so she doesn't freak out!"

Courtney let his words sink in.

He was right and she knew it—*literally*!

Guess this meant she had no choice but to hop on the next plane to Montana!

THIRTY-FIVE

Margot sighed and closed her eyes in surrender when she saw what Ken was dangling in front of her. It was the plastic FBI visitor's pass she'd forgotten about, that had been hidden deep in the recesses of her purse. *Damn* George—who was standing beside her husband with his hands on his hips. *Damn* him for knocking it over at home and finding it. Now she had to explain and she literally didn't know where to start. "Spill it!" George had said. "At the beginning." Ken specified. "Don't leave *anything* out."

And so, having no other choice, she did just that. From the phone call she'd received at the beginning of the week, down to the details of her meeting with the two agents and the necklace that she'd identified in the photo, as the one Kelley was wearing that fateful day.

"Agent Fields said it had been found at the Pirates Lair."

"The *Somalia* Pirates in Africa?" Ken questioned. "The one they just seized that's on every news channel?" Margot confirmed it by nodding.

"Well I'll be *damned*!" George said, shaking his head.

"Damned is right!" Ken agreed. He studied the photo of the necklace and then glanced at the exhumation paper. "And Frank never said a word to you about having suspicions that the caskets might be empty?" Ken asked.

"No." She simply said.

Later, outside her room, Ken spoke to George in confidence.

"There's something that's not adding up here." Ken said.

"You think she's holding back on us?" George asked.

"No, not her, the *feds*! There's something about *their* story that just doesn't add up."

"Like what?"

"The call they made to Margot in the *first* place." He said.
"Why? What did they say?"
"It's what they *didn't* say." Ken mused. "They called Margot up there because they already *knew* there was something in those items they recovered, that she would recognize."
"Why would you say that?" George queried.
"The inscription on the back was *not* what pointed them in Margot's direction." Ken said. "There's a million Kelley's and Jack's that are couples in the US. There was no last name on that inscription to identify it belonged to this family because I asked her. But *yet* they centered right on Margot, so there has to be something else that gave its owner away. The necklace was just a part of a *bigger* find."
"Bigger find? Of *what*?" George asked.
"I have no idea at the moment, but I *intend* to find out." Ken said.

THIRTY-SIX

Lydia stood over the crockpot in the kitchen, loading it up with all the fixings of a southern pot roast dinner. The thick slab of meat took up most of the bottom of the ceramic cooker. She had cut up some russet potatoes and layered them in, adding carrots on top and then raw onions next. The signature roast sauce she had drummed up years ago, was already made beforehand and was waiting in a glass measuring cup on the counter. She grabbed the handle, poured the thick brown liquid slowly over it all, added a sprinkle of pepper for good measure, then finally put the lid on top. She set the proper cooking time and left the appliance to do its job, as she wiped the counter down and rinsed the cup she'd used and slid it into the dishwasher. She let out a sigh and glanced at her watch. It was close to ten in the morning and everything was moving along like clockwork. Lydia mentally checked off the list in her head; Baby Tristan had been bathed earlier and laid down for his morning nap. Sage was upstairs showering and getting ready for the start of her weekend with Meg and Courtney. Hans had headed off to the airport over an hour ago, to pick them both up and Brandon had already retreated to the barn, where he would probably *stay* until the women left on Sunday afternoon. And now, that was dinner was started, that about wrapped it up, the major parts of it anyway. Yep, everything seemed to be coming together without any hitches and she could not be happier for Sage. With Meg and Courtney coming, she hoped it was the beginning of many more memories, towards growing the family bond and support system, that the girl so desperately needed. With Lydia not having any blood family herself, she truly *understood* what Sage was going thru which was another reason why she had pushed so hard with Brandon, to make today happen. She hoped in the long run, it did not come back and bite her in the ass.

Her cell came alive on the counter and began vibrating. She figured it was Hans, who by now had arrived at the airport and was just confirming with her, that he had them both and was headed back. But when she glanced at the screen, she was wrong. It was Margot.

Please God, she prayed, *don't let this be the monkey wrench that disrupts the serenity of the cabin and the moment*, she silently prayed before she pushed the button. *"Hello."*

"Lydia *darling*, how are you today?" Margot said, sounding sort of groggy.

Margot never sounded groggy.

"I'm fit as a fiddle Margot. How are *you*?" Lydia was almost afraid to ask.

"I've had *better* days." She began and immediately Lydia knew her gut was right.

"What's *happened* now?" She asked, not wanting to beat around the bush.

Margot let out a rather heavy sigh and begin telling Lydia about her collapse coming back from a business trip, the day before.

"And you're just now calling us? Are *you* ok? Dear *God* what's wrong?" Lydia was irritated but at the same time, she was also very concerned.

"Well, I got released today. It was really just exhaustion and being overwhelmed with everything that's happened recently. I'm feeling a little better now but they have me on these damn valiums, which makes me see rainbows and butterflies everywhere! I guess I thought my life was going to be *business as usual* after the Karly incident, when in reality, it messed with me more emotionally, than I thought. My doctor says with enough rest and relaxation; I should be as good as new."

Lydia walked towards the opening from the kitchen that led to the staircase in the hall. As far as she could see past the railing, it was quiet and deserted which meant Sage was still, *hopefully*, upstairs and occupied. She wondered if Margot had already called her and began to worry about the damper it would put on the weekend now. Sage would be feeling guilty *and* worried about her grandmother, *instead* of enjoying herself for once, with *no* worries pressing in the background.

Suddenly, Lydia wanted to *curse* out loud at the timing! She had worked *so* hard to make this a *flawless* visit and now *this*!

She was not angry *at* Margot for the interruption, she was angry that *it* had to have happened on *this* weekend! Not the one *before* or the one *after* but this *effing* weekend! Then Lydia did a flip and began chastising herself for not having enough *compassion* for her friend, in a time of need. Thank *God* it had not been *more* serious than it was! So, *between* the anger and compassion, she met somewhere *in* the middle.

"Margot, *why* didn't George or Ken *call* us?"

"Because I asked them not to. I was worried they'd make it sound more dramatic than it is. I didn't want to upset Sage until I knew what was wrong either. It isn't anything serious and I didn't want her flipping out and jumping on a plane."

"Sage is going to be *furious* to find out that she wasn't called right away. Speaking of, have you called *her* yet?"

"Not yet." Margot said. "That's why I'm calling *you* first. I thought maybe you could do me the favor and *tell* her for me. You're there with her and you can calm her better than I could and make her understand that I will be fine and there's no reason for her to come check on me."

"You *think* that will stop her?" Lydia asked with sarcasm.

"If I know my Sage, the answer is no, but it's worth a try.

Besides, that's where you come in Lydia darling. You were always better at handling her emotional needs, then I was." Lydia just stood in the kitchen, knowing that her mouth had to be hanging open in shock, after that remark. Never in all the years that she'd helped in raising Sage, had Margot given her *any* credit. Those valiums suddenly seemed like the *miracle* drug.

"Margot, as much as I *appreciate* the compliment, I really don't *feel* it's my place to *tell* Sage." She stressed.

"Tell me what?"

Lydia turned to see Sage, standing in the doorway, not a *few* feet from her, a look of serious concern on her face.

Too late, Lydia thought, *I just did*!

THIRTY-SEVEN

"*OMG!*" Meg exclaimed from the backseat of the limo.
"Holy *shit!*" Courtney said, which was her way of agreeing.
"Are *you* serious?"
"That's what I'm saying." Meg agreed
A smile spread across Hans' face, as he listened to the ladies' reactions, once he cleared the canopied driveway and they got their first glimpse of the spectacular cabin before them. The magnificent views of the mountains in the distance, the lush green landscape and the dense forests on either side, just added to the splendor. He remembered in the beginning, when he'd set eyes upon it himself, for the *first* time, how it had taken his breath away, in the same manner.
"You should see it in the winter months." Hans said, glancing back at them in the rear view mirror. "A good cup of tea in front of the fire while the world outside the window, is a blanket of white. I *guarantee* the beauty and magic of the moment is just as exquisite!"
"I can *just* imagine!" Meg said, getting antsy in the back seat. "I bet it can get really cold here, right? I mean, *obviously* it snows hard enough that you can be stranded out here for days." Meg said, then she laughed. "Oh *God*, now I can see *why* Sage chose the title *Stranded* for her book."
"I'd kill for office views like this." Courtney said, still staring out towards the mountains.
Hans guided the limo to a stop in front of the main entrance. Both women literally jumped out as soon as he opened the back door, to get a better view.
"I can envision waking up here every morning, for the rest of my life!" Meg confessed, hand over her eyes, shielding

it from the sun. "You can *see* forever! Peter would *love* this place!"

"Anybody in their right mind would *love* this place." Courtney said. "My God, this is exactly what the doctor ordered right now. I can feel the stress melting away, just standing here. It's so open."

"And so quiet." Meg added. "And listen Courtney, do you *hear* that?"

Courtney stopped and listened. All she heard, other than a few birds singing, was silence on a clear sunny day.

"Hear what?" She finally asked.

"No horns blaring, no sirens…it's as if someone *turned* the volume down in New York." Meg said smiling.

"Oh yeah, like *way* down!"

"It's like being on a totally different planet." Meg said.

"That's the truth." Courtney said. "No wonder Brandon picked this place to hide in. Who the *hell* would have found it?"

"I'd like to see them news bitches find us here!" Meg added and laughed. "Right now they are so stumped, on *where* we all are. They are probably still camping out on the doorsteps of *our* empty houses!"

"Speaking of," Courtney said, turning to Hans who was still unloading their bags from the trunk of the limo. She was holding her cell phone in her hand. "*Please* tell me Hans, that you guys *do* have Wi-Fi out here because right now, my phone says I have no *signal*!"

Hans simply smiled and said, "Follow me, ladies."

"*Hello*!" Lydia greeted them with a smile, when they stepped inside the foyer.

"Hell-o—*OMG*!" Meg said again, staring past Lydia's shoulder, to the staircase that led to the second floor. "*Look* at that! Was this *hand*-carved, like, by a *real* person from the area?" With her mouth agape she walked past the housekeeper, her hand outstretched. It made contact with the railing and she stroked it as if it were a pet.

Lydia nodded. "Why yes, as a matter of fact, it was. His name was Henry and he was not only *one* of the men who built this beautiful cabin, he later became the caretaker of the property when he retired. Mr. Hartford gave Henry free reign when it came to the details, since he was a man with so many talents."

"What an interesting story. It's just absolutely fabulous!" Meg said, still stroking the wood railing.

"Did he do this too?" Courtney asked, her head tilted back, as she looked straight up, at the massive ceiling above them. "Look at those *beams* and the way the wood is perfectly aligned up there!" She pointed upward. "It looks like a *real*-life cabin made out of Lincoln Logs!"

"Oh it *does*!" Meg agreed, following her gaze up above, mesmerized herself by the architecture. "*Wow!*"

Hans reappeared in the hallway, minus the luggage he had carried in earlier.

"If you would like to see your rooms, I have deposited your things inside." he said to the two women.

"You might want to freshen up." Lydia suggested. "And then we can see about getting you some refreshments, after your long plane ride. Sage is just finishing up with little Tristan's feeding time and then she'll be right down."

"Oh, I can't wait to see baby Tristan." Meg said, beaming a smile at everyone. "I want to hold him again. He's such a sweet little guy." She cooed.

"Oh I can guarantee you, Miss Meg, Sage will be bringing him around quite enough while you're here. Follow me." Lydia walked past them and down the hall.

Meg and Courtney followed her into the kitchen, where they oohed over the entire layout.

"What a *beautiful* place to cook." Meg said.

"How would *you* know?" Courtney asked. "You don't cook, *remember*?"

"It makes me *want* to cook." She said, laughing. "But Peter does and he would be *drooling* if he saw this kitchen."

Lydia led them down the short hallway and stopped at the first door on the left.

"This will be your room during your stay." she said, opening the door. The women followed her inside.

"This is just gorgeous!" Meg said, eyeing the two full beds with mounds of fluffy blankets and lots of pillows that Lydia had just made fresh, a few hours ago.

"Those beds look like heaven!" Courtney said.

"I have stocked the adjoining bathroom with plenty of towels and toiletries, just in case." Lydia said. "The remote to the TV is in the top drawer of the nightstand between your beds and so is the one that controls the fans overhead. Do not hesitate to ask me or my handsome husband if y'all need anything during your stay. We want you to be as comfortable as possible. With that being said, you have no idea how happy we are that you both came. This is exactly what Sage needed." She flashed another smile at the women and then walked towards the door.

"Thanks Lydia." Courtney said, dropping her bag from her shoulder and tossing it in the nearby chair. "We both really needed this too and are so grateful for Sage extending the invitation. It couldn't have come at a better time."

"I second that." Meg said. "The media back home were getting out of control!"

Lydia stopped and smiled from the doorway.

"No one will bother you here." She assured them. "Make yourselves at home. In the meantime, I'll get some wine uncorked for ya and something to nibble on, that will tide you over until dinner. I'll leave a tray for you in the den when you're ready. It's the room that's right across from the kitchen, off the hall, from where you came in. Sage will be down shortly."

Twenty minutes later Courtney left their room in search of the den, *solo*. Meg had already left ten minutes' prior. When she stepped into the hall, the place seemed as silent as a tomb and the smell of wood was more prominent, along with another aroma that had her suddenly feeling famished.

The something that smelled wonderful was coming from an oversized crockpot on the counter. It obviously was the intended dinner that Lydia was referring to. If it tasted anything like it smelled, then Courtney's empty stomach had just won the food lottery.

She started to pass the island and head straight for the door to the hall in front of her, when her phone vibrated in her back pocket. She stopped and pulled it out and saw it was a text from Michael. He was simply asking for confirmation that she'd landed and was safe. The concern made her smile. She quickly texted back and confirmed that she was safe within the walls of a luxurious cabin in the middle of nowhere and couldn't be happier. It was only after she pushed send that she realized, she'd truly spoken from the heart. She returned it to her pocket. That's when she noticed that there was a second doorway leading off from the kitchen.

The curiosity of the reporter in her took over and she detoured off the beaten path, only to find out she'd come upon a formal dining room with a massive table, that took up quite a bit of space in the middle. The piece looked like it had been constructed by the same hand, that had made the stair railings…probably the same *Henry* that Lydia had spoken about earlier.

 The wood gleamed where the sunlight bounced off the surface, making it look polished and velvety smooth. The chairs were solid wood as well and carved intricately on their regal backs. Courtney stepped further inside the room, marveling at the rustic but elegant chandelier that hung over the middle of the table. She could just imagine what it looked like turned on at night within the rich walls of wood, light bouncing off the overhead beams and the *portraits* on the wall...

Courtney froze on the portraits, everything else around her forgotten, as a spark of surprise tingled inside. Chills came over her, as she stared at the faces, of who she believed, were Sage's parents. She took a few steps closer to inspect them.

They were huge portraits and had been hung evenly, side by side. Whoever had painted them had done an extraordinary job in capturing character. They were so real looking, that she felt, any moment, one of them would start talking to her.

The man who was obviously Sage's dad, was indeed handsome and looked *nothing* like his twin, Charlie Vega. The twinkle in his brown eyes and the unruly curly hair, gave her the impression there had been a hint of mischief about his character. The slightly crooked smile that the artist had captured perfectly, confirmed it. The portrait of the woman next to him, was a natural stunning beauty, complete with blonde-hair, blue eyes, and the face of a delicate angel. Her shoulders were draped almost in the same shade of blue, as her eyes and a simple gold heart hung from her neck. She looked young, vibrant and happy. Courtney glanced around her. There wasn't a soul or the sound of one, in sight. She slid out her cell, shut the flash off on the camera and quickly snapped two pictures of the portraits. She slid the phone back inside her pocket, *fast* because she knew what it would *look* like if someone were to catch her, *especially* Brandon!

But she couldn't *help* herself.

There was a nagging feeling in her gut that had strongly prompted her to do so.

She would study them both later in private, to figure out why.

She stared a moment longer at the male and then finally left the dining room in search of Meg.

THIRTY-EIGHT

It was late afternoon on a Friday when Charlie finally called it quits in the office and began preparations to head home. The majority of his staff had already left after the morning's first meeting, since there was not really much to do at the moment. Most of his clientele were either already signed to upcoming projects or were in the middle of fulfilling contracts, schedules and tours or on vacation. All except for Lola…

As if she had ESP and was channeling into his thoughts, a text from Ava popped up just then on his cell.

Lola just finished her test and she is perfect for the part! Can't wait to view it with you. Let me know when would be a good time??

Charlie typed back, *what about now?* and then hit the send button.

He hated to admit it but he was itching to see Ava. Within seconds, another soft beep from his phone indicated she'd responded.

The test copy won't be available until tomorrow!

Charlie typed a response.

Too bad. I was going to ask you to dinner after. There was a slight pause before the next text from her, came through.

You still can!

Charlie smiled to himself, then typed; *I'm talking about tonight!*

She replied; *So was I…*

With no hesitation he sent back; *What time?*

She responded with; *What about now?*

Charlie smiled even bigger.

Now was *perfect*.

THIRTY-NINE

After a wonderful meal and full bellies, the three women retired to the new space that Brandon had created for Sage, off their bedroom balcony. Hans had added additional seating beforehand—by borrowing the chairs from their bedroom—and had grouped it intimately around the fire pit, which he had already turned on as well. Resting in an ice bucket on the table, were two chilled bottles of wine, alongside a tray that held three, long-stemmed, crystal glasses, that sparkled in the firelight.

Baby Tristan made his last appearance for the night and both Courtney and Meg drooled and cooed over him until they wore him out. Sage gave his brow a final kiss as he yawned and then Lydia whisked him off to bed. Hans handed each of them a glass of Moscotto, then he too soon departed, pulling the French doors halfway closed behind him, to give them privacy.

All three women toasted to one another and quietly sipped, as they each admired the breathtaking view of the mountains bathed in moonlight, beyond the railing. It was a quiet night with the crickets singing softly in rhythm and the owls hooting in the background. To Sage, it was the textbook ending to a *good* first day.

"This home is like a Western paradise." Meg said. "I don't think I've ever felt so *comfortable* in a place that wasn't my own."

Sage smiled and glanced over at her. "Thank You. That's quite a compliment."

Courtney piped up. "I'm quite relaxed myself...*and* stuffed! *Damn* can that Lydia cook!"

"That's for sure." Meg chimed in, lightly rubbing her stomach. "That homemade bread she made was to *die* for. I couldn't stop eating it! She could make a *fortune* if she owned a restaurant in New York!"

"It's just one of her many skills." Sage admitted. "Wait until you eat one of her pastries or pies. She'll pop out one of them before the weekend is over. They just melt in your mouth."

"Oh *God*, by the time I go back home, I'm not going to fit in my clothes." Meg said. "How do you keep your weight down with food like that at your disposal?"

Sage laughed. "I'm not necessarily a size *zero,* in case you two haven't noticed!"

"*Girl*, don't even!" Courtney said. "You have curves in all the *right* places. I had to *buy* some of mine!"

"Ditto!" Meg said. "Jack and I took after my father's side. His mother was a beanpole, so I had to enhance some of my assets as well. Where Charlie, he's *all* my mother's side. She had the curves, like you!"

There was a pause of silence. While they all sipped and enjoyed the night sounds and the light breeze rolling through the upper deck, Sage took a second to think about the conversation they were having. She had to keep reminding herself that when Meg talked about *her* parents, she was talking about Sage's *actual* grandparents. Looking back on the day she'd read that newspaper article to Brandon, she'd had no clue she was talking about her own *blood* relatives or her *father,* as one of the famous missing children. And now here she was, sitting with *two* more of them, who had long ago been presumed *dead* by the world. It was too incredible sometimes to absorb.

"We needed this." Courtney said, breaking the silence. "I don't think I could have taken another minute being cooped up in my apartment."

"Tell me about it." Meg agreed, looking over at Courtney. "I've *never* had the media camping out like that, at *my* doorstep. It's very disturbing when it's *you*—generally speaking—that they're after. I'm used to being the *chaser* of the story. Now that the shoe is on the other foot, I'm getting a taste of my *own* medicine!"

"It's because the tables can turn at *any* time and we just get *too* comfortable in our positions, thinking it won't." Courtney offered.

"Your absolutely right." Meg agreed.

"What really gets to me, is that I've *worked* with over half of those *assholes* on my doorstep, on different projects throughout my career!" Courtney said, with a touch of anger in her tone. "And *some* of those vultures have been in my apartment as *guests,* at one time or another. Since the news broke about Karly, they are so hell bent on getting the story, they could give a *shit* less about respect for me or my privacy!"

"No *one* is your friend in this business!" Sage said. When both the women sent curious glances her way, she added, "At least that's what *Brandon* warned me about, when it came to the entertainment business." She shrugged her shoulders.

"He's right, you know." Meg said. "People you *think* are your friends, can be plotting behind your back and you don't even know it. Give them an offer they can't refuse and they will sell you out in a minute."

"It's definitely a cut-throat business." Courtney agreed, a slight furrow in her brow forming. "Everyone has their price."

"I believe everything happens for a reason." Sage said. "It's the spiritual world's *way* of giving us a wakeup call. There's always a lesson to learn in its aftermath. I know that's not comforting to you now while you're in the mist of it but I can tell you from experience, I've always been better off where I land, once the dust settles, then where I started."

There was a second too long of silence, as both women stared at Sage. She wasn't sure by the look on their faces whether they agreed with what she'd said or thought she was nuts. Then Meg spoke and eased her fears, entirely. "Your absolutely right! If it wasn't for Karly coming after us, we would not be sitting here right now. None of us would know the truth."

"I don't think *all* of us *wanted* to know the truth!" Courtney's tone was slightly sarcastic.

Sage knew right away who she was referring to. "It's going to take some time with Brandon. He's trying to wrap his mind around it."

"Is that *why* he's been MIA all day?" Courtney asked dryly.

"It's a lot to deal with all at once, Courtney! Give the guy a break, will ya?" Meg said, coming to his defense.

"It's a lot for *any* of us to deal with." Courtney said, unyielding.

"And *each* of us does so at a different pace than others!" Meg interjected with a smile.

"I could cover for him and say he's just been busy in the barn, doing what he loves best and I wouldn't be lying." She smiled at Courtney.

"Why? What's in the barn? A wall of mirrors, so he can stare at himself?" Courtney wasn't giving an inch of compassion.

"*Courtney*!" Meg said, chastising her lightheartedly. Sage laughed. "No, there is no wall of mirrors in his man cave, that I'm aware of."

"Man cave?" Meg asked. "What sort of man cave?" "His man cave is a workshop!" Sage said.

"What *kind* of workshop?" Courtney asked, perking up with interest.

"A *woodworking* kind of workshop. I write as a hobby and he builds with his hands, as *his* hobby." Sage said.

"Is he any good?" Meg asked.

"He built *this* for me." Sage pointed to the end table next to her chair. Both women studied it while she told them about his crafty use of the raw material he'd recycled from the tree in the yard. "And it moves easily on wheels so I can use it to rest my laptop on, in front of me." She pushed the table edge with her hand to demonstrate.

"That's pretty cool!" Courtney said, genuinely admiring his handy work.

"I like the *wheel* idea." Meg added.

"The wood is so heavy that for me to move it without wheels, would have been a nightmare. So he added them for easy mobility."

Courtney was so enthralled, she got up from her seat and walked over to examine it closer. She stooped down and ran her hand over the edges. "Nice!" she muttered. "He's talented."

Meg laughed. "Of course he is! He's the *biggest* movie star of the decade!"

"That's not what I'm talking about!" Courtney said, standing back to full height. "The *world* knows about the acting talent he has but I don't recall ever reading in my research, that he was talented in the woodworking department."

"I was just as surprised as you are." Sage admitted. "I was a hardcore fan before he and I met. I read everything on him that was out there for twenty years in print, especially when he gave interviews and I never read anything that indicated he was into woodworking." Both
women looked at her.

"A fan?" Meg repeated. "So the story of Stranded was not just made-up?"

"Sort of!" Sage said. "The real story is a lot more complicated!"

"But the handyman was real?" Courtney asked.

Sage nodded. "Jeb was *very* real!" she confirmed.

"Sorry to pry." Meg reached out to touch her arm. "I can see that just the mention of his name, upsets you!"

"He betrayed my family in the worst way. I don't know *what* would have happened if it wasn't for Brandon and Hans. I probably wouldn't be here right now to even talk about it."

Courtney returned to her seat and for the next half hour, the two women listened as Sage told them the *real* story that prompted her to write the book, from the moment Hans showed up at her door, to when the helicopter took them both away, two weeks later. She admitted then, that she thought she'd never see Brandon again. When she finished, neither of them spoke for a few seconds.

"Oh my God!" Meg said first. "That was an *awesome* love story in itself! And you saved Brandon's life!"

Courtney stayed quiet but moved towards the ice bucket and extracted the bottle. She topped off her glass and then passed it to Meg.

"I did what anyone would do under those circumstances."

"And all this time it was your idol laying in that bed!" Meg giggled, topping off her glass and passing it on to Sage. "Damn that's like a fantasy dream come true."

"But don't forget, she said he was a complete *asshole* when he first woke up!" Courtney reminded Meg. "And if it wasn't for *you* nursing him back to health, he would be *dead* right now." She directed this to Sage.

"Yeah but it was because he was missing some very *vital* things in his life." Sage said gently, defending him as she took the bottle and topped off her own glass. "Brandon was so busy *building* up his career in the beginning, that it took priority over his home life. While his friends were graduating from college, getting married and starting careers and families, he was immersed in the Hollywood lifestyle, quickly losing his true identity to this *fantasy* persona the PR people helped him create. It wasn't until he hit the top, that he realized how many sacrifices he had made in his personal life, to get there. He was already beyond frustrated and bitter about it, when he showed up here. I think the near-death experience helped him along a little faster in realizing, that life is too short to take it for granted. His career is what makes his living but being content at home, is what makes his life."

Again Courtney didn't comment, Sage noticed. She was listening but she also seemed to be turning something over in her mind.

"Any time death knocks at your door; it wakes you up!" Meg agreed, also deep in her own kindred memories.

"It definitely made him take a hard look at his life." Sage added. "I was just lucky enough to be there at the right time, when he did."

"I'm surprised he even listened to you, he's so hardheaded." Courtney finally muttered into her glass, as she took a sip.

"He had no choice." Sage laughed at her comment. "We had a blizzard literally beating down the door, a madman on the property that was threatening his life behind my back and no communication to the outside world. Where was he going to go?"

"I'm glad he and Hans couldn't leave." Meg said. "It makes me ill to think that you would have been here alone with that madman—Jeb!"

"You know; I never came across anything online about you being stalked by your handyman." Courtney said, looking directly at Sage.

"That's because Ken, the wonderful man who puts up with my grandmother, was Sheriff then. He and his boys were the ones who arrested Jeb. He did a good job of keeping it just under the radar and Brandon's name out of the printed piece in the paper, so it wouldn't draw too much attention. The world is a little different out here in Montana, then where we all come from, Courtney. People aren't so quick to air out their dirty laundry and the town of Darby is very protective of who they consider their own. They are also very *proud* to have a superstar in their mist and they will scratch someone's eyes out who jeopardizes it."

"Does Brandon go into the town of Darby?" Meg asked.

"All the time." Sage said.

"What does he do there?" Courtney asked.

"He shops with Lydia and Hans when they go in. Sometimes he and Hans will go alone and have coffee at the diner during the week and hang out with Buster for a while before heading back home."

"Who's Buster?" Meg asked.

"He's the current sheriff of Darby. He took over Ken's position when he retired and moved to Florida to be with my grandmother. He's also a very big fan of Brandon's." Courtney rolled her eyes.

"Does anybody bother him when he's in town?" Meg was still curious.

Sage shook her head. "No. Once they learned what Jeb had done and how Brandon risked his life to save me, well he became their town hero after that."

"So they treat him like royalty." Meg laughed.

"Pretty much!" Sage agreed, smiling at her.

After another brief pause, Courtney said, "So have you learned anything new from the two journals you found in the safe?"

Sage treaded lightly on this answer, only repeating what she learned about the suspicious package that was sent to her grandfather, along with the slogan '*Eye for an Eye*' that, without a doubt, came from Victor Rocha.

"Did you know anything about that?" Courtney asked Meg. She shook her head no. "Not about the package but I did hear Everett talking about the *eye* slogan to Charlie and

Frank in the office one night, when we were all together at the mansion."

"What was the occasion?" Courtney asked.

"Something like what's happening now. We were waiting out the verdict on whether they were going to charge Everett with the shooting or deem it self-defense."

"And we all know the outcome of that." Courtney said.

"After reading my grandfather's take on it, I can't see why they wouldn't consider it self-defense. Victor and his brother broke into Everett's place of business in the middle of the night, heavily armed. He had every right to protect himself."

"I would have shot *both* their asses too!" Courtney made a face and then took a sip of her wine.

"I have to agree." Sage said. "Courtney, you're not *worried* that charges will be brought against you for shooting Karly, are you?"

She shrugged her shoulders. "Not really. It's a case of history repeating itself. She did the same thing her father did, by entering an occupied dwelling with clear intent of bodily harm *and* armed with a deadly weapon. And not just *once* but this is her *second* offense on the *same* person, on top of him being a very famous *public* figure. I just happened to get caught up in *that* drama because I was there, *invited*. I have a right to defend myself, no different than Everett did that night. Should be pretty cut and dried."

"I don't think you have anything to worry about. Brandon's got a PI he's acquainted with. Word is, they are about to close the case, citing insanity and stalking with deadly intent, *second* offense. He's more worried about them making the *family* connection, than he is about your chances of being charged with anything." Sage said.

"Now you sound like Michael." Courtney responded without thinking. "He worries that someone might listen to

Karly's story about us, a little too close and put the pieces together."

Meg and Sage glanced at each other.

"*Who* is Michael?" Meg asked.

"Oh, sorry!" Courtney let out a short laugh. "Michael, my boss at the station."

"You *told* him who *we* are?" Sage asked, suddenly alert.

"Y*es* I did *but* there's *nothing* to worry about!" She said, holding her hand up, suddenly realizing what they were thinking. "Michael would *never* do anything to jeopardize my safety, including telling any of my deep, dark secrets. And besides, I was between a rock *and* a hard place. He found out about Karly while we were in Africa covering this Pirate raid. I hadn't really had a chance to sit down with him somewhere private and tell him before *someone* else did. He was pissed when he confronted me about it. Michael is the kind of boss that wants to hear about your screw-ups from your *own* mouth. The shit will hit the fan if he hears it from a second or third party. Since this was the case, I had no choice but to come clean with him or chance losing the only *true* friend I've ever had, in my adult life and believe me when I say, he's definitely someone you *want* in your corner. And the ironic part of this whole thing was, no one, was more *knowledgeable* about the Benenati murders, *than* Michael. He was the first journalist from the US to *cover* that story in Italy. He researched the hell out of it and wrote an excellent piece and it became his big break that started propelling him up the corporate ladder. The story *belonged* to him is how I justified it. And it was only fair that he knew the truth about what happened to those missing kids." She glanced over at Meg. "I owed him that much after all he's done for me and I can promise you he will not tell anyone!"

"If you think he's safe…" Meg said.

"I do." Courtney said. "There's also a plus side to surrounding yourself with men that think ahead of the game, when you're a single girl." She laughed. "He knows a lot of very influential people who owe him a lot of favors."

"Do I detect that you are *crushing* a little on this boss of yours?" Meg asked.

"*Please*!" Courtney said, shaking her head in denial.

"You are!" Meg said, smiling.

"Looks like it to me!" Sage chimed in, smiling too.

"Honestly, it's *nothing* like that. We have a *solid* working relationship. He's hot, I'm not going to lie." Courtney said, breaking into a grin. "But I have a rule, I don't *mix* business with pleasure."

"Well," Sage said, smiling at her. "*Sounds* like you broke your *own* rule the night you confided in him about your *true* identity."

"*Touché*." Meg laughed. "And now that he knows, we'll have to kill him!" she added jokingly.

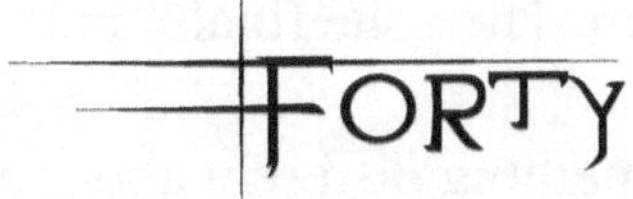FORTY

As the car slid smoothly to the curb, the doorman stepped out of the building and opened the back door, when it came to a complete stop. "Good evening, sir!"

"Good evening, Lawrence." Peter emerged out of the backseat and stepped onto the curb. He bent down and smiled at his driver thru the open door. "I'll call you when I'm ready." He said.

The man nodded and the doorman shut the rear door, quickened his step and opened the glass door to the highrise, just as Peter reached it. As he strolled past him, he pressed a hundred-dollar bill in the man's gloved hand.

"Thank *you* sir!" the doorman called to him, as he headed to the elevator.

"Your always welcome, Lawrence." He called back and pushed the button. The doors opened at once, almost soundlessly, as if it were waiting there just for him. He stepped inside, punched in *her* floor number and after the doors closed, the car began to move upward. Once it stopped and the doors opened again, he stepped out into her private foyer and pushed the doorbell.

She was waiting for him; he could tell by the happy look on her face, the moment she opened the door. There was a brief hesitation and then she launched herself forward and threw her arms around his neck, hugging him tighter than she ever had, raining his face with kisses.

"Oh my *darling*, I'm so glad you're okay!" she said with emotion.

He wasn't expecting this much of a reaction from her, after all it had *only* been a couple of weeks, since they'd last seen each other. So without hesitation he wrapped his arms around her just as tight and they stood that way for a moment on her doorstep. Then she finally pulled back, just enough to be face-to-face.

There was a hint of something different about her tonight, he noticed. Those exotic eyes of hers were dancing just a bit. Her dark hair which was always sculpted to the nines, was pulled back in a ponytail and her famous face was scrubbed clean, void of any makeup. To him, she was perfect this way, just being her natural self and not the persona she played to the public.

"I've *missed* you Peter." She said.

 He returned her smile with one of his own and replied, "I've missed you too, *Lola*!"

 Forty-One

George headed to the back terrace shortly after nine, toting a bottle of ice-cold beer in each hand. He gave one to Ken, who was already seated and was puffing mindlessly on a cigar. He took it gladly from him, twisted the top and deposited it in the ashtray on the side table to his left. George took a seat and glanced over at Ken, as he tossed his cap with it. The man seemed a bit preoccupied in the mind, as he tilted the bottle up and took a long pull of his first drink.

"Everything alright?" George asked, a little concerned. "Margot ok?"

Ken swallowed and rested the bottle on his jean-clad leg and winced a little at the bite of the yeast. "She's sleeping." He said, still staring straight ahead at the dark vast gardens beyond. "She won't be up for a while. I made her take one of them *magic* pills that the doc prescribed, that will put her out when she doesn't want to do it by herself."

George nodded. "She was animated when I was in earlier. I found myself almost wishing I had grinded up some valium in her dinner before I gave it to her."

Ken chuckled. "You make any leeway with her about seeing a therapist?"

"That's what she got so wound up about. She doesn't see any *need* to meet with one. She says she's fine and everybody is overreacting."

"Of course she *thinks* she's fine." Ken said. "She also *thinks* that tomorrow morning she's going to get out of that bed and walk across the hall to her office and conduct business as usual."

"I'm sure you shot that down." George smiled.

"Oh *hell* yeah! She's all worried that the world is going to collapse without her for a few days." Ken took another sip of his beer.

"I've been in the office twenty times today and everything is running smoothly. She seriously has nothing pressing to worry about."

"I know that," Ken said, turning to him finally. "It's not me you gotta convince! I caught her up earlier, trying to sneak across the hall to her office. I chased her back to her room and told her that's what answering machines were for. She tried to argue the fact that it was *just* across the hall. She wanted to *debate* with me about *what* the hell the *difference* was between sitting *up* in bed and sitting *up* in her office chair. It's safe to say, she wasn't too happy with me right then."

"If she got up out of bed every time the phone rang in that office, she'd never get any rest." George said.

"That was my point, *exactly*." Ken agreed.

"Speaking of the phone," George said, turning to glance behind them, to make sure they were still alone. "There was a message on the recorder I caught right before coming out here, that I think ties in to Margot's little *jaunt* to Washington."

Ken was about to take a sip of his beer when he paused and looked over at him.

"What kind of message?"

"It was a message to Margot from a secretary who was calling on behalf of *Judge Frederick*." George said. "The *Judge* who signed the exhumation paper?" Ken asked.

When George nodded he continued. "So he's still alive?"

"Sounds like but might not be for very long. The secretary didn't go into detail but mentioned in her message that he was *indisposed* at the moment and unable to return her call due to *ongoing* medical issues."

"What's he got to be by now? Eighty? Ninety?" Ken asked.

"Something like that."

"You think he's still working the bench? Otherwise why would he need a secretary?" Ken mused.

George shrugged his shoulders. "I guess as long as his mind stays sharp, what else is there to do?"

There was a short pause as they both sipped quietly on their beer and stared out into the night.

"Time might be running out when it comes to questioning him about the past." Ken was the first to break the silence. "Better let Margot know about it tomorrow morning if that's her intent for contacting him. I guess if anyone has the answers as to why Frank had his daughter's casket dug up, it would be him, since he signed the order."

"You think it's in Margot's best interest—emotionally—to be talking to the Judge about that right now?" George asked.

Ken took a few extra puffs off his cigar before he turned and spoke. "Looks like we *might* not have a choice. The man is more apt to talk to her, than to us."

"That's true."

"Now when it comes to the FBI and their little tricks…well, they just have no idea *who* they're messing with!" Ken said and smiled in a menacing way before he took another sip of his beer.

The edginess in his voice made George curious. "Why, what are you thinking?"

"It's not *what* I'm thinking, it's what I *know*." Ken said. "First thing in the morning, I'm going to call on this Agent Fields and ask her *why* she gave my wife a glass of water!"

George sat there for all of a half second, thinking that Ken was trying to be funny. Then for the other half, he wondered if he was beginning to lose his mind.

"Let me get this straight." He finally spoke up. "Your *pissed* because they offered Margot a glass of water?"

Ken nodded. "It would have been different if they'd offered her a *bottle* but she *specifically* told me it was a *glass,* that the male agent brought in."

"Okay, Sherlock Holmes. If I didn't know you so well, I'd think that you need to join your wife in therapy but my gut says this glass of water has some *meaning* behind it?"

"It does." Ken said, nodding his head and turning to look at him. "When I was talking to Margot earlier, I asked her to go over her visit again with the FBI. It just so happens at the time; I was handing her a cold glass of water to take her pill with. I guess it triggered something she forgot about, from the interview. Seems that towards the end of it, when she started getting all emotional, the male who was the forensics agent, disappeared and returned with a glass of water while the woman stayed behind and tried to comfort her. The *slick* little bastards!"

George studied Ken for a second and wondered what part of the story he missed.

"Ok, I'm *completely* lost here." George said. "Why would the FBI be *slick bastards* for giving Margot a glass of water?"

"Because, it's one of the oldest tricks in the lawman's book." Ken said. "If you have no intentions or suspicions towards the subject your questioning, you offer them a *bottle* of water. When you want to obtain *DNA*, you give them a *glass*."

George didn't respond right away. Maybe it was because his mouth was hanging open. "What did you just say? *Are you serious*?"

"I've been doing this for a long time, *son*!" Ken simply replied.

"But *why*?" George was literally blown away by what he was hearing. "Why would they *illegally* take her DNA?"

"They didn't take it *illegally*." Ken said, looking over at him. "Margot *gave* it to them *willingly* when she picked up the glass they offered and drank from it. It's no different than her unwrapping a piece of gum and throwing the wrapper in their trash. They can do anything they want with it because it becomes automatically their property, when she *leaves* it behind."

Silence filled the terrace for a full minute. Finally, George found his words.

"This sounds *scary*, Ken. Just what in the *hell* would they want Margot's DNA for?"

Ken took the last puff from his cigar, then stubbed the fire out in the ashtray. He looked over at George with equal fire in his dark eyes.

"That, my boy, is *exactly* what I'm wanting to know!" he said.

FORTY-TWO

Brandon was rocking out to a Cd from Candlebox, as he swept up sawdust. With excellent music and no interruptions, the morning spent in the workshop had turned out to be quite productive after all. He'd gotten all the pieces to Sage's desk cut out and they were lying in sections on the table, ready to be put together. At this rate, he might be able to start staining it, by the beginning of next week.

When he turned to grab the dustpan, he saw Hans coming through the door. He had a silly grin on his face. Brandon abandoned the dustpan and instead walked over to the control panel and turned the volume down. The music now wavered in the background.

"I see you made it back in one piece." Brandon said, glancing his way.

Hans grabbed the dustpan and met him halfway. "Of course I did sir. It was a pleasant ride. Miss Courtney and Miss Meg are quite charming."

Brandon stopped sweeping and looked at Hans.

"That's part of their *trap*, Hans. They go to school to learn how to be charming. It's a way of luring you in to trusting them, so you'll spill your guts. Sounds like your falling for it."

"My lips are sealed, sir!" He replied, the grin still intact.

"They better be. You need to take this seriously. You better watch out for Courtney, she's smooth. How do you think she got the network to pay her so damn much, to sit in a chair and run her mouth?"

"By having talent sir?" Hans answered with a touch of sarcasm. He walked the dustpan over to the trash container and dumped it.

"Talent my ass." Brandon said, leaning the broom against the wall by the workbench. "She's reading a script off a *damn* teleprompter!"

"A tele—who?" Hans asked.

"Never mind." Brandon said and shook his head. "So what is happening right now? Are they tromping all over my home, poking their noses in every room and closet?"

"No sir, as a matter of fact, they are having some refreshments with Miss Sage on the back patio."

"*Humph.*" Brandon said and began muttering under his breath. "It's only a matter of time before Courtney starts snooping!"

"What was that sir?" Hans asked, not quite sure what he said.

"I'm curious." Brandon said, instead. "Does refreshments include some afternoon wine?"

"Yes sir, I believe so." Hans confirmed, with a perplexed look on his face. "Lydia is in full control of Master Tristan and I'm back-up, so you two can relax."

"That's not *what* I'm getting at. Sage can have wine whenever she wants. It's the loose tongue that comes with it. I hope she doesn't tell them *too* much."

"I think they will be fine sir. Dinner is not far off…and speaking of, it's the sole reason why I came out here. You are taking your dinner in the office and not *inside* with the women, correct?"

"*Absolutely* correct, Hans! That's the *plan* remember? For me to stay as *far* away from either one of them, as I can. You and Lydia said it was only for *two* days!" Brandon reminded him.

"Just confirming sir, that you didn't have a change of heart." Hans said.

"Do I *look* like the freaking *Grinch* to you Hans?"

"Well sir, now that you mention it…" he said with a grin.

Brandon purposely ignored him, walked over to the control panel and turned the music back up. Candlebox was belting out one of his old favorites—*Bitches Brewin'*.

How appropriate, he thought.

 That was Hans cue to exit and he quickly disappeared thru the door.

Much later, he appeared again, this time motioning to him that his dinner had arrived! Brandon again cut the volume to his music and the workshop grew silent. He surveyed the pieces he'd already begun assembling a few seconds longer and then he headed to the office. He noticed it was close to dusk outside, when he'd stepped inside the bathroom to wash up.

No wonder he was starving!

The aroma of something delicious hit his nostrils the second he entered the office. Laid out like the perfect picture on the desk, was all the fixings of a pot roast—tender beef, potatoes, carrots, green beans and a slice of cornbread—steaming on a plate. A glass of iced tea sat next to it. He sat down and dove in.

"Lydia has outdone herself on dinner this fine evening, sir." Hans commented.

"Lydia outdoes herself *every* night, Hans!" Brandon said, in-between chewing.

"Of course she does sir. Miss Courtney and Miss Meg thought so too."

Brandon paused in-between bites to speak. "Everybody already ate inside?"

"Yes sir, they finished up about an hour ago."

"What are they doing now?"

"They have retired to the space on the balcony that you created for Miss Sage. They are sitting around the fire and sharing a bottle of wine. Baby Tristan made an appearance and was coddled and kissed from his fingers, down to his little toes, by his great aunts. They do adore him sir." Hans smiled.

Brandon grunted as he chewed. "You know Hans, I've been thinking." He said, changing the subject.

"Yes, sir?"

"I think maybe I want to invest in some sort of tunnel." He said, pausing from shoveling food in, to take a long drink of the tea.

"A tunnel sir?"

"Yes, you know, sort of like the one my grandfather escaped through, from the Benenati house?"

"Sir?" Hans questioned, definitely looking puzzled. "Not an *underground* tunnel." He added. "One that's *above* the ground."

"For what purpose sir?" Hans asked, sounding a little uneasy. "To escape?"

"No, not necessarily. I'm talking about one that's attached from the barn to the cabin. Something that can be used as safe travel between the buildings. Think about it…during the winter it wouldn't have to be shoveled. You could just walk right out to the barn without even trudging through the snow and if I wanted to stay out here late at night, it would make it safe for any of us to walk to and from the barn, without the worry of wild animals near."

Hans obviously was seeing his vision by the expression on his face.

"I could see something like that being useful, sir."

"If I had a tunnel I wouldn't have to worry about how late it is."

"No sir, you wouldn't."

"I could use solar grids to light it up, so there would be no need for electric."

"Why that's a splendid idea sir." Hans agreed.

Brandon's cell interrupted him before he could respond. It was Madison.

"Hold on, I gotta take this." He said to Hans.

"*Madison.*" He said into the phone.

"I have some rather *interesting* information that I thought you'd like to hear about." The PI said.

"I'm always interested in beneficial information." Brandon retorted.

"First off, Victor's live-in love and his daughter were at his last known residence the night the news broke that he'd been shanked. A few days later, they were gone. No hints, no traces, no notes left behind, no nothing. There was a substantial number of belongings that were left in the house. I got a look at the inventory list and other than a few personal items that can't be accounted for, everything else was—furniture, food, TV's, clothing, toys of the child's."

"What about photo albums?" Brandon intervened. "Was any personal family photo albums listed on that inventory sheet?"

"None whatsoever." Madison said.

"She left that house alive." Brandon stated.

"*Or* she was smuggled out in a body bag along with her daughter, by Victor's mobster friends and they destroyed them." Madison offered.

"To make people like us *think* that she's still alive."

"Absolutely. To throw us off the trail my friend. It's a known fact these days that the police start looking for photo albums, when someone disappears. It's one of the most *common* things a person will take with them, other than their cell, keys, purse or wallet."

"Which her purse was probably not on that list either." Brandon said.

"Right you are again. Also there was not any documentation or files found either. No birth certificates, no shot records, nothing that was personal on either the mother or the daughter."

"More obvious signs that she fled with the kid into the night somewhere."

"That would be my guess." Madison agreed. "And it just keeps getting better."

"How so?" Brandon asked.

"The FBI agent who died in Venice?"

"Yeah?"

"I talked to my friends who use to work with him. They both confirmed at the time he died, he was working on a high-priority case."

"Really?" Brandon said, as he stopped eating altogether. "Don't tell me, it was the investigation into Victor Rocha's crimes." Brandon offered.

"No, it's something you'd *never* guess." Madison said. "Agent Greene was *lead* investigator on the plane crash that your wife's *parents* were on."

FORTY-THREE

Lola lie on her back on the bed, naked, just staring at the ceiling. It was close to four in the morning and Peter had left hours ago, leaving her in a state of panic.

Sleep was not going to come easy tonight because her mind was racing in circles, rehashing everything that he had told her, surrounding his life-altering night, at Margot Hartford's Mansion.

The story was unbelievable from the start and the cast of characters that had somehow assembled under one roof—added to it. As Peter got deeper into the story and told her about the one Charlie had to tell, she felt the chill of dread creep slowly up her spine.

The famous Benenati murders in Italy, were pretty well-known worldwide, thanks to a few dozen documentaries that had been made over the years. Every one of those airings, always closed with the question, *"Whatever happened to those poor Benenati children?"* And now, here sat Peter in her living room earlier tonight, claiming to *know* the very answer, that had mystified millions of people for years.

The fact that his wife Meg and her agent Charlie, were *both* living under assumed identities and were really *two* of the *three* missing Benenati children, was incredible enough to believe. Then he revealed that Sage Cassava's father was the *third* child, the one who had died in a plane crash, when she was just eight. And as if that wasn't enough to blow her mind, he then told her about *Courtney,* who was really *Isabella*—the missing *love* child, whose father was the late Everett Calhoun, Brandon Parrish's grandfather. Of course, after telling her all this, he had sworn her to absolute secrecy. Since most of the people involved were close friends and acquaintances of hers, who the hell was she going to tell? And besides, Lola had something else much more *important* on her mind, then spreading rumors that could have an indirect hand, in ruining her career. Because landing the *lead* in the *Stranded* saga that Sage had created, would be the opportunity of a lifetime. It was simply a no-brainer. Especially when the male lead was a legendary actor like Brandon Parrish. With his name on the bill, fans would come by the *thousands* to watch it—no, make that by the *millions*. A role such as this one, would send her celeb status, sky rocketing in the numbers game. It would finally give her a chance to prove that she could act. That she wasn't just another voluptuous, air-headed actress who made the grade because she had big tits, a healthy rump and curves in all the right places. No, this would be her chance to show everyone what she was made of. It was just within her grasp, the closest it's ever been in her life and she would do everything in her power to not let *anything* get in her way.

A sequel was already in the works and rumor has it, that Sage was possibly going to add even as many as *two* more books to the storyline. That meant *guaranteed* work for a while. And of course *other* offers would pour in, once this franchise was done. The possibilities were endless which was *why* she had to stay quiet for now.

Not dumb but quiet.

She let out a weary sigh and sat up. She grabbed her terry cloth robe from the foot of the bed and slipped her arms inside the sleeves. She leaned over and pulled the top drawer of her nightstand open and extracted a silver case. She took one of the cigarettes from inside, returned the case to the drawer and closed it. She lit it up, taking a few deep draws before abandoning the lighter on the nightstand and grabbing her empty wine glass. She blew out a trail of smoke as she stood up and headed to the kitchen. After filling her glass from the chilled bottle in the fridge, she left and headed back to the master, sipping as she walked, her mind ever working. Instead of returning to her bed, she wondered over to the desk and sat. She took a couple more drags of her cigarette, then laid the butt on the lip of the ashtray, next to her laptop. She also abandoned the wine glass and began tapping on the keys, *curiosity* overtaking her.

Within a matter of minutes Lola was able to bring up a newspaper article dated back in the early 70s. The piece was covering a charity event, along with its A-list of attendees. It included a picture with several men, dressed in black tuxedos, standing shoulder-to-shoulder, in a straight line, facing the camera. The Hollywood playboy, Everett Calhoun and his partner, the billionaire business tycoon, Frank Hartford, were among the seventeen strangers who were spotlighted. Lola continued tapping the plus key, zooming closer. When the two were the only ones filling her screen, Lola reclaimed her cigarette and smoked it, as she studied their faces, *intently*.

FORTY-FOUR

Any time Agent Belinda Fields was knee-deep in a case, or had trouble making the pieces fit, she couldn't sleep. Years ago she'd learned not to fight it, just to give in because her relentless mind had its own agenda. And it wasn't about to let her rest, until she figured it out. This morning was one of those days.

Up since five AM and in a recliner at home, she was still clad in pajamas, re-reading the thick file the FBI had compiled on the Hartford's, when her cell began to vibrate around ten. She sat straight up and planted her feet on the floor, when she saw the contact's name, that filled the LED screen.

"Sorry to bother you, Agent Fields, but something has come up that you should be aware of." Director DiBernardo said, in his distinguished, baritone voice.

"It's not a bother, sir." She said, quickly. For her boss to call her at home, on the only day she'd had off in weeks, meant the nature of his call must be important. "I just got off the phone with a man by the name of Ken Barker. He's the *husband* of Margot Hartford, who you interviewed a few days ago?"

"Yes sir."

"Apparently he called in this morning looking *specifically* for you! Since you're out today and he was threatening to sic his attorneys on us, the call got re-routed to me—at *home*!"

Belinda cleared her throat. "So sorry sir," she began

"He was not a very *happy* man, Agent Fields." He said, before she could speak another word. "He claims his wife was not only disrespected while in *our* care yesterday but that you *and* Agent Metz tricked her into leaving her DNA behind on a glass! He's demanding to know why."

"How in the hell…?" she said.

"He's a retired *sheriff*!" He said, answering the question she never got to finish. "and he's been in law enforcement for thirty-eight years. Apparently he just retired from a small town out west, in Montana. His peers describe him as extremely sharp for a country boy, with an incredible nose for sniffing out bullshit, so you need to be careful with this one. He's an old hat to our tactics and obviously knew the right questions to ask his wife, upon her return home. Seems she took a spill after leaving your office, which could be why he was so damn pissed. He says she collapsed at the airport in Florida and was rushed to the hospital."

"Oh no!" Belinda said. "Is she alright?"

During the interview, in the beginning, Margot Hartford had been so terribly uncooperative, so rigid and angry. But once she'd laid eyes on that gold heart that Metz had handed her, the hard shell had cracked—without warning—right in front of Belinda. She saw the immense pain pass for a moment too long, in the eyes of a mother, who was still in a great deal of pain, over losing her daughter. It had touched her in a way, like no other case had and she'd been feeling crummy about it ever since. Which was why she had spent half of her morning *off,* re-reading about the Hartford case, hoping to find something that she hadn't seen before.

"She's at home resting after a few days in the hospital. Emotional stress was the bigger factor of her diagnosis. If Mr. Barker wanted to pursue this, he wouldn't have a problem finding a *tight-ass* lawyer, who would gladly take the case and make it *difficult* for us to continue our investigation, in a timely manner."

"Sir, I already discussed legal representation with Mrs. Hartford during the interview."

There was a pause on the other end of the line.

"The interview I assume was recorded?" Director DiBernardo asked.

"Yes sir." Fields said.

"Both audio *and* video?"

"Yes sir and in that recording, Mrs. Hartford agreed with me that involving any lawyers on her behalf, would impede our investigation. She seemed as anxious as we are to progress forward, so that *both* her *and* her granddaughter, could finally have some kind of closure. When she left us, she seemed pretty steady."

"When did you end the recording?"

"After she left the room, as per policy sir."

"So Agent Metz is *recorded*, offering her the *glass* of water, on a *copy* that was *archived* and logged into our central file system, by *you* yesterday, *correct*?" There was a second of silence again on the line. Belinda closed her eyes and nervously pinched the bridge of her nose in frustration, with her free hand. The message he had wanted in a roundabout-way, to convey to her, had come through loud and clear. "And per policy, it caught the tech on it, taking the glass by clamps and putting it into a bag. I already watched it, Agent Fields and their attorney would be able to *view* it as well, should *he* pursue it. So let's not *poke* the bear. I'm also told that our Mr. Barker has some pretty good *political* ties that, as you well know, is who *we* take our orders from. I can't express enough, how *important* it is, that we find that damn plane, Agent Fields. It's been an ugly mark on this bureau long enough, especially with the recent *findings* on Agent Greene!" There was another short pause and Belinda could hear what sounded like a shuffling of papers on the other end. "I *think* I may have derailed this problem *temporarily*—enough to *buy* us some time to get this show on the road. Did you *get* the results back yet from the lab?" He sounded annoyed.

"No sir, not yet."

"Notify me the *second* you do!" he said curtly.

"Yes sir!"

The phone went dead in her ear. She cursed silently and hung up on her end.

Ten minutes later the phone rang again. This time it was a private number that shared no ID information. She snatched it up.

"*Fields*." She said.

"It's Agent Metz." He said, speaking quickly. She wondered if he was calling to tell her, he'd just gotten his ass chewed by the director as well. Instead, his next sentence caught her by surprise. "The *results* are back on the *DNA* comparison!"

 FORTY-FIVE

"Say something!" Ava demanded, where she stood next to Charlie, her arms crossed, with a self-satisfied grin on her face.

"Play it again." Charlie said, leaning back in his office chair.

Ava let out an overdramatic sigh, uncrossed her arms and leaned in to maneuver the mouse. Lola's audition video started over. Charlie watched intently and—he couldn't lie—he was floored by what he was seeing.

First off, Lola didn't *look* like the *Lola* that he knew—on the screen. It was almost like looking at her twin but with all the *opposite* coloring. Her eyes were no longer dark chocolate brown but blue, her face—no, her *skin*—were several shades lighter and her dark hair had been replaced by a blonde wig that closely resembled Sage's hair. Her wardrobe consisted of a jogging outfit in a deep gray, that cleverly hid all her curvy assets. In other words, her tits and ass weren't on *display*, as usually was the case, when Lola was allowed to dress herself. Because of the bagginess of the outfit, she looked almost like a *body* double of the *real* Sage.

He tried to shut out the perfect visual image, long enough to get a feel, of what she sounded like. As she spoke her lines to the camera, the flirty, *heavy* tone of her voice she was famous for, was gone and in its place, was this light, slower-paced, *sweet* sound that was laced with innocence. In fact, it took him the third time of viewing it, before he realized she was *emulating* Sage to a tee and the problem was, *no one*, outside of Sage and their immediate family, knew that the story Stranded was based on her *and* Brandon's *real* life. So who told Lola to project this image so *like* his niece, that it was downright *creepy*?

When the piece ended again, he shook his head slowly in disbelief while Ava fidgeted at his side.

"Admit it!" she insisted, re-crossing her arms and staring him down. "Go on!"

"Has Lola had personal access to the author?" he asked, right off the bat.

"What do you mean?" Ava asked, drawing her brows together.

"Did she *talk* to the author, Sage Cassava, prior to this screen test?"

"No, not that I know of. Why?"

"Who told her to *act* like that?"

"Nobody did. That was what she got from reading the character's personality from the script."

"How long has she had access to the script?" Charlie asked.

"Two hours." Ava said. "The first hour was in makeup, the second in wardrobe."

"And wardrobe came up with this look?" He asked.

"Not entirely! Fiona and her team got the description from the book and then Lola added some of her personal touches. *Why*?"

"Has Lola *read* the book?"

"Yes, as a matter of fact she has. She mentioned it when I talked with her about the screen test, at our first meeting. You know, one of her best friends is Meg Jackson. Her husband Peter is the very man who *published* Sage's book."

"Hmmm." Charlie said.

"What is *that* supposed to mean? That '*hmmm*' part?"

"It just means that I don't know how in the hell you pulled this off, Ava…," he began, covering up the fact that he was suddenly suspicious of Lola's intentions. Why would she pick Sage to mimic her traits, if she had no *idea* she was the female in the storyline?

Ava pointed at Lola on the monitor. "I didn't *pull* it off, *she* did. I told you that you were truly underestimating her ability to act in *any* role she puts her mind to. This is my proof!"

Charlie shook his head again from side to side, staring transfixed at Lola's motionless image, where the video stopped.

"She's convincing," he finally said.

"More than *convincing*!" Ava said. "She's your *lead* and you *know* it!"

Charlie continued to stare at the screen, going over a criteria list, he'd stored in his brain. So far, with what he'd seen of Lola's test shot, she checked off several of the *must-haves* on that list.

"Charlie Vega, I can *see* your mind smoking. *Talk to me!*"

Charlie tore his eyes away from the monitor long enough to see that the arrogant smirk on her face was still there. It was the *I-told-you-so* grin and she had every right to bear it. Lola and Ava both had made him literally *eat* his words about her not fitting the part. And as much as he hated to *ever* be proved wrong, he couldn't deny that Lola had nailed it.

"Brandon is going to *shit*!" he simply said.

Ava let out a squeal, bent down to his level in the chair and planted a smooth kiss full on his lips!

FORTY-SIX

Mid-morning, Courtney made her excuses to visit the ladies room and left Sage and Meg on the back deck, chatting away. She stepped inside the double doors, walked through the expanse of the living room, through the hall, into the kitchen and down another hall to the door on the left, that was currently serving as her temporary bedroom. It was quite a jaunt from one end of the cabin to the other. No wonder everyone who lived under its roof stayed fit. You got quite a workout just navigating your way around, on a daily basis.

She shut the door softly behind her and went straight to the nightstand, where she had left her cell phone charging. She sat on the edge of the bed, picked it up and pressed the button on the side, to light up the screen. She skimmed through her messages and found none of them to be *that* important. Until she came to the one from her friend in the graphics department, who she'd asked to *enhance* the piece from the footage of the dead woman's leg, back in Kenya. She read the text twice.

Hey Courtney, enhanced the piece you sent me
to your specifications. Can't send it from here.
You know why. Will email it to you once I get
home later this evening from my comp. Tia!

Courtney had forgotten all about asking for this small favor. With everything going on surrounding Karly's arrest and fleeing New York, it had completely slipped her mind. She made a mental note inside her head, to make sure she checked her phone later for the promised image. In the meantime, she needed to get back to Meg and Sage on the terrace.

She laid her cell on the nightstand and walked around the beds, to the main door. She turned the knob and started to step one foot out in the hall, when she heard voices close by. She hesitated and listened.

"Are you sure they're not in the house?" It was Brandon speaking.

"Yes sir, I just checked on them before coming inside." The British accent was—no doubt Hans, that he was talking to.

"What's wrong with Margot?" Brandon asked.

"She had some kind of fainting spell at the airport." It was Lydia's southern voice that answered him. "She was taken by ambulance to the hospital and from there, they notified Ken."

"Is she okay?" Brandon asked, real concern in his voice.

"She is for right now. She called here yesterday, right before Courtney and Meg arrived. I wasn't going to ruin the day for her but Sage, she snuck up on me and overheard us talking. Anyway, I knew Margot wasn't giving me the full story, so I called George last night."

"What did he say?" Brandon asked.

"He said she was sneaking around and got herself *caught*, is what!" Lydia said. "She was *supposed* to be going to see a friend in Tennessee, at least that's what she told Ken and George anyway. Instead, she took a flight to Washington and met with the FBI!"

Courtney heard a veil of silence come over the cabin. It was so thick she was afraid to move. She took a step back anyway and prayed that the hinges would not make a sound as she closed the gap in the door, barely leaving a crack. She turned her face to the left and put her ear flat against the opening, so she could hear better.

"The *FBI*?" Brandon finally spoke.

"What on earth for?" Hans asked.

"George said they called and requested her to come. It has something to do with the seizure of that Pirate's lair in

Kenya, that's been all over the news. They found something in their camp that they *think* is somehow linked to Sage's mother."

Another few seconds of heavy silence filled her ear from the hallway. Courtney felt like she was breathing loud and that her heartbeat was doing the same. She couldn't *believe* what she was hearing and to validate it, goosebumps raised on both arms, when she thought about the plane number, hanging on the wall in the hut, she'd seen, back in Kenya.

"You haven't told Sage any of this?" It was Brandon's voice that was asking the question.

"*Heavens* no!" Lydia said.

"Good!" Brandon said, his tone thick with relief. "Don't say anything until *they* leave."

"I'm not saying *anything* a 'tall!" Lydia said. "It's not *my* place. Margot *needs* to do that!"

"I agree." Hans said.

"So did George tell you what it was they found?"

Before Lydia could answer, the door pushed with force into the side of Courtney's face and literally knocked her backward. Meg appeared in the opening, with a look of surprise on her face.

"*OMG!*" she exclaimed rather loudly. "Are *you* alright?"

"*Damn!*" was all she could reply at the moment while she smartly rubbed the throbbing side of her face, where the door had connected with her cheek.

Within seconds, Lydia, Hans and Brandon appeared behind Meg in the hallway.

"I had *no* idea you were *behind* the door when I went to open it, I swear!" Meg said again, coming closer, concerned.

"Are you hurt, *dear*?" Lydia asked, a look of worry on her face.

"No, I'll be fine." Courtney said, as she waved them away, hoping that everyone would just let it go.

"What *happened*?" Lydia asked, stepping into the room.
"I was coming in and she was…" Meg stopped
midsentence, when Courtney shot her a look.
"*Coming* out." Courtney finished for her, still massaging
the area.
"I'm *terribly* sorry!" Meg said. "I swear I had *no* idea you
were even *in* here! I thought you went to the *other* restroom
in the hall. That's why I came to this one."
Courtney's eyes locked with Brandon's. He stayed back,
observing from the hallway, with a look on his face that
was not of concern but *suspicion* and Meg's comments just
kept adding fuel to the fire. He wasn't easily fooled and it
didn't take long for him to connect the dots either. "Maybe
you'd better sit down for a moment, madam!" Hans urged.
He stepped closer to her, stopping just inside the doorway,
temporarily blocking her view of Brandon. "I'll get you
some ice." Lydia said and turned to head to the kitchen.
"I'm fine, *really*." She continued to play it down. Han's
expression was of deep concern, as he ignored her
protests and stepped closer into the room to examine her
cheek. In doing so, it gave her a clear shot of the hallway.
She *dared* to glance once more in Brandon's direction but
when she did, to her surprise, he was already *gone*!

FORTY-SEVEN

Brandon stomped his way furiously out to the barn. He was livid—*seething* with rage—and it was the *only* place he could go right now, to let off some steam. Or at least punch a wall or two without anyone hearing. But instead he cursed out loud, as he entered the vacant structure, his voice echoing off the dead space, overhead.

It didn't take a rocket scientist to figure out that Courtney *had* been spying on them from the bedroom across the hall. She'd had her ear *pressed* to the door, when Meg had tried to enter. Otherwise, if she'd been walking straight ahead, her injuries would have consisted of a busted nose instead of a red angry lump, that was rising on the *side* of her cheek.

Lord only knows how much of their conversation she'd heard. With his luck, probably *everything*. Even if it had been just a sentence, it was *one* too many.

This was exactly *why* he did not want *her* or Meg as a guest in his home. Both were journalists, out for *any* tidbit of information that they could report. They were nothing but trouble and Courtney proved that just now.

Isabella, my ass!

Courtney didn't *act* like she had *his* grandfather's blood running through her veins. And she *damn* sure didn't have this family's best interests at heart! In fact, if the truth be known, the only reason she'd accepted the invite to the cabin, was blatantly obvious! If Lydia and Hans believed she was here to help sort out this family drama, they were *dead* wrong! She was only here to spy and gather data for a story that would take the spotlight off her *narcissistic* ass and put it front and center, on *his* family. Brandon cursed again to himself as he walked over to the bar and grabbed a beer from the fridge. He had it halfway to his lips, when his eyes caught the ticker tape on the TV screen.

Somalia Pirates Captured Off the Coast of Kenya!!!
Legendary Hideout Found and Seized by US Military!!!
And right then Courtney Curwin's face appeared on the screen. She was talking animatedly in a microphone, but he couldn't make out a word she was saying because the volume was muted. Curious now, he searched out the remote and unmuted the volume.

It was what the stations called a *teaser*, a sneak peak of what was coming up in an hour, on the nightly news. A video of Courtney flashed on the screen and there she stood, in all her glory, somewhere in a jungle in *Africa*, spewing some bullshit about pirates. Lydia had said she'd been coming back from *location* when she'd basically forced him to agree to this bullshit idea in the first place. The more highlights he heard in the teaser, the more he was further convinced, that little old *frail* Isabella was not here to *support* her new nephew and his wife. *Hell* no, *all* she was here for, was to gather *more* information for her *already* existing headliner and it just fueled the anger that was already brewing within!

 Forty-Eight

An hour later, Courtney slipped quietly out the back door of the cabin, the crisp air immediately nipped at her exposed skin. She pulled on the collar of her jacket, bringing it tighter up against her bare neck and took a quick scan of the area around her. Since her short arrival in Montana over twenty-four hours ago, she had learned rather quickly, that it's nights were a polar *opposite* in temperature, compared to its warm, sunny days, at this time of year.

Since it was well into the evening hour, the dew had already set in, making the emerald grass look as if it were glistening under the moonlight. The hoot of an owl echoed in the distance, while the sound of crickets hummed all around her in rhythm. Beyond the clearing of the property, the forest that bordered either side, no longer projected that fairytale-like image of more friendly pines, as it had in the day time. In fact, *even* the mountains now looked intimidating and spooky like the forest did from ground level. The warning Hans had given her and Meg about the dangers of wild animals that could be prowling at night, popped up in her mind. At the time, she hadn't given it a second thought because she'd *never* expected to be on ground level past dark…but, now *here* she was! Putting herself out there.

But she quickly reminded herself about the electric sensors that Sage said had been installed throughout the perimeter of the property—*courtesy* of Brandon—as a deterrent from any animals coming *too* close to the cabin. And it seemed to have worked, she'd said, because they hadn't seen any in a while, not even the deer. Courtney didn't speak her thoughts at the time but knowing Brandon, it was also probably some high-tech system that was designed to keep out the *human* race as well. Along with the tall tale he'd instructed Hans to tell them about dangerous animals prowling at night, that would keep *ordinary* women inside, shaking with fear. Well, Courtney was no *ordinary* woman and she wasn't afraid to take the walk needed to reach the barn.

Armed with mace in one hand and a pen flashlight in the other, Courtney cursed under her breath and walked softly across the span of the back deck, in the dark. She did not dare turn on the beam of light until she'd safely cleared the windows of the cabin, for fear someone inside might see it. The last thing she wanted to do was alert anyone of her absence—at least for the next twenty minutes anyway. She took the deck stairs, stepped down into the dewy grass and began walking briskly towards the direction of the barn. Continuously alert, she scanned the dark perimeter around her—checking in front, back and side-to-side, straining her ears, listening for any sounds of unusual rustling or movement.

The distance to the barn in the daylight, hadn't seemed that far from the cabin. But now, walking it at night, alone, it seemed further than the actual three hundred-foot span. Two different times she thought about turning around. She wasn't the typical scaredy-cat but she wasn't a damn *fool* either. She'd been in enough sketchy situations because of her career and where it took her, to know better than to be an easy target. But the little voice inside wouldn't allow her to back out now, so she listened to it and kept going.

Thank God someone had left the outside light burning above the outbuilding's main door because it served as a welcoming beacon—up ahead—to guide her. Apparently it had been on for a while because when she got closer, she could see a cluster of moths gathered under its glow. She mumbled a silent prayer as she reached out and grasped the cold knob, hoping like hell that it wasn't locked. To her relief, it turned with ease, all the way to the right. She wasn't expecting the door to be so heavy and it took a considerable effort on her part to open it and *keep* it that way while she stepped inside. The extra weight made it even harder on the inside to close quietly. What in the *hell*, she wondered, was Brandon trying to keep out, that made him end up installing a door like that?

Then just as quickly, the story of Jeb Perkins entered her mind. This was where the psycho handyman had taken Sage, bleeding and bruised and scared to death. It's where Brandon had saved her and baby Tristan's life. Suddenly the heavy door with two deadbolts and a steel bar made perfect sense on an old pole barn. Then she turned around and realized, there was nothing *old* about it.

The immediate space laid out in front of her was a huge, open, two-story floor plan just like the cabin. The first part that caught her eye, was a small fleet of cars that were parked neatly under a second story balcony, to her immediate right. Among them, were the limo Hans had used to pick them up from the airport, as well as a black Tahoe, a black Range Rover and a John Deere tractor. There was a nightlight-type fixture above them on the wall, that illuminated the area in a warm glow that bounced off the shiny hoods.

She looked further to the right and caught sight of the hand carved stairway, that led to the upper floor. It looked like it had been designed for a real treehouse that was located somewhere in an enchanted forest. The balcony overhead had been structured with the same railing, in a very rustic style. Beyond, it was complete darkness, giving no hint of what was up there. It didn't matter anyway; Brandon was who she'd come to see.

More of Brandon's obsession for security, was evident in the initial entry of the barn. To her left on the wall at eye level, was a massive panel, lit up about three quarters of its span and was covered with green, LED lights. The sound of a TV, came from a dimly lit hallway straight ahead.

Without further hesitation, she headed in that direction and soon spotted a pool of light, spilling from a doorway on the left.

This was where she found him.

He had his back to her and was watching something intently on a huge flat screen, mounted on the far, right wall. She was surprised when she looked up and saw her *own* image staring back. It took another second for her to realize it was the segment on the Pirate's raid, she'd just covered in Kenya. The station had probably figured *now* was the best time to air it, hoping it would take the public's attention in another direction and away from the current story of their popular news anchor, who shot a woman in the leg. The topic of Pirates would appeal to the audience more than a justifiable shooting, thanks to *Disney's* invention of the character, Jack Sparrow. She secretly hoped it worked so she could head back home tomorrow and get on with her life.

Before she could announce her presence, Brandon abruptly spun around, the sudden movement even making her flinch. His eyes were full of alarm and his body language looked stiff and on guard, when he caught sight of her.

"It's an extremely *bad* idea these days, to be *sneaking* up on me like that!" He warned, his tone not friendly at all. His arms that had been crossed when he'd turned, were now down at his sides, hands clenched in fists.

"I wasn't *sneaking*!" She said, going into defense mode. "I merely *walked* up to the door. You just didn't hear me because your *attention* was elsewhere!" She glanced up at the screen where the segment was still playing. He did the same and then they looked back at one another.

"*Africa*, eh?" He simply said, thru clenched teeth. His tone was accusing, *already,* as he nodded his head in the direction of the TV. If it was only one trait she admired about Brandon, it was the fact he wasn't one to beat around the bush. Just how she liked it!

Courtney nodded. "I was there, covering the investigation of the Pirate's lair, as I'm sure you know by now," she said, walking further into the room, closing the gap between them. She raised her hand and gestured at the footage of the horrible discovery outside of Kenya. "And I *know* what you're thinking." She said, coming to a stop just inches from him. "You don't think that it's a coincidence that Margot was just probed by the FBI, over that same Pirate's hideout, that I was just covering." She stopped squarely in front of him where he stood just inches from the desk. He really had nowhere to escape. A flicker of surprise registered in his eyes but only for a moment before the anger behind them, pushed through.

"What gave you *that* idea?" he demanded, crossing his arms.

"Lydia," she said, not letting him rile her. "I couldn't *help* but overhear what she was telling you, concerning Margot, when everyone thought I was *outside*!" It was meant to be a jab and by the look on his face, he wasn't *feeling* it.

"You're a *pro* at sticking your nose in where it *doesn't* belong, Courtney!" he said, his jaw twitching which was a sure sign that he was trying to keep control of his temper. "But then again, I shouldn't expect anything *less* from you!" he added.

"*Think* what you want of me, I frankly don't *give* a shit!" Courtney said, trying to keep her cool. "But it *wasn't* intentional and it's not *why* I came here!"

He gave her that look of doubt. "Of course it's not *why* you came here, Courtney." he said, his handsome face settling into a smirk. "The real reason you jumped on this opportunity, was so you could *pry* some information from my wife. That and you needed to get the *hell* out of town and hide. What's the matter? Don't you *like* being *hounded* by the press?"

"*Brandon...*"

"How does it *feel* to have them camping outside *your* front door?" he pushed, cutting her off. "Does it make you *feel* like a prisoner to the point, that you have to *leave* in order to find *peace*?"

Courtney studied him for a moment. She had to keep reminding herself that this was not just the *famous* Brandon Parrish she was talking to but her *blood* relation, her nephew, her half-brother's son and probably the only thing close to family, that she would ever have. Basically, she didn't want to burn a bridge that wasn't even built yet.

"Look Brandon, I *get* it that your pissed about the clusterfuck that we've both been thrown in to. Believe me when I tell you, that I'm *just* as pissed—if not *more*—than *you* are. At least *you* know your *true* birthright! I've lived my life believing that I was someone, that *suddenly* I am not! And with that being said, I didn't come out here tonight, to get in a war with you, over what I do for a living."

"I'm not discussing the details of Margot's FBI visit with you!" He said, shaking his head to convey his decision was firm.

"Sure you are," she said with confidence. "because what I'm about to tell *you,* will make you anything *but* speechless on the subject."

He just stared at her for a second, no doubt skeptical. And it was only in that moment that she realized, the late Everett Calhoun's *good* looks weren't the *only* genes he'd passed on to his grandson. It suddenly made complete sense *why* this so-called nephew of hers, was so *damn* famous. Brandon sincerely seemed to saturate the air around him with an unmistakable command of confidence and charisma, the same kind of dominate traits she'd been hearing about, when others had described the man *who* had given her life.

"You have ten minutes, Courtney!" he finally said, glancing at his watch, as he casually leaned a hip against the edge of the desk. He reached for a remote lying beside him and paused the segment on the TV.

The time stamp must also be a family trait, Courtney guessed. She'd taken the same '*let's get this over with*' attitude with Michael, whenever he interrupted her, putting a kink in her agenda. It clearly sent her the message that Brandon was of the opinion, that he had *better* things to do. She was about to change his mind.

"I *think* I have a pretty good idea *why* the FBI asked Margot to meet with them." she began, jumping straight to the point.

"You *think*?" he asked, his tone dripping with sarcasm.

"Yes Brandon, I *think*! The facts aren't all in yet *so* it's the only foundation I rely on until they do! That's *why* I used the word *think*. Now, are you going to pick apart every word I say or are you going to let me tell you what I *know*?"

He stared at her for a few seconds, jaw still twitching, then reluctantly nodded his head.

"*Thank you*!" she said with equal sarcasm and let out a heavy sigh. "I've wanted to talk to you about this since I arrived here. But you've been *hiding out* in this barn the *entire* time, making the opportunity next to impossible. That's when I realized, it was better anyway, if I just came out here to you. It gives us the privacy I need, for what I have to say."

"Which is?" he asked, interrupting her again.

"The Pirates lair outside of Kenya and the plane that Sage's parents were on, are somehow connected. I saw the proof while I was there *with* my own two eyes."

"What proof?" Brandon asked, obviously still not buying any of it.

"You remember the number that Ken found scribbled under the desk in Frank's old office? The one that opened the safe? It was the *serial* number of the plane that Sage's parents were on."

"Yeah, what about it?" he asked sarcastically and glanced again at his watch.

"That number was hanging *on* the wall in one of those huts *in* the lair." She said.

Brandon just stared at her with a blank look on his face, for all of thirty seconds. Then he spoke. "What in the *hell* are you talking about?"

"The flight *number* 317537 was *on,* what looked like a piece of *sheet* metal, *hanging* from the wall in one of the huts. It wasn't written, it looked like an *original*. It was mixed in with a bunch of maps and sailing coordinates, that were tacked up. It was in the shape of a perfect rectangle and looked as if someone had just cut it off the side of the plane."

"Is this a *joke*?" He still wasn't buying it.

"Don't *be* stupid!" she spat, slightly losing her temper. "I wouldn't *joke* about something as *delicate* as this. Regardless of what you think about *me,* I've come to really *care* about Sage!"

"That's enlightening. Not too long ago, you were *hunting* her down like a dog to get a *five*-million-dollar interview!" He said, anger flashing from his eyes.

"That was *before* all this fell into my lap!" she said back at him, with just as much heat. "*Before* Charlie's little speech, *before* I knew *who* I really was, *before* I found out that *she* was my *nephew's* wife or that I even *had* a nephew, for Christ sakes!" She said it out loud before she could stop herself. Both of them knew it. Using the family term had caught him off guard too, but it caused the harsh look on his face to soften, if just a little. She counted to ten inside her head, before continuing. "Look," she said, throwing her hands up in surrender. "I'm not a big fan of the *tit-for-tat* game and furthermore, I didn't risk coming out here to compare incomes with you and what we both think, is way *overpaid* for what *we* do. So let's just put the egos aside for a second and discuss something *mutual* we both do care about—*your wife*! Because the plane *her* parents were on, is somehow *connected* to these *damn* pirates in Africa and that's all that should matter to you right now!" There was an intense silence that followed her words. It hung thick between them in the room. Brandon stayed stoic—giving no hints outwardly, of what he was thinking. For all she knew he was on the brink of throwing her out of the barn and off the property. Pulling the wife card had been her only option to steering his focus back on the *real* problem at hand. Sage was his world. He was vulnerable when it came to her. All anyone had to do was watch his reaction when she entered a room, to see that.

"Are you trying to tell me my wife is in danger?" He asked, point blank. The cockiness and the smirk was finally gone from both his face and his tone.

Progress…even if it was only going to come in smidges…

"I don't think so," Courtney had to think about that for a second before answering it honestly. "not in any *immediate* danger that I know about. But depending on what they find out, as far as *how* they are connected, could open old wounds and bring her a lot of pain."

"Did anyone in charge know how the plane number ended up on the wall?"

"Nobody knew at the time what it was until I saw it and told them. After that, we were pretty much banned the very next day from returning to the site. It is Africa's rainy season, so it was pouring buckets for days, which kept us all inside with little to do and a lot of time on our hands.

One of our cameramen made friends with the house boy in charge of our rooms and he just happened to have a cousin, who was a local cop in Kenya. He had been sent to the camp to help translate between the natives and the generals. Through him is how we learned about the FBI sending out a *second* team."

"For what?" he asked.

"That's what I tried to find out the entire time we were there. It's customary for the FBI to be brought in automatically, when Americans are involved. But when I got wind that a second team had been sent, it definitely indicated that something much bigger was in the works. I had this theory in the beginning, that maybe it was because the leader of the pirates, had somehow managed to escape the raid."

"Why would you think that?"

"Because of the way everyone was acting. I've been around the military long enough to know, that when they capture the ultimate target, afterwards, they gloat! But in this case, no one was reveling in the fact that they'd just taken down, one of the most infamous pirate's lair of all time. Not the generals running the show and not the soldiers who were guarding it. And right before we were hustled out of there, I saw and heard that they'd put more troops on the ground and were instructed to scout the perimeters. I found it odd but my boss, Michael, didn't. It wasn't until we got back in the states, that some of the things I'd said, began to stand out in his mind. Coincidently, Michael and *the* general— who is in charge of the lair—are childhood friends. Since my boss has direct access to his private number, he called him up. They agreed to have a conversation that was *off the record*. He more or less told him that something they'd found while investigating, is what prompted the second team to come in."

"So you think they shut you guys down and called in reinforcements because *you* identified the plane number on the wall?"

"I think the plane number was just the beginning of a complicated avalanche. At first, Michael thought that they made us leave the camp early because they'd discovered that one of the pirate's boats were unaccounted for. Knowing now that Margot was called down to identify an item that could have belonged to her daughter, just proves that it was something else they had discovered." Courtney went on to tell him about the steel footlocker that was found buried in the ground and its contents. "My boss says there was something inside those ledgers *or* the diary they found in the box, that caused them to disperse the extra team."

Brandon pondered this over for a second before he spoke.

"Do you know who the diary belonged to?" he asked.

"No," Courtney said, shaking her head. "That's why I was curious if the diary was what they wanted Margot to identify."

"What would make you think that?" he asked. "When Sage was talking about her mother earlier, she mentioned she had been fond of keeping a personal diary and that her last one she had been writing in, at the time of her death, was missing from her room. Margot assumed that Kelley had taken it with her. She said it was possible because her mother was notorious for documenting all her different life experiences and travels." "Coincidence?" He asked, being serious.

"I don't believe in coincidences, Brandon."

"Then what is your take on this?"

"I think whatever the FBI found in that lair, they deemed it important enough to take a second look at a twenty-five-year-old case."

"What are you getting at?" he asked, his brow furrowed in a frown.

"I'll show you what I'm getting at *if* you just answer my question. If it wasn't a diary, then was it a gold chain?" Brandon hesitated just a little in his response. "Was *what* a gold chain?"

"The item that Margot recognized when she went to the bureau?"

"I already told you, I'm not going to discuss the details with you."

"I saw the portraits in the dining room of Sage's parents." She said, ignoring his insolence and taking another angle. She dug her cell phone out of her back pocket. "Or I assume they are of *her* parents." She said. He nodded. "Ever *notice* the gold chain that is hanging from her mother's neck in the portrait?"

Brandon's jaw began to twitch again, in spurts. "Of course," he said, arms still crossed. "I see it *every* time I sit at the table."

"Well, this is where it's going to get *weird*." She cautioned. "Remember when I mentioned in the beginning of our conversation, about the cameraman on my crew, Tony?" Brandon nodded. "He has mad skills when it comes to silently filming what's going on around us without anyone being the wiser. He's the stations go-to-man, whenever we head into tough assignments like this one, for just that reason. As with any segment we cover, there are always a list of rules going in. The one they rode on us the hardest about, was that we were not allowed, under any circumstances, to shoot any video of *either* the pirates they'd captured or the victims they'd kept prisoner. But Tony did it anyway, not intending to *ever* use it as a public piece, but more for our private viewing behind the scenes. I happened to watch it while I was bored in the hotel, waiting for the rain to stop. On it, he captured a few of the soldiers removing a dead woman on a gurney. Michael later told me she was found in a hut.”

“How do you know she was dead?” he asked.

“Because I know someone who confirmed it for me. I also know someone who I asked to enhance the frame of the footage when she was closest to his camera, on the stretcher.”

“Why would you *ask* someone to enhance footage of a *dead* person?”

“Because I wanted to see what she was *wearing* on her ankle.” She located the picture, then handed her cell over to Brandon. “Here, take a *look* for yourself. I just got this a few minutes ago.”

He uncrossed his arms, took the phone and looked at the image. “So what does this prove?” He asked, looking back up at Courtney. “The dead woman in Kenya just happens to have an ankle charm on her leg, that resembles the one Sage’s mother was wearing in the portrait. The jeweler probably made a million of these at the time.” “I thought about that, *until* I was told about the *missing* plane that is also *connected* to the lair.” She said.

“What *missing* plane?”

“The *one* Sage’s parents were on.” She said.

Brandon stared at her for a second. “What are you *talking* about? Their plane isn’t *missing*. It was *found* and their remains were brought back.”

Courtney shook her head and proceeded to fill him in on what Michael had revealed to her, right before she came to Montana.

“Someone has their stories mixed up!” he said, shaking his head in disbelief.

“No, someone went to *great* lengths to deceive the Hartford’s, into believing their daughters plane was found. *Why*—is the *mystery* here.” Courtney stressed. “You and I could stand here all night trying to come up with scenarios

and never figure it out. What we should be asking ourselves instead is—where's *that* plane and what *really* happened to the *people* that were on it?"
Brandon's face paled slightly and the shock in his eyes grew more prominent. "Wait…*you* don't think that *this* is..." Courtney knew Brandon was a very smart man. She also knew it wouldn't take him long to digest the facts. And like clockwork, the first sign came when he ran his hand nervously through the top of his hair while taking another glance at the image on the phone, he was still holding. "*Oh my God…*"
"According to Michael's source, they've only *recently* confirmed she was *American*. They're guesstimated her age to be somewhere around the *fifty* mark and there's proof that she's lived in that camp for a very long time. I however, do not *believe* it's a coincidence, that she's around the same *age* as Sage's mother would have been, had she lived. Or that she's *wearing* a piece of jewelry from the eighties, that is almost *identical* to the one around Kelley's neck in the portrait. Or that the *serial* number of their plane, was *found* in an adjoining hut."
He tore his eyes away long enough to lock them with hers. The realization there, confirmed to Courtney, that—*finally*—they were both on the same page. Brandon handed the phone back to her and rubbed both of his hands over his face in shock. That's when she decided to drive it home. "Brandon, what *if* that plane *didn't* crash? What *if* Sage's mother—by some *miracle*—has been *alive* all this time and held *hostage* by the pirates, only to *die* just hours *before* she would have been rescued? And what *if*, they sent this *second* team, to *cover* it up?"

 FORTY-NINE

Jane Doe's DNA was back!
Belinda thought it would take forever to hear Agent Metz say those words.
"*Please* tell me this woman is not *who* we think she is?" she stressed, waiting with baited breath.
"You got your wish. Our Jane Doe is *not* Kelley Cassava, unless she was adopted. She is nowhere near a match to Margot Hartford's DNA!" he said with conviction.
"*Thank God!*" Belinda said out loud before she could catch herself.
"There's more." he said.
"Go on," she urged, regaining her business-like composure.
"We got the toxicology tests narrowed down to cause of death. It looks like it was intentional."
"How?"
"Her blood work contained a large dosage of a plant native to Africa called *Devils Berries*."
"*Devil's Berries*?" Belinda questioned.
"Yes, here in the states it's better known as *Belladonna*. It's one of the most poisonous plants in the world because it contains Tropane alkaloids, which will, at first, cause the victim to become delirious and experience hallucinations. What follows next is the loss of voice, dry mouth, headaches, breathing difficulty and convulsions, then eventually death. The berries on this particular plant mock the appearance of blueberries and have a very sweet taste. Consuming ten to twenty berries is enough to kill an adult, but it only takes one *leaf*—in which the poisons are much more concentrated—to kill a full grown man."
"So, if these Belladonna berries resemble blueberries, what makes you come to the conclusion that someone poisoned

her? Who says she didn't consume the berries on her own?"

"I'm way ahead of you. I connected with Agent Murrow, who was head of the investigation at the scene. He confirmed that the remains of the plant, Belladonna, was found in one of the other huts and positively identified by a local. Someone had simmered a leaf of it in a kettle of tea. Since one of the cups contained less than a third of the liquid, this is how we think Jane Doe ingested the poison. Dr. Cafferty says the contents found in her stomach during the autopsy is consistent with that theory but he's having more tests conducted to make sure."

"You said *one* cup?" Fields asked. "Was there more?"

"Yes, Murrow says there were *two* cups at the scene."

"Don't tell me, the second cup was never touched?" "You got it." He confirmed. "It was an easy crime scene since everything was left as it was. Someone didn't bother cleaning up."

"That, or they were in too much of a hurry." Belinda said, then hesitated for a moment, her mind working quickly, devising a plan. "Do me a favor." She finally spoke again into the phone. "Can you get Dr. Cafferty to clean our Jane Doe up enough for a head shot?"

"We are way ahead of you. He's already done that."

"Good! I need it emailed to me, asap! I want to see if any of the survivors *or* the pirates captured in Kenya can identify her. I have a hunch that once we find out *who* she is, maybe it will tell us *why* someone would want her dead."

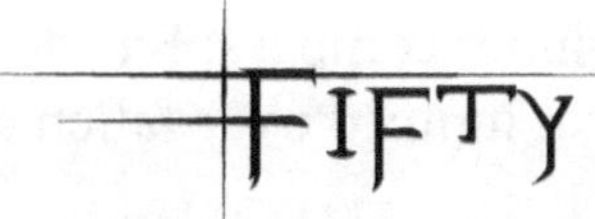FIFTY

The woman's entire body was covered in a mixture of sweat and blood…*her* blood! Her bare arms, face and neck bore deep scratches and cuts. The thin tank was drenched and stuck to her skin from running. The knee-length shorts, left the lower part of her calves exposed, the skin now raw with nicks from low-lying creepers and briar. The high-tops on her feet were covered with muck so thick, that she could no longer see their vivid color. And the buildup was adding weight to her already-fatigued legs that she didn't need. The burn in her lower abdomen and thighs, matched the burning in her lungs. Her heart was pumping excitedly in her chest and no matter how much her body wanted to quit, her stubborn drive would not allow it. So, her thighs continued to keep their rhythm, like a smooth precision machine. Her arms that were outstretched and continuously used to shield her face from passing branches and leaves, were beginning to feel like dead weights. She wondered how much longer she would last before she fell flat on her face and passed out from exhaustion.

The sounds of wild birds calling out to one another, echoed in the jungle. Somewhere behind her the shrill scream of a monkey rang out and was soon followed by another further off in the distance. She had learned a long time ago that their presence was *always* a good sign. It meant that the threat of a predator was not near—in animal or *human* form. Subconsciously her hand brushed the side of her waistband and the bulge there reassured her that she had the means to deal with either one, should the need arise. She refocused straight ahead and pushed harder, navigating recklessly at a high rate of speed. She crossed over rough terrain, in and out through dense vegetation blindly, with no clear path or plan to guide her, depending solely on insane prayers and her inner compass. She dodged trees and low-hanging foliage, jumped over fallen debris and twisted vines.

More sweat poured from every inch of her body. It trickled down her neck, her spine and under her breasts. It slid into her eyes, burning and impairing her vision. She repeatedly wiped them with the back of her injured hands, the salt burning her fresh wounds.

A sharp pain began to work its way into her side, wedging itself up under her ribs. Her breathing became more labored because of it. She applied pressure with her right fist, trying to contain it, as she continued to run…. faster and faster, pushing herself to her limit.

The lump of fear threatened to rise again in the back of her throat. She wanted to scream and cry with frustration and anger but knew if she allowed it to take over, it would distort her focus and slow her down.

She conjured up an image of the last time she'd seen her *lover's* face. Regardless of the brave smile he projected to her, his eyes were filled with fear. When he hugged her goodbye, she'd felt it in his embrace and when he'd whispered harshly in her ear, his last words had resonated their meaning in chills, that had gripped her to the core… "*RUN!*" he had pleaded in a harsh whisper for only her to hear. "Don't *look* back! Don't *think* about *me*! *Don't* try to justify, *don't* try to plan…for *God*-sakes, *just RUN*!" She'd felt his breath hitch when he had spoken the last sentence. She'd felt his body shudder against hers right before they'd been separated. Their eyes had locked for only a few seconds but a million words had been silently passed between them. The *secret* message he was trying to convey to her had been *loud* and *clear* and she had to accept the fact that they both might *die* and never see each other again!

Fear began to creep up her spine again. The lump was pushing back up in her throat. Fresh tears began to spill from her eyes and mix with her sweat and blood. If she didn't stop soon and rest, she would collapse from exhaustion! But the fear inside was greater. So she ignored all the signs and kept running for her life!

FIFTY-ONE

Michael had just walked through the door of his Manhattan brownstone when his cell began to vibrate. He shut the door and locked it behind him securely and reengaged the alarm.

"*Patrol found the boat*!" General Bradley said, the moment he answered.

Michael shifted the cell from his right ear, to the left. He dropped his keys onto a table in the foyer and turned on a few more lights in the dim corridor.

"So there *was* one missing." He stated.

"Yep! One of them four-seater speed boats. They found it about six miles up the river towards Kenya. It was hidden up under a canopy of trees. The outboard engine was still warm. Whoever took it can't be too far ahead of us. I have troops all over this *damn* place and yet, not *one* alert has sounded from anybody!"

"Maybe they didn't stay on land. They could have hidden theirs to throw you off and boarded another boat." Michael suggested, as he navigated his way through the silent hallway and into the kitchen. He loosened his tie with one hand just enough to undo the first three buttons on his shirt.

"We already thought about that. I got eyes in the water too. No alerts coming from there either. These son-of-a-bitches are sneaky!"

"They've been living and navigating in that jungle for years, Bill. Don't beat yourself up about it." He opened the fridge and pulled out a cold beer. "Got any idea how many of them escaped?" He unscrewed the top and took a long sip.

"Not at the moment but once the interrogator gets done with the ones we captured, we'll know soon enough."

"So tell me this—are the pirates being really *stupid* right now or really *smart*?"

"From what I hear, so far everyone is being *really* stupid. Course, they're ruthless pirates without a *damn* conscience, so what do you expect?" the General said.

"Did you find out who the Jane Doe is?" Michael asked.

"The FBI is working on that. Apparently they had a strong lead that fell through so it's back to the drawing board."

"Anything on the location of that missing plane yet?" Michael asked.

There was a brief pause and then the general said, "That's what they brought the interrogator here for. If it still exists, we'll know soon enough!"

 FIFTY-TWO

"Where's Courtney?" Sage asked, when Meg appeared solo on the balcony.

"She complained of an annoying headache, so she took some meds and said she was going to lie down for a bit." Meg replied as she reached out and accepted the glass of wine Sage offered, then took a seat next to hers.

"I'm surprised the headache didn't start sooner." Sage said. "She had a nice little knot on her cheek."

"*I know!* I *feel* so bad!" Meg said with a sigh. "I can't believe *I'm* responsible for marring that *perfect* face! I just hope the bruise is gone before she has to go back on the air."

"It was an accident. You didn't do it on purpose." Sage reminded her "And besides, by the time she boards the plane tomorrow, it will have almost disappeared. You'll see." She leaned back in the chair. "But you're right about one thing—she *does* have a *perfect* face. Of course she's related to Brandon, so it makes sense. He has a perfect face too." She added and giggled.

"The apple doesn't fall far from the tree in that gene pool." A smile spread across Meg's face. "Everett had a perfect face too and he was so damn charming!"

"I barely remember him, except for the fact that he smelled good and had a voice that tickled my tummy!" Sage laughed.

"You remember him from a *child's* point of view but *I* knew him as a young woman." Meg said. "I loved him—of course—because he saved our lives but I wasn't blind to the fact that he was also drop-*dead* gorgeous! And I wasn't the *only* female who thought so. Women of *all* ages and walks of life would just *gravitate* towards that man like he was some kind of—Pied-Piper-*Casanova*! All he had to do was *lay* on some of that *movie-star* charm and the knees would instantly go weak on any female within a fifty-foot radius!" She let go of a short giggle herself and took a sip of her wine. "Brandon has that *same* charisma Sage," she then said, almost as an afterthought. "Which is *why* he has *triple* the fan base then most of his *peers* in the entertainment business. Honey, you've seen it for yourself—*hell*, you were *one* of them!" She stressed. "You know all your man has to do is step one foot on the red carpet and the fans are screaming like maniacs and falling all over themselves like maggots behind the barricades. It's the number one reason *why* we journalists hound him like we do. If we're lucky enough to acquire a story that puts his handsome mug on the cover, our magazines literally *fly* off the shelves! He's a walking money machine for all of us affiliated with this industry! And Courtney—another reason why she's at the top of *her* field— she possesses it too! She gets the same reaction when she walks into a room. People literally stop *breathing* just to stare at her— it's crazy! And the extra attention and the chaos she creates, doesn't *even* seem to affect her." Meg said. She took another sip and then added. "Both of them inherited the charisma gene from Everett—no doubt!"

They sipped in silence, both taking a pause in the conversation. Sage was enjoying this side of Meg, having her *all* to herself, to reminisce about the old days. She was also quickly learning quite a few things about Brandon's legendary grandfather. The side of him that Sage had not seen through the eyes of a child, as Meg had pointed out. Since her newfound *aunt* seemed to be in such a chatty mood, Sage figured that *maybe it was the* perfect time to also learn more about the dynamics between the four men. "So…my father and Everett were close?" Sage said, more as a statement than an actual question.

Meg averted her eyes from the view beyond the balcony and studied Sage for a second before answering.

"They were *very* close." She said.

"Closer than he was with my grandfather?" she asked.

Meg hesitated briefly again before answering.

"He *adored* your grandfather *but* Everett was *his* idol. And Frank, he was Charlie's. The fact that my brother made himself *one* of the most sought-after agents in the business, gives that away." Meg said.

"There's no doubt that he knows what he's doing." Sage agreed.

"Charlie has a motto that he lives by. I'm sure by now you've probably heard him say it. He'll tell you, 'N*obody taught him anything in his line of business unless they failed'*."

Sage couldn't help herself. She laughed out loud, not because of the humor but because of the irony. "I have never heard him say that but *boy*, can I totally relate."

"Charlie is a brilliant, *self*-made man." Meg smiled. "And if anyone knew him better than I did, it was *your* father. He often reminded me, that Charlie's gruffness in manner, was because his mind sped faster in his brain, then most people on average did. Sort of like a mad-scientist *kind* of theory. Because of that, thru Charlie's eyes, it seems like half the world is a *little* too lazy for his liking. He's not one who gets along with slackers or people that stick their nose where it doesn't belong. Like his sister, for instance." She laughed. "but for those of us who *really* know him, he's a teddy bear underneath all that anger."

Sage felt a tug on her heart when she heard the emotion come through in Meg's voice. She wanted to say something to comfort her but their situation was still in the early stages and Sage didn't want to step on any toes by saying something wrong or insensitive.

"If I may speak freely Sage," Meg said, saving her from her rampant thoughts. "I don't think it was fair for either Everett or Frank to burden my brother with the responsibility of telling Andy, Brandon and Courtney about their true past. Charlie didn't *create* it, he was just the *messenger*, making good on a promise. I know you and Brandon are not too happy with him right now because of the timing issue, but that was not entirely his decision to wait this long. Life kept happening, is what he explained to me. It wasn't until you and Brandon met, that it stirred the pot and forced his hand. He knew this would be the outcome—the anger and discord—the disbelief and some sense of betrayal. But keep in mind what's happening on *both* sides of the fence. *We* lost *our* home, *our* parents, *our* identity, *our* country of birth, with a bounty on our heads. Charlie was *only* fourteen when our parents were murdered. And then he lost his brother, Sage—he lost his *twin*! Jack was part of his *soul*…and your mother was a part of his soul too because Jack loved her so deeply." She paused and took a sip.

Sage waited a moment before she spoke. "How *was* the relationship between my father and Charlie?"

"They were like typical twins," she said ironically, with a faint smile tugging at the corners of her mouth. "They had their own *secret* language. They finished each other's sentences and they were always together. Charlie was the tougher one of the two. He will tell you he watched over Jack and not the other way around. That's why I never understood why they paired up the way they did when it came to their mentors. Everett was obviously the tough guy while Frank walked the straight and narrow. You would have thought that Everett and Charlie would have been more compatible and the book-worm men like Frank and Jack, would have found more common ground. But that wasn't the case!"

"How did Charlie feel about my mother when she stole my father away and married him?"

"He was ecstatic for them both." Meg said.

"No jealousy on Charlie's part?" Sage asked.

"Absolutely not!" Meg said, wriggling up her nose. "Charlie adored your mother and your mother adored him right back. People would joke around, that Kelley got *two* husbands for the price of one. That's how much time they all spent together. They were like *The Three Musketeers*!" She said, a shimmer of tears threatening her eyes as she paused. "Anyway, enough mushy, sad stuff. I'm just glad I'm here and I finally get to know you. You're all that *we* have left of our brother, our precious Kelley and Frank. Brandon and Andy is all we have left of our heroic Everett. Too much time has already been wasted."

"We *both* had a right to know. They should have told us sooner." Sage said.

"Your grandmother had a lot to do with Charlie keeping his mouth shut, when it came to telling either of you. They both also knew that Brandon was too much like his grandfather and it would have been no time before he ended up at Margot's door, asking questions and she wasn't having any of that. She thought she was protecting you."

"And her plan might have worked if I hadn't of found my grandfather's journals." Sage said.

"Who would have thought Frank was secretly keeping a journal for years." Meg mused.

"Obviously *none* of us did." Sage said.

"He just didn't seem like the type that would write his thoughts down on paper." Meg added. "Frank was a very *private* man."

"But yet he was committed and faithful to his writing, back when my mother was just elementary age and before he ever met Everett!"

"And your grandmother swears she didn't know anything about it." Meg said, cocking an eyebrow at Sage. "You would think your mate of almost *fifty* years would know." Sage said.

"I would know it if Peter were keeping one." Meg agreed.

"I would know if Brandon were keeping one too." Sage admitted.

"Well, who am I to judge?" Meg let out a short laugh. "I was married to my husband under an *assumed* identity and he didn't have a clue!"

"Very true." Sage agreed.

"Goes to show you, just when you think you know a person…"

Sage didn't speak, just nodded in agreement. Both of them lapsed into a moment of silence as they sipped and enjoyed the magnificent view beyond the balcony.

Sage noticed that it was quite clear and cooler than the night before which meant snow would not be too far behind. The owls could be heard periodically off in the distance. Their call to the night paired perfectly with the full moon, whose glow silhouetted the mountains. Sage's mind began to wonder—as it always did—to that fantasy place inside her head, where the 'what ifs' existed. Like, *what if* her parents were still here and not dead because they had never boarded the plane? Or, *what if* her grandfather were still alive and right now, just sitting in his office in Florida, working on some kind of deal? To push the dream a little further...*what if* her father were right *next* door, in his *own* cabin, with her mother, getting ready for bed, or better yet—he was out in the barn, tinkering in the man cave with Brandon while her mother was sitting out here, on this very balcony, with her and Meg, sharing a glass of wine?

What if?

What would be different *if* everyone were still alive today? Would Everett have given up Hollywood socializing and moved out west permanently, to be closer to Brandon and to see his great-grandson grow up? Would her grandfather have persuaded her grandmother to sell the mansion and move on the property, to be closer to her? Would Charlie have left the micro-managing of Hollywood's elite, to be next to his twin brother? Would her father already be retired and living on the property, after a long running successful practice as a lawyer?

"You know Meg," Sage said breaking the silence when the thought came to her. "You said earlier that *my* grandfather taught Charlie and my father the *business* side of life." Meg nodded. "So if that's the case, then what did Everett teach *them*?"

Meg hesitated a moment, then said, "Survival instincts."

"What do you mean?" Sage asked.

"Frank taught them how to *deal* with the business world but Everett taught my brothers how to be *street* smart. Of course they had no choice, thanks to that *asshole* Victor Rocha." Meg stressed. "Everett knew he wasn't going to be around forever to watch over us, so they wanted them prepared!"

"Do you think Victor had any idea what really happened to you guys?"

"No, because if he did, we would be dead." Meg said, shaking her head. "The vendetta against Everett became obsessive when Victor found out his wife was having an affair with him. Victor, to this day, never had proof that Everett was even at my parents' house, the night he murdered them nor could he confirm, that Everett was the one who had Isabella. Since Catalina was dead, he couldn't get any answers, so he was driven on assumptions only. Karly was riding on assumptions; she didn't have proof either. Catalina's maid was the only one who could pinpoint her itinerary that day to an extent. She told the authorities that her mistress never left the house all morning and that the baby was there with her. But by late afternoon, after the gardener discovered her face down in the pool, there was about three hours that were unaccounted for. Since Everett is not here to ask *how* he acquired the baby before Catalina drowned, we can only assume it happened in that time frame. I'm not sure I buy the story that Karly is telling. I think she had a love/hate relationship with her father and she's covering for him when it comes to which one of them really caused Catalina's death."

"Wait a minute," Sage said, sitting up in her chair. "You said the gardener found Catalina?" Meg nodded. "I thought Victor was the one who found her?"

Meg shook her head. "It was all over town, the story of her drowning was on everyone's lips. That's how my parents found out. The gardener himself is the one that Everett first heard it from. From the way Jack told it, he was sitting in the pub on the corner, waiting for Catalina to join him and the baby so they could fly to the states. She never showed at the designated time, so he continued to wait. The gardener was so distraught after discovering her, that he headed to the *same* pub for a few shots. When he told the bartender what had just happened, Everett was right there and heard every word."

"*Oh my God*!" Sage said. "How awful!"

"Tell me about it." Meg said. "It makes me all weepy inside for Everett. That poor, *poor* man. He lost his first wife to cancer. Then he had to give his son away right after because he lost his home from all the unpaid medical bills. Then he gets a second chance at love, only to lose her shortly too, which then forces him to give up yet *another* child because to keep her, would surely get them both killed. I mean, *seriously*, the guy just never caught a break." Meg said, leaning forward in the chair and resting her wine glass on the table. She picked up her cigarette pack and fished for one. In one swift motion she stuck it between her lips and lit the tip. Smoke, in thick clouds, rose above her head.

"You don't mind me asking all these questions, do you?" Sage asked, not wanting to overstep her bounds.

"*Never*!" She said without hesitation. "I've told you before Sage, you ask me anything and if I have an answer, I'll tell you. *Especially* about your father. But if you need details, then Charlie is your man. Have you read any of what I just told you, in Frank's journals?"

"No. I thought it would have the answers to some of my questions in there but instead, most of it is just causing me to ask *more* questions." Sage stressed.

"Like what?" She asked.

"Like why he kept blaming himself for the deaths of my parents."

Meg took a drag and blew more smoke over her head.

"Frank *always* blamed himself for their death. He figured if he hadn't gotten sick in the first place, then he would have been the one on that plane and not the '*kids*', as he called them."

"What did he have? The flu?" Sage asked because there were parts of that time she really couldn't remember either.

"No, it was food poisoning." Meg said. "The *worse* kind."

"Where did he get it from?"

"Not sure. It was so long ago and sometimes my brain gets all foggy on the facts. I really don't remember it being discussed in detail, not with me anyway. Charlie would be able to tell you more since he and Frank were joined at the hip." Meg said and shrugged her shoulders. "Why?" she asked. "What are you thinking?"

"I don't know just yet." Sage said, staring off into the distance. "There's still a lot of things that don't add up."

"Talk to me!" Meg urged, perched on the edge of her chair now, fully alert. "Like what?"

"Like this court order we found to have the graves exhumed. What was he looking for?"

"That might not be something that any of us will ever know, Sage. But the one thing I can tell you, Frank was a very *smart* man all by himself. He didn't petition for those graves to be dug up on a hunch. Knowing him like I did, he had something *factual* to back his request. That's the only way he operated, strictly on facts. Everett too."

"What do you think about the remains not being in the caskets?" Sage asked.

Meg released a heavy sigh. "I've no doubt *thought* about it—a *lot*—ever since we found that paper in his safe. I can't *imagine* the pain Frank must have felt knowing his baby girl's remains, weren't in that coffin where they were supposed to be. Hell, I'm not going to lie. Knowing that my brother was never in there either, well, it hurts and pisses me off at the same time. But in the long run, it was over twenty years ago and there's nothing we can do about it now, right? I mean, maybe there was nothing left to send back, you know? Maybe, they lied to give the families some decent closure. They probably figured their secret was safe and that no one would ever take a peek inside, for the *morbid* purposes of it."

"Your probably right." Sage said. "But it's still not right."

"Nothing about this my darling, will ever be right." Meg agreed.

"So what's my grandmother's beef with Charlie?" Sage dared.

A laugh escaped Meg and in the process almost caused her to choke on the wine she was sipping. "Nothing gets by you, does it Sage?" She asked as she delicately wiped the corner of her mouth.

"Obviously *some* things do!" Sage said and returned the smile.

Meg just eyed her for a second. "You're a *lot* like your father." She mused. "You have his traits but when it comes to handling your straight-laced grandmother, well that is strictly traits *from* Kelley."

"Really? What kind of relationship did my mother and grandmother have with each other?"

"It seemed at times *strained*." Meg admitted. "Kelley had her mind set to do one thing and Margot had her mind set that she should be doing the opposite. They loved each other, don't get me wrong, it was just that they had two totally *different* opinions on how Kelley was supposed to live her life."

"Like *what* for instance." Sage probed.

"Well like Kelley's *choice* in a husband." Meg said, hesitated, then added. "I don't want to step on any toes here." She interceded, looking Sage directly in the eye.

"It's time for the secrets to be over." Sage said. "Besides, I'm a grown woman and I have a right to hear things about my mother that obviously Nana will never tell me. And I need to hear it from someone else's perspective. All my grandmother will ever do is paint a picture that makes her look good in it."

"I'm sure that Margot thought she was doing the right thing…at the time!" Meg said.

"About what? The fact that she tried to keep my mother and father apart in the beginning?" Sage asked, wanting to know more about that, as well.

Meg nodded. "We were dumped on her out of nowhere. I can understand better now as an adult, *how* that must have felt. She went from having one child in the house, to four overnight. We invaded her space, her quiet sanctuary, her home and we brought danger with us, danger that threatened the safety of her *own* child. Who could blame her?"

"What happened?" Sage prodded.

"Well, Jack *saw* Kelley and Kelley *saw* Jack—is what *happened*." Meg said. "It was love at first sight for them two. You would have to be blind not to see it when they were together in a room. Margot, of course, thought she was going to put an end to it right away. And again, who could blame her? With Jack as a walking target, she didn't want her precious daughter to get caught up in the crossfire."

"But my mother married my father, so her plan didn't work?" Sage said, more as a statement than a question.

"Kelley was a very strong-minded person and so was my brother. They fell in love and that was it. No one else existed or mattered when it came to their act as a duo. And the more time they spent together, the more they bonded almost into one person. They could just look at the other and talk silently between themselves without saying a word and when they did talk out loud, they literally could finish each other's sentences. It was obvious to anyone that knew them, *including* Margot, they were a package deal and nothing or no one was going to interfere. Besides, your grandmother chilled out towards Jack after they were married and Kelley became pregnant with you. I always thought it was because he agreed to move into the North wing. That way, she could keep an eye on the *both* of you, living in the same house which made her tremendously happy."

"So back to my original question, what did Charlie *do* that put a wedge between him and my grandmother?" Sage asked. When Meg didn't answer right away, an uneasiness stirred in her gut. "Is it something *bad*?" she persisted. Meg turned to look at Sage. "No, unless you consider *innocently* falling in love to be a *bad* thing!"

"Never!" Sage said. When again Meg didn't elaborate, she asked. "Are you referring to the union between my parents? Surely Nana isn't blaming Charlie for their attraction to each other?"

Meg shook her head. "No, it was mostly Frank that had to take the backlash from her about *your* parent's union. If he hadn't of let us stay in the mansion that first year, Kelley would have never *met* Jack!"

"So how did Charlie end up on her shit list?" Meg took a sip of her wine and put her cigarette out. A heavy sigh released from within her chest and the smile waned from her face. "I'm not sure if my brother would be pissed at me for telling you this, so do me a favor and let's keep what I am about to tell you *between* just us for now, ok?" she asked, looking straight at Sage.

"Absolutely!" she agreed.

Meg nodded but seemed to be struggling. "About a year before your parents boarded that plane, Charlie fell in love for the first time. Her name was Serenity and she was a beautiful girl with long blonde hair and pretty green eyes and a super sweet personality to match. In fact, she favored your mother so much, she could have easily passed for her sister. And she was so smart like Kelley *too*!" She added, then paused for a second, as if reflecting. "They dated for a few months and then it got serious and we were all ok with that because we soon grew to love her the same. She fit right in with our families, as if she'd been a part of us from the start. As you can imagine, your parents got to see more of her, than any of the rest of us. The four of them spent a lot of time together, they went on double dates constantly and on a few vacations here and there, as well. During that time, Kelley and Serenity became the best of friends. They would periodically do a solo act and meet up with me somewhere in the world for a girl's weekend. When we did, we'd have a blast!" Meg smiled briefly and then her face turned stoic again.

"So what went wrong?" Sage asked. "Why did they break up?"

Meg swallowed hard and turned to stare out into the night beyond the balcony, almost as if she were trying to collect herself.

"She *died,* Sage." She finally said.

Sage was stunned. That was not what she had expected to hear. "Oh no! *Meg,* I'm *so* sorry!" She said when she saw the shimmer of tears gather in her aunt's eyes. "What *happened*?" she leaned over and placed a comforting hand on her arm.

Meg took a deep breath and turned back to Sage. "You remember when I said a moment ago that she was smart like your mother?" Sage nodded. "The reason I said it was because she had paved her way through a man's world, much like Kelley had in your grandfather's corporate world. Serenity had earned her wings long before she ever met any of us."

"She was a *pilot*?" Sage asked.

It was Meg's turn to nod. "Yes! An *Ace* of a pilot!" she confirmed.

"So what does Charlie's girlfriend being a pilot have to do with the wedge between him and my grandmother?" Sage was almost afraid to ask, fearing the answer but the curiosity won over.

More tears shimmered in Meg's eyes. "Margot was looking for someone to place the blame on after she lost Kelley. Serenity was her likely target but because she wasn't around to unleash her wrath on, Charlie was next in line."

"Why was her target on Serenity?" Sage asked, totally confused. "What on earth did she do?" Meg
sighed heavily again.

"Serenity was *one* of the pilots flying the plane that your parents' were on that day."

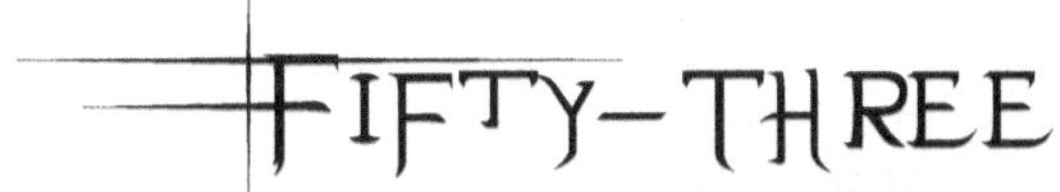 FIFTY-THREE

Charlie stared up at the stars and thought about how perfect the night had turned out to be. The moon was casting a glow, bright enough, that no artificial light was needed. The air was cool and a soft breeze blew periodically across the deck. Other than the light trickle of water coming from the fountain at the end of the pool, the evening was quiet. He was quite comfy, stretched out on the lounger. His feet were up, his tie was loosened, his belly was full and he had a fresh cocktail in his left hand and a grin on his face. And for once, his mind was *completely* off work.

At first he thought maybe his newfound mood was because he was celebrating a small victory, when he realized he might be *closer* to filling the female lead for Sage's movie. Or maybe, he thought, it could be the fantastic dinner he'd just shared with an equally fantastic woman, a few hours ago. Or maybe, it was the fact that he had finally found someone that didn't bore him, after being around them for longer than an hour. Either way, something in the air had changed. Charlie could *feel* it.

"So, *when* are you going to call her?"

He turned towards the seductive female voice in the lounger next to his. He could see every inch of her features clearly in the moonlight.

"Tomorrow." Was his short reply.

"In the morning?" Ava pushed.

Charlie shrugged. "We're not supposed to be talking business, remember? We're supposed to be *decompressing* under the stars." He took a sip of his cocktail.

"We've already decompressed." She said. "When we both agreed Lola should be the lead in Sage's movie!"

"It's not *final*, Ava. Not until Sage approves of it." He said, somewhat firm.

"Sage will approve." Ava was so sure when she said it. "She's going to agree with *us,* that Lola's *nailed* it."

"Doesn't matter what *we* think. Sage might not *like* her." Charlie said. He pulled a new cigar from his shirt pocket and shoved it in his mouth. He fumbled in his pants pocket for his lighter and came up empty handed.

"Of course it matters what we think!" Ava said, then leaned over and produced a lighter and stuck it under Charlie's unlit cigar. "*We* are the experts and her advisors after all. That's what she's paying us for."

"You know how this game's played. She has the rights to tell us *both* to keep looking." He toked on the cigar to get it going under the flame.

"Nonsense!" Ava said, retracting the lighter, once the cherry on the end began to glow. "And besides, *why* would she not *like* Lola? Does she even *know* who she is?"

Charlie nodded while he puffed on the cigar. "Who the *hell* doesn't know *who* Lola is?" he asked, somewhat ironically.

"That's *my* point, exactly! She would be *crazy* not to hire her." Charlie grunted in response, so Ava asked. "Have *they* ever met?"

He shook his head no. "As far as I'm aware, Sage has never *met* Lola. She was invited to their wedding but never came!"

"She said something about that in makeup." Ava said. "but says something more pressing got in the way."

"Hmmm." Charlie said.

Ava glanced over. He could see her in his peripheral vision. "There you go with that '*hmmm*' again. What am I *missing* here?"

"You're not missing anything." At first Ava didn't respond, just studied him, even when he finally turned and met her eyes. It made him nervous when she did that. "*What?*" he asked, not being able to stand it.

"*What?*" she repeated, finally answering. "*What*—is the question I should be asking! What is it about Sage Cassava, that has you so *protective* of her?"

"She's a *valuable* client!" He simply said, as if that should explain everything. Charlie had learned rather quickly that Ava was very good at reading people. After all, it was her *specialty*. This could be a problem if his drink were too many some night and his tongue too loose and he were to *like* her too much.

"Is this how you are with *all* your clients?" she pushed. He nodded. "Like a papa bear?" she added. He nodded. "Your *so* busted, Charlie Vega, because you're not like *that* with Lola and she's *your* client too!" She let out a short laugh.

"It's Sage's project. Lola is merely a possible asset on this venture. The hierarchy dictates and I enforce."

"Your *stubborn*, Charlie Vega." Ava said, amused. "But since that's your only crime, I'll leave you to your fears. Nonetheless, you better not make them someone else's, by trying to *sway* Sage from taking Lola on, as her lead. Cause if you do, I *won't* have dinner with you anymore." A grin tugged at the corners of her mouth.

"I won't have to *sway* Sage; Lola's reputation might *do* that all by itself!"

"What's *that* supposed to mean?" A slight frown clouded Ava's brow.

"It *means* that Lola could be the perfect actress for the part…," Charlie began.

"She is!" Ava cut in.

"And we could scour the Hollywood A-list and never *find* another actress that could do it better…," he continued.

"You won't!" she cut in again.

"And we *both* agree that she has all the right *body* dimensions, height, sound, personality…," he added.

"*All of it*." Ava echoed. "Sage would have no reason to say no!"

Charlie smiled and removed the cigar from the corner of his mouth. "Sage *could* say no because she doesn't *want* a voluptuous *sex* kitten rubbing up against *her* husband, is why—*even* if it is *only* make believe. Could be something really *simple* like that, Ava. You know *how* this business works!"

Ava didn't speak for a moment. Then she began shaking her head no.

"*Nah*! I'm not buying that Brandon Parrish's wife, is a jealous *type* of woman. After all, she *married* a legend whose been labeled the sexiest man alive, *more* times than *any* actor dead *or* alive. There's no way she could handle his outrageous fame if she had a jealous streak in her. If so, their marriage would have already been over when his costar *fondled* him to death in front of the camera, at his last premiere."

Charlie sighed. "*Ava*, Elvis and Jim Morrison weren't around when the public started voting on *who* they thought was the sexiest man in Hollywood. Since the title only pertains to *living* legends, then that comment you made about Brandon has *no* merit." He said, raising his eyebrows.

"Stop being difficult *and* anal!" she said, shooting him a smile. "You know that Brandon Parrish deserves that title just like Sage is not full of the green-eyed monster."

"So, you're an *expert* on the character of our author now, eh?" he said, shooting her a smile in return.

"I'm a pretty good judge of character Charlie, I told you that when we first met. I can read people and situations very clear at times. Almost too clear for my own good. So yeah, you could say I've studied your client in advance before I accepted this job. And from my observations, Sage is a *very* confident and patient woman who can put together a hell of a story. Anyone with half a brain knows that *good* writers are very passionate people, who are guided more by their heart—when making decisions—than through their mind. Jealousy to me is a mind issue and Sage is obviously someone who's ruled by her heart, *not* her head. Her story, if you read it, will tell *you* that."

He stubbed his cigar out in the ashtray on the table next to him. "Oh, *believe* me when I tell you, I *know* Sage's story, inside *and* out!" He sighed and relaxed his head against the back of the lounger. "And on that note, let's *drop* the business talk for now. It's *too* beautiful of a night to waste on endless possibilities."

Ava stared at him for a few seconds too long before she said, "Ok," *too* easily. She leaned back, sipping on her glass of red wine. From his peripheral, Charlie could see that she had turned her attention back to the view beyond. He let out a quiet but heavy breath and hoped she would not hear. He was more than glad she agreed to get off the subject. He was beginning to feel burnt out over the whole entire process and this feeling too, was something new to him.

Charlie welcomed the silence that enveloped them on the patio, once again. He sipped on his drink and heard the hoot of an owl somewhere above, on the hillside. He glanced back over at Ava.

She broke her gaze from the view and glanced his way.

"It's a beautiful night." Charlie said.

"Gorgeous." Ava agreed.

"Want to do this again tomorrow night?" he asked.

"Supposed to be a full moon!"

Ava smiled. "Absolutely."

Charlie smiled back. "What time?"

"How about right after you get off the phone with Sage?" She asked.

Charlie didn't answer, he just nodded and returned to the view beyond.

Ava was definitely not like anyone he had ever met. She was driven when it came to getting what she wanted. He found that trait in a woman to be *quite* attractive. Although, in the beginning, her *good* looks would have done him in, all by itself. Too bad a woman of her stature was only hanging around him to get the job done. She would never be interested *personally* in a guy like himself. Hell no, he was *way* out of her league.

"So, *now* that we're talking about *personal* stuff, would this be considered a *date*?"

Charlie let the silence speak for a moment, then he said; "We are here and *not* in a boardroom and we didn't *actually* say we were going to *do* this—we just did—so *technically*, no."

"Ok," she began. "You *technically* just asked me to *do* it again tomorrow. So would that be considered a *date*?"

Charlie pondered for a moment and then nodded. "To some people it would be considered a date, since I *asked* you and we're planning it."

"But I don't give a damn what *some* people think. I give a damn what *you* think." She said.

Charlie mentally told his racing heart to slow down. He feared once Ava got what she wanted, she would be gone. Such was the way tinsel town worked.

"I would call it a date." he simply said.

She smiled, really big. "Then that's all I needed to know." They both turned back to the view and the conversation ceased between them.

Within a few more seconds of silence, Charlie felt her soft hand slide into his big one he had resting on his lap.

Without looking her way, he gave in and closed his fingers around hers.

 FIFTY-FOUR

The call Agent Belinda Fields had been waiting for, came in shortly before noon.

"The Jane Doe has been *positively* identified. Her fingerprints popped up within a half hour of running them." Mullins said, with excitement in his voice.

"She has a record?" Belinda asked. They were *finally* getting somewhere.

"*Surprise, surprise!*" Mullins said. "Her real name is Winifred Gentry. Most knew her by a nickname, Skinny Winnie because she was terribly *thin* from all the drugs she did, back in the day. She was fifty-eight years old but coroner says she looks seventy. She had some priors in her early teens and twenties—prostitution, petty theft, possession of drugs, paraphernalia and so on. I guess after a while that bored her so she moved on to bigger things. At thirty-two she was charged with Grand theft, burglary, assault on an officer, and another drug possession—this time it was heroin. Not long after she did her time and was released, she simply *disappeared.*"

"Do you mean that *literally?*"

"I have the missing person's report right here in my hand."

"Who filed it?"

"Her mother."

"And her statement?" Fields asked.

"Mother says she was seeing a character by the name of Josef Gates at the time she disappeared. Local sheriff did an investigation on him as well and said you could wallpaper a small office with his rap sheet. Seems he disappeared too, around the same time, according to the few people who knew him, that was interviewed. Looks like the final word was that they believed the two of them took off into the sunset together which there's no crime against that. I spoke to Winifred's mother a short while ago. She still has no idea what happened to her daughter. I'm sure someone from our office will be on her doorstep shortly to change all that."

"Can you send over a copy of Josef Gates record?" Agent Fields asked.

"He has two. One here in the states *and* the other where he's originally from, in Italy." Mullins said.

"*Italy*?" Belinda repeated. "That place just keeps popping up in this investigation." She observed out loud.

"Tell me about it!" Metz agreed. "There's *definitely* a connection here when I tell you the rest."

"I'm listening." Belinda said.

"Gates was a problem from the start." Mullins said. "The first charge he caught, was drug trafficking, here in the states. He was twenty. The second time, he was trying to smuggle a *large* amount of cocaine into Florida, on a speedboat. The Miami coast guard were the ones who shut that little operation down. He was twenty-eight then and only a year out of prison. He was arraigned and later deported back to Italy, to serve his time. He was released seven years later. Apparently he stayed clean for a while and then it was rumored that he was back into the drug trade—this time in his homeland of *Italy*. Not long after the rumor surfaced, Mr. Gates went missing. Speculation *was* that he *stepped* on the toes of a well-known and *established* drug lord in the area, who was very territorial. And when Gates chose to ignore *his* warnings of infringing, he took him out, most likely. I checked our records. I found it odd that no one ever filed a missing person's report on him. And guess what the *senior* Mr. Gates *did* for a living?"

"What?" Belinda asked, on the edge of her chair.

"He was a *coroner* for the city of Milan. In fact, he's the one who signed off on our *late* Agent Greene's *death* certificate, when he came up floating in their ocean."

"Now why, do you suppose, a man in his *position* never contacted the authorities when his *only* son went missing?" Belinda mused.

"That's what I wanted to know. The investigation that Winifred's mother started back in the states, is how they eventually ended up on his doorstep. When the father was questioned, he claimed that he and his son weren't very close and hadn't been in touch for years. The investigator at the time thought he wasn't being entirely truthful but had no way to prove otherwise."

"Interesting," Fields said. "But yet, he *knew* that day they visited him and he still never filed *even* then."

"My thoughts exactly!"

"So *who* was the drug lord in Italy, that Josef Gates pissed off?" Fields asked.

"An *dead* ex-mobster by the name of Victor "*The Roach*" Rocha. His *daughter* Karly, just got arrested *here* in the states, for *attempted* murder!"

"Oh, that's *definitely* a connection!" Fields said, as she immediately envisioned in her mind, the *face* of Margot Hartford.

FIFTY-FIVE

Both the investigator and Brandon had agreed to touch base around one on Monday. By noon he had already escaped to the office in the barn and made a checklist for Madison, from the outrageous claims that Courtney had made over the weekend. Before he would *ever* think of approaching his wife with such an extravagant theory, he needed the facts to back it up. There was no sense in getting Sage all upset with hope or hurt, over something that could later *pan* out to be false.

What had started to convince him, was the part where Courtney had found the serial number of the plane, *hanging* in one of the huts. The second was the cover-up about the plane still considered missing, that the FBI said twenty years ago, was found. Now, he just needed Madison—who had more access to answers than he did—to verify any of it. With the FBI so heavily involved, Courtney had stressed how *tight* of a lid was on their investigation. Any leaks, could be easily traced back to its source. Michael Buchanan's easy access to the General, was a *privilege* to them right now. The last thing they needed was for their only avenue to be shut down, should someone open their big mouth and start spreading information. He knew a gift horse in the mouth, when he saw one. He had to be *delicate* when conveying what he needed to Madison. And he also felt their time was running out.

After all, how long would the General continue to update his friend, was anybody's guess. There would come a time, deeper into the investigation, when the creed of silence that the military and the FBI demanded, would supersede the obligation to a long-time friendship. Once that happened, they might never learn the whole truth.

He yawned and shook his head, to rid it of the fog that seemed to gather there. He had lost a ton of sleep last night and now that it was afternoon, he was beginning to feel it. But how could he get any sleep after what Courtney had told him? It was devastating enough for *him* to try to absorb her words, how in the hell was Sage going to? And what would be the impact on her mental state afterwards? And suddenly, he wondered whether Courtney had told Meg and Charlie about her suspicions of the cover-up? She hadn't mentioned it that night and he'd been too shocked at the time to ask. Surely she had since Jack was *their* brother. He made a mental note to find out. Maybe Courtney had only confided in *him* since they both weren't directly blood related. He stopped on that note and thought about what he'd just admitted in his mind. He'd automatically referred to Courtney as his *blood*. He let that sink in a moment and came to the result that he *still* didn't like anything about it. Regardless of what she'd came to him with, he still didn't trust her.

She *could* have her *own* agenda in this fight. Her *kind* always did. After all, she was a very aggressive *investigative* reporter—she was notorious for it! And with all the heat on her right now—with the Karly shooting at Margot's—the story about Kelley Cassava would overshadow *her* recent baggage. The world would be so fascinated by the discovery of Sage's mother being held captive off the coast of Kenya, that the mystery surrounding her death would go on for weeks, months, maybe even a couple of years unless they got one of those pirates to *sing* early. The press would forget about her and Meg and would zero right in on *his* wife.

And they'd be all over Margot's front gate again, making them a prisoner in their own home. Not to mention the fear he always had of anyone ever finding *this* private paradise. That just added another worry on his mind. Too many people were learning the location of this secluded cabin and before too long, someone would tell the wrong person and then they would need barriers at the ends of the driveway. They would have to install huge iron gates that would mechanically lock by remote and connect an electric current through it for the *shock* factor, in case some crazy-ass decided to scale them or the fence. And cameras…he'd have to install *more* motion detectors and security *and* guards...

He was beginning to feel the edges of a headache coming on. It made him ill to think that this beautiful mountain hideaway would ever be violated by the likes of the paparazzi or become to them all inside—a prison. It was the only place in this world that he could walk around, *anywhere* on the property and not feel like he was on display. And the only solace he had, was knowing that *if* the media did discover this place, at least they lived under a restricted no-fly zone and they could not spy on them from overhead.

He stood up and walked over to the fridge by the bar and pulled out a cold beer. He was able to take a few sips before the vibration of his cell on the desk, caught his attention. He quickly walked back and sat the beer down, snatching the phone up in one swift movement and put it to his ear. "Madison!"

"Mr. Parrish." The investigator confirmed.

"Talk to me!" Brandon said, anxious.

"I have some more info concerning Victor Rocha's mistress. One longtime resident claims that the woman was at *least* six months pregnant before she disappeared."

"Great!" Brandon said. "Instead of leaving one bastard behind, Victor leaves us two!"

"*Unless* she was murdered. Then there would be none." Madison offered.

"Still not finding her trail, huh?" Brandon asked.

"Not yet. If she's still alive, then someone was really good at hiding her, Mr. Parrish. Of course back then, people didn't have credit cards, computers or ways of tracking data to find someone. It was very easy to get lost in the shuffle, if you wanted too."

"You think they killed the daughter too?"

"Maybe. Or they sold her into the black market and she became someone *else's* daughter. Children in that time period, could fetch high dollar at an auction or through a private broker. A lot of wealthy women were barren and would pay anything to adopt a child discreetly. Fertility options were zilch at the time so a child that age was very highly in demand and would easily have been sold for a tidy profit."

Brandon said. "So if this child survived, she'd have no idea *who* she is?"

"She was very young when the adoption would have taken place. Unless the adoptive parents were straight with her later in life, she would have no way of knowing *where* and *who* she came from or that she was even adopted."

"That's only a *little* comforting on our end. I hope for our sakes that her parents did take that secret to the grave. Did you find out anything else about her?"

"Yes!" Madison said, as if he were ready to move on as well. "Several years after the mistress disappeared, her mother was found suffocated in an assisted living facility."

"*Really*?" Brandon said, totally intrigued for the moment.

"The nursing home was thoroughly investigated after the incident." Madison continued. "They had a reputation to uphold, after all. And because it was a five-star facility, it didn't look very good when one of their residents had turned up murdered. A few hours later, during dinner rounds, was when they found the woman deceased. The pillow that was used to suffocate her with, was still covering her face. Of course the staff was questioned first and one of the nurse's recalled a woman coming around lunch time to visit the victim. She claimed she was the woman's daughter."

"Did anyone confirm it was the *missing* daughter?"

"No, of course not. Victor's mistress had been missing for several years by then. Everyone at the facility knew it, except for the nurse on duty, who allowed the imposter in. She was a *new* hire and did not know the history."

"Anybody figure out why the mother was targeted?"

"An address book that the woman kept in her bedside drawer, was the only thing unaccounted for."

"If that was the only thing they were after, why not just wait until the woman is asleep and take it? Why kill her?" Brandon asked.

"Maybe tying up *loose* ends, Mr. Parrish? It might not have been just the address book, that was *full* of delicate information. As I mentioned before, the woman was living in a five-star assisted living, which *means* the bill every month to keep her there, was *not* cheap. Her financials, were a mere pittance and would have not even begun to pay for the meals, much less the housing and round-the-clock nursing care. *Someone* with very *deep* pockets was footing the bill on her behalf."

"And did you find out *where* the money was coming from?"

"No, not yet. It was a long time ago, before the age of computers. I'll be lucky if I can even find a paper trail leading to the contributor. The answer to that question might be easier for my guys to find, that I have on the ground in Italy."

"Did the mistress' mother possibly have other children? Maybe one of them were paying the bill!" Brandon suggested.

"She had no other children. Victor's mistress was her *only* child. I'd say given the facts—the mistress, her child and her mother—all *presumed* dead, your family should be pretty safe for now. That is *if* Victor's partners were the ones who wiped them all out!"

"Interesting." Brandon muttered. "Anything else?" He glanced at his watch. Brandon was anxious to discuss his new request of information before Sage came out to the office. She had mentioned putting the baby down for a nap and then heading his way to access the damage done to the pic of the four men on the wall. He didn't want to be discussing any part of this with Madison when she did.

"No, Mr. Parrish. That about wraps it up on my end for now."

"But not on mine." He said. "I've got something a little more serious that I need you to check into." Brandon hit the highlights surrounding the story that Courtney had told him about the night before as he cautiously peeked out the hallway for signs of Sage. As he talked, Madison was silent on the other end. When he finished, it took a moment for the man to comment.

"That's quite a story, Mr. Parrish."

"Your reaction's a lot calmer than mine was, I can tell you that." Brandon said.

"I'm sure! What part would you like for me to check out?" He asked.

"*All* of it!" Brandon said.

"Ok. I'll see what I can find."

"And one more thing, can you get your hands on a list of *all* the passengers who were on that flight with my wife's parents?"

"That should be easy." Madison said. "But may I ask exactly what it is that you are looking for?"

Brandon hesitated for a moment and then he replied.

"*Anything* out of the ordinary." No sooner had he said it, he heard the main door slam on its hinges. Sage had *entered* the building.

FIFTY-SIX

Sage got sidetracked from making the trek out to the barn earlier because of Charlie. At first when she saw his name show up in the display screen of her phone, she almost let it go to voicemail. But then some sixth sense in her gut told her to pick up and she was glad she did. He sounded a little too cheery compared to the last time they had talked but she was glad he kept it strictly business, as he declared that he had some rather *great* news, concerning the casting in her movie. He thought he'd found a possible candidate to play the lead in her story opposite of Brandon's character. Sage promised she would view the video he'd already sent to her email within the next few hours and get back to him some time tomorrow. After small talk concerning the baby and Brandon's welfare, she ended the call and headed downstairs to find Lydia in the kitchen making tea. As she brought the baby's monitor closer to her on the counter with one hand, she was sliding the other into the sleeve of her sweater.

"Do you mind taking over for a while? I need to go out to the office and handle some business."

"I'm already on it!" Lydia said and then suggested. "Why don't you take some fresh tea out to Brandon on the way."

"Thanks but I'm sure by now, Brandon has something a lot *stronger,* already open out there, celebrating now that Courtney and Meg are gone." She rolled her eyes, slid her arm in the other sleeve.

"That man *loves* you to death." Lydia said smiling. "That's all that matters. The rest in-between can be dealt with."

"Easier said than done!" Sage said, returning the smile and walking towards the door that led outside. "I'll return as fast as I can."

"No hurry, my darling. You know I *live* for the moments when I get to have that precious baby, all to myself." Lydia smiled and winked.

"You're learning to be *greedy,* Lydia." Sage threw over her shoulder and then laughed as she closed the back door behind her.

When she arrived to the barn and walked into the office, Brandon was sitting at the desk staring off into space. A yellow legal pad was laying in front of him, his cell phone on top of it. The page on the front was blank but yet there was a pen beside it and a beer in his hand, that was already half gone.

"Penny for your thoughts." She teased when he finally focused on her. "Everything ok?" she asked, a little concerned.

"Yeah babe." Was his reply. "Everything is wonderful." He rested his beer on the desk and stood up to give her a kiss. "Tristan sleeping?"

"Yes, I have Lydia watching over him while I came out. Charlie called not ten minutes ago. He said he has a possible lead for my movie. He already emailed me the audition tape. Can you pull it up for me?" She nodded towards the keyboard that was only inches from him.

"I got a better idea. Why don't *you* set down and pull it up," he said, moving out of the way and pulling the chair out for her, "while I get *you* a glass of wine."

"Brandon," she said as she walked over to the chair and sat down. "It's in the middle of the day and my fun weekend is over. I have a baby to take care of when I go back in." She protested as he pushed the chair, with her in it, closer to the desk.

"One little glass is not going to hurt, besides, I already talked to Lydia and Hans about taking on diaper duty for a few hours today, so I could spend a little one-on-one time with my wife." He kissed her again on the cheek and then headed to the bar. "Since I haven't had you one minute to myself, *all* weekend." he added. "I've missed you!"

"I missed you too!" She replied, giving in and began pecking away on the keyboard. She signed into her email, located the file Charlie had sent and started it downloading by the time Brandon returned to her side.

"So who is the actress in the screen test?" he asked.

"Charlie said he didn't want to influence me with any *celebrity* names, so that part is a surprise." Sage said.

"Ok," Brandon said. "Let's see!"

She clicked the play button and then turned the volume up and both her and Brandon stared at the screen. When she saw the word Stranded on the clapperboard, she wanted to pinch herself. Then the second most astonishing thing happened. The audition tape began to play and Sage and Brandon—for a moment—were totally speechless.

"*Holy shit!* That's *Lola Watters*!" Brandon said.

"I was just going to ask you if my eyes were *deceiving* me!" Sage replied, with equal excitement in her voice.

"I had to look closer myself just to make sure. *Damn* Sage, how in the hell did they get her to look *so* much *like* you."

"Of course they got the description from the book. But how crazy is that?"

"Rewind it." Brandon said. "Start it over."

Sage put the mouse over the controls and restarted the video. Both of them watched intently this time. When it was finished Sage turned to Brandon.

"*Wow!*" Was all she said.

"*Wow* is right."

"What did *you* think?" she asked.

"Looks like we've just *found* our lead!"

"I can't believe she's Charlie's *first* pick. I would have *never* thought I could land an actress of her *caliber* in *my* movie!"

"So, your happy with Lola?"

"*Extremely*!" she gushed. "In fact, I'm *honored*!" Brandon laughed. "What?" she asked.

"Most wives in Hollywood, wouldn't want an actress like Lola doing *love* scenes with their husbands, no matter how much money, they're offering to do it! And *my* wife is just sitting here, *all* excited." The grin on his face was full of mischief.

"And…should I be *worried*?" she asked, which she *really* wasn't. She truly trusted her husband at this point.

He leaned over and kissed her, then pulled away a few inches to look directly in her eyes. "I owe Lola *big* my love, for a favor she did for me a while back, if you remember." Sage nodded to acknowledge she knew exactly what favor he was referring to. "But that's *all* she'll ever get from me. I've *already* sowed my wild oats when it comes to the Hollywood scene, Sage, long before I *met* you. I'm not in the *least* bit interested in revisiting *any* part of it. I'm perfectly content with where I'm at. I'm also head over heels *in* love with the mother of *my* child. Lola is *not* the mother of *my* child." He said, assuring her. "Now that we've got that out of the way, it's time to celebrate." He flashed that infectious smile at her that she loved.

"Brandon, is this *really* happening?" Sage's eyes filled with happy tears, just thinking about her book becoming a movie.

"Yes, baby, everything you've worked so hard for, is finally paying off!" He bent down again and kissed her.

"So what happens now?" She asked, once he pulled away.

"If you want her, you need to call Charlie and confirm it!" he said.

"Do I call him back now or wait until tomorrow?"

Brandon shook his head. "No, *let* him stew. You never want to seem overanxious in this business!"

"Ok, and once I confirm with him, what happens next?"

"Well, if all of the casting is done, sets are designed and

locations are chosen, then it will move into production."
"Which means?"
"Production *means* that I will be leaving you and Tristan behind for a little while to begin shooting for my scenes."
"Of course the baby and I will be coming too?" she questioned.
"Not if I can help it! Sequestered in a trailer on the movie set, is no place for *either* of you. I will be shooting anywhere from 12-14 hours a day. It's safer and more comfortable for you two, to just stay here."
"Charlie says I should be on the set while they're filming, to make sure everything is as I wrote it. If they find the location somewhere here in Montana, that won't be too bad!"
"If they find a location close, I would go for that."
"Charlie said they had a strong lead not far from us and that they were in negotiations for a lease now but he didn't say where."
"Typical of him. He never gives out any details until someone signs on the dotted line *in* blood." Brandon joked.
"Speaking of blood," Sage began, pointing at his hand that was holding his beer. "Did you cut yourself?"
Brandon looked at his palm and wrist where faint smears of blood tainted the skin.
"Yeah, I did earlier. I was trying to get the rest of the broken glass out of the frame." He sat his beer down and walked over to the bar. Sage stood up and followed him. He'd put the frame, in its entirety, inside a shallow box. There were still pieces of glass jutting out in a haphazard fashion along the edge.
"Did it come apart?" Sage asked, leaning over his shoulder as he gripped a safe edge of the wood.
"Not yet." He said. "The back of it is sealed up tight against the picture. I'm hoping we can pry it loose and not do any damage."

Brandon took the corner that had broken free on impact and began to apply pressure to separate the frame. The wood groaned and creaked. At one point he paused long enough to grab a towel on the bar to wrap around the glass, to avoid further injury to his hands. "*Damn*!" he said. "They don't make frames like *this* anymore!" At last, with quite a lot of effort, he broke it in half and managed to slide the pic, intact with the backing, into Sage's hands. Brandon walked past her with the small box and headed in the direction of the trash outside the office door. She took it over to the desk, laid it down on the surface and gently began to pry the photo free from the thick backing. It was almost like an adhesive had been applied around the edges, possibly to make it stay in place. She worried for a second that it wouldn't come off without tearing the photo. But then, little by little, it began to separate, much to her relief. And only once it was separated, did she take a closer look. The padding was actually a *real* newspaper and it was covered in some kind of clear plastic. At first she thought someone had used it to give the photo a base or was used as a filler. But it was not until she glanced at it the *second* time, that she saw someone had written across it, in *red*, angry, thick marker the words; EYE FOR AN EYE!! A chill sliced through her spine as she fought to control her emotions. Her eyes scanned the articles beneath the writing and immediately was drawn to a photo of a plane in the middle of takeoff. Across it, the heading shouting— *MISSING PLANE!* It took Sage only ten seconds more to realize what she was looking at.

An involuntary wail escaped from somewhere deep inside of her, echoing off the walls of the office. A cry so distressful, that the sound of it, brought her husband *running*.

 Fifty-Seven

Courtney was fresh out of the shower, still in a robe, with a towel wrapped around her damp hair, when she heard the doorbell chime in the apartment. Slightly puzzled, she made her way across the living room and over to the panel on the wall. Accessing the camera outside her door, she was a little surprised to see Michael. She silently shook her head and disengaged all the locks.

"I pay top dollar for security and a doorman to keep the riff-raff away from my door." She said, being her snarky self, as she always was with him.

"And I pay top dollar for the riff-raff downstairs that you call *security*, to let me in!" Michael said, walking straight past her and into the living room. "Got a beer?"

Courtney turned to look at him, still holding the door. She shook her head again and shut and engaged the locks and turned to face him. "Well, *hello* to you too!" She tightened the belt on her robe.

"This is no time for formalities, Princess. Go get dressed!" He barked "We need to talk!"

She shrugged her shoulders. It had to be something important because Michael would not show up, otherwise! "Beer is in the fridge." She said, walking towards her bedroom. "Grab one for me too!"

Courtney shut the door to her bedroom and began disrobing in haste. She quickly dressed into a pair of yoga pants with an oversized tee and slipped into the bathroom to do something quick with her wet hair. After combing it out and leaving it to hang loose while it dried, she slipped back out her bedroom door and headed towards the living room. Michael was already seated on one of the twin couches and he was sipping on a bottle of beer. On the coffee table between the two, sat hers in a frosted glass. The man had *class* and a great memory, she had to give him that. "So what do I owe this unexpected visit? Are you coming to tell me I'm fired yet?" she asked, taking a seat across from him.

"Did you have a *good* time in Montana?" he asked instead, ignoring her question. "You look rested, *except* for that bruise on your cheek. Can't wait to *hear* the story behind that?"

"I had a *great* time in Montana!" She said, playing it his way. "Their property is a mountain oasis! The cabin is *beyond* magnificent and the views were so incredible to wake up and go to bed with, that neither Meg *or* myself wanted to leave. Sage is an *absolute* doll, Lydia is a *master* at cooking, Hans couldn't be *more* gracious, baby Tristan is the *cutest* thing in the world and Brandon is *still* being an ass!"

"Sounds like *you* had a great time." Michael said, sounding cynical. "So which one of them gave you a shiner?"

"None!" Courtney said. "I sort of tangled with a door, but *on* accident. Meg was coming *in* the bedroom as I was trying to walk *out* of it."

Michael just stared at her for a second. "*So*, since when do *you* walk towards doors with the *side* of your face?" He wasn't buying it.

"*Ok*! So I was *accidently* eavesdropping on a conversation when *Meg* decided to walk in—*same* difference!"

Michael just stared at her for a second. And then he asked. "Spying on the family so soon into your relationship?" His tone was just slightly sarcastic.

"I wasn't *doing* it intentionally! I just happened to be leaving the room at the same time that everybody decided to have a conversation directly *outside* in the hall! Well— *down* the hall." She added and raised her eyebrows slightly.

"Hear anything that was worth getting clobbered for?" He

asked, rather amused, a slight grin trying to make its appearance at the corners of his mouth.

"Yeah, in a round-a-bout way." She admitted. "It opened up an opportunity for me to speak with Brandon, like we talked about."

"And?" Michael asked.

Courtney filled him in on the *entire* conversation she'd had with Brandon in the barn, on her last night at the cabin. Then she added bits and pieces of the highlights between Meg, Sage and herself during their conversation, out on the terrace. "I think," she said, wrapping up the end of her visit in words, "Brandon now realizes that he and I are on the *same* side when it comes to his wife's welfare. Sage is a great person and she doesn't deserve any of the pain that will come her way *if* her parents or their plane were tangled up in this Pirate's mess. Speaking of, have you heard anything else from your friend since I was away?"

"Yes, I have." He told her about the boat being found not far from the Pirates Lair, shoved up under a clump of trees but no sign of the occupants.

"Any news about the dead woman on the gurney?" Courtney asked.

Michael shook his head. "He didn't go into too much detail about *her*. He just said the FBI were looking into it."

"*Dammit*!" Courtney said. "I was hoping there was something to tell Brandon."

"You know Courtney, when they do identify this Jane Doe, I'm not sure if Bill is in a position to even discuss that with me."

"I've thought about that. And if that's the case, there's a good chance we may *never* know who she is. The FBI has already told one big lie years ago. I can't see them doing the right thing now."

"Let's hope they do, if it *is* her." He said. "I think this infiltration is too big to put a lid on this time, Courtney.

Too many people—including the military—are involved. The world's infrastructures have drastically changed since the FBI screwed-up over twenty years ago. Social media is alive and well and everybody's talking about the Pirate's hideout. It's been trending online since we got home from Africa. The public is watching their every move. It's a little bit harder these days to cover shit up. Somebody within is always willing to sell out for a price. The truth will come out, sooner or later."

"Let's hope! Sage has a right to know if that's her mother."

"Of course she does. You said they reached out to Sage's grandmother. What for?"

"Brandon finally admitted to me it was a necklace that they showed Margot that belonged to Kelley. She was wearing it the day she left with her husband to the airport. But as far as it being the *same* gold heart that was on the dead woman's ankle that I saw in the video, there's no way to prove it. The FBI told Margot that they think the pirates looted the wreckage, was how it made its way to their camp which shoots down any hopes that the Jane Doe was Sage's mother. And Margot never mentioned anything to Lydia about the FBI finding a diary which we know that they did, we just can't prove that either."

"There's always a strong possibility that it *does* belong to Kelley Cassava and they decided *not* to tell her mother." Michael offered.

Courtney stared at him hard. "Why not?"

"A piece of jewelry pilfered during a raid of a wrecked airplane, is easier to swallow Courtney, because over time, gold is not going to perish in the outside elements. But a *diary*, full of paper and bounded by a cardboard cover, now that's a *different* story. In twenty years something like that would eventually disintegrate into nothing, just lying over there in the heat, exposed to the weather, day after day. Introducing a book like that into their story of finding it intact in the jungle like a piece of gold, is a lot harder to swallow for a sharp, shrewd business woman like Margot Hartford, don't ya think?"

Courtney pondered this over for a moment. "You think the old bird is on the level with this one?"

"Why wouldn't she be? She's angry over the loss of her daughter and looking to blame someone for a couple of decades now. I doubt there's much they will get past her and they know it." He said. "And common sense tells me, just as it would tell a detailed-thinking woman like Margot Hartford, that no pirate-looting-thief is going to find a personal diary intact from a wrecked plane and want to carry it back to camp, just to shove into a footlocker and bury it under the ground."

"I see your point." Courtney agreed.

"The inventory logs are invaluable, according to Bill, since it seals the fate on all the pirates that were captured! Those I can see someone burying because its evidence. But not a dead woman's diary!" He shook his head in confusion.

Courtney shrugged and took a sip of her cold beer. "Did the General ever find out who was occupying the hut?"

"One of the prisoners said it was a foreigner, named Don. Nobody has acknowledgement of a last name."

"Don sounds *American*, not foreign." Courtney pointed out. "So do they think this Don guy was the one that was keeping the logs?"

"At this point, there could be several suspects."

"So I take it they haven't found this guy among the captured?"

"Not yet. But they're working on it as we speak."

"Maybe he's the leader who escaped on the boat they found." Courtney mused.

"As I've said before Princess, *anything* is possible."

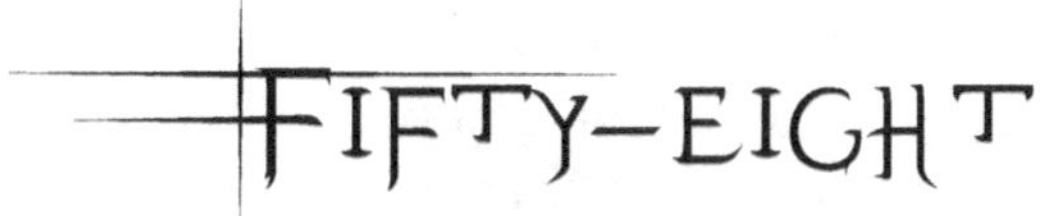FIFTY-EIGHT

She had been completely knocked out for half the night in
the jungle and later awoke, still laying where she had
fallen. She was exhausted and her body was sore. She
could see her arms and legs in the moonlight and they were
covered with cuts and bruises, making the flexibility in her
limbs, stiff *and* painful.

Her ankle was swollen, caused by landing wrong, when she
had been coming down a steep slope. The end result had
been a bad twist. Luck was not on her side. Not being able
to run efficiently could slow her down and cause her death
if she could not get away from her captor or an animal that
meant to have her for a snack.

Putting just a slight bit of weight on her injured left foot,
had her swearing under her breath. She was hoping that
with a little gentle manipulation and stretching, that it
would carry her long enough, to get to her destination
before it was too late. The call of the owls and other
tranquil noises that were typical at night in the jungle, was
a good sign that she was alone in the immediate area. But
she still moved with caution, making as little noise as
possible, just in case.

She had no clue since falling asleep, how long she'd been
out. She was miserable and wet—her clothes were sticking
to her skin and she had matted, dried blood on every inch
of her legs, arms and neck and she'd been bitten by either
ants or something else while she'd laid out cold, on the
earth floor.

While waiting for her foot to adjust and cooperate, she
removed the flask that had been secured to her hip and
drank the water hungrily from the spout. She'd not realized
how parched she'd been until the tepid liquid slid down her
throat, making her swallowing a lot easier. She took a piece

of beef jerky that was wrapped in her pocket and began chewing vigorously, studying the compass while she ate. She was still turned in the right direction but how far away she was from the building, was anyone's guess. She spotted a long stick, from under some brush and with some practice, she began to make small strides, using it as a make-shift cane. Before too long, she managed to hop her way out of the bottom of the slope and back on even ground, where it wasn't so difficult to walk. She forged ahead with determination and stubborn will. Eventually she picked up the pace and was actually making progress. Another hour passed before she came to the edge of the jungle and into the clearing she'd been looking for. A smile of triumph tugged at the features on her face. She limped cautiously towards a clump of trees that would be easy to hide in.

FIFTY-NINE

August, 2012
My dearest darling Sage,

I felt compelled to write this letter because I feel my time here on earth, is getting short. This may be my last trip to the cabin for a while, so I must prepare you when it comes to the events, surrounding your parent's death. I highly doubt that your grandmother has done her duty by telling you herself. She took your mother's death hard and after, in order to heal, she just wanted to put it all behind her. She thought it was in your best interests, not to know the truth. However, I do not.

The story the FBI told us, concerning the plane crash, was an outright lie but I didn't know that in the beginning. It was not until a few weeks after that fateful day, that I became suspicious enough to start checking out the facts. What tipped me off was a special delivery that came directly to the house, addressed to me. The newspaper wrapped in plastic and bound to the back of this frame, was what was inside. The caption, 'Eye for an Eye' was already written in red across the front. It was accompanied by a single photo. There was no return address on the envelope, but I didn't need one to know where it came from, or an explanation of its meaning.

Victor Rocha was an evil man who was riddled with jealousy and a chip on his shoulder, that weighed him down to the point of scum. If you're not familiar by now, as to who he is, then you should get in touch with a man named Charlie Vega. He is an exceptional human being who will explain everything if you hand him this letter and tell him who you are. From this point forward he will become a

very important figure in your life. Be kind to him, my darling. He is just as much a victim, as we all are. As for your grandmother, if she is still with you, tell her it's time to spill her part in this as well.
God speed my child!
I love you with everything I have.

Your loving grandfather, Frank!

Sage stared at the old newspaper in front of her on the coffee table. The sight of the thick, red, angry letters written in rage across the front of the black and white paper, still clearly carried the message of its wrath. Just as it had meant to do a long time ago when it was sent to her grandfather. The photo that accompanied it, was a perfect image of what looked like her mother's gold heart, the one she'd been wearing in the portrait and had on the day she left for the airport. It was carelessly lying on a background of sand. The sun was reflecting on the tip of the heart and Brandon had already pointed out that the clasp was broken in the picture.

"*I feel so bad for Frank!*" Lydia said, staring at the documents on the table. She had taken a seat next to Sage and intermittingly would place a comforting hand on her back. "That bastard Victor was sending him this while that *poor* man was grieving for those kids. How sick can you be?" she stressed.

"Filthy, *bloody* bastard!" Hans echoed, where he stood hovering over his wife's shoulder. "He's beyond sick!"

"He had to have arranged this from inside the prison," Brandon said, staring at the newspaper as well, from his position next to Sage. "He was already incarcerated, when this was sent."

"So where in the *hell* did he get a picture of *my* mother's necklace?" Sage said to no one in particular, in the room.

"And *what* was the meaning behind it? Was he just pouring salt into an already *open* wound, or was he trying to *imply* that *he* was the one behind the crash?"

"Just because Victor had a picture of a heart similar to the one your mother wore, doesn't mean it's the *same* one." Brandon said. "He could easily have had someone find a duplicate, just to make it appear more genuine."

"How would he know something like that?" Sage asked, finally turning her eyes from the documents to look at her husband. "Our grandfathers went through hell to keep that man away from everyone they loved! Don't think my mother wasn't *high* on that list."

"Victor didn't have to get *close* to her, Sage, to see the necklace. He could have had Frank and Everett on camera surveillance and your mother was all over both those equations. At any point they could have noticed the necklace *if* she wore it often. It wouldn't have been too hard for them to find a similar one and snap a picture of it. That style was very popular then."

"He's right, my darling." Lydia said, patting her shoulder again in comfort. "They were very popular. All that peace and love *bullshit* those hippies raved about back in the seventies—why they hung hearts and butterflies and mushrooms on their necks, in their ears and had them symbols printed *all* over their clothes. I remember when your sweet daddy got your mother one. She just *gushed* over it and the sentiment to her he'd had engraved on the back, sent her *over* the moon. I must be getting old because for the life of me, I can't *recall* just what it said."

"What do you think my grandfather is talking about, concerning Nana?"

Sage directed this question to Lydia.

"I don't know, Sage. That is obviously something that you'll *need* to ask her."

"Which is *exactly* what I plan on doing after finding this!" Sage said, waving her hand at the documents in front of her.

"I *knew* she was holding back when we were all at that meeting with Charlie." Brandon said. "There were moments when she'd get this look on her face, during parts of his story. You know, that *troubled* look that says something *real* heavy is weighing on your mind?"

"This could be *what* made my grandfather force someone to open the graves." Sage said, looking first at Lydia and then at Brandon. "And as far as his letter to me goes, I think it's *time* I pay my grandmother another visit!"

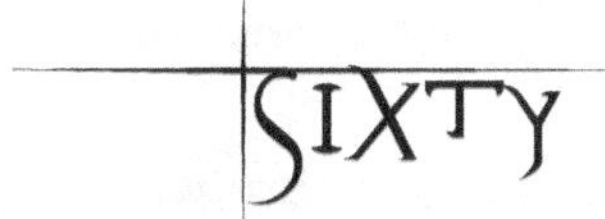

SIXTY

Nearly two-thousand miles away, Agent Fields sat in a conference room, with two other fellow agents and the director, in an intense meeting. They were discussing the evidence, that were spread out on the table between them. "Were all of these items found in the footlocker buried under the ground?" Director DiBernardo asked, directing this question at all three.

Mullins spoke first. "The newspaper and the diary were located in the footlocker, sir. The heart was discovered in a separate hut, on the body of the female Jane Doe, who has now been identified as Winifred Gentry, a missing person out of Louisiana, some twenty years ago."

"Miss Winifred Gentry had quite a rap sheet." The director remarked to no one in particular. "Which looks to me like she would have been 'right at home' living among a bandit of thieves."

"It was obvious to our investigators that she'd lived in the hut she was found in—for quite some time—from the amount of personal effects." Mullins responded. "Did this Winifred Gentry have access or live in the hut where this footlocker was found?"

Again, this was Mullins territory. "The hut where the footlocker was found belonged to another couple, according to a few of the victims who we've been allowed to talk with."

"That doesn't answer my question, Agent Mullins. We need to find out *if* Gentry had access to that hut. Because if she didn't, then we need to find out *who* wrote this cryptic message on this newspaper," he pointed to it laying between them on the table, "Which would then tell us who wrote the *same* message in *bold* letters on the wall in

Gentry's hut! Do we have any names yet, of this couple that lived there?"

"The man's name was Don. They are working on getting the females name. Most of them are still too weak and sick and the doctors are holding my guys at bay over at the hospital, from asking anymore questions for now."

"So I take it, we don't even know *if* we have this Don *or* his girlfriend, in our custody with the other prisoners?" The director asked.

"That would be correct, *sir*!" Mullins answered. "Some of the pirates are trying to play the hero and keep their mouth shut. They aren't being cooperative when it comes to identifying themselves *or* their leader. We've been notified that a rather aggressive negotiator arrived on scene yesterday to help loosen their tongues. We should know more about the workings and the people in this camp very soon. I hear he's really good."

"I don't agree," The director said, rather dryly, glancing at his watch. "He arrived yesterday and it's already two in the afternoon and we *still* have no answers yet." Silence fell thick in the room. "Don is an *ordinary* American name. Are there any *white* men *or* women among the pirates? After all, a *white* couple wouldn't be that *hard* to pick out among a slew of Africans!" Again, he directed this to Mullins.

"There were *no white* people among them, sir. The only ones accounted for were the victims in 'the hole'."

"Was the newspaper loose in the footlocker?" He asked Mullins.

Mullins nervously cleared his throat. "No sir, it was folded and tucked inside the cover of the diary."

"And this Winifred Gentry's cause of death *was* poison?" This he directed to Metz.

"The toxicology reports are not back yet to confirm a hundred percent." Agent Metz began.

"But your *lab* guys have pretty much *confirmed* in your heads, that she *was* poisoned?" He cut in.

Metz nodded. "Along with the investigators on the scene, we have both agreed that it's a ninety-percent chance she *ingested* the poison in her tea, from a plant known as Belladonna."

There was a pause of silence as the director wrote something on a pad of paper in front of him.

"What year was it, that this woman and her boyfriend went missing?" DiBernardo directed this to Fields.

"1987." Agent Fields said, glancing at Gentry's personal sheet in front of her.

"And the plane went missing also in 1987, correct?" "Yes sir!" She didn't have to consult notes to answer that one.

"What an *odd* coincidence." He said in a tone that let all three know, he believed the opposite. "Did you *check* the passengers list and see if this Winifred was on board?"

"Yes sir, I did!" Mullins said. "She was not listed among the passengers."

"But there was *one* female passenger on board that I can't seem to verify yet." Agent Fields said, stepping in. Mullins glanced over at her.

The director turned his attention from Mullins to Fields and said, "Please, *elaborate*."

Fields began. "As we are all aware, back in '87, our national security wasn't as advanced as we obviously are now. Taking that into consideration, virtually *anyone* could have created a fake passport and cleared security if it was good enough. So, knowing that, I decided to do a background check on all the females on board, which were a total of five, just to be sure. Four of the women checked out right away—which included Kelley Hartford-Cassava. There was one that did not. She was one of the stewardesses. I'm running her name through our system now and as of thirty minutes ago the comp was still searching.”

“What caused the red flag?” DiBernardo asked.

“She was the only one *without* a paper trail in the system. The name, date of birth, social security number and the address listed on her passport, didn’t match up in any of the other data searches, I’ve conducted. She also had a note in her file that specified *‘next of kin not found’*, when the plane first went missing.”

“Was that note made by our *infamous* Agent Greene?” The director asked.

“Yes sir.”

He nodded his head slowly in deep thought, then again jotted something down on the pad in front of him, on the table. The room grew thick with a suppressed silence until he finished. He laid the pen down and clasped both his hands together and looked up at all three.

“So right now, we know *two* things for sure.” The director began, releasing a heavy sigh. “Winifred Gentry is no longer *missing* and she was found *dead* in a camp that belonged to a bunch of murderous thieves, in Africa. What we *don’t* know for sure, is *how* she got there, *how* long she’s been there and what *role* she played in the camp. I don’t believe she was one of the pirate’s prisoners, considering her colorful past and the fact she had her *own* hut. If your hunch turns out to be right,” he said this to Fields. “and she *was* a passenger on that plane, under an assumed name and a fake passport, then our problem doesn’t get any better, it grows!”

“If she’s alive, then how did she survive if the plane crashed!” Fields spoke aloud before she could stop herself, the realization and the excitement of the idea hitting her full force.

Director DiBernardo smiled in an odd, yet smug way, as he faced her, from across the table. In her peripheral she could see Mullins and Metz, in unison, turn their heads and look in her direction.

"Which is *more* the reason why we need answers immediately, on *how* this woman arrived into this camp." The director said calmly, too calmly. "And since her so-called boyfriend went missing with her at the same time, has anyone checked on the passengers list to see if he was among the men?"

"I did." Mullins spoke up. "Josef Gates was not listed."

"I doubt very highly that a criminal *such* as Gates would *fly* under his *real* name. Did you look as deep into that list as Agent Fields did?" he asked him directly.

"No sir." Mullins said. "None of them waved any flags on the initial search!"

"If this Gentry woman slid by on a fake passport, then I'm sure Mr. Gates did the same! I highly doubt it's just a coincidence that they disappeared *together*!"

"But, if she's alive—or *was*—and we find Gates among the prisoners…," Fields couldn't find the right words to finish, so the director did it for her.

"Then your next question would be the same as I was about to ask. Are the *other* passengers that were aboard that flight *still* alive if these two cons are? Am I correct, Agent Fields?"

"Yes sir!" she responded.

Another lull of silence filled the room. Then the director spoke. "If the pirates planned the ultimate theft by hijacking a jet, then *where* in the hell is that *damn* plane? It's not like it's a *small* object that one can hide easily, even though it's a jungle out there, so to speak. We're talking a *Gulf Stream Jet,* that weighed over sixty-thousand pounds. You'd think it wouldn't be that hard to locate, correct? So we need to find out if they sold it, parted it out, traded it— for all we know it no longer exists. And my last question for now would be—*Who helped Gentry and Gates pull this off?* I don't see them doing it alone. They were cunning but not smart enough to execute this, all by themselves. *Agreed?*" Everyone nodded. "We've got a lot of work to do!" the director reminded them. "And the best way to approach this, is to get some of the toughest questions answered, which means our GI Joe needs to use whatever *means* necessary, to get these dirty pirates to talk! *Now!*" he shifted his glance to Mullins.

"I'll contact General Bradley right away and pass the message on sir!" he assured him.

DiBernardo then turned his attention to Fields.

"Let me know what the results are on this female passenger your running. And in the meantime, while you're waiting, check the backgrounds on all the male passenger list as well." She nodded as the director began gathering his pad and papers and shoving them in his open briefcase. "Agent Metz, as soon as your confirmation comes back on that tox-test, I want a copy of it on my desk, *asap*. Mullins, tell the General I expect to receive some kind of answers *today*, concerning the pirates and check the backgrounds on the pilots that were flying that plane!"

"On it right now, sir!" He fished his phone out of his inside suit pocket and began scrolling through contacts. The director closed his briefcase and left the room. Mullins was the next to go and then Metz muttered something and left himself.

Agent Fields sat for a moment longer, staring at the newspaper that was still lying in front of her on the conference table. On the front page of the Billings, Montana paper, was an article featuring a couple from Florida who had built a cabin retreat in the middle of nowhere, to serve as a second home. While many retirees were known for escaping to Florida to avoid the frigid northeast and west temperatures during the severe winters, the couple featured, did just the opposite. They used it to escape the extremely hot and brutal heat in the summers, that the sunshine state was known for.

She studied the faces and the body language of Margot Hartford and her husband Frank, smiling heartily as they posed arm in arm, in front a monstrosity-sized cabin, that was so vast, that only a portion of it could be seen behind them in the background. It gave the viewer a sense of a happy time in their lives and of a couple who looked as if they were on top of the world…that is, until you looked at the *angry* red scrawl of words, written across their happy faces…

EYE FOR AN EYE!!

Beside it, was the photo that the investigators at the Pirates Lair had taken of the wall in Winifred Gentry's hut. The same vicious quote, that survived through the ages—thanks to the King of Babylon—was scribbled in what appeared to be red lipstick, in huge letters on the wall made of sticks and mud, just inches above Gentry's head in the photo. The only problem was, the same person that wrote it on the newspaper was *not* the same one who wrote it on the wall. The paper handwriting was rough and slim lettered and boxy, more like a man's writing. The one on the wall had more of a rounder, fatter font, with a flair in the tail of the letters, more *feminine*.

The message was *not* meant for law enforcement.

It was *personal*.

Call it *gut* instinct, call it intuition, call it *whatever* but the *passion* behind the manner, in which *both* of the messages were written, *screamed* of an incredible vengeance of *two* different kinds to her!

The *first*, was written on the newspaper, like some sort of *revenge* or atonement. But the *second* one, on the *wall* in the hut…it spoke to her *more* in the form of a reckoning or what was known back in the day, as a *retribution!*

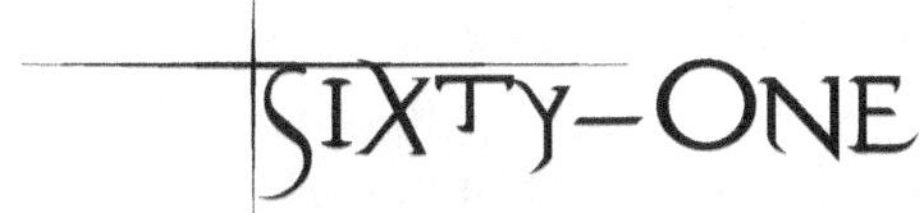

SIXTY-ONE

Courtney typed for thirty minutes straight, adding to the never-ending notes she'd compiled on her laptop, surrounding the Pirates lair. While the conversation with Michael was still fresh in her mind, she wanted to add important *key* parts of it, to the ever-growing list of questions, that she needed answered.

When was this nightmare ever going to end?

She sighed deeply, massaged her temples for a few seconds to lessen the tension, looked at her phone and made herself turn away from the screen. Her eyes immediately were drawn to the chair by the door. In the seat was the binder that Charlie had given her, with Everett's memories tucked inside.

She'd forgotten all about it, with everything else going on. Her eyes shifted immediately to the bookshelf on the right. The teddy bear, the one she'd been holding in the photo, the one she *now* knew Everett had given her, sat on the top shelf, haggard, but looking back at her with it's big, brown, button eyes. She thought about the kind words and warm description of the man Meg had told them about, back at the cabin. The man who was *supposedly* Courtney's biological father, that had saved them all. The man she would *never* know or have the *chance* to meet. The man who was legendary and *feared* among his peers at the same time. Who bore through his genes, another *legendary* icon of her time, her nephew, Brandon. Another one whose peers *feared* him but for *different* reasons.

The apple didn't fall far from the tree…of course, she was part of that tree and her peers obviously didn't *fear* her at this moment. Had they ever?

Whether she wanted to admit it out loud to anyone or not…she could not *deny* it to herself, any longer. The restlessness, the bouts of becoming unfocused, the disorganization of her usual routine and her short temperament, were all due to the fact, that she had *not* come to terms with the story of *her* birthright. The two people she *thought* were her parents, in fact, *weren't* and not far away, all *that* time, and most times just a *step* behind her, was her *real* father. The one *who* had given her life, the one *who* had given up *his,* so she could have a *normal* one. Suddenly, since the first time this all began, she was curious to know more.

She made herself stand up and walk across the room to the chair. She hesitated twice before finally picking up the binder. It was cold on the outside and felt heavier than the day she'd carried it in here. The teddy bear came down next and with it, she headed out the door to the hall.

Ten minutes later she was propped up in the comfort of her bed, leaned against a mass of fluffy pillows, holding a frosted glass of cold beer, with the binder on her lap—still closed. The teddy bear was just a few inches away. She stared at it for a few seconds longer before she released a deep breath and opened the cover.

The first page was a quote written in a black, felt-tip, bold ink.

Then I said goodnight and tucked you away
inside a place called Nostalgia, where
you'll always remain unspoiled.
Somewhere between my lungs that used to breathe ocean
air and my belly that fluttered with hope.

~Victoria Erickson

Below it was a five-by-seven envelope that had been glued to the page. Courtney sat her glass down on the nightstand

and used both hands to carefully open the flap. Inside was what looked like a picture. She gently slid it out and turned it over.

A woman with dark chocolate eyes, rimmed in long, silky fan of black lashes, stared back at her. The perfect rose-colored hues on her cheeks, blended in flawlessly with the bronze-colored complexion of her skin and her nose was absolutely perfect. Her full red lips gave just a hint of the flirtatious nature, behind the personality of its owner and framing her face was a thick, wavy mane of black hair. She wore a beautiful blue-flowered sundress that displayed a graceful and petite pair of bronze shoulders. She looked to be in her mid-to-late-thirties. The background looked like it was taken outside, somewhere tropical, maybe. Courtney had no idea who she was, but there was no doubt she was drop-dead gorgeous—stunningly gorgeous beyond words. She flipped the photo over and scanned the back to see if there was anything written, that she had missed the first time. But it was blank except for a small heart, drawn in the same black felt marker that had been used to write the quote above the envelope.

Courtney turned it back over and stared at the picture for a few seconds. The woman's eyes seemed oddly familiar and she found that she couldn't stop staring at them. She wondered briefly if this was Brandon's grandmother, Everett's first wife, Andy's mother. She remembered him telling her that he saw a picture of her one time, that his dad had. He described her as having dark hair and dark eyes, the total opposite coloring of his famous dad. After all, this was Everett's binder, something he had made up of his memories, his life and she would make sure that when she was finished with it, she would give it to Andy next. He would probably be grateful to know, he had at least one good picture of his biological mother to hold onto. She gently slid the photo back inside the sleeve, closed the flap and turned the page.

It didn't take long for her to get lost in the mementos of Everett's binder. Page after page held tokens of his travels, all the way from postcards to matchbook covers of casinos, musicals and famous icons of the fifties, sixties and seventies. Pictures were scattered throughout of both he and Frank, Charlie and Jack, even a few of what looked like Meg, when she was about fifteen. Everett was impeccably dressed in every one of them exactly as Meg had said, when describing him back at the cabin! He was an extremely handsome man and at least a head taller than most of the men he posed with. He looked sturdy, strong and built pretty solid, during a time when gyms weren't on every corner, like they were today. She also couldn't help but notice he seemed very popular with the ladies. There was always an abundance of women, when he was photographed at parties or places that looked like casinos or clubs.

Another photo she came across, was of Everett and Frank, standing outside the doors of the furniture store they had started together—the one where he'd shot Rocha's brother dead and filled Victor's body with three bullets before the cops showed up. Then another below it, of a couple, who was no doubt Kelley and Jack, on either side of him, as they smiled sincerely at the camera in front of the same doors. Sage looked so much like the both of them, yet neither one looked like the other. It sort of reminded her of the two sons of actor, Martin Sheen— Emilio Estevez and Charlie Sheen. They both looked *just* like their father, yet the two brothers looked *nothing* alike. DNA to Courtney, was such a random and crazy thing.

The next page was a single photo, of a newborn in an eight-by-ten size. By first sight alone, she knew it was *her* as a baby but it was one she had never seen before. The page opposite held about four more, in a three-by-five size. She looked like she was encircled in a pink blanket, just as beautiful and delicate as the dress she had on. It was a very fancy, beautiful white satin dress with tons of lace and ruffles. A fancy bow was bound around a head full of medium-shade of brown hair and matched the lace on her dress. It reminded her of something a baby would be dressed in, for a Catholic christening.

She studied the photos for a moment longer and then gave in and turned the page. A sharp intake of breath escaped from her lips involuntarily. In a five-by-seven sized-photo, was the *same* dark, exotic woman that was on the first page she'd come across in the envelope, under the quote. This time she was not alone in the pic but was cradling Courtney, as an infant, in the same christening-type-dress, with a smile that was…*adoring*, as she looked down at her, in her arms. Baby Courtney was laughing and looking up at her with the same adoring smile.

"*Oh God!*" she said, out loud as she read the words, *Catalina and Isabella, 1969* written with the same black marker underneath. "*Oh God!*" She repeated, not able to control the crazy emotion that was producing sudden pressure in her chest. She pushed the book away quickly, off her lap and onto the bed. It slid too far to the side and ended up falling to the floor with a thud. It landed open to the first page. Gravity caused the photo of Catalina to spill out and stop within centimeters of the last sentence of the quote written there.

Somewhere between my lungs that used to breathe ocean air and my belly that fluttered with hope.

Courtney flipped her legs around and sat on the side of the bed, trying to steady the rush of rapid breathing, that had come up out of nowhere, working her lungs into a frenzy.

She could not tear her eyes away from the dark ones in the photo, that were staring back at her from the floor. Nor could she stop re-reading the last line of the stupid quote. She mentally tried to calm herself, averting her eyes off the woman that she thought in the beginning, was Andy's *birth* mother, when instead, it was *her* own! Something suddenly brushed up against her leg. Spooked, she jumped and turned to see it was just the teddy bear, *not* some nostalgia monster that had crawled out from under her bed. The sudden movement had caused it to roll over, resting next to her thigh, face-up. It was the bear that Everett had given to her as a child. The bear she'd loved and held for comfort, when she'd been scared. The bear that now suddenly *seemed* menacing.

She dared to glance down at the photo of Catalina again. She had been cheated by life and God and everyone who had a hand in the finality of it. She would never know what it was like to feel *either* parent's hugs, their kisses, their words of encouragement, their advice, their life story in their *own* words. She would never *hear* their voices and what they sounded like, or know what their habits were—their likes and dislikes, their goals and their failures, their lessons and their love…their *love*…she would never have a chance to know *real* love.

The rage within always led her back to here, led her back to the emptiness she'd felt all her life. Suddenly out of anger, she grabbed the bear, stood up and threw it across the room, as hard as she could, just wanting to get *rid* of it, get it *out* of her sight!

It sailed in the air, it's back connecting with the wall, making a *clank, clank, clanking* noise, as it slid down and fell to the floor, resting on its side.

She grabbed her beer, took a healthy drink and started to pace and then abruptly stopped, *mid*-stride. She stared straight ahead for a second in pause, as a thought barreled

its way through the anger, that was crowding her head.
Something was way out of sync here...
Slowly she turned and glanced over her shoulder where the
stuffed toy was resting on the floor. She tilted her head as
more confusion clouded her brow.
The bear was made of stuffing...
Sure it had buttons for eyes but the rest of him was *stuffing*!
So *why* then, had it made that *clanking* noise, when it had
connected with the wall?
She abandoned her beer on the night stand, quickly walked
over, bent down and picked it up. The button eyes were
made of *hard* plastic, and embedded in the fabric. If the
eyes had *made* contact first, no doubt they would have
made a noise.
But they didn't.
She began squeezing along first one leg and then the other.
Finding nothing, she moved on to the arms, then around the
neck and began making her way down the stomach, then
stopped...
There was something *hard* in its back.
Possibly a small music box?
A lot of stuffed bears came with them, to soothe a baby in
the crib when played, so it wasn't something out of the
ordinary. Most music boxes had batteries inside to make
them play. The manufacturer would have provided a flap
for easy access, whether it be by zipper or by Velcro, to
change them out periodically.
Just seemed odd that she had never noticed it before or
remembered that it was there. She flipped it over on its
back, feeling along the seam, looking for an opening. It
turned out to be Velcro.
The seam had yellowed and looked really worn with age.
She could tell it hadn't been opened in a very long time. It
took her a few tries to break the bond and at one point she
thought she was ripping the wrong seam. If there had been

any batteries left inside, they were no doubt rusted and probably had crystallized the acid to the box *years* ago. She dug around just inside the opening, fishing with her finger and instead came across something cold and flat. Not knowing *what* could be in there after all this time, she jerked her finger out, feeling the creepy crud rolling up her spine and walked out into the hall and into the kitchen. She turned on the bright overhead light, slid the kitchen drawer open and pulled out a set of slim, silver tongs. They were a perfect fit as they slid inside and did the fishing where her finger had been. She heard and then felt them *brush* up against something hard and thinking she had it in the right place, gave it a tug.

All that came out was old, musty stuffing.

"*Dammit!*" she said, to the emptiness of the kitchen.

Trying not to damage the bear, she tilted it once more in better light and slid them in again. This time she felt on the outside of the fur to help guide them in.

That's when she realized the object was no longer in the same spot. Whatever it was, had slipped down further towards the top of the leg and it was definitely not square *like* a music box.

She pushed the tongs deeper. Again, she gave it a pretty good yank and this time, struck pay dirt. The object came out with a force and it pinged off her chest and fell to the floor with a thud. Courtney stepped back and looked down. It didn't take her long to find it.

Just inches from the baseboard of her island, lie a tiny Ziploc clear bag. It held what looked like a *gold* chain inside. Courtney picked it up with shaky fingers, opened the zipper and it slid out smoothly onto the counter. She stared at it disbelievingly.

In front of her, under the harsh light, lie a gold *heart* on a chain—*identical* to the one Sage's mother was *wearing* in the portrait

SIXTY-TWO

Around five PM Montana time, Brandon's phone became quite animated. The *first* of two, multi-media texts came in from Courtney, then shortly after, she stopped texting and *started* calling. The only problem was; he couldn't answer because Sage was right there, *inches* away. They were deep in a discussion about their impending trip to first California—to see Charlie—and then on to confront Margot in Florida. Thank *God* he still had the ringer on *silent* and in his hands, facing *away* from her because he could *imagine* what would have happened if she'd just now seen Courtney's name popping up on his screen. Brandon hated the sneaking around and felt guilty as hell for not coming clean right away with Sage, about Courtney's findings in Kenya. But he needed a little more convincing before he would put his wife through anymore unwanted stress. That's why he'd wait until she was engaged elsewhere before he would return any calls or dare look at the images Courtney had sent.

He continued to engage in a conversation with Sage while texting his pilot Johnny, about their upcoming plans. Halfway through sending the date they wanted to fly out, the phone began vibrating again and he saw Madison's name pop up on the screen—another *call* he couldn't take in front of her.

Damn!

Why was everyone calling at the wrong time!

Sage eventually left the conversation and their bedroom to call her grandmother out on the terrace. Brandon put some distance between them as he took off downstairs to the den, trying to access the pictures on his phone Courtney had sent him, at the same time. While the first one was downloading, his phone vibrated again and this time the caller was Ken. Hoping that nothing was wrong, he quickly hit the green button and put the cell to his ear.

"Hey Ken!" He said, as he stepped through the doorway of the deserted den. "Sage is on the other line, calling Margot." A nice fire had warmed up the room and he took a seat that faced the doorway, just in case Sage come looking for him.

"That's *why* I'm calling you, son. While they're yacking, you and I need to *talk*!"

"Is everybody ok?"

"Margot's resting, if that's *what* you're asking but her stubbornness will *never* get better."

Brandon laughed. "A *trait* she passed down to her granddaughter!"

"Lord *help* us both, right? Anyway, I know Lydia brought you up to date concerning this FBI business with Margot. There's something about it that just doesn't sit right with me and I wanted to run it by you."

Fifteen minutes later, he called Madison back. He was still waiting on a copy of the passengers list but as far as breaking into the FBI code to find out what they were up to, he had not been successful.

"They got a lid on the investigation alright. Nobody will touch it and the few that will, hasn't been able to hack anything yet." Madison said, sounding defeated for once.

"Whatever is going on over there, they've got it under lock and key. Nobody knows anything. Not even my fed buddies, retired *or* active. Only a select few are allowed to be involved. An FBI agent by the name of Belinda Fields is heading the investigation. She's known among her peers to be pretty determined to seek justice and she's fair." Ten minutes later he hung up with Madison and looked at the images in the text, that Courtney sent. He wondered why she was sending him a picture of the *same* necklace that she'd shown him before. This time it looked like it was laying on a kitchen counter instead of around a dead woman's ankle. But when he looked at the second photo, his throat went dry. The inscription on the back said, '*Isabella*'. He didn't even bother to listen to the voicemail. He phoned her directly.

"Where in the *hell* did you get *that*?" he asked, again glancing at the empty doorway.

"I take it you didn't *listen* to my voicemail?" she said, in a sarcastic tone.

"Why would I *listen* to your voicemail, when I'm going to *call* you?"

"Because if you had, you would already *know* where *that* came from, when I was hysterically *screaming* it into your recorder *twenty* minutes ago!"

"*So…*are you going to tell me *now* or should I hang up and go *listen* to the voicemail?" he asked, sarcastically.

"*Where's* Sage?" Courtney asked, in a huff.

"She's upstairs talking to her grandmother on the terrace and I can tell you the conversation won't be a long one, if I know my wife. You better hurry up and start talking." Courtney began hastily telling Brandon about finding the pictures of Catalina, which led to finding the heart necklace with the name engraved on the back, inside the teddy bear that had been in her possession for years. She told Brandon there was some kind of significance behind the gold hearts.

"You know how I *feel* about coincidences, Brandon." All he could say was, "This is just getting, more and more confusing by the minute." Then he filled her in on what Ken had just told him.

"We both know there's only one reason that the FBI would want DNA from Margot." Courtney said. "It has something to do with *Kelley*!"

"DNA is for *living* tissue comparison." Brandon said.

"The feds did it to compare the Jane Doe." Courtney said.

"They wanted to be sure it wasn't Kelley."

"There's no *other* explanation." He said.

"Have you *told* Sage yet?" She asked.

"*Hell* no. I was waiting on more info. She's already been hit hard once today."

He told her about the newspaper they found behind the frame, along with a picture of her mother's heart necklace.

"Victor was taunting Frank it sounds like. I wonder why he singled him out? I thought it was Everett he was always after because of the affair."

"Sage thinks it's because he went after what mattered most to Everett and that was Frank. What mattered most to Frank was his daughter. After that, next in line was his granddaughter Sage."

"Karly took care of that."

"Karly came after *me*!" Brandon said, correcting her. "*Both* times."

"Oh there's no doubt she personally wanted a piece of you too. Not sure why, but yeah, I can see your point. I even remember her saying something to the effect of not being interested in *any* of us, except *you*, back at Margot's."

"We're missing *something* here."

"I agree. She was trying to *kill* the baby which is *your* bloodline. Then you would have been next. Wonder if she has any clue about Andy being Everett's son?"

"Or that *you're* his daughter! She did mention Isabella was on that *death* list of hers."

"I think Everett plays a bigger role in this than anyone is giving him credit for. Too bad *he* wasn't the one who kept a journal." Courtney said, being flippant.

"Yeah, too bad!" Brandon agreed.

SIXTY-THREE

"So according to *one* of our victims, the Gentry woman was the leader's long-term girlfriend." Agent Barbara Ross said to Fields, in the privacy of her office.

"Who we already suspect is Josef Gates." Fields added. "He made everyone address him as *Shetani* which means *'the devil'* in Swahili. While the poor woman told me this, she began violently shivering in her bed when she said *his* name. I asked her if she could identify him in a line-up. She started flipping out when she thought I was going to put her in the *same* room as him and had to be sedated. Doc said she'd been in that hole for three years and was very traumatized. Several of the pirates had been taking turns raping her for a while and he doubted she would ever be able to live a normal life again. The next victim to talk to me was an older woman, who had spent more time around the tribe. Apparently they used her as a regular cook for the camp instead of their dick's pin-cushion. She was taken out of the prison 'hole' quite often and left out, sometimes as many as a few days at a time. She also confirmed what our first victim did, that the Gentry woman was the leaders' girlfriend. Towards the end, Winnie suspected that she wasn't the *only* female the leader was bedding in the camp. Gentry went into a rage at both him and who she *thought* was the rival. She was out for blood and physically attacked the woman in front of everybody during dinner time. It took several pirates to pull her off and break it up. The cook said the devil was present the entire time but he did nothing to stop it. It was obvious that he was enjoying the fact, that two women were fighting over him. She also said that Gentry was as feared in the camp as the leader was because they *both* had a sick, *twisted* way of viewing life. She said Winnie liked to fancy herself as a *witch*. She was always spouting off at the mouth to someone, threatening to curse or conjure up spells to wound or kill them. She acted no different the night she attacked the *other* woman in front of everyone. She claimed her rival would be dead for messing with her man. That next morning, at the crack of dawn, we moved in our military and seized the camp and found Winnie dead, instead."

"Did anyone mention the *name* of this *other* woman, the rival?" Fields asked, feeling a twinge of excitement beginning to surge through her.

"Her supposed rival was referred to as '*the herbalist*'. She was valuable to the leader because she knew how to combine a mixture of botanicals to heal, soothe and cure a lot of illnesses *holistically* within the camp. She was a prisoner, no different from the rest but she was granted limited freedom like the cook because of her skills. Gentry, on the other hand, thought the woman was having sex with him to gain favors. The gossip just added to it. The old woman says the herbalist hated the leader and his girlfriend, even more."

"So it looks like the herbalist is the likely one who poisoned Gentry with the Belladonna." Fields observed. "Since she previously attacked her, with intentions to kill, it's obvious she had a score to settle which gives her motive and access to the poison."

"Whoever the herbalist is, she did us all a favor by taking Winnie out. Gentry did things to those victims that was just inhumane! She deserved what she got." Agent Ross said, shaking her head in disgust.

"This woman you interviewed, the cook? She's a great witness. Can she identify the leader if we do a line-up?"

"Mugshots have been taken of all the pirates that we have in custody. They've been shown to all the victims that were in stable condition and would cooperate. Many confirmed that the Devil wasn't among them which means he's still out there *loose,* in Kenya somewhere. I've sent one of our top sketch artists over to work up a likeness with the cook. I'm hoping we have something to use by this afternoon, that we can work with. We'll find this prick, one way or another." She promised with an edge to her voice.

"What about the man who worked out of the hut that the footlocker was found in? Did anyone know him?" Fields asked, feeling somewhat deflated.

"The cook knew a little about him. "Ross said. "She said most of the pirates referred to him as the *bookkeeper* and that he was really nice. He would roam the camp freely during the day time but before dusk, he was made to return to his hut and he was padlocked in. They wouldn't remove it until the next morning. He was no doubt one of the prisoners just as she and the herbalist were. And like them, he had a skill that bought him a little freedom in the camp and a hut to call his own."

"What the hell would a band of thieves want with a bookkeeper out in the middle of a jungle?" Fields asked. "And what's with all the titles for the people within the camp? Didn't anyone have *normal* names?"

"She didn't know much else about him except his name was Don, that he talked with an accent and he and another woman tended to the wounded and the weak during the day."

"The herbalist?"

"No, she said it was *another* woman, who she assumed had a medical background of some sort because she was always summoned when one of the pirates fell seriously ill. She also dictated to the leader, *when* he should summon the herbalist for her. It sounded to me like she had some kind of control over him the way the woman talked because he seemed to do whatever she asked. There were dynamics between them, of some sort. He didn't take orders like that from any other prisoner."

"Interesting." Fields said. "Did she say what this woman looked like? Was she white, African, Spanish?"
Ross shook her head. "No, the cook is in her sixties and very unique. I had to get a translator involved because she doesn't know a word of English. She said she'd never been up close to the woman in question, only saw her from afar a few times. She said she never saw her face. Apparently, anytime the woman would come outside of the hut, she was always wrapped from head to toe, because of the hot sun."
"What's the cooks story? How did she end up as a prisoner in the camp?" Fields asked.
"She claims her family was very poor back in her country and couldn't afford to travel in the past. Her grandson was the first to go to college and he was the one responsible for her being in Africa, at the time she was captured by the pirates. He bought her a surprise cruise for her birthday—which included a safari trip near Kenya. It was during that trip, that their jeep suddenly became surrounded by a bunch of natives, with lots of guns aimed at their faces. The guide was forced out of the vehicle and then shot dead on the side of the road in front of them. The jeep with the passengers still on it, was driven to a place not far away, where a van, that had no windows in the back, waited. They were transferred from the jeep into the van and then driven for what seemed like *half* the night. The next time they pulled her out, it was early dawn. It took a few seconds for her eyes to adjust from the dark, smelly, sweat box they had all been traveling in for hours. When she began to focus, she realized they had stopped near a huge building that looked like it had just been plopped down in the middle of nowhere. She described these thick, dense, canopied trees and brush that surrounded it to the point that it just blended in with the scenery. '*If you didn't know it was there, you wouldn't see it*'—was her comment."

"Did they take her inside the building?" Fields was hoping she would say yes but Ross was shaking her head again. "No, they had them standing outside the van for a good twenty minutes. It was then that she first laid eyes on the *Devil* himself. He came with a few other men who were also heavily armed, from a thick of trees, to what she thought was the west. It didn't take her long to figure out he was completely in charge. She describes him as a very tall, dark-skinned, very fit man, in his early fifties. At first she thought he was a native of Africa, like his minions that do his bidding but later, she realized he was just really dark from repeated abuse under the direct sun. It wasn't until the rainy periods, that his skin began to lighten enough on his face, for her to realize he had some sort of tattoo-marking near his eye. She *also* seemed extremely *nervous* when she talked about the leader, like the other victim did, only she didn't end up having to be sedated after. But she did warn me that if I ever were unfortunate enough to meet him face-to-face, I would forever have a chill in my spine that would never go away. She's convinced he's the *real* devil sent from hell and he's roaming our earth right now, disguised in the likeness of a man."

"I can't say that I don't agree with her." Agent Fields said. "If he's not the real one, he's close enough to it from the stories I've heard about him and he has to be captured. How long has this woman been held captive by the pirates?"

Agent Ross replied. "She was one of the luckier ones, with only a little over a year under her belt. Because of her age and the fact that she was a master at cooking, she escaped the horrors that her younger, fellow female victims had to endure. Eventually, she'll re-acclimate successfully back into the normal life she once knew. Can't say much for the others."

"What about this herbalist? Anybody know where she went?" Fields asked.
Agent Ross shook her head. "We have no idea at this moment, where she is. All of the victims have been positively identified. She's not among them."
"That's because she poisoned Gentry and then ran off with her *lover*—the leader." Agent Fields said, matter-of-factly. "My mother used to say, *'where there's smoke, there's fire'*. So let's just say, *maybe* the rumors in the camp were true about the two of them having more between them then just her healing qualities. Winifred was the only one to stand in their way, which is why she's dead and the herbalist isn't. Aren't any of the pirates talking yet?"
"They're playing the usual, *foreign* game. Using the excuse that none of them speak or understand English. We have a translator now on scene to fix that. Between him and the negotiator, they should learn something very soon. As for the victims, most are seriously ill and protected by the doctors in attendance right now. No one wants to talk and who can blame them? They've been tortured and beat down and made to live no better than pigs at the slaughter. Frightened beyond repair doesn't even began to describe their present state of mind. Most just want to put this nightmare behind them and reconnect with their loved ones who thought they were all dead."
"Someone needs to talk and *fast*! We need to find out *where* this building is that the cook was first taken to. It might be a second hideout where the leader and the herbalist are now. If it's so obscured by nature's landscaping that we can't find it on our own, then we need someone to take us there."
"The pirates are the only ones who can guide us. The victims know nothing. I've already asked." She said, shrugging her shoulders.

Ross and Fields soon ended their meeting and two hours later, Mullins appeared at her door.

"You got a second?"

Fields nodded and paused in her paperwork as he came all the way in and shut the door.

"Any luck on the prints yet?" she asked.

"The prints for the boat just arrived and are being fed into the system as we speak but the partial thumb print on the tea cup we took from the hut, is not getting any hits so far." He walked over and took the chair Ross had vacated not long before.

"How about you? Any luck on the male passengers yet?" He nodded at the list laying in front of her, that she'd been going over when he came in.

"Nothing jumps out at me. I'm running backgrounds now. It will take a while." she said. "What's up?" she asked, nodding towards the file folders he had in his hand.

"I've been checking into relatives and acquaintances of the pilots aboard the flight." Mullins said. "Most of their statements were really nothing of value in the past, when Agent Greene was running the show. Since we all know he *faked* some of the documents surrounding the crash, I decided to go back and re-interview some of them to see if anything of significance had been jogged from their memory, after all this time. Mrs. Gail Rueben was an aunt to one of the pilots on the flight and the third one I contacted on the list. An elderly gentleman, who claimed he was her former husband, said Mrs. Rueben had passed away some years back. I expressed my condolences and explained the reason for my call and before too long, he began to yak away. He tells me that back in the day, he and the Mrs. were quite the traveling duo. Once they both retired, they began taking year-round trips and visited countries all over the world. Since her only favorite nephew was an ace pilot who flew internationally, he said their airfare to get to these destinations came fairly cheap. Once she died, he slowed way down. On the tenth anniversary of his wife's death, Mr. Rueben decided to take one last trip to Italy, as a dedication to her memory. According to him, it was her favorite vacationing spot. While there, he made it a point to shop the farmer's market, where he and Mrs. Rueben would go every time they visited. During his stroll, he saw a man about a hundred and fifty yards ahead of him, that looked a hell of a lot like his wife's nephew, who was supposed have died in that '87 crash. He said he was talking to another man in the doorway of a pizzeria. He tried to cut through a thick throng of people to get a closer look, when someone accidentally bumped into a loaded cart filled with grapes, that ended up spilling all over the ground. It generated quite a commotion and took his focus off the duo up ahead for a few seconds. When the pathway was finally cleared and he could get by, he looked up and the doorway was empty— both men were gone."

"We all have a doppelganger." Fields said, not really ruling it out.

"That's what I said to myself when he told me. But I thought I'd run it by you anyway."

"Ok. So if hypothetically, let's say the pilot is still alive and faked his own death. Why would he do it?"

"Well, we did discuss the theory that the plane was possibly hijacked and never crashed. So I would say money, the usual suspect."

"No doubt money is always the most popular motivation and if so, he had to have been *involved* from the beginning." Fields debated.

Mullins said. "And what better way to successfully hijack a plane than to be the one who is *in* control of it."

She stared at him for just a second while the wheels in her brain began picking up pace. "If that's the case, you can bet the *other* co-pilot was done away with, long before the plane ever reached the Indian Ocean." Fields said.

"Unless *she* was in on it too." Mullins said.

"*She*? The co-pilot was a woman?" Fields asked.

"Yeah! I just noticed it when I was looking over the reports!"

"Between Gates and the pilot, it would have been easy to overpower her. And Winnie, acting as one of the stewardesses, could have easily allowed her boyfriend on, if she were the one working the door where the passengers boarded. It would have been a piece of cake for her to have lifted a uniform with no one the wiser back then." She glanced quickly down at the list of males in front of her on the sheet of paper. "Which one was the nephew of the Rueben's?"

"His name was Lorenzo Martin." Mullins said, then slid a sheet of paper from the folder he had in his hand and laid it on the table in front of her. It was a printed copy of a passport picture. A man who looked to be no older than late twenties, early thirties, smiled back at the camera. He had brown eyes, medium brown hair, a rather large nose for his deep-set eyes, followed by a wide mouth, thin lips with a deep dimple that rested in the middle of his chin. A signature pilot's cap adorned his head. Flight stripes and colorful pins decorated the right breast of his matching flight jacket. The points on the white collar peaking just above the deep navy blue coat, was also bejeweled with a few honorable pins the size of an eraser head. His smile would have looked genuine to some but to Fields the deadpan stare from the eyes painted a darker story of his soul.

"This was taken a year before the crash. He started flying at age twenty-six on small, single-engine planes—Cessna's, Beechcraft's, Pipers—then he flipped over to the commercial side and began training and flying for Pan

American. That was short lived. Within two and a half years he left the company and obviously struck gold when he began flying *independently* for private charter flights. At the time he disappeared, he'd invested five years and he was thirty-eight. The aunt, Gail Rueben, was his father's older sister and she was very close to both her brother and his son. Lorenzo's mother died in a car accident only three years into their marriage and two after giving birth to their only child. Lorenzo Sr. raised his son alone and Gail Rueben was a big help. By the way, Mr. Rueben was Gail's second husband, so all this info, he said, came from her after they were married. Lorenzo was already in flight school in California when they met. As you and I already know, an aviation education doesn't come cheap and Lorenzo senior didn't make that much money slinging a hammer to cover tuition, so I'm guessing his aunt helped pay that ticket, since she had some hefty money bags in her financial dossier. Her first husband left her his entire estate when he died and he was apparently quite wealthy. Neither had any extended family other than Gail's brother and son. Because the brother was already dead and Lorenzo was presumed *legally* dead at the time *she* passed, Mr. Ruben took claim to what was left, other than a sizeable portion that was automatically withdrawn and donated to a facility in Italy somewhere."

"*Italy*?" Fields asked.

"The husband said she'd been going to visit there every year, long before he came into the picture. He said it was a beautiful and romantic spot and he had no qualms about her picking it for their honeymoon. It was the reason they'd gone back every year on their anniversary. She owned a nice villa there. Purchased again before their union. He thought it odd that she had arranged for it be sold upon her death without consulting him. Her reasoning behind it had been written in her will. In it, she claimed that she didn't want him to go back there and grieve for her. He said her attorney sold it within a few days after she was buried and it brought twice the amount than it was worth. So he counted himself blessed because it cushioned his retirement immensely."

"Back to the sighting of Lorenzo in Italy, did he say if he ever went inside the pizzeria to see if the two men were in there?" Fields asked.

"He did. Figured that was the likely place they could have went. Although the little eatery was busting at the seams with people, none of them resembled the man he had been talking to or the one that looked like Lorenzo. He stayed at the market for another full hour, walking around and looking, but never laid eyes on either one again. Since Lorenzo Sr. and Mrs. Rueben were deceased, there was no one to tell the story to back home. So he had never thought about it again, that is, until I called."

"So he can't make a positive ID." Fields said.

"He's eighty-four and this was fifteen years ago. He can't be certain."

"But it's a possibility that it was *this* Lorenzo Martin."

"He swore it was. But he said he couldn't imagine why Lorenzo would do this to his aunt, make her think he was dead, after all she'd done for him. It was a sick trick to play, was how Mr. Rueben said it."

"Maybe *Mr.* Rueben was the only *one* who didn't *know* he was *still* alive." Fields mused. "And just maybe *Mrs.* Rueben did."

Mullins stared at her for a few seconds and then began to shake his head. "I would have thought the old man was seeing things earlier, before we found out about this Winifred character. But now knowing that she might have been *on* that plane and *she* was still alive, it changes everything."

"It makes perfect sense." Agent Fields said, wheels still turning at a fast rate in her head. "Mrs. Rueben goes to Italy after her *first* husband dies with all that money. She's already invested a fortune in her nephew's education, so what's another several thousand to drop on a villa for her and the dear boy? A safe place in their favorite spot to seek refuge whenever they both were in town, separate or together? After all, if Lorenzo was hiding from the world and wanted to make them believe he was dead in America, what better place to hide, then in a quaint villa in another country? Do you happen to know who bought the villa after she died?"

"I haven't dug that deep yet."

"I bet somewhere through all the red tape we'll find out they have a connection to Lorenzo. Probably purchased it with the money she supposedly donated to the orphanage so as not to raise any suspicion. If he's still alive, really alive, he'd be in his mid-sixties by now and living scott-free in that villa under an alias."

"If it was him in the market, then all the commotion with the vendor's cart caught his attention too. The minute he took in the scene, he had to have recognized Mr. Rueben among the crowd and rabbited while he had the chance."

"Probably straight back to the very villa his aunt used to own and hide out in until he was certain his step-uncle had left town. I don't doubt that somehow he still has ways of hacking into the airport's flight manifests and can see a list of its passengers."

"How brazen Lorenzo is." Mullins said, still shaking his head. "But just like all criminals we profile and go after, he's no different. They always return back to the place they are familiar with and this is how they get caught. The paper trail is so easy to follow and they just don't realize it."

"Most people aren't going to think like we do. A woman dies and in her Will she wants to liquidate her assets and donate a little to charity and leave the rest to family. That's not something out of the ordinary to raise an eyebrow about. He thinks he's been smart enough to pull off a hijacking and his own death but never counted on the fact that old step-uncle would just appear one day in the same farmer's market he's at. I'd say that's pretty brazen if he's still holing up in that villa today. In fact, it's pretty stupid on his part if our guys find him there. We better bring this to the attention of the Director and stake the place out. If we find the pilot alive, then we might get our answers faster from him, then the tight-lipped pirates."

Mullins gathered the papers he pulled from the folder still clutched in his hand. He shoved most of them back inside, except for one that was still lying on her desk. It was blank except for a set of two names written in ink. One of them immediately caught her attention.

"What is this on here for?" she pointed, when Mullins looked down. He paused in organizing and tilted his head to look.

"That's the name of Gail Rueben's first husband and his business partner." Mullins explained. "I didn't figure it mattered but looked it up anyway, since we're trying every avenue we can, to find a connection."

"I think we just *did*!" Agent Fields said, as that familiar twinge of excitement she always felt, began to rise in her gut.

"What do you know that I don't?"

"What did Gail Rueben's first husband do for a living?" she asked.

"He was an importer." Mullins said. "He dealt in real fine Italian art and furnishings as a distributor, of course. Worked out of a few warehouses scattered throughout California and New York. Did well for himself. But that little bit of info wasn't acquired from any digging on my part. That came courtesy of Mr. Rueben, who really likes to talk, once you get him going. So now, it's your turn. What do you know about this guy? If he's still kicking, I can have him hauled in immediately for questioning." he offered, pointing to the name she was asking about. Fields shook her head.

"Don't waste your time. He's not among the *living* anymore."

"Everybody with any ties to this case is turning up corpses. Tell me *how* this one ended?"

"Tito Marconi was shot *point* blank between the eyes during a robbery, that he and his half-brother were committing at the time."

"Who was his half-brother?" Mullins asked.

"The notorious mob-boss from Italy, *Victor Rocha*!"

SIXTY-FOUR

She had stood as still as a statue by a cluster of palms, camouflaged, about two hundred feet away from the main door to the building, for the last thirty minutes. The threat of dawn was at her back. She held the 6-inch blade down at her side, ready for any movement, as the sweat rolled down her arms, the salt stinging the fresh wounds, her breath as silent as the morning, coming deep within her diaphragm. The silence around her was deafening, the isolation engulfing. But before she dared to move a muscle, she had to be sure that she was entirely alone before making the dangerous trek, across open terrain, without being seen. Because being sure was the difference between life or death, at this stage in the game.

Another ten minutes slowly ticked by in her head. Within that time, nothing in her surroundings changed. It began to give her a little bit of hope. If the *Devil* and his pirate pigs didn't make an appearance by the time the sun began to rise in the sky, they wouldn't try to approach the building again until the sun had set well into the night. And they wouldn't dare come near the building between then. It was one of the leader's strict rules.

She knew their routine so damn well, knew their filthy habits, the way their minds worked. They were cowards and bullies who liked to move around in the dark, who liked to wreak havoc when people were caught off-guard, sleeping and vulnerable. Like typical bullies, they tortured the weak and defenseless. Like pigs, they became gluttons who annihilated everything in their path. Like scavengers, death would not come soon enough for what they would do to her, if she were caught.

When birds began to sing in the distance, she moved quietly but quickly towards the direction of the structure. Another cluster of trees conveniently edged the south corner. She slid into the middle, blending into the landscape and again slowed her breathing and watched with eyes of a predator, waiting for the prey. Again, the silence immersed her and she settled there for a few minutes, listening. The dew lay heavy on thick leaves just inches from her face and seem to glisten as the sun became brighter on the horizon. Soundlessly she raised her arm and cut a few off the branch, then slid the blade back in its sheath at her waist. A pain shot up her leg from the ankle, reminding her that she needed to get off it soon. She extracted a key from the pouch at her side, then stepped from the cluster. She slid the key in the bolt lock and stepped inside, closing and locking the door behind her in a matter of seconds. The interior of the building was not only cool but pitch black. She waited, breathing deep again from the diaphragm, listening for any sounds inside *or* out. After another five stressful minutes ticked by, she released a small breath and took two paces to the right. Reaching out, she found the matches on the ledge and lit the lantern hanging on the wall, just inside the doorway. Her eyes darted from one end of the space to another, scanning for any movement and found nothing. Another small sigh escaped her, as she released more of the bound-up stress within. She was alone for now and she'd best make use of the time. Using it as a neutralizer, she slid the dew side of the leaves she still held in her hand, down both of her arms to stop the salt from her sweat, that was burning the open cuts. In the light of the lantern, she could see just how caked with mud, her entire body was. After all, she'd spent a few days in the jungle, without shelter, proper rest or food, much less the luxury of finding water to bathe with. She might be a little banged up, slightly dehydrated and extremely dirty, but she was *still* alive, wasn't she? Who cared what her appearance looked like at the moment. She'd escaped and made it to the building, safe and in one piece. And now all she had to do was prepare accordingly and wait for them to come. And eventually *they* would come, no doubt by nightfall. By now they had to know she was missing...

She folded the leaves, shoved them inside her pouch on her hip. She turned the lantern flame higher, raised it out straight in front of her and stared at the monster of steel. The huge Gulf Stream Jet loomed *eerily* under the radiance of the lantern.

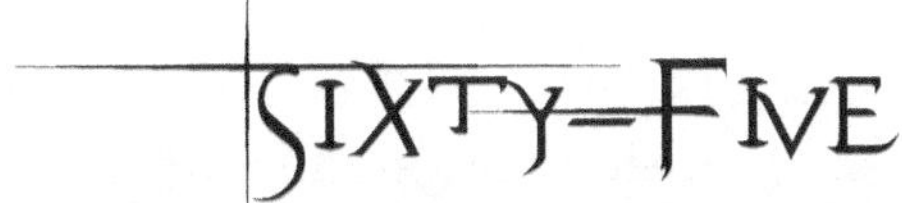

SIXTY-FIVE

A few days after the arrangements had been made, Brandon and Sage reluctantly kissed baby Tristan goodbye and left their beloved cabin in Montana. Their first stop was Charlie's office in LA. Once there, Sage was going to meet Lola for the first time and discuss the plan of attack to start filming Stranded. Before that meeting was to take place, both of them hoped to get some answers from Charlie, concerning the comments her grandfather had written in his journal and their findings that were attached to the back of the photo. Then from there, they would hop back on the plane and head to Florida, where they would confront Margot.

Not ten minutes in the air, Sage began second guessing whether they should have left Tristan behind with Lydia and Hans. It took Brandon a good twenty minutes to convince her he would be fine. And another ten after, to convince her they weren't bad parents for leaving. He knew she was nervous about being on a plane. Add in the fact, she was *almost* a little *too* excited about her upcoming meeting with Lola and extremely apprehensive about being away from Tristan for the first time. The mixture of it all made it hard for her to relax during the two-hour ride and it wasn't until the wheels had finally landed on the runway of LAX airport, that he actually saw some color flow back into her cheeks.

He had flown on so *many* airlines, to so *many* destinations throughout his career. He'd taken a million trips on his plane, since he'd owned it. And not one time, had he *ever* entertained the idea, that something could go wrong in the air.

But *his* parents hadn't *died* in a plane crash either.

They made good time across town to Charlie's office. Once the driver had them safely inside the garage with the door closed, Brandon guided a calmer Sage out of the limo. When they reached the designated floor, the doors opened and Charlie was already waiting for them in the hallway with his open.

The only other door on the left, that led to Peggy's office, was already closed and locked, according to the flashing red '*security*' light above it. Charlie made eye contact with Brandon first, as they stepped out into the hall. He nodded briefly and then turned his attention on Sage. Brandon noticed his eyes lingered on her for a second longer and an effort to smile formed briefly at the corners of his mouth and then quickly disappeared.

He suddenly felt sorry for him, even though he didn't want to. It was probably because of the vulnerability he saw flash in the big guy's eyes. She was his niece after all. He'd lost his brother in all this mess. She was all he had left besides Meg and the memories.

It still didn't change the fact that Brandon, himself, was angry. But as Lydia had asked, he'd come to hear him out and that was the best he could do for now.

"How was your flight?" Charlie asked, once he closed the door behind them.

"Nerve-racking, as usual." Sage said, not missing a beat, the hint of irritation still in her voice. "I hate airplanes!" Charlie walked around his massive desk and took a seat in his equally big, black leather chair.

"You'll hear no argument from me! I share your pain!" Two leather-clad, wing-backed chairs, sat at a comfortable distance from the front of his desk. Brandon took the right one, Sage settled in the left. "You *both* look exceptionally well." He remarked. "Looks like spending some time in the countryside suits you Brandon. You've got nice *color* in your cheeks. Your eyes are still full of shit though."

"Not as full as *yours* is, *big* guy!" he retorted.

 Charlie ignored him and looked over to Sage. "Baby Tristan didn't come with you?"

"No." Brandon replied for her, rather curtly. "We thought it best if he stayed behind *with* Lydia and Hans, where he's *safe*!"

"This place is like a fortress," Charlie said, locking his dark eyes on Brandon. "but *you* know that!"

"So is *my* house *now*, since I've learned it's not just the *fans* that I need to keep out!" Brandon replied, in a *snarky* tone. "Thanks for the *pre*-warning pal!"

"*Oh* stop!" Sage said, shaking her head at them both. "We don't have *time* for this, the great battle of the *testosterone*! Put your personal grievances aside for now and let's get on with it, shall we?" She threw her hands up in frustration. "Or clear the air right now, take your pick!"

"*I'm pissed*!" Brandon said, not taking his eyes off Charlie.

"So I've *noticed*!" Charlie said, holding his stare.

"You *should* have told us in the beginning." Brandon pointed out.

Charlie nodded slowly. "Yes, I *should* have, although it's debatable at the time whether *you* would have believed me or not."

Brandon thought about that for a few seconds. He was right. He would have thought he'd taken a serious bump to the head or something. It was a crazy story to swallow, especially when someone is trying to convince you that your grandfather fought mobsters—*dangerous* mobsters—back in his day. As a kid, he'd fondly remembered Everett as a kind man, with an incredible sense of humor, who was always up for an adventure and who was basically—*cool* as shit. Totally the *opposite* of the man Charlie had described that night.

"Regardless, you *should* have told me." Sage took center stage. "Instead of letting me *think* I was alone!"

"Margot made it abundantly *clear* that it was best to stay away, concerning *you*." Charlie said. "Meg was told you were off limits too!"

"Oh, don't *you* worry. My *Nana* is going to get an *earful* when I stop at her place next!" Sage said. "But right now, *we* have lots of questions that *need* answers."

"I can only answer what I know." Charlie said.

"Did my grandfather order the hit on Victor in prison?" Brandon asked right off the top. "Don't *bullshit* me!" he warned. "I *need* to know."

"I have *no* intentions of bullshitting *either* one of you. That's Margot's department." He said.

"You didn't *answer* the question." Brandon said.

"Everett told me he had *nothing* to do with it." Charlie shrugged his shoulders.

"When did he tell you this?" Brandon asked.

"During the meeting at Franks, the day after it went down. Both Everett and I met there to discuss it in person with him. None of us trusted talking over the phones."

"Did you *believe* him?" Sage asked.

"*Yes!*" Charlie nodded. "If he had ordered it up, he wouldn't have hesitated to tell either one of us. In fact, he would have been *gloating* over it. I don't think I've hid the fact from any of you that Everett *wanted* Victor dead. Hell, he already tried once."

"What about *my* grandfather? Did either one of you ask him if he ordered it?" Sage asked.

"*Yes!* That was the first topic that was discussed the second we were all three alone. He swore he had nothing to do with it either but he wasn't acting right."

"What do you mean?" Sage asked.

"Everett arrived before me at the mansion that day and later, he told me he found Frank in a *severely* agitated state. He was pacing the office and your grandfather had a hard time calming him down, which was unusual." He said this to Brandon. "He was still pretty riled when I got there. Everett and I thought it was time for a celebration because the bastard finally got what he deserved. But not Frank. He acted like he was upset that it had happened. We were both stumped on his reaction."

"So, surely all three of you discussed your theories on who ordered it?" Brandon asked.

Charlie again nodded. "Of course we did."

"And what was the conclusion? Did you come up with a list of suspects that fit the bill?" Sage asked.

This time Charlie shook his head. "If he pissed anyone else off in the states, we were unaware of it. As for an old rival back in Italy, there's a million possibilities, again unknown to us at the time. As I said, Everett and I were ready to celebrate, knowing that it was finally over. Frank, on the other hand, was not."

"Did you ask him why?" Brandon asked.

"Yes, even after I left, Everett had a one-on-one with him. He said Frank just kept saying that whoever had done it, had *ruined* everything."

"Ruined what?" Sage pressed.

"Ruined his chances of getting your mother and Jack back...*alive*!" Charlie said.

The silence in the room was heavy. Both Brandon and Sage stared at him.

"What in the *hell* are you talking about?" Brandon finally demanded while he automatically reached over and covered Sage's hand with his own. He felt her fingers tighten like a vise around his, in response.

Charlie's gaze left Brandon's for a second to study Sage. His eyes stayed on her as he spoke a bit more softly. "Someone anonymously sent Frank a package shortly after your parent's plane went missing."

"Why didn't you tell us that back at Margot's?" Brandon demanded.

"I didn't think it was something I needed to share with everyone." He then turned his attention to Sage. "I thought a more private setting was appropriate."

Sage disengaged her hand from Brandon's and bent to retrieve the tote bag she'd carried in and sat by her chair. She opened it up and pulled out the newspaper and the photo of her mother's necklace they'd found. She leaned forward and placed them both on the desk in front of Charlie. He looked down at the items and slowly began to shake his head.

"I wondered if he kept this shit. I was hoping he'd burned it." He said, sounding more like he was talking to himself.

"Where'd you find this?" He tore his gaze from them to look first at Brandon and then Sage.

Brandon commenced to telling him about coming home from Margot's and finding the photo on the floor, the glass broken, to the day they took it apart and Sage finding it practically glued to the frame in plastic.

"Sorry you had to see this." He said this to Sage.

"Who sent this to my grandfather? Victor?"

Charlie nodded his head yes. "Frank got it shortly after the plane went missing and whoever did it, was clever. Both Everett and I tried to trace it. The mail system was different then, not like today where tracking is on every piece of paper that goes through the post office and with no return address, we quickly hit a dead end."

"Where was Victor at the time?" Sage asked.

"In prison, on death row, in San Quentin. Right here in

California. If he was going to send something like that to Frank, it wouldn't have mattered if he was in Bangkok. Victor would have found a way to get it to him."

"What was the intended message?" Brandon asked.

Charlie sighed and once again levelled his eyes on Sage. "The message was clear. Let's drive this *grieving* father insane, by making him believe that his daughter and son-in-law *died* because of a Vendetta someone had against his *best* friend. Hence the red scribbling across this newspaper," he said, nodding towards the offensive words. "*Eye for an Eye*! It was something Victor said to Everett right before he got locked up, so it was *obvious* to us that we didn't need a return address to know *who* the package came from. On the other hand, Frank believed that Victor was sending another message. He thought that Victor had somehow *hijacked* your parent's plane and was holding them hostage somewhere."

Sage sat up straight in her chair. "But that's impossible! The plane crashed and everyone on it perished." She looked from Brandon to Charlie. "Surely my grandfather knew that, regardless of whether their remains were in the caskets or not. Why would he let Victor get under his skin like that?"

Brandon was starting to feel *really* bad that he couldn't just come out and tell Sage and Charlie that at this point, *anything* was possible. But the answers that Charlie was giving, was starting to add pieces to a puzzle he and Courtney were already putting together. And the fact that Charlie knew of the package and the possibility the plane *might* have been hijacked, was adding more credibility to Courtney's farfetched theory about the Pirate's lair. "What did Frank say to a judge that would make him open the caskets? He had to have had something *very* incriminating."

"Frank and Judge Fredrick, were longtime friends." Charlie began. "Never met the guy myself but sometimes, when your grandfather needed a sitting judge's influence in his business deals, he always turned to him for legal advice. Frank contacted him about his theory, without consulting me or Everett first. We all four had a rule with each other— we were *never* supposed to discuss *anything* about Victor or the longstanding Vendetta to anyone *outside* of our small circle, unless we agreed unanimously as a group. Frank took it upon himself that day, to break his own vow. When Everett found out he had consulted the judge for his help in the exhumation, he was pissed. He was worried that it would bring suspicion from the FBI, down on all our heads. But Frank reassured him that Fredrick would *never* do anything to jeopardize his position or ours."

"What was my grandfather's take on that?" Brandon asked.

"Everett told me later that he almost believed Frank had leverage on the judge, in order to manipulate him so well."

"Do you know what he had on him, if that were the case?" Sage asked.

Charlie shook his head. "Your grandfather was a dignified, class act Sage. He was not a dishonest man. He couldn't intentionally take someone down back in the day, if he wanted to. But when that plane went missing, when he lost your mother, something snapped in him and he was never the same. He wanted revenge and he wanted it from Victor any way he could get it."

"What did he discuss with the Judge? How much did this man know?"

"He told him that the FBI was hiding something and shared these documents from the package. I guess it was enough to make him sign the order. Everett later told me the judge did it, in order to prove to Frank, they were in there, so he would let it go. It created just the *opposite* effect, when the caskets turned out to be empty.”

“What happened then?” Sage asked.

“Fredrick initially talked Frank out of going after the FBI publicly, once the exhumation had taken place. He warned that it would bring down some heavy scrutiny on his family. Then, for shits and giggles, the judge was kind enough to contact Everett, *personally*. He told him about Frank’s visit to his home, where he had brought the newspaper and the photo of the necklace. He then reminded Everett about what the consequences would be *if* Frank pursued his wrath on the agency. He stressed that the feds had a way of digging into your past and finding things that should stay buried. Everett thanked him for the heads up and then hopped on a plane to go see Frank and convince him that if he didn’t quit, he was going to put all of us in danger, including his precious granddaughter.” He said this to Sage. “Apparently during that conversation is when Frank told him about his belief that his ‘kids’ were still alive and that Victor was behind it.”

“So your saying that everyone thought Frank was delusional with grief?” Brandon asked. “That there wasn’t *anything* that added any credibility to his theory?”

“Not that Everett or I knew of.”

“Did he receive any other mysterious packages?” Sage asked.

Charlie shook his head. “If he did, he never shared them with us.”

“My grandfather left me a letter that I found with the newspaper and the photo.” Sage said, finally laying the sheet of old paper on Charlie’s desk in front of him. Charlie did not hesitate as he slid his reading glasses on and began to read it. When he was done, he wasn’t so quick to remove them. Brandon swore he saw his shoulders slump lower, somewhat.

"*Damn* you Frank!" he finally muttered. Both Brandon and Sage gave him a moment as he seemed to be trying to compose himself. "He was a *hell* of a man." Charlie finally said. "Where I grew up in Italy, the man was always looked upon as the masculine bull, the head of the family, the hard one with a magnitude of overzealous pride. Being around Frank gave me a whole *different* perception. He was the total opposite." Charlie paused again, straightened up in the chair and sighed as he finally made eye contact with Sage. "Frank never hesitated to speak softly and compliment someone on a whim. He was so open with that shit. He'd hug us all the time and always remind us of how important we were to him, to each other, to life. And he was always telling me how proud he was of the man I was becoming, how much like my father I was and how proud he would have been. I always thought he was so wrong about me. I remember my father as a loving, kind man. I was nothing but an angry, detached kid, who was mad at the world for what had happened to us. But Frank, he was like the perfect role model for a dad, not that we didn't have one of our own before Victor took him out." He paused a moment to collect himself. "It's just that Frank and Everett knew how much we missed our parents so they tried to make up for it. But when we lost Jack and Kelley and …" he trailed off. "then Everett, it affected Meg and I in a bad way. All the steps we'd taken forward to put this nightmare behind us…well their deaths just set us way back…mentally and emotionally in ways I can't even explain. Losing more people in our lives…it did something to me that I've never been able to shake. I guess that's why I *unintentionally* put distance between Frank and I. I was afraid if I openly showed him too much love, he would die too. So my visits to the mansion became less. Being in that house, where the good memories were, when we were *all* together, it hurt too *damn* bad." He shook his head in distress.

Sage knew that somewhere in all that misery was the pain he was still carrying from losing his girlfriend Serenity too but she wouldn't dare bring it up because she had promised Meg that she wouldn't. It was a subject that she hadn't even brought up to Brandon yet but she would rectify that on their ride back home when they had a chance to talk. So instead, she tried to steer the conversation back to the topic at hand.

"What was my grandfather hinting at, when he made the comment in the letter to my grandmother?" Sage asked.

Charlie sighed, removed his glasses and rubbed his eyes. "Frank confided in Everett later, that he believed Margot was the one who *ordered* the hit on Victor Rocha in prison."

This clearly took Sage aback. Her eyes grew wide, her mouth slightly agape. "*What?*"

Charlie nodded. "You have to understand that your grandfather was at the top of his game until this plane deal happened. I don't want to say that he was losing it. He just kind of unraveled for a while and he had every right. Losing a child is a devastating thing. It did something to them both. Margot withdrew from life for a while. Frank was the opposite. He wanted someone to blame, somebody to take it out on. A lot of his accusations and assumptions about the whole affair, never truly panned out. He called the incident everything in the book—a government cover up, a conspiracy, an international kidnapping—all the way to thinking someone had hijacked the plane. Like I said earlier, for a while, he actually *believed* that your parents were still *alive* and Victor was the only one who could tell them where they were. When he was iced in prison, Frank lost all hope they would ever be found and did a downward spiral, for a while."

"Is it possible that he wasn't just grasping at straws? That maybe Margot had something to do with it?" Brandon asked.

"*Brandon*!" Sage said, turning his way, eyes still wide. "My grandmother is *guilty* of a *lot* of things, but a *murderer* is not one of them."

"It's a *fair* question, Sage. Don't think she's as pure as that lily white hair on her head!" Charlie said, coming to his defense. "She can be quite the manipulative viper, *both* in business, as well as in her personal life. But I have to go with my gut on this one and say *no*!" he said this to Brandon. "At the time, Margot was in no condition to make an executive decision like that. She was so distraught, that she couldn't even hold down a cup of broth or put two words together. Hell she didn't come out of her room for a few months. How could a woman in her state of mind, orchestrate a successful hit on an inmate? Especially in a federal prison?"

"When you found out that Victor was shanked, *who* was your first impression?" Brandon asked.

"*Everett*!" he said immediately.

"The motive being the revenge for killing Catalina?" Brandon asked.

Charlie nodded. "If the FBI would have known about her and Everett's affair at the time, they would've been at his front door in a matter of minutes. Hell, if they'd known about us, or *Isabella*, they would have put them in jail. When I look back on it now, I realize how much Frank and Everett both, really put their lives on the line for us. Not too many people would do something like that today."

"So my grandfather thought my Nana had a hand in Victor's death? Is that why there was talk of divorce?" Sage asked.

Charlie studied her for a second. "So I take it you've been talking to Meg?" he simply said, more as an observation.

"Yes, their marriage took a bad hit when this happened. Both were heavily grieving and that left them to attack each other. But neither were ever serious about throwing in the towel permanently."

"So my grandfather was the likely suspect—according to your theory—not Margot?" Brandon asked.

Charlie nodded his head yes. "It would have been a piece of cake for Everett to pull off something like that. He had *lots* of friends in *lots* of places. A few phone calls would have sealed the deal. Or knowing Everett as I did, only *one* call would have sufficed in his world."

"Then why didn't he do it? He had the means and the motive? What would stop him?" Brandon persisted.

"*Respect*." Charlie answered immediately. "He *loved* Frank. The man changed his life. Changed *your* father's life and ultimately *yours*. If it wasn't for Frank, he would have never gotten to meet you, to watch you grow up, to be a detrimental part. You were his world, as Sage was to Franks. You two became the focus that they both needed to move forward. You were the reason they mellowed out and why they decided to let go, once Victor was dead. If it wasn't for your grandfather believing in Everett from the beginning and giving him a second chance to do the right thing, he would have probably been dead too. Shot down by some lowlife in a bad part of a neighborhood somewhere. Everett felt he could never pay him back for giving him the opportunities he did, but the respect part, he could deliver by the tons. So when he threatened to finish him off, Frank asked him to back off after the package arrived. Everett obliged. He would do anything for Frank, *anything*." He stressed. "And everybody knew it!"

"Including Victor." Brandon surmised and looked over at Sage. "Which is why he went after Frank."

"Killing Catalina wasn't enough for Victor. He wanted Everett's head and it became his main focus in life."

"If my grandfather knew this, why didn't he just put a bullet in Victor's head, like he did his brother in the furniture store that night?" Brandon wanted to justify his grandfather's actions in the beginning. Now, understanding his frame of mind a little bit more, he wondered why Everett hadn't done away with the asshole when he had the chance.

"I can *only* tell you what was going through his head at the time because he told me. Everett regressed into thug mode when he came face to face with Victor in the store that night. The only reason why he didn't just take one shot and blow him away like his brother, was because he said it was too easy of a death for the likes of him. So he shot him in both kneecaps first, so he couldn't get away. Victor somehow dragged himself behind the sofa for cover. Since Everett had the night goggles on, he could see Victor clearly. He shot him in the arm, the one that was still holding the gun, and was about to shoot him in the other, when he heard the sounds of sirens and tires, screeching outside the building. Knowing he had only a few seconds to end it, he stepped back in front of the sofa—to make it look authentic—and opened fire, hoping one or more of the bullets would go through the wood and take him out. To his surprise, he was still alive when the cops found him cowering, behind it, in a pool of blood."

"What did he shoot him with?" Brandon asked.

"A 357 Magnum."

"*Damn*!" Brandon exclaimed.

"It was Everett's weapon of choice. He would always tell me and Jack that if he was forced to use one, then he intended on making it worth his while."

"No wonder Victor was bent on seeking revenge. No doubt he had crater's in his legs from the bullet holes, as a constant reminder."

"He could barely walk straight in prison because of the injuries." Charlie said. "That's why he was such an easy target to kill. A man with a disability like Victor's, made him no longer intimidating."

"Which made him hate them even more."

"Absolutely!" Charlie confirmed.

"Do you remember what my grandfather was sick with, that prevented him from taking the trip in the first place?" Sage asked.

Brandon turned to look at her.

Charlie shook his head. "He was throwing up, visiting the bathroom a lot and was extremely weak, is what Jack said. I really didn't see it firsthand because Margot wouldn't let anyone go near their room, for fear at first, that he was sick with something contagious. I just assumed he had the flu? Why?"

Sage shook her head. "Just curious. Meg had no idea either. I guess it's totally irrelevant to the chain of events that followed."

Brandon wanted to ask Charlie if he knew about the agent, Phillip Greene, that had been found floating in the Venice river, near Victor's old stomping grounds, back in '87. But he couldn't with Sage present. Until he came clean with her about what he'd learned from Madison and Courtney concerning her parents, he had to keep some of it to himself. Including the FBI finding a dead woman with a gold heart in her possession, that was identical to Sage's mothers' she wore in the portrait. The same one that

Courtney found in the stuffing of the teddy bear, that Everett had given to her years ago. *Or* the serial number of the plane Courtney saw in the hut, where the steel footlocker with the meticulous inventory logs were found buried inside with a diary. Or the fact that the same coroner who signed off on Catalina's death certificate, was the *same* one who signed off on the *dead* agent who had been assigned by the FBI, to work the plane crash case. Before Brandon could ask another question, the buzzer on Charlie's desk phone, interrupted him.

"Excuse me!" Charlie said, as he picked it up and held it to his ear. "Yes, Peggy?" There was a pause as he listened. "Ok, can you make sure she gets an escort up the back? Thanks!" He hung up the phone and looked at Sage. "Lola has arrived downstairs. She should be up shortly. We can resume this conversation after."

Without waiting for a response, he stood up and made his way around the desk and headed towards the door.

SIXTY-SIX

Lola couldn't stop staring at her.

Sage Cassava, had this *aura* about her, almost to the point of intoxicating. She was a *natural* beauty, even more so *in* person, than she had appeared in the stock photo on the back of her book. She had an incredible amount of curly, wild, blonde hair that hung in ringlets down her back, with amazing true-blue eyes that dripped with kindness and perfect pink coloring of the lips that were enhanced with a soft shimmer of gloss. She was the Bohemian side to a different kind of Barbie, that Mattel had never thought to create.

She instantly liked her, something that Lola had never experienced before. And the realization of *why* she had snagged the biggest bachelor in Hollywood, needed no further explanation after ten minutes of being in the room with her. She would become the new 'breath of fresh air' for tinsel town because she was *nothing* like the *others*. She was *genuine*, with a flair about her around the edges that spoke of class, down to the hint of the silver, shiny, slim hoops that hung from her ears and peeked out between the tangle of curls, when she moved her head a certain way. She was a fuller-figured woman, like Lola herself, with all the right curves in all the right places. The bell-sleeved, V-necked, blue top she wore, hugged her full breasts, flattered a surprisingly trim waist that blended smoothly into a healthy set of legs. Lola found herself wanting to mimic her style, right down to the choker at her neck and the x-shaped, diamond ring, she wore on her finger. *So this was the woman that had taken the legend to his knees?*

Brandon Parrish, as handsome as ever, was sitting next to his wife, on the couch in Charlie's office, listening to her talk about her book, *Stranded.* He hadn't hardly taken his adoring eyes off of her, the entire time.

He was dressed in a dark blue, button-down Henley and a pair of faded blue jeans that were ripped at the knees. The aroma of his cologne reached her in waves and smelled absolutely delicious. His gorgeous mane, with shades of blond and caramel strands running through it, was long— laying a few inches just past his shoulders. Lola couldn't help but notice the sparkle in his blue eyes and the way his smile reached them. He was happy, *sincerely* happy and the glow that saturated him, was bright enough that a blind man could see it.

She felt a twinge of jealousy. The *good* kind—when you were extremely happy for your friend but sad to not be there yourself—*kind* of envy.

She then glanced over at Charlie and watched him react to her while he and Sage exchanged information about the shooting location. He was dressed in his usual sport coat, dark dress pants and Italian loafers—no socks. He sat to Lola's left, in a black, winged-back chair. His curly hair was out of control and was in bad need of a good cut. So was his black beard that appeared to have even more gray in it, than the last time she'd seen him. He handed all three of them an aerial shot of the cabin in question, but other than that, he wasn't saying much during this meeting, which she also found quite unusual. Except for the few times that Sage asked him a question, he seemed to be content on letting her have the floor.

And that was fine with Lola. So was the fact that apparently Sage was already a *big* fan of hers. It had obviously lent leverage to her decision in casting her, so she'd use it to her advantage. Who wouldn't in her shoes?

Whatever it took to secure the part, she was willing to do. She was no dummy. This woman, Sage, was a gold mine, *especially* since she had Brandon in *her* corner. And Ava had reminded her on the way here, that Sage was *still* writing sequels and as long as she was doing that, it guaranteed work in her future.

You scratch my back, I scratch yours.

This was the break she'd been looking for. The opportunity of a lifetime, to finally star in a role that would make everyone take her as a serious actress. She wouldn't let anything stand in her way. Not anything.

She glanced over at Charlie, who was still staring at her. She smiled at him and he winked. Sage and Brandon began talking about the location of the cabin. They both confirmed that it was the ideal spot to shoot the movie in. Lola watched them as they interacted. The big guy was definitely not acting like his usual self. She studied him while his head was turned, listening to Sage. It was hard to believe this burly looking caveman, was *really* Rodolfo Benenati, heir to a *billion*-dollar fortune. Him and his sister Meg, who was *actually* Laviana Benenati.

Meg…she still couldn't *believe* that she was a part of this or that Peter was *married* to one of the missing children, who disappeared from their home in Milan, decades ago. Their murdered parents had gone down in the history books as one of the most famous, unsolved crimes of the century. Lola could just imagine the frenzy that would ignite a media firestorm *if* their *true* identities were exposed. She turned her sole attention back on Sage. Here sat the daughter, who had been the focus of another tragedy, who was also *sole* heir to a vast fortune all her own. Sage, the granddaughter of the billionaire, Frank Hartford and daughter to the late Roberto Benenati, who had also died as a billionaire.

She was *worth* more than Brandon or Charlie *combined*! Lola let that *sink* in for a minute and then, without hesitation, she signed on the dotted line.

SIXTY-SEVEN

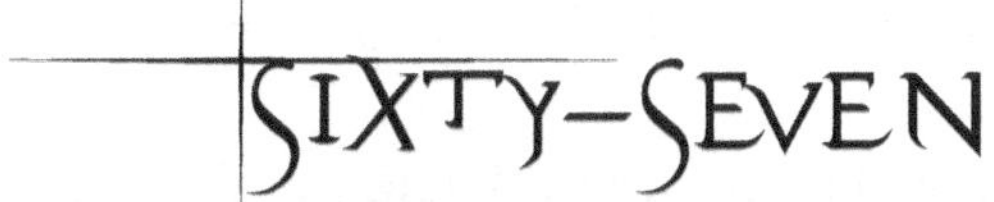

Courtney sat in her private office in the newsroom, staring at her computer. On the screen, was a listing of several flights and times to Italy in the upcoming days. She'd aired her last piece on the Pirates lair, not an hour before. Until the investigation was over, there would only be updates to keep the viewers informed which could be done by anyone. The station had made it clear that she was to disappear for a few weeks, maybe even a month, before they would start shooting her first Interview with Brandon and Sage, to kick off her new show.

Suddenly, she had mixed feelings about leaving the anchor desk for a more committed assignment. At least while airing the news, the material was continuously available because the world was always going to be evolving with scandal and mischief. But when it came to tackling these strange and eccentric people and convincing them to do personal, one-on-one interviews, it was going to be tricky. For now, she did not fight the station and their unanimous decision for her to take the much-needed time off. With the way she was feeling, she couldn't agree with them more. After talking with Brandon the night before, she had decided to take the trip. Italy was a beautiful place all of its own but the secrets it might hold about her mother and Everett, was what she was really after. That and the fact that she needed to see the house that Catalina had lived in, the Benenati's home where they'd been murdered and where her biological mother had been laid to rest. It was something she had to do…needed to do in order to put the pieces together in her head. And then, maybe after, she would take a plane to where Everett was buried, just to see it and know that once in her life, even in his death

under the cold ground, that she had been in the same place
with him at the same time.

She absently reached up to her neck and felt the gold,
dainty heart that hung there. She'd decided on this last
airing, that she would wear *her* necklace on camera, just to
give it some significance, to give Catalina, Everett and
Sage's parents some form of respect, even though they both
would never know she'd done so.

In her peripheral, a body suddenly filled her doorway. She
turned to see Michael, standing there in all his handsome
glory, in a dark navy blue suit, smiling at her.

"How are you doing, Princess?" he asked. Her face stayed
stoic as she slightly shrugged. She didn't even have the
fight in her anymore to holler at him for calling her that
ridiculous name. He stepped in the room and walked over
to stand beside her. "Going to Italy?" He asked, glancing at
the screen.

"I'm thinking about it." she replied.

"Do you need some reinforcements?" He was sincere and
she appreciated that.

"No, this is something I need to do on my own." she said.

"It's a beautiful place to visit and decompress but don't
make the entire trip about the *past* Courtney." He lightly
patted her shoulder. "Remember to stop and smell the roses
and don't dig too deep to raise any suspicion. It's an *old*
country with *old* ways. People are close knit and talk to
each other. Gossip and a newbie in town spreads fast."

"I don't intend to bring attention to myself." She said. "I'm
planning on looking like the American tourist, that I am."

"Gee, for some reason, that doesn't reassure me when it
comes to you." He smiled.

She wasn't in the mood and he knew it. Next he said: "I'm
just a phone call away if you change your mind or get in a
little trouble. I got people *over* there."

"Humph!" Courtney said, "That sounds like something Everett would say." Michael didn't comment, so she turned and looked up at him. "And speaking of—you never told me," she began.

"About what?" he asked.

"About *how* you knew him? *Everett.*"

"Yes, I did." He said.

"Tell me again." She urged.

He sighed. "It was at an intimate cocktail party both of us were invited to. We just happened to have the same idea at the same time which was escaping to the terrace for a cigar. Once he found out what I did for a living, we engaged in a conversation that lasted for a while. He was quite interested in *how* our side of the tracks worked and I obliged him."

"And what happened from there?"

"I gave him my business card and he gave me his and a few hours later, I left the party."

"Don't tell me, let me guess. You were working on the Benenati case at the time." she said.

Michael's eyebrows knitted in deep thought and then surprise. "Yes, as a matter of fact, I was."

"He already *knew* that…knew *who* you were." She said. "It was no coincidence that you both decided to hit that terrace at the same time. He *wanted* that connection to happen."

Michael didn't comment. It was obvious she had given him something to think about. "He set you up from the beginning, probably in part to keep an eye on you concerning the story and of course, to later *prime* you into hiring me."

"You impressed me on your own."

"But *he* led you to me." She said. "I guess I owe him something for that."

"I don't think he did it as a marker, Princess. When are you going to get it through that beautiful, thick head of yours that the man *really* cared about you?"

"Oh I know. Everyone who knew him keeps reminding me, that he did it *out* of love." She said, with a note of sarcasm in her words.

Michael suddenly bent down to her eye level. His face was a few inches from hers. It was so unexpected and he did it so fast, that she was taken aback. With him being so close, her senses betrayed her by consuming the intoxicating richness of his cologne. She could literally feel the power behind his charisma and his intense blue eyes pinned her in a serious manner.

"The *sacrifice* Everett made to ensure that *you* lived a long, healthy and prosperous life, should be enough *proof* to you of his love. You don't need any of us to substantiate that for you." She was drowning in his eyes and the soft timbre of his voice. "Sometimes Princess, love can be *all* about the *action* and doesn't *need* any words!" Before she could react, he moved in and took her mouth with his. It wasn't by far the usual, friendly peck on the lips, nor did he go to the extreme of forcing his tongue down her throat but the message behind it, however, was clear. So was the pounding of her heart and the lurch in her gut… He pulled away, it seemed, just as quick as he had started. His eyes stayed level with hers, searching for a second or two, or three in them for...something. Then in a sultry and sexy voice, she had never heard come out of his mouth until now, he said, "Be *careful* in Italy, Courtney. Don't make me have to come down there and *rescue* you!" Still not being able to say a word, she watched silently, as he turned and left her office.

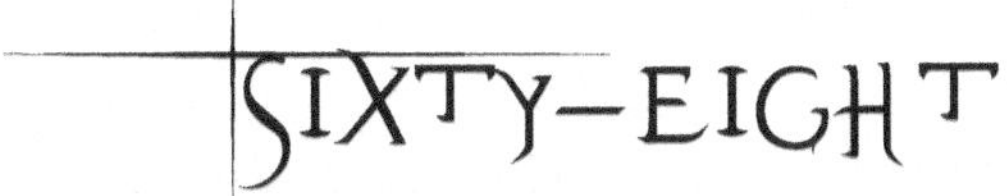 SIXTY—EIGHT

Agent Fields sat in the repressing silence of her home office. The only light on in the room, was coming from the glow of a single desk lamp. She'd been sitting in her chair for over an hour and a slight headache had begun to push pressure near her temple area. She was on the verge of calling it quits and just going to bed. But who was she kidding? Sleep was the last thing that was going to come easy to her tonight. That or the answers to this ever-growing mystery surrounding the plane that went missing in '87.

An assortment of paperwork covered the top of her desk, some in neat little stacks, some fanned like a deck of cards. In the largest stack were files that held the case surrounding the missing plane, as well as personal files on the Hartford's, Victor Rocha, Everett Calhoun, Karly Driggers, Winifred Gentry, Josef Gates and what they gathered so far on the Pirates lair. On the wall next to her desk was a standard-sized corkboard, full of visuals also pertaining to the case. One of them that kept catching her eye was an eight-by-ten photo of the hut in Africa, that Winnie's dead body had been found in. The angry words that had been scribbled in red on the wall above it, *'Eye for an Eye!!'*, screamed out at her but held no answers. Nothing in all of the paperwork she'd dragged home, gave her any either. Not the ones she was looking for anyway. But yet her gut kept telling her that she was missing something. Something so elementary that in its simplest form, it was eluding her. To the point that she told herself to get up and walk away and come back with a fresh mind.

She took her own advice and left her office, walked down the hall and quietly turned the knob on the first door to the left. Inside, the room was dark except for a nightlight to the far right of the wall. The soft glow lit up the twin bed skirt, trimmed in soft pink ruffles and lace, that jutted out under a thick matching pink comforter. The small silhouette of her precious daughter's form was illuminated, snuggled and sleeping soundly under it where she had been the last ten times she'd checked on her.

Fields' daughter was only eight years old. The same age that Sage Cassava had been when she'd had both parents ripped away from her. For some reason tonight, she could not get that out of her mind. She doubted that every night, for twenty-two years, Margot Hartford had not let it leave her mind either.

She released a heavy but silent breath as she closed the door quietly and made her way back down the hall. Instead of going straight into her office at the end, she turned left and headed to the kitchen. The light over the stove was on and strong enough to see by, as she poured herself a glass of white wine. She was hoping it would help her relax— free up her brain or put her to bed. Either one would work at this point.

She took a few refreshing sips and then wandered over to the windows that took up nearly the entire wall, above her kitchen sink. It had been one of the main features that had sold her on the purchase of the apartment. Somehow, at the time, she had thought the sunshine that came through them, would make up for the missing swing set in the yard. After all, the public park was only six blocks away and they would need the exercise after being cooped up in a high-rise, *right*?

The guilt of raising her daughter in such a busy and congested place, always plagued her the strongest, when she was frustrated with a case. She tried to clear her mind again and concentrate on the world outside her windows. Below in the streets, cars were there but sparse. The lamp lights that dotted the sidewalks, glowed under a heavy, mist-like fog. The office windows of opposing buildings that faced hers, were dark and almost menacing. It had been raining long enough that the surfaces of everything outside was slick and gleaming. She had been too deep in thought the first time, to even notice.

Your missing something…

A voice whispered inside her head.

"What in the *hell* is it?" she said, speaking out loud to herself, as she searched the murky landscape beyond.

"I'm sorry, could you repeat the question?"

A female, robotic voice sounded from somewhere behind her. She jumped, almost dropping her glass and in the process, spilled wine on her hand and on the floor. Years of training had her reaching to the left side, grabbing at the air, where her shoulder holster held her gun. In a panic, she remembered she had put it away in her room, locked up safely from the little girl asleep down the hall. Her heart raced as she turned and scanned the dark room for the perpetrator who had somehow broken into her house. And then it donned on her *who* and *what* was happening. Her shoulders began to relax. Her breathing calmed and she rolled her eyes and silently whispered *"stupid"* to herself. The tower device sat a few feet from her on the counter. Her mother, who lived in Maine, had sent it just recently as a gift to her granddaughter. She thought it would come in handy when helping Grace with homework, or just to answer the dozens of questions that an eight-year-old needed answered. Against Belinda's better judgement, she'd allowed it, as long as it *stayed* in the kitchen. Being an FBI agent and working with classified, top-secret cases, it was not particularly a good idea to have a random recording device that interacts with the household and records—according to suspicions on the Internet—anything that's said in the home. So Belinda had compromised by keeping the device *in* the kitchen and her conversations and discussions concerning work, *out* of the kitchen. Being out of sight and out of mind, she had forgotten the thing was even in the house.

She stared at it for a few seconds, also remembering all the reviews that claimed the machine seemed too eerily lifelike, to be just a conversation between a computer and its owner.

"Elsa?" she said, calling out the name her daughter had selected for the device.

The tower blinked a green light a few times at the base and then responded automatically. "Yes?"

"I didn't ask a question." She said, not sure how to shut the thing down. Maybe it operated like a real computer and went into sleep mode whenever it sat still for too long.

"If there is anything that I can help you with, please let me know." The personal assistant said.

Belinda chuckled softly in the dimly lit room.

"If only you could help me *solve* this case, you would be *priceless*." she said, ironically.

"I'm sorry. Did you say you want to order a case of something?" the smooth robotic voice asked.

"No." she said, shaking her head. "I don't want to order anything."

"I am ready when you do." Elsa replied.

Belinda turned around, dismissing the device and continued to stare out into the night, looking from one twinkling light below, to another. The streets were still empty, as were the sidewalks and the pier beyond. The roads were still slick and shiny, with a car passing here and there, leaving tracks behind on the asphalt.

She sipped on her wine. She watched drops of rain on the window make their sliding decent down the panes of glass. The hum of the refrigerator kicked on and the air coming from the ducts overhead, picked up the hum where it left off. The apartment was deathly quiet, but in a good way and it allowed her mind to wander back to her task, nice and easy.

She thought about the pirates who were now in a prison of their *own* making, under the careful watch of the U.S. military and her own bureau, the FBI. She wished they would surrender and start talking. Didn't they realize their leader had abandoned them and had no intentions of coming back, much less to rescue them? Weren't they smart enough to realize that he didn't care about anyone's ass but his own and that now it was time to look *out* for themselves? Did they even care how much *trouble* they were in?

By now Josef Gates—if indeed it was Gates who was the leader—was probably so far underground, that they would never find him, no matter how many resources they had at their disposal. He lived in that jungle for a long time, long enough that he knew where to go and how to disappear if there was trouble. A criminal like him always knows where the exits are, it's a cardinal rule.

And where were all the key players that the victims had talked about in their interviews? The herbalist? The foreigner named Don that manned the hut? Or the mysterious woman who had tended to the wounded alongside him that hid her identity from head to toe in fabric.

What was it that someone thought her *name* was?

Debbie?

Donna?

Dolly?

"*Daisy!*" She confirmed to herself, this time out loud.

"*Daisy is a noun.*" Again, the personal assistant came to life behind her. "*Daisy is a small grassland plant that has flowers with a yellow disk and white rays. It has given rise to many ornamental garden varieties. It is also used in names of other plants with flowers similar to the daisy, e.g.,*

Michaelmas daisy, Shasta daisy." It paused, then started up again. "*The parts that grow above the ground can be used to make medicinal tea. People take*
wild daisy tea for coughs, bronchitis, disorders of the liver and kidneys, and swelling and inflammation. It can also be used as a blood purifier."
The device fell silent again behind her. Belinda, unnerved this time, continued to stare out into the dark night, deep in thought. The devices definition of the name Daisy intermingled with the facts swimming around in her head. How odd it was that Elsa had given her medicinal facts on the name. She would have never thought the daisy flower was considered a plant that could be administered as a medicine. The herbalist came to mind again, the one the witnesses had talked about. She wondered if the two women had become friends, considering that they shared a few things between them—the knowledge of herbs and the hatred they had for the leader.
"Thanks for the definition of *Daisy*, Elsa!" she said, feeling the effects of the wine starting to take the edge off her headache but not too happy that the information was causing her mind to ask more questions.
"*Daisy is a noun.*" The personal assistant repeated. "*The meaning for the name Daisy is Day's eye and is the name of a flower with a bright yellow disk in the center, framed with white points.*" Belinda immediately noticed this version was different from the first. "*Its origin is English.*" The device continued. "*The name Daisy was popular in the eighties. Daisy is also the name for Daisy Duke, from the television show, Dukes of Hazard.*" An image of Linda Bach, from one of her favorite childhood shows, flashed in her mind. "*Daisy is also the name for the railway engine from Thomas the Train. Daisy is also a character's name in Toy Story 3.*" Thanks to her daughter Grace, she knew that character well. "*Daisy is also the name of Daisy Duck,*

girlfriend of Donald Duck." Elsa said and then went silent again.

Belinda knew that last tidbit *personally.* When everyone else was worshipping the mouse and his spouse, she was one of the few, who liked their friends better. Daisy and Donald Duck had been the stars in her eyes as a kid, not Mickey and Minnie. Sure, she had liked them too but the Ducks, they were the hit with her. For hours after school and on Saturdays, she would watch every cartoon that had a duck in it—Donald Duck, Dark Wing Duck, Huey, Dewey and Louie and Scrooge McDuck. In fact, she was so nuts over them, that her parents drove for almost two days to take her to the Magic Kingdom in Florida, just so she could see them in person. That trip had been one of the best memories of her childhood. She suddenly wondered why she had never thought of taking the same trip with Grace. The rain had begun to fall heavy again. The soothing sound of the drops hitting the glass, buffered her too-quiet surroundings. She suddenly wondered if Jack and Kelley Cassava had gotten the chance to take their daughter to Disneyworld before they had disappeared on that plane. Surely they had, her mind reasoned. They *lived* right there not far from Orlando and everybody who lived in Florida went to Disney, even if it was just once, *right*? What would they have been, just forty-five minutes away from its magical gates, from Margot's mansion? And back in the eighties, tickets were cheap and the Hartford's were loaded, so Belinda was more than sure they'd had no problem making *lots* of trips to the theme park with their daughter before they'd taken a plunge into the Indian Ocean.
Or had they?
Belinda began to wonder if the bureau would ever learn the truth about what happened to the charter jet all those years ago? In reality, probably not.

And they probably will never know what happened to the herbalist or the damn leader of the lair or the real identities of the man named Don and the woman named Daisy—obviously *fictional* names—like the rest of the prisoners in the camp. And just where in the *hell* had all these key players disappeared to?

Don and Daisy. Just saying their names together sounded so *cliché*.

"Don and Daisy." She said this time out loud.

"*Donald Duck and Daisy Duck.*" Elsa said, behind her.

"*Donald and Daisy Duck are fictional characters created in 1940 by Walt Disney Productions. Disneyland is located in California and Disneyworld is located in Florida.*"

The shrill ring of her cell in the distance broke the silence and her concentration. Who in the *hell* would be calling this late? She quickly left the kitchen, entered her office and snatched it up.

"*Hello*?" she said, almost in a loud whisper, caught off guard.

"*Fields*?" She heard Mullins familiar voice on the other end.

"Yes, it's me! What's *wrong*?" Something had to be, for him to call this late.

"You're not going to *believe* this!" He said, sounding wide awake, out of breath and quite excited. "They *found* the plane, Fields!" He said with emotion cracking his voice.

"They *what*?" she asked, not entirely trusting her ears to what she'd just heard.

"They *found* the *damned* plane, Fields!" Mullins repeated, the sound of joy trying to break through the strong emotional tone of his voice. "And *not* in pieces either, it's *intact*! We were right all along; the plane was *hijacked*! The *damn* thing is like it was the day it left the ground in '87 and it's been *hidden* in a hanger all this time, in the *middle* of the African jungle!"

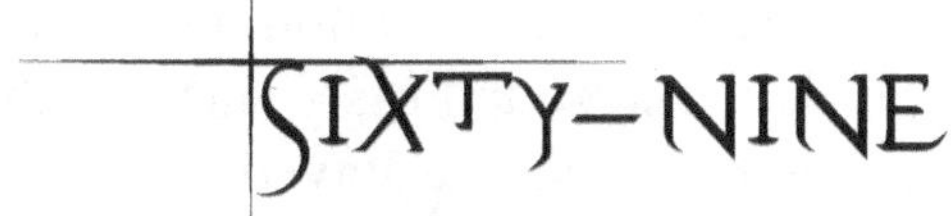SIXTY-NINE

Something awoke her...

She jerked her eyes open, blinked a few times and let them adjust for a second in the darkness. Other than her eyelids, she allowed nothing else to move on her body, for fear she would draw attention to herself if she was no longer alone.

Twenty seconds ticked by and nothing…

Then thirty, forty…

She began to make out shapes on either side of her but none of them were moving. Staying completely still, she continued to count off seconds in her head, as she scanned the area in front of her, back and forth. A full minute now passed and nothing…

Feeling no immediate threat, she slowly dared to move her hand to the makeshift bag at her side. The cold handle of the knife jutting out from it, reassured her that she was still armed. She took in several slow, deep breaths—breathing through her nose and soundlessly exhaling through a small part in her lips. Sweat trickled down her back from a mixture of fear and the intense heat inside the cockpit. But she would not move from her position on the floor, until she figured out *what*, if anything, had awakened her. The Devil and his men would not dare approach the hanger during daylight, for fear of being seen. Knowing she had at least ten hours until sundown, she'd climbed into the plane, headed to the back end of the row of seats and had slid down to the floor. She'd kept her back to the wall and sat there, where she had intended to wait. She drank enough water to re-hydrate herself, ate another small portion of the beef jerky and then had somehow fallen into a dead sleep. She suddenly worried that maybe in her slumber, she had made a noise that had alerted someone that she was in the plane.

After another two minutes went by and nothing stirred, she slowly moved to the right and soundlessly slid into the floor space between the last row. She stayed there, listening, for at least another two.

Nothing…

She dared to get on her knees next and moved slowly upwards, between the space of the twin seats. The musky smell of old fabric assaulted her senses and she avoided touching them, in case it generated dust and made her sneeze.

The door to the plane was still cracked open, the way she had left it because initially, it was the way she had found it. She had made sure upon entering the building, that she not disturb anything that would announce her presence, including the tracks her shoes had made in the dirt floor. The pirates might be dumb in other areas but they were masters when it came to tracking. She had studied all of them, including the Devil, for way too long.

So, to be on the safe side, she waited, listening too hard to the deafening silence, for any kind of sound or movement beyond the crack of the door. Still nothing…

Slowly, she slid the knife out of its hiding place at her side. Several more seconds ticked by, then another full minute. More sweat trickled down her back, from her hairline at the base of her neck and down her collarbone.

The hanger beyond the door stayed deathly quiet. The minutes and seconds still ticked off in her mind. By now, at least ten more had gone by since she'd been startled awake. The Devil and his goons could not have stayed silent for this long, if they were in the building, especially in the dark. One of those klutzy, obnoxious fools were bound to do something that would make a noise. Believing more by the minute, that she had simply woke up on her own, she cautiously moved a step forward from behind the seats and stood up. *Nothing…*

Another scan of the cockpit proved she was still alone. Her eyes had adjusted well in the dark now and she could make out every inch of the space, all the way up four rows, to the door that was ajar on the left. She stared at it for another full, two minutes. Nothing outside moved or made a noise. She released a bigger breath, stood up taller and tried to calm herself from the nerves jumping inside. Maybe it was a branch that had been moved by an animal outside, or a monkey had used the roof to scuttle across into another neighboring tree. There were a million reasons why something would make a sound *outside* that could have awakened her.

Another five minutes counted off in her head. If nothing had moved inside by now, it meant she was still alone. It was nearly impossible for her to swallow with a parched mouth, that had just been awakened from a deep sleep. Now would be the time to access the water supply and fill up her container and take a much-needed piss in the makeshift bathroom. While she was at it, she would take a look out the peephole to the outside, just to get an idea of what time it was.

Motivated by the fact that she was about to pee herself, she moved quietly to the opening of the door and hesitated. Again she listened and still nothing.

She pushed slowly on the door, just enough to squeeze through but didn't do so right away. She just stood there and listened, to be on the safe side.

Still *nothing…*

Feeling confident that she was truly alone in the structure at this point, she exhaled a breath, slid the knife back in its sheath and opened the door a little wider, just enough to slip through.

The second she got on the other side, a bright light hit her directly in the face out of nowhere, *blinding* her. She instantly put her hands up to shield her eyes. Her heart was pounding as she heard a male voice shout: *"FREEZE! Don't move!"* More lights lit up inside the structure and she began to make out matching shapes beyond the glare. This was *not* the *Devil* and his band of idiots, her mind quickly processed.

The feel of it was way too professional and organized.

So, who in the hell was it?

"It's not him." she heard someone say. "It's a *woman!*" The spotlight that had blinded her in the beginning, immediately shut off. The rest of them stayed on. With the decrease in the glare, she was able to see who was doing the talking. Spread out strategically around her and the plane, were at least a couple dozen men. They were all dressed identically in camouflage. The lights were coming from the end of their scopes, mounted on the top of their assault rifles, which were all pointing directly *at* her.

But she could care less *about* the guns because her eyes had leveled on the insignia, on their *right* shoulders. They were all wearing the patch of the *American* flag and they were speaking *English*.

She fell to her knees, let out a wail as if she were suddenly wounded and began *hysterically* sobbing.

SEVENTY

It was close to seven-thirty that evening when the limo from the airport, finally pulled in front of the private gates of Margot Hartford's mansion.

Brandon looked over at his wife and reached for her hand and gently squeezed.

"You ok?" he asked, noticing the deep sigh that she released from within while staring out the window. She nodded and released another. "It's been a *long* day baby, but it's almost over." He said. She nodded again in agreement.

The gates in front of the car began opening, the huge wrought iron arches moving soundlessly back, to allow entry. The driver pulled forward and once cleared, he moved past them and began the decent down the long winding drive to the mansion. He came to a smooth stop in front of the expansive entryway to the front doors. George was already outside and came bounding down the stone steps.

Sage exited first. George took her in his arms for a muchneeded hug while Brandon instructed the driver on the few bags they had in the trunk. Ken came out of the door just as the driver got back inside the car and proceeded to pull away. He shook hands with Brandon, as a few of the staff grabbed their bags and headed inside. George took them straight to Frank's old office.

Margot was already there, seated in a leather recliner, looking very pale and fragile. She was dressed in classy pajamas, with a lap blanket tucked around her legs. Her hair was combed but not as elegant as it usually was and she was void of makeup except for an attempted effort at lipstick, in a shade that wasn't doing her bland complexion any favors.

Sage walked hurriedly over to her chair, bent and hugged her, worry in her tone as they exchanged pleasantries. Margot waved away her concern, as if what had happened to her, was merely a summer cold and she would be back on her feet and fine by next week. Sage turned to take a seat on the couch next to him and he saw her averting her eyes, as they filled up with tears.

The fact that he was worried about his wife, was an understatement.

It suddenly donned on him that questioning Margot, was not going to put an end to this sordid tale. And Sage would finally see that too, once Courtney shared with her, what she'd witnessed herself, during the coverage she did on the Pirates lair. There were just too many avenues that branched in all directions, to probably ever *really* know the truth. Anyone who would have been able to fill in the gaps, were all simply dead.

"I wanted us to talk in this room, because we all know it's soundproof." Ken began. "From now on, considering the circumstances, I don't think we should talk freely around the help. Regardless of how long they've worked here before Karly." Margot rolled her eyes at that comment.

"And on that note Sage, Brandon," he said, looking at the both of them. "I have done an *extensive* background check on *all* the staff Margot has in her employ."

"Including me," George added, waving his hand. "I insisted."

"None of them have any connections to Italy or have any shadiness in their past. No criminal records, no family members with serious records, not even a traffic violation, so you can relax."

"Security alarm is on, no one is getting in." George reminded them.

"No one!" Ken assured them. "So your stay here this time, is perfectly safe."

Sage nodded and Brandon spoke. "I trust you." He said. "We *both* do." He added. Ken nodded.

"So how are you *really* feeling, Nana?" Sage asked, right off the bat. "*What* happened?"

Margot again waved her hand in the air. "I'm fine! Haven't felt better as a matter of fact."

"She's lying." George said, nonchalantly as he sipped on his glass of white wine. "It took both of us," he said, gesturing at Ken. "to get her down here from her room and that was even traveling by elevator. She's *still* that weak."

"Oh *nonsense*!" Margot said, making a face of disdain up at George. "Don't worry the poor girl with your exaggerations."

"Nana!" Sage said, rather firmly. "I'm *past* the point of worry. In fact, there's a whole lot of *other* words I could use that would better describe my present state at the moment. But that's beside the point and thank you George for the bit of truth that obviously my grandmother doesn't want to share with me." Margot whispered something under her breath but Brandon couldn't make out what it was. "How long do I have?" Sage asked, looking from George to Ken.

"What is *that* supposed to mean?" Margot hissed, glaring at Sage.

"She lasts about an hour and then she gets weak again and has to lie down." George said, knowing full well what Sage was asking.

"Would you *two* stop talking about *me* as if I were an *invalid* in the room. I'm not *dying* of a terminal *disease* for God's sake. I'm just *exhausted*!" Her voice rose an octave. Brandon could clearly see that, just getting angry, was quickly depleting what energy she had. Ken stepped forward and gently began to massage her shoulders. Surprisingly, she did nothing to push him away and seemed to give in to it. Obviously the woman was still in distress

from something that had physically attacked her and he
wondered if she hadn't suffered a mild stroke. Sage's next
words told him she wasn't buying it either.

"It's obvious that your more than *just* exhausted, Nana."
She began. "I'm not blind.

"As it is obvious my darling Sage, that you didn't *just* come
here to check on your old grandmother, when you found
out about my *little* mishap. All of you call it what you will
but I'm the one it happened to and I've been through
worse, I can tell you that." Margot insisted, keeping up that
brave front.

"Nana, *please* answer my question. *What* happened?" Sage
said.

"It happened after her little visit to the FBI." George
interjected, looking over at Margot.

"Oh for the *love* of God!" Margot said, shooting him
daggers.

"The *FBI*?" Sage come up for air. "Why would *you* be
visiting the FBI?"

Brandon felt his heart drop. This was where he was going
to get tangled up in not telling his wife about something he
already knew.

"I take it you haven't filled her in about the *shit* they pulled
on her grandmother?" Ken asked him directly, with nothing
more than mere curiosity.

Sage turned and looked at Brandon. "You *knew* about
this?"

Yep, Brandon thought, *here* comes the *tangled* part!

"Sort of." He said, sheepishly.

"What *shit* are you referring to?" Margot suddenly
demanded of Ken.

"The shit about the *DNA* off the glass!" George said.

"*DNA*?" Both Sage and Margot said at the same time,
looking at Ken and Brandon.

"I thought it was best to *wait,* so we could talk about it when we were *all* together." Brandon said, in his defense.

"So *someone* better start explaining!" Sage said, throwing her hands up at them all. "*Nana*?" She focused in on her grandmother.

Margot sighed deeply and then began telling her granddaughter about the facts leading up to her collapse. She started with the phone call she received early one morning, not long after everyone had parted from the mansion, requesting her presence at a meeting in Washington with the FBI. She summarized the conversation between her and the Agents, about the missing plane still technically *missing*, the bogus paperwork that claimed the FBI had *paid* for the burials, then tearfully broke it to her granddaughter about finding her mother's necklace, among the Pirate's belongings. While Margot tried to collect her emotions, George picked up where she trailed off, from the time they received the phone call from the hospital, to the diagnosis of Margot's mental breakdown. Ken then explained the comment behind the glass and how he discovered that they had used it as a trick, to obtain her DNA.

"What does the FBI want with my grandmother's DNA?" Sage questioned right away.

"I don't know." Ken said.

"What would they *normally* want it for?" Brandon asked Ken.

"The only reason of course, to match up to *other* DNA left behind from either the subject themselves or…of a *living* or recently *deceased* relative to prove a match."

"Then why are they interested in Nana's? Has anyone bothered to ask them?"

"I did." Ken admitted. "I called straight to the top. Spoke to the director myself. All he did was lie and wouldn't tell me a *damn* thing. They're *sneaky* little bastards!"

"They knew about the exhumation." Margot said. "The agent in charge wanted to know why Frank pursued it, what was the grounds for his suspicions. Of course I had just learned about it myself when you all did. I had no answers for her."

"We think we have the answer to that." Brandon said.

"Victor Rocha sent grandfather a package *after* the plane crash." Sage began. She told them in detail about what they found behind the picture frame and handed the contents of the newspaper and the necklace to Ken while she handed the letter Frank had penned, to Margot, who sighed when she finished reading it.

"What does my grandfather *mean* about you in that letter, Nana?" Sage asked.

Margot closed her eyes all of ten seconds, then released a deep-seated sigh. "Your grandfather was a *wonderful* man." She began. "I loved him with *all* my heart. We were best friends, *soulmates*, partners in everything that we did. And then, when all this happened, when we lost our little *girl*…" Margot trailed off for a second. George took a step over and squeezed her shoulder for support. It must have given her the push to move on. "We were *devastated,*" she said, with intense emotion. "And at *odds* with each other. Grief has a way of doing some pretty crazy things to the loved ones *left* behind. When Victor was killed shortly after, in prison, Frank went off the deep end for a while. He suspected everybody of being the one behind the hit, *including* me."

"So your saying he was out of his head with grief and grasping at straws?" Brandon asked.

"Basically." Margot replied.

"So you had nothing to do with the hit on Victor?" Brandon asked.

"At one point I will admit, I suspected Victor had something to do with Kelley and Jack and I'm not going to lie, if he did, I wanted him as *dead* as Everett or my husband did. But he did not *die* by my hand. Someone *else* got to him first!"

"And none of you *ever* found out who had it done?" Margot shook her head no. "Not even a hint of who it could be?" Sage pushed.

Still Margot had the same answer. "No. At that point I didn't care who ordered it up, I was just glad it had happened."

"Did you know that Victor was sending Frank packages and taunting him?" Brandon asked her.

"No, I did not. This is the first time I've seen any of this."

"Ever hear of the *'Eye for an Eye'* message, written on the newspaper?" Brandon asked.

"No." Margot said. "My husband and Everett had powwows in this office *without* me present and half the time *without* my knowledge. I'm sure it was to discuss things like this."

"It was Victor Rocha's *mantra*." Sage said. "He used it when informing his enemies, they were in *his* sights!"

"The asshole sent your husband *hints* that your daughter and her husband were still alive and being held captive somewhere." Brandon said.

"Frank tried to *convince* me of that." Margot admitted. "But holding onto that kind of hope, that she was possibly alive, hurt *worse*. I came to the decision, to *accept* that she wasn't *with* us anymore and Frank could not. I had a responsibility to raise you," she said, looking at Sage. "and I couldn't heal, if another part of me thought that your mother was out there, *still* alive and being held *captive* by savages. I laid in bed for months, *thinking* about his farfetched theory and it was driving me nuts. By believing it, we were falling right into one of Victor's games and I wasn't having any part of it. And now, I don't know what to think!"

Brandon subconsciously cleared his throat and checked off another box on the list of facts, that Courtney had told him about. The dots were connecting too easily and he vowed on the flight home, he would come clean with his wife and contact Courtney as soon as they arrived back at the cabin, to bring her up to speed.

"This is getting way *too* big." Brandon commented. "What legal recourse do we have for making the FBI tell us *why* they wanted Margot's DNA?"

"Well," Ken began. "I'm no attorney but standing on the other side of the fence, they operate behind the guidelines and protection of the government. First you would have to prove that they took her DNA before we could demand the reason why. And that's the part that is going to be hard, unless they admit it which they won't."

"Don't get any ideas about hiring a fancy attorney." Margot warned Brandon. "Because I already used that tactic and it won't do you any good. Agent Fields explained to me that it would only hamper the progress of getting to the truth. I agreed not to, on the grounds that I wanted this nightmare to end, for both Sage and I."

"What did you agree to, Margot?" Brandon asked.

"I want it over. I want *closure* Brandon. I agreed to give them *space*, to get some answers for me."

"You shouldn't have agreed to *anything*." Brandon said.

"She didn't *sign* anything." Ken interrupted.

"I'm not that stupid." Margot said with sarcasm.

"They can't hold her to anything in a court of law, so you can relax." Ken reassured him.

"Agent Fields knows more than she let on to me, about this current investigation." Margot said. "But aside from her secrecy bound by her civic duty, she was credible in assuring me that something was about to bust wide open. I will set back and wait to see if she makes good on her promise. If they can't give me answers by then, I will

assemble one of the *best* legal teams in the country, you can bet your sweet *ass* on that, Brandon. One way or another, we will get some answers. The only reason I held back, was because I believe they are on the verge of *finding* the plane, through these pirates."
"*Finding* the plane?" Sage asked, looking from one face in the room to another. "*What* plane?" Tears began to shimmer in her eyes.
Brandon's heart sank!
This was not the way he wanted her to find out.

SEVENTY-ONE

Twenty-four hours later…

Agent Fields exited the car in front of the FBI building on Wilshire, in California. Mullins wasn't far behind. He tipped the driver and then caught up to her. Once they cleared the front desk, both rode the elevator to the tenth floor. They were quickly directed to a private office, where Agent Barbara Ross was waiting.

"How is she?" Fields asked, immediately.

"Doc says she's been napping for a few hours now." Ross said, glancing at the watch on her wrist. "I'm waiting on a call for clearance."

"Has anyone from our office, been in to see her?" Fields asked.

"We had a team that flew her in but they said she was conked out for most of the flight. When they found her, she was severely dehydrated, weak and starving. She had cuts, bruises and bites, all over her entire body and layers of mud caked on her skin. Her right ankle was acutely sprained and severely swollen. Apparently she'd been in the jungle for over a week but in her state of mind, she thought it had been more like a few days."

"That's a perfect estimate of the timeline when the lair was seized! She has to be one of the women *missing* in that camp!" Agent Fields said, with excitement.

"Did she give them a name?" Mullins asked.

"No, she's not been very cooperative. The psychologist that was assigned to her said she seemed to be scared out of her wits and kept watching the door, like she was expecting something or someone *bad* to come through it. She flat out refused to take any pain meds or allow the nurse to put an IV in her arm. We're thinking she's the herbalist I told you about back in Washington." She said this to Fields.

"Because she was asking for chamomile and not in a tea bag form."

"Ok, so while we're waiting on that call, tell me about the plane."

"Our military boys found it on the first try. From my understanding, all the Pirates carried a compass. They used them to find the structure also by coordinates. The building was so camouflaged into the environment, that you wouldn't know it was there, unless you were looking for it. General Bradley said the plane fit perfectly inside, as if the building were custom made just for it. All the original pieces, down to the *damn* seats were intact. The serial number on its side was the only thing that had been changed. Someone had modified it with a new slew of numbers. They had welded it to the original body so no one would know the difference, when it was spotted in the air."

"So the one hanging in the hut, that the reporter spotted, was *obviously* the original." Fields said.

"It matched up perfectly, even though we already know it's the plane that was missing in '87."

"You mean they've been flying it all this time?" Mullins asked.

Agent Ross nodded. "And without a doubt to commit more crimes. But they haven't had it out for a while. *Why*, we don't know but the landing strip they used, it was way overgrown with debris. Someone had recently been clearing it which meant they were going to use it soon."

"I wonder if the leader got word we were raiding the camp?" Agent Fields said.

"We thought about that." Ross said. "Either someone tipped him off or it was just a coincidence that he was readying the plane to go somewhere. The fact that the woman was waiting inside the cockpit, makes it more plausible."

"She admitted to waiting for Gates?" Fields asked.

"No but for what other reason was she waiting in there?"
"Maybe hiding because she was scared out of her wits?"
Mullins offered.
"Not to mention extremely exhausted." Fields added. "So
still no answers as to what happened to the passengers on
the plane?" Agent Fields asked.
"Hopefully we will get that answer when we talk to this
woman. She obviously knew it was there, is why she went.
So maybe she has some info we can finally use."
"I still can't believe it's intact." Mullins said.
"Which means our theory of it being hijacked, is exactly
what happened." Fields said.
"They stole a plane, is the bottom line." Ross agreed.
"Which now we need to find out why?" Mullins said.
"There's always a gain."
"And I don't buy that Gates just stole it to say he could.
Even though he had a penchant for having sticky fingers."
"No, I agree." Fields said. "There was definitely a much
bigger plan behind it, than just taking a plane for shits and
giggles."
"Could it be because he needed it to continue his drug
smuggling operation? A zebra never changes its stripes!"
Mullins said.
Both Ross and Fields looked at each other.
"It's a possibility!" Fields said.
The vibration of Ross' cell indicated a call coming in. She
swiped it off the desk and answered just as quick.
"Ross." There was a moment of silence and then she said,
"We're on our way!"
She hung up and stood at the same time. "She's awake and
we have clearance. Lets' go!"
They hustled to the elevator, rode down to the lobby and
caught a car to the hospital, not ten minutes away but it
took them twenty because of the traffic. Fields was antsy.
She couldn't wait to lay eyes on this woman's face and ask

her who she was. It was too much to hope that after all this time, it could be the Hartford woman. But it didn't stop her from wishing.

The car finally pulled into the parking lot of the hospital. The line to the entrance was long, with cars and taxi's and lots of people weaving in and out. Ross mentioned that visiting hours and shift changes were happening which made sense for the delay. Two cars before theirs, Fields couldn't stand it any longer and informed the driver and her party that she was just going to get out right there. She exited the car, as did Mullins and Ross. Walking with slim briefcases in hand, all three entered the building and followed the elevator up to the fifth floor where they were greeted by Dr. Nolan, who had been the attending physician. After pleasantries where exchanged, he led them down a series of corridors, talking all the while.

"Jane Doe's condition has greatly improved. She's slept for four hours straight, ate everything on her tray and drank 3 pitchers of ice water."

"Sounds like she's recovering nicely." Ross said.

"Definitely much quicker than I expected. But that's due to the fact that she's in phenomenal shape. I believe it's the only thing that kept her alive in the jungle all that time." They turned another corridor and walked through a set of double doors into a private wing. Before the doctor could open the door, a male nurse came hurrying out.

"*She's gone!*" he said to the doctor.

"*Gone?*" Dr. Nolan asked, confused.

"The *woman!*" He gestured back at the door. Ross stayed behind while Fields and Mullins entered the room. Sheets were awry. The tray was pushed aside and the bathroom door was open and empty.

"*Dammit!*" Fields cursed under her breath and joined Ross outside in the hall while Mullins continued to look around.

"Security has been notified!" Another nurse said, when she approached the doctor.

"Is it *possible* she just took a walk?" The doctor asked, mainly to his staff.

"Not likely." Ross broke in. "How long has she been gone?"

"I don't know." The male nurse replied.

"When's the last time anyone *saw* her in the room?" Agent Fields asked.

"About thirty minutes ago, right before I called you." The doctor said to Ross.

Mullins came out of the room. "What floor is your security station on?" He asked, directing the question to the doctor.

"First floor, south wing. Someone from the information desk will take you."

Mullins hurried past them and headed to the elevator.

"Did she say anything to anyone while she was awake?" Agent Ross asked the small group that had assembled around them. But all shook their heads, except for the doc, who was still quite bewildered.

"She asked me about a half hour ago, what *country* we were in." he said, shaking his head.

"And what did *you* tell her?" Fields asked.

"I told her she was *in* the United States, *California* to be exact."

"What else did she say?" Fields prodded.

"She wanted to know what *part* of California and I told her *L.A.!*"

SEVENTY-TWO

Charlie and Ava had agreed to hook up, after his initial meeting he'd had with Brandon, Sage and Lola, for a pre-celebration of the signing of the contracts. Unfortunately, she'd been tied up last night with some unexpected function out in Vegas and had caught a plane just in time, to meet up with him tonight for dinner.

In the meantime, while he waited for her arrival, he carried a freshly-made whiskey and sour to the rooftop, to enjoy the view. The sun was just setting in the sky and everything around him was descending into darkness. He walked over to the roof's edge and surveyed the traffic down below. It was moving at a steady pace and was actually beginning to thin out. The street traffic wasn't as congested either. It was not the typical Friday night crowd. Even the drug pushers were nowhere in sight.

He thought about his conversation with Sage and Brandon after Lola had left. He thought it had been productive. He also hoped it was the *end* of the story, for a while. There was nothing else to tell. It was all up to Margot now. And then his mind lingered a little too long on Lola's reaction to meeting Sage. It had struck him as *odd*. Lola always acted kind of quirky but last night, he thought she acted *too* calm. And she stared a hole in Sage when she was unaware. Almost to the point of studying her, inch by inch. Brandon was too googly-eyed over his wife, to have even noticed. But Charlie had watched her, while she was watching Sage and the look on Lola's face was that of someone who was merely more than curious. And it had bugged him to the point, it became a *mental* note. He drained his glass and decided to head back downstairs to recreate another. Just as he turned, his attention was caught by the door to the roof, where it was propped open about five inches with a brick.

It was moving against the draft that was coming up from the stairwell.

Which meant someone had entered the door to his floor. He smiled as Ava's face entered his mind. He'd left a key hidden in the fountain out back, like he had in the *older* days. He'd instructed her on where to find it, in a text message. She must have gotten here *quicker* than she'd anticipated.

Wonderful!

He crossed the distance, opened the door and took the steps down. Just before he reached the bottom, he felt his cell vibrate in his jacket pocket. It was probably Ava letting him know she had arrived. He was one step ahead of her. He took it out and glanced at the screen.

It was indeed Ava, just as he had suspected but what it said was *not* what he had anticipated. He stopped on the landing, dead in his tracks and stared at her message.

I'll be there soon, got two more stops!

Charlie heard the door to the outer hallway open and shut, the one that led directly to his office. He glanced down at the screen again and *re*read Ava's message. It was sent a minute ago. So if she was still out running errands, then who the *hell* was in his building?

The entire staff had already left *hours* ago! He sat his glass down on the last step very quietly and pocketed his cell. He then silently opened the door that led to the hallway. From this position, he could see a straight shot to his office door. Both were empty and *too* quiet. A trickle of sweat began to roll down the middle of his back. He carefully stepped inside and took his jacket off. He bundled it up and stuck it in the door jamb to keep it from latching and making a noise. He grabbed an umbrella from the stand as he passed by, in case he needed a weapon. He neared his door soundlessly, looked slightly to the left and saw nothing. Then he dared to move to the right. He heard a shuffle and it had come from the direction of where his desk was—the desk where his gun was hidden deep within the third drawer and not doing a *damn* thing to protect him there.

It's all over, right? Meg's words last week echoed eerily in his mind as chills shot up his spine. And that *strange* feeling he'd been experiencing for a while, began to spread thick and heavy in his gut. Part of him wanted to back away and call 911 but the other part wasn't having none of it. He inched a little closer to the door frame, leaned slightly forward and that's when he caught sight of the *intruder*…

The woman was standing with her back to him. She was dressed in what looked like scrubs that someone would wear in a hospital and he couldn't help but notice that the top was several sizes *too* big. The pants however, seemed to fit better. Her light colored hair was bunched up in some kind of clip in the back of her head and it was tilted at the moment, while she seemed to intently be thumbing her way through *his* file cabinet.

What in the hell?

Charlie's first thoughts were that she was possibly a *stalker* fan, who had hidden in the building somewhere until they'd closed, so she could try to steal *personal* information on one of his clients. Then he began to wonder if it was *someone* from the media, disguised as a hospital worker, looking for the next big story!

He began to really get *pissed*!

Whoever this thief was, his evening with Ava was going to be ruined because the cops would have to be called, to get her *ass* removed. And he'd press charges. Oh hell *yes*, you better believe he'd *press* charges and *that* would take a while!

Then, without warning…everything *happened* at once…

As he slid his cell slowly out of his pocket, it began to

vibrate and the *sound* of it, in the *silence* of the room, was *magnified*.

The woman's head snapped around and when Charlie saw her *face*, he lost all faith in *his* existence.

~ THE END~

*For more information, updates on the next release,
or to contact the author, visit the website at
<u>www.Marina-Cox.com</u>*

Or Facebook @Marinacox13

Printed by: *LULU Press, Inc.*
Lulu.com

Publisher: *Marina Cox*